Lake Season

Center Point
Large Print

Also by Denise Hunter and available from
Center Point Large Print:

Married 'til Monday
The Goodbye Bride
Just a Kiss
Sweetbriar Cottage
Blue Ridge Sunrise
Honeysuckle Dreams
On Magnolia Lane
Summer by the Tides

**This Large Print Book carries the
Seal of Approval of N.A.V.H.**

Lake Season

DENISE HUNTER

CENTER POINT LARGE PRINT
THORNDIKE, MAINE

This Center Point Large Print edition
is published in the year 2020 by arrangement with
Thomas Nelson.

Unless otherwise noted, Scripture quotations are taken from
the Holman Christian Standard Bible®, copyright © 1999,
2000, 2002, 2003, 2009 by Holman Bible Publishers.
Used by permission. HCSB® is a federally registered
trademark of Holman Bible Publishers.

Publisher's Note: This novel is a work of fiction. Names,
characters, places, and incidents are either products of the
author's imagination or used fictitiously. All characters
are fictional, and any similarity to people living or dead is
purely coincidental.

The text of this Large Print edition is unabridged.
In other aspects, this book may vary
from the original edition.
Printed in the United States of America
on permanent paper.
Set in 16-point Times New Roman type.

ISBN: 978-1-64358-461-4

The Library of Congress has cataloged this record
under Library of Congress Control Number: 2019950805

Dear friend,

I'm so excited to start a new series with you! This one is centered around a historic inn and three adult siblings who have already found a special place in my heart.

The seed for this first story began when my husband and I were renovating a one-hundred-year-old lake cottage. When the drywall was peeled away we were delighted to uncover signatures on the wooden walls beneath it—the boards had served as a guest book of sorts. The signatures dated back into the 1920s and '30s and, to our surprise, included some notorious gangsters of the day—John Dillinger and Baby Face Nelson among them. That gang was known to have roamed the area and was rumored to have hidden out around the lakes where the cottage was located.

Unfortunately, after consulting with some experts, we found out those signatures were not authentic. But the potential discovery was so exciting that it got my creative juices flowing. What could my protagonist find behind the walls of her historic inn? *Lake Season* is the direct result of that inspiration. I had so much fun conceiving and writing this story, and I'm thrilled to share it with you. I hope you enjoy the journey as much as I did.

Blessings!

Denise

Lake Season

Prologue

The house was eerily silent. Molly Bennett leaned against the closed door, too weary to move another step. Her throat ached from swallowing tears, and a headache throbbed at her temples.

Her older brother, Levi, was still on the sidewalk saying good-bye to the last of the friends and neighbors who had come to offer condolences. The last few days had been exhausting beyond anything she'd ever experienced, but Levi had been like a rock.

A sound on the steps drew her attention, and she looked up the grand staircase to the landing, where the stairs turned for the second floor.

Her eighteen-year-old sister, Grace, peeked around the balustrade. "Are they gone yet?"

"Every last one." Molly straightened, feigning more energy than she felt. Grace had disappeared from the gathering about an hour into it. Who could blame her?

"Come on down," Molly said. "I'll make you a cup of tea."

While Grace settled in the living room Molly went to the kitchen, the old, scarred floor creaking under her feet. Miss Della had already set the kitchen to rights and hugged them good-bye. Molly didn't know what they would've done the last few days without their mother's best friend. She'd guided them through the funeral process, organized today's luncheon, and when it all got to be too much, simply enveloped them in warm hugs.

The whole town had come together to get the Bennett siblings through the last few days. Mama's beautician of many years did her hair and makeup. Nonnie Hartwell sang Daddy's favorite hymn. Food flooded in from the ladies at church along with offers of help.

When Molly returned, Levi was in the living room with Grace. His dark hair stuck up as if he'd just run his fingers through it. He'd ditched his suit coat in the July heat, and now his tie was loosened, the top shirt button undone. He suddenly looked much older than his twenty-six years.

Grace was faring no better. Her blue eyes were bloodshot, her color wan, and even though it had only been a few days since that awful phone call, she seemed to have lost weight. Her cheeks had hollowed out, and the navy dress Mama bought her for homecoming last fall seemed loose on her lanky frame.

Molly handed Grace the tea, then turned to Levi. "You want something? Coffee, iced tea? Valium?"

"No thanks." Not even a smile.

Molly sat on the sofa next to Grace and kicked off her heels. She hadn't realized until this very moment how much her toes hurt after being squeezed into them for five long hours. She wondered, not for the first time, why society continued these rituals that only exhausted the recently bereaved. Even she, extroverted and chatty, was out of words and the energy to use them.

Levi, letting his guard down for the first time since the accident, slunk back in the recliner across from them. His shoulders gave in to gravity, his eyes closing on a deep sigh.

None of them had taken their parents' seats, Molly noted. Daddy's brown recliner and Mama's corner of the couch sat empty. She could close her eyes right now and almost catch a whiff of Mama's sweet perfume and the leathery scent that followed Daddy as closely as a shadow.

"What happens next?" Grace asked, tears in her voice. "What are we going to do?"

It was the question that had been rolling around Molly's mind when she wasn't finding dress clothes in which to bury their parents or scouring picture albums with her best friend, Skye.

"We don't have to do anything for a few weeks," Levi said. "My boss is giving me some time off."

"And I can finish my summer courses online," Molly said. "My advisor already approved it."

At twenty-three Molly was only one semester away from her hospitality degree. Her fall semester would consist of an internship, which she'd already secured at a prominent boutique hotel in Italy.

"But what about after that?" Grace asked.

A look of reluctance came over Levi's face as his eyes toggled between them, finally settling on his younger sister. "I thought you might come to Los Angeles and stay with me for a while."

"What do you mean, 'a while'?" Grace said. "Like till the end of the summer?"

Levi took his time in answering. "Until you finish high school. We'll have to sell the house and—"

"No!" Grace popped to her feet. Her chest heaved, and her face flushed with emotion. "All my friends are here! And I can't give up my volleyball team! You can't take that away from me."

Grace had been held back in elementary school, so she was only starting her junior year even though she'd just turned eighteen.

"I know it's not ideal," Levi said, "but we have to be reasonable, Grace."

Molly reached for Grace's hand, but her sister jerked it away.

"I'm staying in Bluebell. I don't care what you say, I'm staying. We can't just sell the house. How can you even say that?"

12

"Honey, we can't afford to keep it," Molly said. "There's still a mortgage to pay. Mama and Daddy borrowed from the equity for all the renovations. They still owed a lot of money on it."

Grace's eyes turned glassy. "This is my home. Mama and Daddy's home. They wouldn't want us to sell it, and you know it."

Molly couldn't dispute that.

Their parents had been slowly restoring the historic building to its original purpose: an inn. They'd planned to run it together when their dad retired from his medical practice next year. It had been the town's first inn, built in 1905, and featured ten bedrooms. Early on it had been a stagecoach stop, then for years it housed the post office, till it was sold and turned into the governor's summer home. Their parents purchased it when the kids were little, and they'd grown up here.

But four days ago everything had changed.

"We don't want to sell the house," Levi said, "but we don't have another option."

"Who's going to buy it like this anyway?" Grace asked, gesturing wildly. "The whole upstairs is in shambles."

Not an exaggeration. Their parents had been in the process of taking down walls to give the rooms en suite bathrooms.

"It's not ideal, but it can't be helped," Levi said.

"Stop saying that. You could quit your job and move back here. At least until I finish school."

"Where would I earn enough to support this household? Bluebell's small, and you know how seasonal it is."

"You could work in Asheville, couldn't you? There's lots of jobs there."

"That's too far away, Grace."

"I'm not leaving my friends!" Grace's tears spilled over. "We can't sell the house. All our memories are here. It'd be like losing Mama and Daddy all over again!"

"Our memories are in our hearts, Gracie," Molly said. "We won't ever lose them."

"That's just the baloney people say to try and make you feel better! Every time I sit on the porch swing I feel Daddy with me. And every time I walk in the kitchen I see Mama at the sink. I don't want to forget them." Her words wobbled.

Molly's heart ached in her chest. "You won't forget them. None of us will."

Grace crossed her arms. "I'm not leaving. I'm eighteen and that makes me a legal adult. I'll stay with Sarah's family if I have to."

Sarah's family loved Grace, but Mrs. Benson was being treated for breast cancer, and Molly doubted the family could take Grace in for two years. Besides which, Grace needed family right now. They all did. They had one grandmother left, but she was in assisted living in Georgia.

Molly looked at the stubborn tilt to Grace's chin, the spark of will in her eyes. Then she met Levi's gaze and held it for a long moment.

The idea that had been forming in the back of her mind the last few days surfaced once again. Crazy. Sheer madness.

But was it really? Was selling the house and moving Grace to a strange city a better option?

"What if . . ." Molly said. "What if we opened the inn just as Mama and Daddy planned?" The idea sounded as crazy on her lips as it had in her mind.

Levi stilled.

"Yes!" Grace said. "We should do it."

Molly looked at Levi. "You could move back home and get a job here. We have the rest of the equity loan in the bank—maybe enough for the remodel and to float us until it's complete. We could remodel over the fall and winter just as they were planning to do and open in the spring in time for lake season."

"You have no idea what you're asking," Levi said. "Remodeling this thing would be a full-time job, Molly. And two of us, running an inn this size?"

"*Three* of us." Grace dropped to the edge of the sofa. "I can work evenings during the school year and all summer, and after I graduate I can work full time."

"You're going to college," Levi said firmly.

Even Molly prickled at his bossy tone. "You have a business degree, Levi, and I'm almost finished with my hospitality degree. We couldn't be more suited to this."

"I can do the website," Grace offered. "And all the artsy stuff. We can make this work. I'll do whatever you tell me to do, and I won't complain."

"I don't want to be an innkeeper the rest of my life," Levi said. "And you were aiming for something a little grander than a small inn on Bluebell Lake."

"It wouldn't have to be forever." Molly did want more than this eventually. But all that could wait, couldn't it? Wasn't it more important to do what was best for Grace right now?

She shifted to business mode—her brother's love language. "Look, if we sell the place now, we'll get pennies on the dollar. Who's going to want a building that's half house and half inn? If we finish the remodel and make a go of the place, even for two or three years, it'll be much more attractive to potential buyers. You know I'm right."

Levi leaned forward on the chair, resting his elbows on his knees. He gave Molly a pointed look. "What about your internship? You've been talking about it for months. *Italy,* Molly. Your dream. You can't just throw that away."

Her heart shrank two sizes at the thought of

giving up the opportunity. She'd worked so hard to secure that internship, and they'd chosen her over dozens of applicants.

But one look at Grace's pleading expression solidified her decision and eased her discomfort. Grace needed her now. Needed them both. Their parents would expect them to look out for each other, not their own interests.

"Not going to lie . . ." Molly said. "It'll be hard to turn that down. But everything's changed, Levi. Everything has to be on the table. We can't just go back to life as usual. All we have now is each other."

Her words hung in the air, suspended like a spring fog over the valley. Their parents had taught by example that family came first. Molly hadn't always gotten that right.

They needed to do this. Not only for Grace, but because of what this inn had meant to their parents. It had been their dream; how could their children just let it die?

"Please, Levi?" Grace said quietly. "You know it'll work."

"What I know is that half of businesses fail in the first five years," Levi said, but his tone had softened.

"Mama and Daddy already crunched all the numbers," Molly said. Levi had even helped them with it. "They have a solid business plan, and we have the abilities to carry it out. It's not such a crazy idea. I think we can do this."

She held Levi's eyes for a long moment. It was a lot to ask. He had recently been promoted to project manager at a commercial construction company. He'd be throwing away all that hard work.

But they all would be giving up things they wanted. Even Grace would be investing her time and talents toward this endeavor. Did she know what she was in for? Molly wanted to make sure.

She gave her sister a firm look. "You wouldn't have time for all your extracurricular activities. You'll have to drop everything but volleyball if you're going to help out around here."

"I will. I'll do it. I promise." Grace didn't even blink. "Anything, as long as we get to keep the house."

"We'll be selling it eventually anyway," Molly said. "Once it's a viable business."

Molly had dreamed of running a hotel in Tuscany ever since she'd watched a travel show on the region during high school. She'd taken three years of Italian in preparation and had studied everything she could find on Italy and Italian culture.

"I know. I understand. And I know it's asking a lot of both of you, and I really appreciate that you'd sacrifice so much for me." Grace's wide blue eyes pleaded with them.

"I think we can do this," Molly said again.

Ignoring the brief sting of regret, she stuck out her hand, palm down, as they used to do as children. "I'm on board."

Grace immediately set her hand on Molly's. "Me too."

They looked at their brother.

"Levi . . . ?" Molly prodded.

His gaze shifted between his sisters. His mouth pinched at the corners.

Tension gathered, making the air feel tight and heavy somehow.

Finally he heaved a great sigh and stretched out his hand. "I must be crazy. But . . . all right. Let's do it."

one

Ten months later

Adam Bradford was nobody's idea of a hero. His eyes swept past his reflection in the rearview mirror of his rental car as he pulled up to the curb at the edge of downtown Bluebell.

He did have that crooked nose that seemed so popular on the heroes of romance novels, but he hadn't gotten it in a fistfight. He'd gotten it at the library while unshelving a difficult-to-reach hardcover copy of *Moby Dick*. And while he might be trim and fit, he did not sport rippling abs, a chiseled jaw, or even the requisite cleft chin. It wasn't just his ordinary looks either. He wasn't particularly adept with people, especially the fairer sex. The irony was not lost on him.

But there were certain things at which he was extremely proficient. Writing—that went without saying—academics, research, planning. Adam was a planner and a plotter, but this time his preparations had completely backfired.

He looked at the majestic white house, likely turn-of-the-century, situated on a shady lawn about twenty feet off the busy sidewalk. There was no sign indicating it was an inn, but his app listed it as such, and he was getting desperate.

He exited the sedan, maneuvered around a small Dumpster, and followed a walkway past a dirty Bobcat and up to the massive porch. The front door, an old wooden behemoth, was open, a positive sign. He stepped over the threshold to the sudden sound of a circular saw.

There was a grand staircase directly ahead and, to the left of it, a tall mahogany stand that appeared to be a check-in desk. It was unmanned, however, and devoid of a bell. He opened his mouth to call out, but before he could utter a word a head peeked around the corner to the right of the staircase.

"Oh good, you're here. Help!" Dark hair swung over the slim shoulder of a woman he guessed to be in her early twenties.

She had the kind of natural beauty he associated with soap commercials, and he could easily picture her a few years ago, walking across a football field on homecoming night on the quarterback's arm.

He pushed his glasses up. "Excuse me?"

"Can you just come here and hold this? This stupid, dumb . . ." She muttered the rest too quietly to be deciphered.

The wooden floor squawked under his brown leather Clarks. He found her sitting on the floor of a massive living room amongst wooden boards of various shapes and sizes; a random pile of nuts, bolts, and screws; and an oversize white

21

instruction sheet, unfolded and tossed to the side. A large box featuring the photo of a gleaming wooden stand sat off to the side.

"If you could just hold this end while I finish this . . . I think I'm finally headed in the right direction."

He knelt, doing as she asked.

"Thank God you're here. Grace bet me I couldn't figure it out, and she's due home from school in an hour. How was I to know the directions wouldn't be in English? And the pictures! Do you see those?" She jerked her chin toward the instructions. "It's like a kindergarten class project gone awry."

She tossed her hair over her shoulder, and the clean apple-y smell of it drifted his way. He looked at the picture on the box and tried to make sense of the few pieces she'd fastened together so far.

"I'm Molly, by the way, Levi's sister, but I guess you already know that."

He tried to process the simple sentence but was distracted by that scent. And the smudge of something white—chalk?—on her nose.

She blinked at him, obviously waiting for a response.

Heat flushed his neck. "Adam Bradford. Um, what language?"

"What?" She spared him a glance, her eyes returning to focus on the screw she was forcing into a too-small hole.

"The directions—what language?"

"Oh, they're in French. This is North Carolina, people. I mean, Spanish maybe. But French? I don't know a single soul who speaks it."

With his free hand he reached for the instructions. As he began reading them to himself, it didn't take long to see they would have to start over.

"See what I mean?" she said. "Impossible."

When she finished with the screw, he let loose of the board and scratched his chin. "I, ah, have good news and bad news."

She looked up at him, and he immediately got caught in her wide amber eyes.

"Let's have the good news first. I'm an optimist when I'm not under pressure to prove myself. And okay, there's a bet on the line. But it's only an ice cream cone. And my dignity. Mainly, my dignity."

He noted flecks of color in her irises, ranging from milk chocolate tones to gold. All that intriguing complexity was framed by luscious dark lashes. Utterly mesmerizing.

"Um . . . the good news?"

He cleared his throat, a hot wave of embarrassment sweeping into his face. "I—I can speak it. That is, I'm fluent. In French, I mean." Just not his mother tongue, apparently.

"Are you kidding me? That's awesome. What does it say?"

He gave her a look of warning. "That's the bad news. I'm afraid we'll have to start over."

Her face fell, turning her mouth down in an adorable pout. "Oh, doggonit. It took me forty-five minutes to get this far."

Could she be any cuter? Adam dragged his gaze from her lips. "It'll go fast, now that we have directions."

"Good point."

They made quick work of separating the pieces she'd assembled, being careful not to strip the screw holes. Then he set to work on the instructions.

"Read it out loud, in French," she said brightly.

Okay . . . maybe she was the curious sort, an eager learner. He could respect that.

He did as she asked, translating internally as he went, and directed her through the beginning stages of the project. While the sketches were, indeed, a jumble of splotchy lines, the written instructions were clear and concise.

As they made quick work of the assembly, Adam was barely cognizant of the background noises: intermittent hammering, voices coming from upstairs, and the saw he'd heard earlier, periodically making him raise his voice to be heard.

Molly held pieces in place while he worked in the screws and tightened bolts. She had small hands with long fingers that tapered down to neat, unpainted fingernails. She wore only a utilitarian silver watch that complemented her creamy skin.

She'd make a nice protagonist, he found himself thinking. Though she was delicate in size, he sensed the kind of inner strength imperative in a heroine. Creativity surged inside. It was the first time since he'd turned in *Under the Starry Sky* that he'd felt anything like the stirrings of inspiration. He wished for a pad and paper, because Adam Bradford had just found his muse.

Molly watched as Adam deftly put the last piece in place. The stand was becoming heavy and unwieldy, but she could see it would serve its purpose nicely. She needed the piece to stand just inside the entry, large enough to hold a welcoming bouquet of fresh flowers and a guest book. The Queen Anne style fit in with the home's décor without breaking their budget.

Adam flipped the stand upright, his biceps bunching beneath his button-up. He said something in French.

She looked at the stand. It appeared to be complete, and there were no parts left unused. "Is there more? We're all out of parts."

He ducked his head. "No. I said, 'That should do it.' "

"Oh, good." Her impulsive request that he read the directions aloud had come from a spontaneous desire to hear the language from a man's lips—she'd always thought French to be the premiere language of love. Her eyes drifted over his features. He had brown hair, neither short nor long, and a little messy, as if the wind had caught it on his way in.

The sharp turn of his freshly shaved jaw was his most masculine feature. A pair of scholarly glasses hid two magnificent blue eyes. They were a less intense blue than her siblings'—the color of faded denim, jeans gone soft from many washings.

"I guess your dignity is salvaged after all," he said as he stood.

He helped her to her feet, his hands engulfing hers with warmth. He let go as soon as she got her balance. He wasn't particularly tall, but at five two she barely reached his chin.

She glanced at her watch. "And in the nick of time."

He lifted the stand with ease. "Where would you like me to put this?"

She directed him to the spot by the door, and he set it in place about an inch from the freshly painted wall.

It looked just as she had envisioned. "Perfect. Levi said you were a godsend, and for once he wasn't exaggerating."

"He did? I am? Who's Levi?" He pushed his glasses up on the bridge of his nose in a gesture that was already becoming familiar. She hadn't noticed his glasses slipping, but it was probably just a nervous habit. He did seem a little flustered.

Wait a minute. Molly blinked. "My brother, Levi? The one who asked you over to help me . . . He's no fan of my dignity, but he owed me one."

Adam shook his head. "I'm afraid I don't know what you're talking about. I don't know your brother; I just came to see about getting a room."

Her lips parted as she froze. "Oh no. I'm so sorry! I've taken up half your afternoon."

"It's no problem at all."

"And I can't even give you a room. We're not open yet."

"I couldn't help but notice all the construction. Is this place turn-of-the-century?"

"1905."

"That makes sense. The architecture bears out the trend of the time—reviving previous styles from the nineteenth century. I noticed some regional characteristics—the roofline, for example—but also some eclectic flair brought over from abroad. Tourism of the time was broadening the scope of architecture in the US."

Molly gave a bemused smile. "You must be an architect."

A flush crawled up his neck. "No, actually, I'm not. Don't mind me. I'm just full of useless information."

"You're probably a whiz at Trivial Pursuit.

But back to our situation with the inn . . . We were supposed to open this weekend but . . . life happened."

"I was afraid of that. I've already checked every place I can think of. Everyone's full up."

"It's the start of Memorial Day weekend—our busiest of the year. People book out months in advance—sometimes a whole year."

"Well, that explains it. I actually booked a house on the lake, but there was a mistake with the reservation."

"I feel so bad that we can't accommodate you, especially after you went out of your way to help me."

She thought of the two completed rooms upstairs sitting clean and ready. It was true the kitchen wasn't finished, but they were only days away from completion. What could it hurt?

"Well, thanks anyway. It was nice meeting you, Molly." He was already moving toward the door. Someone had closed it while they were working on the stand, and the air was getting a little stuffy.

"Wait," she said. "Listen, maybe we can offer you a room for a night or two."

"I'm actually planning to stay in town a while—through the end of July probably."

"I see. Well, you could always move someplace else after the weekend. There'll be plenty of vacancies starting Monday night."

He shifted in the doorway. "Are you sure? I don't want to be in the way."

She gave him a wry look. "Have you looked around? *We're* going to be in *your* way."

His laugh was warm and mellow, pleasant. "At this point I'll be happy to have a roof over my head."

"There is a roof, but I can't guarantee there won't be people stomping across it. And saws buzzing, and hammering and whatnot. But everything shuts down by suppertime, and mornings usually don't start till eight or nine. Can you live with that?"

He gave a nod. "I'm grateful. Thank you."

"It's the least I could do after all your help."

As if on cue Grace burst through the front door, backpack swinging from her thin shoulders, wearing her volleyball clothes. Molly had completely missed the sound of her loud car pulling up to the house.

"Hey," Grace said in greeting. Her long blonde ponytail swung as she looked to the space where the new piece of furniture now stood. Her face fell.

"You owe me a cone," Molly said smugly. "Double scoop with sprinkles."

"Fine. But I got an A on my math test, so you have to pay for pizza tonight."

"Well worth it. Great job, kid." Molly high-fived her sister, then shifted her attention to

Adam. "Grace, meet our first guest, Mr. Bradford. This is my sister, Grace, straight out of volleyball practice."

He extended his hand. "It's just Adam. Nice to meet you."

Molly found his shy demeanor inordinately appealing. Maybe because it was so different from Dominic's arrogance.

"You too," Grace said before addressing Molly. "I thought we weren't open yet."

"We're not exactly."

"She took pity on me," Adam said. "There's no place else to stay."

Molly and Grace exchanged a look. Yes, their brother was going to throw a fit, but Molly was willing to risk it after Adam had been so generous with his time.

"Are you sure it's all right?" Adam had apparently picked up on the unspoken message passing between the sisters.

"Absolutely. Let's get you checked in." Molly stepped behind the counter and opened the registration page.

"Need some help with the system?" Grace joined her behind the counter, dropping her bag.

"I think I remember." Molly went through the check-in process step by step, taking Adam's credit card and having him sign in. She quoted what would be their regular rate and offered him 50 percent off for the inconvenience.

He thanked her as he pocketed his credit card.

Molly opened the antique cabinet and withdrew the key for room seven. "Here you are. Let me show you around, then I'll take you to your room."

"I have to get my bag. I'll be right back."

Molly watched through the picture window as he strode across the porch and down the steps. He was dressed business casual in khakis and a blue shirt. She wondered what he was doing at Bluebell Lake alone and for so long. The area attracted mainly couples and families with children who enjoyed frolicking at the beach and riding Jet Skis across the twelve-hundred-acre lake.

Grace nudged her. "What's up with that?"

"What do you mean?"

"Levi's going to have a conniption when he finds out we have a guest."

Molly wiped the dust from the registration stand. "Oh well. This inn belongs to all of us, not just him." She watched as Adam withdrew a suitcase from a small blue sedan. "He kind of looks like that actor from *The Notebook*, don't you think?"

"Ryan Gosling? Are you kidding me?"

"Well . . . at the end of the movie, when he was all lovelorn and kind of scruffy looking."

Grace snorted. "A nerdy Ryan Gosling maybe."

"He's not nerdy. Scholarly maybe." Molly

didn't know why she felt the need to defend him. She watched him bump the car door shut and start making his way back to the house.

"I think somebody's smitten with our new guest."

Molly rolled her eyes. "You know my heart belongs, now and forevermore, to Nathaniel Quinn."

"Most women fall in love with the *heroes* of romance novels, not the authors."

"Book boyfriends aren't real; authors are." Molly waggled her head at Grace and walked away.

two

"L et's start with this side—it's not under construction." Molly beamed at Adam as he entered the foyer, her smile so warm and bright it could probably burn off the morning fog. He noticed a shallow dimple in her left cheek. "It's my first tour, so you'll have to be patient with me. Little warning: sometimes I talk too much."

Adam hitched his laptop bag higher on his shoulder. "I'm sure you'll do fine."

"I'll show you the library first. The dining room won't be of much use to you anyway. Where are you from, Mr. Bradford?"

"Adam, please. I'm from New York. I flew in early this morning, and I've been trying to find a vacancy ever since."

"Well, your search is over. You're a little ways from home."

"Yes, I am." He struggled for something else to say and came up empty.

Molly seemed awfully young to be running an inn. He followed her to the left of the stand and down a short hall. This part of the house seemed untouched by the construction. It featured the high ceilings of a bygone area, original mahogany woodwork, and squeaky wood floors.

"So what's the history behind this place?" he asked.

"Well, as I said before, it was built in 1905," she said over her shoulder. "Bluebell's first inn. Early on it became a stagecoach stop, and it's been many things over the years, including a saloon, if you can believe it. It was even a post office for a while. In the sixties—the lake's real heyday—other hotels opened, but the Bluebell Inn remained *the* place to stay.

"Unfortunately, the area declined in popularity in the seventies, and the inn was purchased by the governor's family and made into a summer home. They lived here until my parents bought it. My siblings and I grew up here."

"If only the walls could talk," he said. "I'll bet they'd have some good stories."

Her smile widened. "I know, right? The last innkeeper's wife kept a journal, though, and we have it right here in our library. Fascinating stuff and as close to talking walls as we're going to get, I'm afraid."

Maybe he'd find a spark there. Although the sixties weren't really his sweet spot.

Molly continued her tour. "The Bluebell Inn—we've kept the original name, by the way—has the distinction of being the only hotel that's both downtown *and* on the lake. The best of both worlds."

"Convenient for me, for certain. So your parents own the inn then?"

Her smile faltered just a split second before she bolstered it. "That was their plan for retirement . . . but I'm afraid they passed away last summer. My siblings and I are opening it on our own now."

He stopped just shy of the room she'd entered, wishing he could call back his question. "I'm so sorry." He wanted to say more. That he was impressed by her resolve and commitment. By her strength. But uncertainty made the words congeal in his throat.

"Thank you." She gestured him inside the room.

It was about twelve by fifteen, had wall-to-wall shelves, a dark leather sofa and coffee table, and an old desk situated in front of a large picture window.

"I never asked what brought you to Bluebell," she said. "Business or pleasure?"

"Business." He smiled politely and began looking around, not really wanting to expound. It got tricky sometimes, protecting his anonymity.

"Oh, all right. Well, let me know if I can be of service in any way. I know most everyone around here, and sometimes connections are everything."

"I'm not really . . . That is, my work is more solitary. I'll be going to the library a lot."

"Oh!" Her eyebrows popped as her lovely eyes lit up. "Are you researching the area? We have some really fascinating town history, and I could connect you to some people."

"Yes, research. Exactly." That much was true. He needed to find a plot somewhere, quickly, and that's where it had always started before.

"I've read every book on the subject. If I can be of help, let me know. Speaking of which . . ." She gestured around the room they'd entered. "Our library. We actually have several good books on the area."

He followed her to a shelf on the far side of the room, taking in the musty smell of old books. It was too warm in the room. Or perhaps he was only nervous. His damp palms were slippery on the handle of his bag.

She set her hand on the hardback spines of a few old tomes. "The downtown library doesn't have all of these, and you're more than welcome to help yourself. We have books on the town's history and a few on the regional history. I'm not sure which you're interested in."

"All of it, actually. Thank you. I'm sure I'll find these helpful." He browsed the adjacent section. *Desiring God*, *Mere Christianity*, and *Love Does*, among others. "Good books."

"You've read them?"

"All but *Anxious for Nothing*."

She dropped her hands to the pockets of her shorts. "Well, you're welcome to them as well. And if you find yourself in need of a quiet space

36

to work on-site, this would be your best bet. The construction is on the other side of the house. It'll probably be quieter than your room. There's the patio too, and it's in the shade. But it can get pretty hot out there even in late May."

He took in the view of the lake through the picture window. A shaded lawn stretched down to the grassy shore where a wooden pier jutted out into the water. A small metal boat, tied to the end, bobbed in the wake of a passing pontoon. He turned to take in the rest of the room. "I can't imagine a better place to work or read."

"I know. My brother wanted to turn it into a guest room. Can you imagine? He's all dollars and cents."

"I'm glad you kept it as it is. I may use it a bit tomorrow, if I won't be in your way."

"Not at all. That's what it's here for."

"Do you live on the premises?" he asked. Muse or no, she might be a little distracting.

"Yes, all three of us do. My sister and I share a room, and my brother took the maid's room off the kitchen."

He stopped by a wall of shelves that housed a generous fiction section.

"As you can see, we're well-stocked in fiction, too, if you enjoy reading novels."

"I do." His eyes scanned the shelves, finding everything from the classics—Austen, Dickens,

Twain, Brontë—to the contemporary genres of mystery, thriller, sci-fi, and romance.

"My dad liked to read a bit of everything, but I primarily read women's fiction and romance—you probably don't read those genres."

"I sometimes do. Actually, men account for 19 percent of those who read romance novels."

"You don't say."

"Of course science fiction is the most popular genre for men at 69 percent, followed by crime and thriller at 62."

She blinked at him.

And still his mouth kept moving. "Overall about 47 percent of Americans read fiction. It was on the rise from 2002 to 2008, but it's been dropping slowly ever since. Men are more likely to read nonfiction than women though." *Shut up, Adam.* He pressed his lips together.

Her head tilted, studying him as if maybe he was an alien from one of those sci-fi novels. "Interesting."

Not to normal people.

His eyes suddenly fell on a series of familiar spines. On the name spanning their lengths. His throat tightened uncomfortably, constricting his airway.

He hitched his bag on his shoulder and moved away from the shelves, distancing himself from the books. He made a beeline toward the door, hoping all his blood hadn't rushed into his face.

She stopped talking suddenly—his first clue she'd been speaking at all. And he'd rudely walked away. *Smooth, Bradford.*

"I'm so sorry," she blurted out before he could figure out what to say. "Here you are, lugging around your heavy bag while I rattle on about books. Let me show you up to your room."

He hated that he'd made her feel bad but couldn't think of a thing to say that didn't involve random statistics or irrelevant details. So he just followed her back down the hall, around the check-in desk, and up the staircase, while she filled the silence with her lovely chatter.

He found her gift of gab charming and was envious of her easy way with people. She'd do well as an innkeeper, despite her youth. She wasn't *that* young, and though he'd barely reached thirty himself, he'd always felt older than he actually was.

At the top of the steps they took a left, and he followed her down the hallway. The faint smell of new carpet welcomed him. Wall sconces shed golden light on the space and made copper highlights sparkle in Molly's dark hair. Her white top billowed behind her, reaching just past the waistline of her shorts.

Whoever her parents were, they would be proud of her, he thought with sudden sentimentality. He of all people knew how important that was.

He hoped he might find the opportunity, and the words, to tell her that before they parted ways.

"Here we are," she said as they turned a corner. The white five-panel door bore many coats of paint and featured the old-style glass knobs. The skeleton keyhole was still in place, but a deadbolt had been installed above it.

She stepped aside so he could unlock the door.

"It's all made up," she said. "But you'll have to adjust the air. I'll be making up the room each day whenever you slip out."

He blinked at her, the idea of her entering his personal space both disconcerting and pleasant.

"Molly . . ." A male voice shouted from down the hall as Adam carried his bags inside. "Where are you?"

"Be right there." Her voice was rushed as she backed away. "If you need anything, please let me know."

Before he could respond a man rounded the corner. He was a few inches taller than Adam with the build of a wide receiver, rugged in paint-stained jeans and a sleeveless T-shirt. He looked like someone Adam might cast as a hero in one of his novels—tall, dark, and handsome. Intelligence—and disapproval—sparkled in his clear blue eyes.

"Hey, Levi," Molly said, her hands searching for a place to land. "What do you need?"

Levi's gaze moved between them, his brows

40

drawing together as they landed on Adam's suitcase. "Hello."

"Hello."

"Um, Adam," Molly said, "this is my brother, Levi. Levi . . . this is our first guest, Adam Bradford." Her injected enthusiasm fooled no one.

Levi's gaze swung back to his sister, and Adam would've had to be clueless to miss the instant thread of tension drawing tight between them.

"Adam's in the area doing research," Molly said, obviously trying to fill the awkward silence. "He'll be staying until Monday."

Levi gave Adam a polite smile. "Nice to meet you."

"Likewise. Is everything all right?"

"Absolutely," Molly said enthusiastically. "Fine and dandy."

Levi's pointed gaze swung back to his sister. "Molly . . . might I have a word with you downstairs?"

three

Molly followed Levi down the staircase, across the foyer, and out onto the porch. He shut the door behind them and turned on her, crossing his arms over his chest.

She tried to focus on the sweet scent of her mother's lilacs emanating from the bushes lining the porch. But it was hard, what with that look on her brother's face. Disapproval rolled off him in waves.

His jaw was locked down tight, his lips were pressed into a firm line, and even global warming wouldn't melt the glacial look in his eyes.

She held up a hand. "I know we're not open yet. I know we're still under construction. But the guy had a rental reservation that fell through, and every place in town is full. He's here on business. You'll hardly even know he's here."

Levi palmed the back of his neck, still eying her.

She set her fingers on her temples. "I know, I know. I turned away the other people this morning, but Adam was so kind to help me with the stand—it took a whole hour, and he didn't so much as complain. He read the directions for me—they were in French! And I thought the least I could do was offer him a roof over his head."

Levi unlocked his jaw. "I sent someone over to help you with that."

"I know—that's who I thought Adam was. Your friend never even came!" So this was really his fault, if they wanted to get down to brass tacks. She knew better than to verbalize the thought.

Levi gave his head a shake. "That's not the point, Molly. We haven't had the final inspection yet. We have no lodging permit. Do you know what'll happen if the Department of Health finds out we're hosting guests already?"

"Guest. Singular." As if it mattered.

He gave her a scathing look. "All this work could be undone by that one impetuous action. Do you understand that?"

"Of course I understand. I'm not dim-witted. But it's only three nights."

"That's three too many."

"It's the weekend, Adam. Who's even going to know?"

"How about all the people we have working their butts off on a holiday weekend to help us open by next weekend?"

"They're friends and neighbors. They won't say a word and you know it."

"We can't take that chance. We have to ask him to go."

Her shoulders stiffened. "I'm not kicking him out when I've already told him he could stay."

She was surprised by the ferocity of her opinion on the matter.

She pictured Adam's warm blue eyes, the shy duck of his head, and that blunt index finger poking his glasses into place. No. She would not budge on this. Her chin tilted up, meeting Levi's stubborn look with one of her own.

"You know what's at stake here," he said.

"Like my word? I gave him my word, Levi. That means something to me."

"It was foolish to give him the room."

"I concede it was impulsive. But I can't undo it now."

A long moment passed between them. A car passed by, bass thumping. A robin tweeted from a nearby branch, and wind-driven leaves scuttled across the road.

Still he stared her down.

She lifted her brows, her mouth set. But something squirmed uncomfortably inside. She didn't want to be at odds with her brother. It downright pained her. So much so that she'd probably give in soon if he didn't, no matter how strongly she felt.

"Fine," he said after a long moment. "But we can't take his money, Molly. As far as the records go, he's not a guest. He's just a friend spending the holiday weekend with us. That's the only way we can make this work. And please, let's not make a habit of this."

"I already checked him in and took his credit card. I don't know how to undo it."

"I'm sure Grace can handle it."

She wondered if Adam would agree to these terms. He didn't seem like the type of man who'd like the idea of freeloading. Then again, with the rentals booked and the other hotels full, what choice did he have?

Levi's eyes pierced hers. "That's my final offer."

"Stop being such a bully. This inn belongs to all of us, you know."

"Someone has to look out for its best interest. You've already admitted this was a mistake. Now you need to undo it."

Molly softened a bit. Maybe he was right. Her actions could jeopardize all they'd been working for since the fall. Jeopardize their parents' dream. His compromise was reasonable. And it would keep peace between them, something that, since their parents' deaths, seemed more important to her than anything else.

"I already promised him breakfast and told him his room would be cleaned."

"We don't have time for any of that if we're going to open next weekend. We're barely getting any sleep as it is, and you promised Grace you'd help her study for finals."

"And I will. I'll take care of Adam's room too, and anything else he might need."

"When are you going to find time for that?"

"I'll figure it out. Do we have a deal?"

Levi's eyes searched her face, softening as he no doubt noted the weariness on her face, in her sleep-deprived eyes.

"Fine," he said after a long moment. He turned to leave, but just before he stepped across the threshold he turned back. "By the way, you have drywall dust on your nose."

Molly brushed her nose. Her finger was covered with a thick layer of white dust. How long had she been sporting that look?

Great. Just great.

four

Molly's eyes were getting heavy, but after the long day she needed at least a few minutes between the pages of a novel. She shifted the pillow beneath her, getting comfortable. She'd had to go to the grocery to get food for their guest's breakfast—lately they'd been subsisting on Frosted Flakes and Cheerios. She'd come home, cut up the fresh fruit, and made blueberry muffins. They weren't as good as Miss Della's, but they'd have to do.

She hadn't seen Adam the rest of the day and therefore hadn't yet told him they couldn't take his money. She'd have to seek him out in the morning.

Grace entered the bedroom, looking as worn out as Molly felt. She'd helped Levi paint the baseboards in the dining room, and her hands sported flecks of white paint.

"You finished?" Molly asked.

"Yeah. It looks good. The floor goes down tomorrow. I'm starting to think this might actually happen."

"We're almost there."

Grace fished her pajamas out of a bureau drawer. "I'm going to take a shower."

"All right," Molly said, not looking up from her book.

"How many times have you read that thing anyway?"

"Four." Molly smirked. "But who's counting?"

"I can't wait to be done with school so I can *stop* reading."

"Are we even sisters?"

"Sometimes I wonder."

"I just love the way he words things. Listen to this."

Grace groaned.

But Molly didn't let that stop her. She flipped back a page and found one of the highlighted paragraphs. Some of the pages were more yellow than white. *"The night sky was as dark and desolate as her soul. The cool breeze brushing her skin gave no comfort tonight. Her heart was a brittle shell, cracked and threatening to splinter into a million pieces, a condition only made worse by one inevitable truth: this time he would not be there to put it back together."* Molly sighed. "Isn't that just delicious? And there's plenty more where that came from."

"That's quite all right. You can stop now."

"Nathaniel Quinn puts words to my thoughts. It's like he's inside my mind thinking like I think and feeling what I feel."

Grace rolled her eyes. "Whatever you say, sis."

"Someday, when you fall in love, you'll understand."

"You know . . ." Grace stopped at the threshold

of the bathroom. "Nathaniel Quinn isn't his real name. It's only a pseudonym."

"Of course I know that. I'm the one who told you."

"Well . . . maybe *he's* actually a *she*."

Molly snorted. "That's ridiculous. Why would a woman use a male pseudonym? Besides, he writes the hero's point of view equally well. They're downright swoon worthy."

"And yet, it's not them you're in love with. How can you still be such a romantic after what happened with—" Grace went still. "Sorry. Shouldn't have brought it up."

"It's fine." Molly waved away her concern. "I'm over him."

And she was. It had been two whole summers ago, after all. Dominic had been unworthy of her love. She'd fallen for his lies, hook, line, and sinker, and he'd made a fool of her. She might be over him, but putting her heart back together was proving a more difficult task.

Adam found a continental breakfast sitting on the buffet table outside his room at eight o'clock the next morning, just as Molly had promised. The orange juice was chilled and fresh, the fruit bursting with flavor, and the muffins, still warm, melted in his mouth. Back home he often replaced breakfast with an Americano from his favorite local coffee shop.

49

He'd slept like a dream on the soft mattress, had a hot shower, breakfast, and two cups of Keurig coffee. There was no reason to stall any longer.

He packed up his laptop, tucked his phone into his pocket, and made his way out. He'd ease into it, just scout out the area today. Drive around, sightsee, take pictures. No pressure.

Except for those pesky emails from his editor, Elaine, and his agent, Jordan. His new book was due October first, only four months away. It wouldn't be so overwhelming if not for the fact that inspiration had all but dried up. Unlike his first eight books, which had all but written themselves, this one was eating his lunch, and he hadn't even started the actual writing yet.

He'd never believed in writer's block. Had thought it an excuse for lazy writers who lacked the discipline to sit down and work.

But he'd tried that. Had been trying for two months just to get the outline done. Before he even started writing a story he completed detailed character sketches and a chapter-by-chapter outline. He could write the actual story very quickly once he had an outline completed.

He had numerous pages of notes—basically drivel. He was a perfectionist, to be sure, but these pages actually were drivel. The wince on Jordan's face after reading them had corroborated his suspicions.

This trip to the setting of his work-in-progress was a last-ditch effort to inspire a plot that would excite him, not to mention Jordan and Elaine— and ultimately his readers.

Because he had plenty of readers. And having hundreds of thousands of people waiting for his next book didn't reduce the immense pressure he felt.

His career sounded like a fairy tale to most authors. Jordan, who was also his best friend from college, had submitted Adam's first manuscript, unbeknownst to Adam, to all five of the big houses. The novel went to auction and fetched a price that most writers, let alone beginning writers, only dreamed of.

It was somewhere between the offers and the contract that the nerves had struck. People were going to read his private thoughts. People were going to make assumptions about him, the author. Assumptions that, he was certain, he couldn't possibly live up to.

He'd already managed to disappoint his father, the one person he'd most longed to please. The thought of disappointing thousands of strangers seemed unbearable.

After telling Jordan he wanted to back out, his agent went to work with the publishing house and negotiated an agreement they could all live with. Adam would use a pen name, and they would keep his real identity a secret.

His book—his very first book—hit the *New York Times* and *USA Today* bestseller lists. And ever since, his house had been trying to convince him to reveal his identity to the general public.

The pressure was on yet again. This time Rosewood Press wanted to reveal his identity during a live interview on *Newsline Tonight* on August eleventh, the date of his next release.

He'd already rejected the idea, but they weren't giving up so easily. Well, neither was he. Better to remain in hiding than to risk disappointing the now-millions of readers who expected the author to look and act like one of his super-masculine heroes. Besides, he was already selling like gangbusters and had even gotten a movie deal. What more could the publisher want?

Was it this elevated pressure causing his block? Or had he finally just hit the wall? He'd pushed on in the past to great success, but for some reason he couldn't seem to break through this time around. He was starting to feel like a hack, and that wasn't exactly helping the situation.

He took the last of the stairs, looking both ways, half hoping for a glimpse of Molly. His heart sped a bit in anticipation, but she was nowhere to be found.

He heard male voices coming from the kitchen area, as well as the sound of hammering. He exited through the front door, disappointment weighing his steps. He was only eager to see her because she was a fresh dose of much-needed inspiration.

As he stepped outside, the cool morning air washed over him, heavy with the fresh scent of lilacs. Birds tweeted from a nearby branch. He'd have to stop in at the visitors' center and get a list of animals and plants native to the area.

He was opening the door of his rental car when a voice called his name. He turned to see Molly traipsing down the porch steps. A pair of shorts revealed tanned legs, and a blue T-shirt hung on her small frame.

"Wait up!" she called.

His memory hadn't exaggerated her natural beauty or her show-stopping smile. And there was that dimple again. His respiration increased, his heart rate kicking into a higher gear.

Take it easy, buddy. And for goodness' sake, no statistics today.

"Hi, Molly," he said, then cleared the frog from his throat. "Good morning."

"I was hoping to catch you before you left," she said as she neared. The sunlight glittered off her hair, which was pulled back into a messy bun. "Did you sleep all right? Did you find breakfast?"

"I slept wonderfully. And the food was good—best breakfast I've had in weeks." Also the only one he'd had in weeks.

Her eyes lit with pleasure. "Thank you. It wasn't much. We'll be offering several options once we open—and Miss Della is a much better cook than I am."

Something happy bloomed inside him at finding the right words to say. "I'm sure that's not true. I mean, your muffins were pretty good."

He winced. Three "goods" in thirty seconds. Where was a thesaurus when he needed one?

Her laughter was like a melody he wanted to hear over and over again. "I'm glad you liked them." She tugged at the frayed hem of her T-shirt. "I uh—I was talking with my brother last evening, and we decided we'd like to offer you a complimentary stay. Since we're not technically open and all."

He sensed trouble beneath her perky tone and too-bright smile. "Complimentary?"

"Gratuitous. On the house. Free of charge."

His lips twitched. "I know what complimentary means."

"Of course you do. I'm sorry." Her cheeks turned rosy.

He was mesmerized by the sheepish look, but also hated himself a little for putting it there.

"It's just the inn is an awful mess and such an inconvenience right now."

"Is everything all right, Molly?"

"Yes, it's fine. Really. We'd like to do this for you. Please."

"That's really nice, but . . . I'd prefer to pay my own way. And I'd like to support your efforts here. It's a noble thing you're doing—opening your parents' inn."

She scratched her neck and looked past him toward the shops across the street. "Listen, Adam . . . I'm going to be completely honest with you. I might have been a wee bit presumptuous in checking you in as a guest. We haven't gotten our lodging permit yet, and I'm afraid the health department would frown on that."

Why hadn't he thought of that? Likely they'd withhold the permit altogether. "I've put you in a bad spot."

"It's not your fault. It's completely mine. But it turns out we could be in a lot of trouble for checking in a guest before the inspection is done."

He held up his hand even as disappointment wriggled through him. "Say no more. I'll go get my things now."

"No, no!" Molly stepped in his way. "I don't want you to leave—where would you even go? If you're just a friend staying here, free of charge, everything should be fine. It's only a couple days, after all."

"I don't feel right about that, Molly. I'm taking up your time and energy and your space, not to mention jeopardizing your business."

"The room's just sitting there anyway. It's no trouble."

"I could pay you under the table, cash."

She was already shaking her head. "We don't want to chance that."

She obviously wanted him to stay, despite the risk. It was written all over her face and in her earnest eyes, not to mention her hopeful tone.

But he really didn't like feeling indebted to anyone.

"I know we just met." Her eyes were wide and bewitching, those flecks of color sparkling. "But I feel as though we're already friends."

His heart gave a squeeze at her sweet honesty. She was really special; his first assessment of her was right on target. How was he supposed to turn her down now?

Besides, she was right. Where would he go? Miles away to Asheville, where he'd have to travel the treacherous mountain roads every day?

His breath leaked out in a long steady flow, like a bike tire with a small puncture. "Okay. That's very generous of you. If you're sure it's all right, I'll stay."

Her smile was reward enough. "It absolutely is. That's great, Adam, I'll—"

"But only if you let me service my own room. And no more breakfasts—as good as it was, I can fend for myself."

Her face fell a little at the compromise.

"That's my final offer." He gave her a steady look. As much as he wanted to be near his new muse, he also had to be comfortable with the terms.

She pursed her lips, calling his attention to them. The top one was artfully arched, and a beguiling crease ran down the center of the full lower one. They were rosy, though he couldn't detect even a hint of lipstick.

"Okay," she said finally, backing away. "It's a deal."

He pulled his eyes from her lips, his face heating at having let them linger too long. He nodded. "Great."

"Thanks, Adam. Have a super day, and let me know if I can be of any help."

"Will do," Adam said. She was already helping even more than she knew.

five

Molly stood over Grace's shoulder at one of their eight dining room tables, peering at the laptop.

Grace opened up a window and leaned back. "These are the ones Mama wanted." She almost had to yell to be heard over the sound of the Sawzall buzzing in the lobby, where Levi and a friend were installing a window. There'd been plenty of grunting and complaining as they tried to cut through the native timber.

"Are you sure?" Molly asked.

"I found it saved to a file."

They were looking at the paper menu inserts that would be placed in holders on each table. The template with its decorative flower border and the inn's logo front and center did look like something their mother would've chosen.

"How long will it take to get them?"

"Three days if I rush it."

"Let's do it. Once we have the daily menu down, it'll just be a matter of printing them up from here, right?"

"Exactly."

They were so close to being ready—just hammering out last-minute details. Fortunately, their parents had been planning for the inn a long time. They'd hit estate sales and inn foreclosures the past couple years, gathering luxury towels, linens, and tableware. In fact, they'd been returning from such an excursion when they had the accident.

Once the siblings had finished remodeling upstairs, they'd just had to purchase odds and ends, install mini-splits to heat and cool the rooms, make room for a large linen closet to accommodate towels and supplies, and install a heavy-duty washer/dryer set.

"She also planned to have the day's weather forecast on each one," Grace said.

"Attention to detail. Mama was all about that." A bit of melancholy settled around them like a lead cape.

"Yeah, she was." Grace turned those baby-blue eyes on Molly. "Do you think they'd like what we've done?"

Sometimes she forgot how young her sister was. Molly wrapped her in a hug. "I think they'd love it. And they'd be so proud of how we've worked together, you know?"

"It's been kind of rewarding, bringing their dream to life."

Molly heard an unspoken *but* at the end of the sentence, so she waited. They'd all had their bad days, when grief crowded out the good memories. She'd been proud of how Grace had risen to the occasion.

"It's just . . . It's been a good distraction. But what if, once it's done, and we don't have that to focus on anymore, all the sadness comes flooding back?"

Molly squeezed her again. "Oh, honey. The sadness is natural, and you've been processing it even though you've been busy. We all have. And anyway . . ." She injected a hint of humor into her tone. "If you really think you're going to be less busy once we open . . . girl, you've got another think coming."

Grace gave a wobbly smile.

"Molly!" Levi called from the lobby, his tone demanding. The Sawzall had finally stopped, but she could hear other construction noises.

Grace rolled her eyes. "Better answer the master."

"What is it?" Molly called as she made her way out of the dining room, through the living room, and into the lobby.

"You're going to want to see this."

"What?" She prayed it wasn't a problem that would further delay the opening. Or cost more money. Nothing made Levi grumpier.

Erik, Levi's friend, was busy unwrapping the new window, which was propped against their check-in desk. They'd cut through the plaster and some of the lath, but the exterior wood still remained in place.

"Look," Levi said, pointing into the opening. "The old mail slot."

Molly gasped as she took in the sight. Indeed it was a letter slot from the days when the post office had occupied this space.

"That's so cool." She moved aside as Erik began prying the lath away from the lower wall.

"The exterior part of the slot must've been covered over years ago."

"There'll be a metal piece on the outside then, right? Can we salvage that part?"

Levi hitched a shoulder. "Don't see why not. Just don't tell the historical committee. They'll probably want us to leave it put. Frame it in gold and add a bronze plate for posterity's sake."

Keeping the historical committee mollified had cost the Bennetts precious dollars. Even the new windows had to meet their exact specifications— and this last one had to be ordered twice.

A large section of lath crumbled down. Erik and Levi began picking up pieces of splintered wood and tossing them into the trash barrel.

Molly stepped in for a closer look at the slot, her imagination running wild with thoughts of all the letters that had come through that opening between 1957 and 1976 when the post office had been housed here.

Her eyes fished through the darkness beneath the slot where the lath had yet to be pried away, and something caught her eye. A square of white, wedged against the inside wall. She reached into the space, wincing as her hand made contact with

61

spider webs. Curiosity beating back the horror of a possible encounter with an eight-legged creature, she felt around until her fingers found what they'd been seeking. She pulled the paper from the depths and out into the light.

An envelope. She flipped it over and found it addressed and stamped. Her heart thudded in her chest at the find.

"What's that?" Levi asked.

"A letter! It was wedged inside the wall. I wonder how long it's been there." She dusted the dirt and webs from the envelope. "There's no postmark."

"Well, open it and find out." He went back to the work of prying the lath from the wall as if— *hello*—they hadn't just found an old lost piece of mail.

She clutched the envelope to her chest. "I can't just open it."

"Sure you can. Slide your finger under the flap and lift it up."

"But . . . what if it's private?"

"Whoever wrote it is probably dead by now," he said over his shoulder.

"Your sensitivity is unsurpassed."

"And yours is off the charts. Open the thing. It's probably just a payment for a bill or something." He shot Erik a look that clearly said *Women*.

Erik snickered, and she shot a look at the back of his head. *Men*.

Molly scanned the envelope. It was from a

Miss Elizabeth Van Buren, whose return address was right here in Bluebell, on Church Street. It was addressed to a Mr. Benjamin Schwartz in Tennessee. The blue ink was slightly faded, the script neatly slanted to the side. She looked closely at the stamp, which bore the American flag.

"It's a five-cent stamp! Can you imagine?"

There was a loud splintering sound as Levi pried more lath away with the crowbar. "That would date it between '63 and '67."

Erik chucked a piece of lath into the garbage. "How do you know that?"

Molly stared at the envelope. She didn't know any Van Burens. "He collected stamps as a child."

Erik snickered.

"Shut up," Levi said. "It was a brief and unfortunate hobby during my awkward adolescence."

Molly wondered what the letter said. Maybe it was just a boring old thank-you note or something. Maybe Elizabeth and Benjamin were distant cousins, and the letter was full of trivial details of her daily life.

Or maybe, her inner romantic sang with a clear, compelling voice, it was a declaration of undying love—one that had never even been received.

"Are you still dithering over that letter?" Grace asked as she entered the bedroom, pulling the holder from her ponytail.

Said letter was sitting on Molly's bed where she'd left it when she went to take a shower and get into her pj's.

"Just open it already. You're building it up so much in your mind it's only going to be a big fat disappointment."

Molly ran her fingers through her damp hair as she studied Grace. She hated that her little sister was so cynical at the tender age of eighteen. If anyone had reason to be jaded it was Molly.

"Not everything winds up being a disappointment," Molly said. "Life can bring good surprises too, you know."

"Well, you'll never know if this is going to be one of them until you open it."

Work on the house had kept Molly busy all day, but not so busy she hadn't come up with at least two dozen possibilities for the contents of the letter, each one more fanciful than the next. Honestly, sometimes a big imagination was nothing but a curse.

She sank onto her twin bed, the mattress giving under her weight, and picked up the envelope. It was light in her hands and not very thick— probably only a single sheet of paper, she'd already surmised.

The mattress dipped as Grace sat at the foot of the bed. "Go on, open it so you can pick up your Nathaniel Quinn novel and get on with your life."

"Skye thinks I should open it too." Her friend would've ripped it open the instant she'd found it. She'd come up with another dozen possibilities about the letter's contents, all of them more realistic than Molly's.

"You should."

Molly gave the return address a lingering look. Grace was probably right. She was going to be horribly disappointed after daydreaming about it all day. She wanted desperately to know what was in the envelope, but there was also a niggling voice that said it was none of her business.

"Tampering with mail is a federal offense," Molly murmured.

Grace gave her a long look.

"Fine," Molly said finally and handed it to her sister. "You read it then."

Grace rolled her eyes and made a big production of gently sliding a finger under the flap and slowly, so slowly, parting the seal.

Molly's heart was thumping in her chest. Her sister was right. She was being ridiculous. Her romantic streak and love of history had combined to tempt her with this old lost letter, which was, in fact, probably just some big cosmic joke.

Grace withdrew a pale pink sheet of unlined stationery. Both sides were filled with the same neat script as the envelope. She took her time smoothing out the page and then began reading aloud.

"My dearest Ben, I can't begin to tell you how grieved I've been since you left. I ache, as I have never ached in all my nineteen years, not only for myself but on your behalf. I know Daddy's words hurt you to the core. I know the hopelessness you must feel at his rejection. I feel it too. It's that hopelessness that made me act the way I did, say the things I said.

"I don't know what the future holds, my darling. I only know that I don't want to face it without you. I shouldn't have said what I did. I didn't mean it, and my eyes have wept buckets of tears for the regret I feel.

"I should've told you I'd wait for you, that even war couldn't separate us. Instead I acted like a spoiled child, and now I fear I've lost you forever, and that is more than I can bear."

Grace flipped the paper over.

"And this is why I will say what I should have said that night. I love you, Benjamin Schwartz. There is nothing I won't give up for you, including my family, my inheritance, and everything that I know. If you will only tell me you feel the same, I will wait for you to come back to me.

I will wait four years or however long it takes, and we will become husband and wife as my heart has longed to do all along. Forever yours, Lizzie."

Grace's eyes lifted to meet Molly's. They held for a long moment, the poignant yearning in Lizzie's written words filling the space between them.

Molly's breath escaped. She hadn't realized she'd been holding it. "He never got her letter." The full weight of that realization pushed at her shoulders.

Grace's eyes fell to the sheet of paper. "It's dated August 18, 1964."

Molly took the letter from her sister. "Who cares what it's dated. He never got it."

"Maybe she called him when she didn't hear back from him. Or maybe he had a change of heart, too, and called her."

"I wonder what she said to him that she regretted. I wonder what her dad said to him. His 'rejection.' "

Grace hitched her thin shoulder. "Maybe he told Ben he wasn't good enough for his daughter. Sounds like something a dad would say."

"It could've been anything." Molly glanced down, scanning the letter for a long moment. "She mentions the war. The Vietnam War was just gettting started in '64."

"Maybe he was drafted."

"Or he enlisted. Maybe that's what they argued over before he left. She said she'd wait for him—only he never got the letter. What if he went off to war, never knowing how she truly felt?"

Sadness enveloped Molly like a heavy cloak. She could hardly bear to think of this lovelorn couple separated by a misunderstanding that could've been rectified, she was certain, if only this letter hadn't gotten stuck in that stupid mail slot.

Molly knew what it felt like to have someone suddenly taken from you. Maybe that's why she was having such a visceral reaction to the letter.

She'd been so excited to find it. It had seemed like her own personal buried treasure, tucked away in her pocket all day. Like maybe God hadn't forgotten about her after all.

Now she wished she'd never opened it. Never found it.

No, she wished it had never been lost to begin with. Instead, Lizzie had likely been left pining for Benjamin. And he'd never have known about her change of heart. The course of their entire lives had likely been changed by a fluke. It all seemed so random, so pointless, so cruel.

Molly released a soul-deep sigh. "This is awful. I wish I'd never found this stupid letter. I hate sad endings." She never even started reading a book unless she knew she could count on a happily-ever-after. This was worse—it was a real-life tragedy. And she was all too familiar with those.

"Look at it this way," Grace said. "Lizzie was nineteen in 1964. That would place her in her midseventies today. That's pretty old. These people are probably dead by now."

Molly gave her a look. "That's supposed to make me feel better?"

"Well, if their hearts were broken, their misery is over now. He could've even died in the war. And look, Lizzie probably found some nice man, got married, and had a houseful of kids. She probably had a long, happy life. Maybe he did too."

"You don't know that."

"And you don't know it ended badly." Grace gave her head a shake. "Wow, it's like we've switched places."

That terrible ache was back. The one that throbbed every time she remembered her last phone conversation with her parents. It hadn't ended badly. Not really. She pressed against the spot, but it did no good. It never did.

Molly gave the slanted script a good hard look. The worry clutching her heart was a tangible thing, like a fist squeezing in a death grip. She couldn't stand this . . . this not knowing.

She was going to get to the bottom of it one way or another, she decided.

"What's that look on your face?" Grace asked. "I'm a little scared."

Molly picked up the envelope and scanned the return address. "Elizabeth Van Buren . . . Have you ever heard of any Van Burens around here?"

"No. But that was a long time ago. People come and go. They could've even been summer people."

"The address is on Church Street, so not a lakefront house. It was probably their residence. I wonder if Miss Della would remember them."

"She's only in her fifties, isn't she?" Grace narrowed her eyes suspiciously. "You're not going to let this go, are you."

"Of course I'm not going to let this go. I have to find out what happened."

"What does it even matter? It's over now, whatever it was. *Long* over."

Molly blinked at her. "What if Benjamin never found out Lizzie had a change of heart? What if he's still alive and has been pining for his first love all his life?"

Grace smirked. "This isn't a romance novel, Molly. More likely he went off to war, came back, and fell in love with someone else."

"You're so cynical."

"And you're such a romantic. Love isn't resilient enough to last years and years without a stitch of contact. People move on. They get over it. They fall in love again."

She wondered what her sister could really know about love. "Maybe so, but they deserve to know what happened. Call it . . . closure or whatever."

Molly looked at the envelope. She had first and last names and addresses. How hard could it be to track them down in this day and age? Then again, she wasn't very good with computer stuff.

She wasn't good at it . . . but Grace was. She glanced up at her sister.

Grace's face froze, her eyes going hard. "Oh no, you don't. This project is all yours." She hopped up from the bed.

"But you're so much better with the internet."

"So go the library route. I've got finals, and after that I've got volleyball practice, and we're running an inn, remember? You're not going to have time to worry about some lovelorn couple from the sixties."

Grace disappeared into the bathroom, the door shutting behind her. A few seconds later the shower kicked on.

Molly looked down at the letter. It was true their time would be severely limited. But somehow, some way, she just had to find out what had happened between Lizzie and Benjamin.

six

Memorial Day, 1964

The warm sun blazed on Lizzie's skin, and a breeze fluttered over her bare legs. Eyes closed, she smoothed out the beach towel at her sides. "Who Put the Bomp" blared from a nearby transistor radio, and Lizzie sang along, tapping her fingers on her towel. The sounds of laughter and splashing and the smell of Coppertone made it official: summer was here. And oh, how she adored summertime!

School was out, the weather was finally warm enough for lake activities, and the summer people were arriving, bringing in a whole new crop of cute boys.

A spit of sand scattered over her feet, and Lizzie squinted open an eye to see her best friend, Nonnie Ludwig, showing off her spiffy red swimsuit.

"Come on, Lizzie." Nonnie reached out a hand. "We're having a chicken fight."

"Cool." Lizzie let Nonnie haul her to her feet, then ran alongside her toward the shoreline. "Who's playing?"

"A bunch of us. My brother already claimed you, and I snapped up Earl Foster—he's such a hunk!"

Lizzie glanced at Nonnie's bouffant that had been an hour in the making. "You're going to get your hair wet."

"Only if I lose!"

The water was cold on her legs as they splashed their way to the group. They were all kids from school, most of whom had graduated with them a couple weeks ago. They paired up, and sure enough, Lizzie ended up with Nonnie's brother, Doug.

"We're first up," Doug said, smiling big at the opportunity to have Lizzie on his shoulders. He was only fifteen, but he'd had a crush on her for as long as she could remember.

She gave an inward sigh but smiled at him as he turned and lowered himself into the water. She took one of his hands, stepped onto his thigh, and swung a leg over. When she was properly seated on his shoulders he rose up out of the water, and Lizzie tucked her bare feet behind his waist.

Across from her, Nonnie sat on Earl's broad shoulders, clutching the top of his head.

"That's attached, you know." Earl reached up and poked Nonnie playfully in the side.

Nonnie squealed and squirmed, making Earl almost drop her.

"Settle down up there."

"Then stop tickling me," she said.

"Then let go of my hair."

"This should be a piece of cake," Doug

muttered to Lizzie. "They're too busy flirting to pay us much mind."

But Doug had underestimated Nonnie's determination to preserve her bouffant. She and Earl plowed forward. Nonnie's stiff arms refused to give way, even though she was laughing her head off.

Lizzie was laughing, too, at the gritty look on Nonnie's face.

"Give it up, Nonnie," Lizzie said.

"Never!"

Lizzie felt herself tipping backward. Below Nonnie, Earl drove forward.

Nonnie squealed, and the crowd cheered.

Lizzie plunged backward, hitting the water with a slap. The sounds of laughter and squealing were instantly muted as water filled her ears. She turned herself upright, then pushed against the sandy bottom.

Her arms brushed against flesh, then hands gripped her, pulling her gently skyward. She broke through the water, sucking in a breath, and opened her eyes, expecting to see Doug. Instead she stared into the eyes of the most beautiful boy she'd ever seen.

He had brown eyes that turned down at the corners. They were framed by wet, spiky lashes. His dark hair was slicked back, exposing a low forehead and the black slashes of his brows.

She was staring, she realized. And clutching his

bare (very muscular) arms. His bare chest was only inches away. She snatched her hands away and put some space between them.

"Thank you." Her voice was shaky.

He was slower to let go, waiting until she had her balance. And seemingly reluctant to look away. "You're welcome. I'm Benjamin. Benjamin Schwartz."

"Elizabeth Van Buren." Someone had turned a million butterflies loose in her stomach, and they'd gone to war with each other. "My friends call me Lizzie."

"Well, Lizzie, I'm here for the whole summer. How 'bout you?"

"I live here," she managed. "Over on Church Street."

Those lips stretched into a smile, exposing a set of perfect teeth. "Cool. Your friends are calling for you."

Only then did she become aware there was anyone else around. She heard Nonnie calling her name, saw Doug's scowl. Another girl was already mounted and ready to go up against the winners, who were apparently waiting for her. How long had she been standing there, caught in his spell?

"I better get back to them." Lizzie gave Benjamin her best smile as she turned. "Thanks again."

"Anytime."

She made her way back to the group.

"Hey, Lizzie," Benjamin called.

She looked over her shoulder, hoping her dripping ponytail didn't look like a dead squirrel hanging on the back of her head.

"You ever go to the dance hall?" he asked.

She bit back a smile, her heart hammering in her chest. "I'm going Friday."

"Maybe I'll see you there, Elizabeth Van Buren."

She went for a coy grin. "Maybe you will, Benjamin Schwartz."

seven

Present Day

Adam grabbed a pair of khakis off the hook behind his door and folded them neatly. He hadn't bothered unpacking for his short stay at the inn, but the clothes he'd worn since his arrival were scattered around the room.

He'd attended church this morning at a little chapel in town. It was like stepping back in time to the days of pews and choir lofts and organs. The stained glass was beautiful, though, and the preaching was solid. The people were probably friendly, too, but he slipped in after the service began and out before the last "amen" had finished echoing through the sanctuary.

He'd had a couple productive days scouting out the area. His mom had been right. It was the perfect place to set one of his stories. He'd been busy capturing the sights and sounds and smells in his trusty little notebook.

This was the easy part—the factual part. All he had to do was take in the town with all his senses. Breathe in the smell of pine and fresh-cut grass. Listen to the distant purr of a boat engine and the slap of a flag whipping in the wind.

The local gathering place seemed to be a

coffee shop, set up in an old fire station. The parking lot was always full, and they kept the garage doors open, the crowd spilling out onto the paved patio.

The history part came next. He needed to ask Molly if he might avail himself of her library after he left the inn. Bonus: it'd give him a chance to continue seeing her. Strictly as his muse, of course. He'd never had one before, so he wasn't sure how this was supposed to work. He only knew that the more he learned about her the more he wanted to write her as his protagonist.

He tucked a folded shirt inside his suitcase. He'd found a lake house that was available this week. Unfortunately their weekends were mostly booked. That seemed to be the case with most of the rentals. So instead of getting comfortable in one home for the summer's duration, it looked as though he'd be drifting from one place to the next. Not exactly ideal.

A knock sounded at his door, and his heart stuttered at the thought of possibly seeing Molly again. Or maybe it was her brother, whom he'd also seen a couple times in passing.

He swung open the door to find his visitor was the former. Her dark hair was down around her shoulders today, her smile bright, bringing her dimple into play.

"Hi, Adam. Sorry to bother you, but I was

just . . ." Her eyes swept past him, and when they returned to his face the sparkle dimmed, as did her smile. "You're leaving."

"Yes, I . . ." He was momentarily at a loss for words. She looked so disheartened, and that was the last thing he wanted. "I found a house that's available now that the holiday weekend is almost over. Their guests had to leave early. It worked out."

She blinked. "Oh. Yes, of course."

He'd thought it was understood he'd get out of her hair as soon as possible. "I didn't want to get you and your family in trouble with the authorities. You've been very generous in letting me stay."

She seemed to recover, her smile back in place. "Not at all. So you found a place for the summer?"

"Well . . . no, not exactly. They have guests arriving Friday, so it looks as though I'll be moving around a bit."

She shelved her hands on her slim hips. "Well, that doesn't sound like much fun. You could just stay here, you know. We're not sold out a single weekend, so you'd have a room for the entire summer."

She hadn't mentioned that before. But then, he hadn't been giving the inn serious consideration for the long-term. "What about the permit?"

"That's what I came up to talk to you about.

We're ready to open. The inspector will be here Tuesday. I was going to ask if you could maybe clear out your things just for the day . . ."

"Oh." He shifted, his palm sweaty on the glass doorknob. He waffled. It was tempting to stay under the same roof as his muse the entire summer. So tempting. It could even make the difference between success and failure where his writing was concerned.

"We'd love to have you." Her beaming smile dimmed a few watts. "But I understand if you'd rather have a full house to yourself. Inns aren't for everyone. Especially old ones."

The dim light from the hallway gave her skin a golden glow and darkened her eyes to caramel brown. "You've been very welcoming, and you have a beautiful face—I mean, *place*. You have a beautiful *place*."

Why did he have to be such an imbecile with women? Heat rushed to his cheeks, and he fought the urge to cover his own face. Or better yet, shut the door and hide. He hoped she hadn't noticed his clumsy gaffe.

"I don't want to pressure you, obviously," Molly continued, "but please know you're welcome here. Full service will begin immediately once we have the permit . . . cleaning and a continental breakfast and extra amenities you won't find at a rental. If you think my muffins are good, wait till you taste Miss Della's. And frankly, you'd be doing us a favor, as we want to keep our rooms filled. Weekends are one thing, but weekdays are harder to fill up around here."

Well, when she put it like that. "I'm certainly open to the idea of staying. I just didn't want to cause you problems with the inspection."

She waved away his concern. "As I said, he'll be here Tuesday. If you're cleared out for that, we can formally check you in afterward, and you'll be set for the entire summer. I can even give you a bigger room if you'd like. Not our suite—it's already booked for quite a few weekends. But the corner room has a seating area you might find more comfortable for a lengthy stay. It's a little more expensive, but—"

He held up a hand. "I'm quite comfortable right here. Frankly, I'll be gone a lot anyway. And I intend to make use of your library if the offer is still good."

"Of course! You're welcome to spend all the time you like in there."

"All right then. If you're sure I won't be in the way."

Her smile was mesmerizing. "Absolutely. It'll be fun to have a guest around all summer. Almost like part of the family." She gave him a pained look. "Sorry. That was probably the wrong thing to say. Not everyone wants to get chatty with the innkeepers. Some prefer to just blend into the background. I'm going to have to get better at this. Levi's always telling me I talk too much and have no boundaries."

She simply captivated him. Her long lashes fluttered down when she was embarrassed. He'd have to jot that detail in his notebook.

"Not at all." He found her chattering ways utterly charming, but it was probably best to keep that to himself. "I look forward to getting to know you all. I can be packed up and out of your hair early Tuesday."

"That would be great. The inspector's not due until ten thirty, but I'll need a little time to clean your room. And we've gone to extra measures to be sure everything is up to snuff, so I'm sure we'll pass the inspection with flying colors. We only need to score 70 percent to get the permit—again, something you probably didn't need to hear."

He bit back a smile. "Check-in is at three o'clock?"

"I can call you when we're all set here. Do you have a pen? Here, just give me your phone."

He did as she asked, and she plugged in her number and sent herself a text. Getting a number from a woman had never been so easy.

She seemed a little distracted as she handed back his phone.

"Are you sure you're all right with this?" he said. "I could easily move into the house for a couple days until things are all clear."

"No, it's not that. It's just . . ." She bit her lip, calling attention to the vertical line down the middle of her plump lower lip. Another detail he should write down before he forgot.

"I was wanting to ask you about a project I'm working on—since research is kind of your thing."

"Of course. What is it?"

She tucked both hands into her back pockets. "If I wanted to find someone, how would I go about doing it?"

"Find someone—like a missing person?"

"Sort of. I'm not very good with computers, so I'll probably have to resort to public documents and the library."

Now he was curious. Was she looking for a birth parent? An old boyfriend? "What information do you have about the person?"

"Two people, actually. I have their names—just the first and last—and former addresses."

"I can't imagine it would take too long to locate them, especially on a computer."

"I know, but that's really not my—"

He was already withdrawing his Mac from his bag and opening it on the desk in his room.

"Come on in." He sank into the wooden chair. "What are the names and address? Maybe we'll get lucky."

"It's actually two names at two different addresses." She read one of them off her phone and came to stand behind him, peering over his shoulder. "This is awfully nice of you. I'm terrible at this stuff. Grace says I was born in the wrong era. I mean, I can get around a little on there, but I've mostly used the computer in school for documents and Excel, though I truly hate spreadsheets."

"Not a problem."

"Well, I am on Facebook. Isn't everybody?"

"I'm not." He scanned the results of the search, but there was nothing that included all the words he'd put in.

"Really? Are you more a Twitter guy? Instagram? LinkedIn?"

His lips twitched. "None of the above. But I can send a mean email. Well, not mean as in hostile but—"

"I understand."

"Social media isn't really my thing. So . . . this information isn't turning up much of anything."

"Well . . . I should've mentioned the addresses are very old—dating back to the sixties."

"Oh, I see. That is a long time ago." He was beyond curious, but he didn't want to pry.

"I found a lost letter," Molly blurted.

He turned and looked up into her sparkling eyes.

"In the wall downstairs, when my brother was installing the window in the lobby."

"In the wall?"

"Remember how I told you this building used to house the—"

"Post office." He was starting to make sense of this. How curious.

"Right. There was a mail slot, and the letter apparently got stuck in there for all these years."

Interesting. Romance may be his genre of choice, but he did love a good mystery. "Are you wanting to forward the letter to its intended recipient then?"

"Sort of." She looked down for a long moment before meeting his gaze again, guilt in her eyes. "I already read the letter. I probably shouldn't have—it's a federal offense to tamper with mail, but I couldn't help myself. And now I almost wish I hadn't, because it's a love letter. Even worse, it's a declaration that might've changed the course of their lives had the letter gone through."

Ah, romance and mystery with a thread of history. "You have me intrigued."

Her eyes lit up as she sank onto the footboard of his bed as if pulled there by gravity. "I know, right? Finally, someone who understands. My sister thinks I'm crazy, and my brother . . . ugh. Would you like to read the letter?"

"And become guilty of a federal offense?" he deadpanned.

She froze for a moment before giving a soft little laugh. "You're teasing me. Grace thought

I was being ridiculous too. I guess it has been sitting around a long time."

"I'd love to read the letter. It sounds like a—"

She was already halfway out the room. "Be right back."

He listened to the sounds of her footsteps going down the hall, a smile playing at his mouth. She was so excited about this letter—not that he could blame her. The mystery intrigued him too. Just not as much as Molly herself did.

He stood and turned his chair so she could have a seat when she returned, then perched on the bed's wooden footboard. She was back before he had time to get nervous about having her in his room again.

She slipped into the room, leaving the door open, and handed him a white envelope. "Here it is."

"Have a seat." He scanned the addresses on the face of the envelope, taking in the feminine script and the five-cent stamp. Then he lifted the flap and removed the sheet of stationery.

Molly watched Adam as he read the letter. His expression remained impassive, a slight glare from the window making it hard to see his eyes behind his glasses.

He held the letter with steady hands. His fingers were long and tapered, the nails neatly trimmed. Nice hands. Manly hands.

Why was she thinking about his hands? Her eyes swept upward toward his face. A lock of hair had fallen over his forehead as he read. He'd shaved this morning, and she found herself missing the slightly frumpy look of the scruff. Although it gave her a clear view of his jawline.

He turned toward her, letting the letter fall to his thigh. "That's quite a letter." His voice had a new husky note.

"*Thank* you. Honestly, my siblings don't have a romantic bone in their entire bodies. You don't think I'm crazy for wanting to track them down?"

"Not at all. I'd do exactly the same."

Molly felt her smile broaden. "I knew you'd understand. So where do I start? How do I go about finding them?"

"They're in their seventies now—or at least Lizzie is. She doesn't give Benjamin's age, but he's at least eighteen, if I'm interpreting the reference to the war correctly."

"Yes, that's a good point."

"I hate to be a killjoy, but I'd suggest starting with death records. They're public, and there's no point looking for them if they've already passed."

She knew he was right. "All right. Where do I find those?"

"The internet would be your best bet since you

don't know for sure where they were living. You could check local records for Lizzie or Elizabeth, but there's no guarantee she stayed in Bluebell her whole life."

"Sounds easy enough."

"If you come up empty, it'll get a little more complicated. There are probably hundreds of people in the US with those names. We don't have social security numbers or birth dates, or even middle names."

We.

Everything else he said went right over her head as she absorbed the unifying pronoun. That word warmed her heart in a way she couldn't describe or even fully understand.

"So . . ." he continued when she didn't respond. "This may very well take a while to work out."

"I'll check the county records first chance I get. Though Levi is kind of on the warpath about the inn. And honestly, I have more to do before opening than I even want to think about."

"Let me help with your search." He shifted a bit, just enough that the glare on his glasses gave way to soft blue eyes, framed in dark lashes.

"I can't ask that of you. You're a guest—I'm supposed to be serving *your* needs." Her brother would have her head. He'd already cautioned her about getting too familiar with the guests. Getting

Adam involved in her little project definitely crossed the line.

"Don't be silly," he said. "You've let me stay here free—for four nights by the time it's all done and said. The way I see it, I still owe you."

She waved his words away. "No, you don't."

"I don't care to be in someone's debt, and this is an excellent way to return the favor. Besides which, I love a good mystery, and this one's aroused my curiosity."

"I couldn't impose. You have your own work to do."

"Not so much that I can't fit in a side project. I'd love to get to the bottom of it as much as you would."

He seemed sincere. That was the thing she liked so much about those eyes. They were very sincere. After the debacle with Dominic, that particular trait meant a lot to her.

"Are you sure you'd have time for it?"

"Please." His lips twitched. "You had me at 'lost letter.'"

And then, as if the movie reference wasn't enough, he lifted the letter and sealed the deal. "These people—if they're still alive—deserve to know what happened. Don't you think?"

Molly's heart gave a hard tug. He did understand. She didn't know him well enough to know if he was a romantic or simply pragmatic enough to realize how important closure was. But right then Molly felt as if she'd found a kindred spirit.

"Thank you, Adam," she said. And she didn't know if she'd ever meant those words more.

eight

Who wants to do the honors?" Levi asked, holding the wooden vacancy sign that would hang below the inn's shingle sign on the front lawn.

Grace elbowed him. "You're the only one who can reach it, doofus."

Levi lifted the sign, not even having to go onto his tiptoes to reach the eyelet hooks.

Molly watched, swallowing past the achy lump in her throat. She wished her parents could see them now. Most of all she wished they were still here, living out their dream. She put her arm around Grace's shoulder.

Can they see us, God? Do they know we're all right? Can you let them know we are? And please tell them I'm sorry about that last call. I didn't mean to brush them off.

"Did I miss the party?" Miss Della said as she came up the sidewalk, all smiles. Her turquoise dress showed off her deep-brown skin, but an enormous bouquet of blue hydrangeas nearly concealed her face. "I heard somebody around here was officially open."

"You're just in time," Molly said. "Buck sent us the Godfather as a grand opening gift. Stay and eat with us." Buck's was the best pizza in town.

91

"I just might at that." Miss Della held out the bouquet to Molly. "Congratulations, kiddos. Your parents would be so proud."

Molly took the vase and gave the woman a one-armed hug. "Mama's favorite. Thank you, Miss Della. They're beautiful. I'll put them on the table in the entry."

Levi stepped back from the sign, having secured it. They admired it for a moment, as worry settled in Molly's stomach. What if—

No. She wouldn't go there. They were going to make a go of this place. Everything was going to be fine.

"Now we just need some guests," Miss Della said, as if reading Molly's mind.

"We already have one," Grace said, following Molly and Levi back up the walkway. "And he's staying the whole summer."

"Is that right," Miss Della said.

Once inside, air conditioning swept deliciously over Molly's skin as she set the flowers on her new table in front of the new window.

"Perfect," she pronounced.

Skye had sent a bouquet of balloons, and they danced on the check-in desk. She'd stopped by first thing that morning to congratulate them on the opening. Cards lined the wall behind the desk. The community had really come together to help them pull this off. From help with the drywall to plumbing to landscaping, Molly wasn't sure they could've done it without their friends and neighbors. It was enough to restore her faith in humanity.

"Now what's this about a summer guest, and why haven't I got wind of it?" Della asked as they made their way to the dining room. Levi began pulling a couple tables together while Molly grabbed the plates.

"I'm sorry," Molly said. "My oversight. Will you be able to set up for breakfast in the morning?"

"Of course. I'm planning to be here every evening to do prep work and come in bright and early to finish up. I already got groceries. Wednesday's menu is fresh fruit with homemade granola and orange spice muffins."

"Yum," Grace said. "Make extra muffins, please. They're my favorite. The menus are all printed up and ready, see?"

"Well, look at that." Della picked up one of the holders from the table. "These look lovely, Grace. And the daily weather forecast is a nice addition."

"I'll have to print them off each day," Grace said, "but we're going to be all about the details."

"Anticipate their every need," Molly added.

"Y'all sound just like your mama. She'd have loved the way this place turned out." Della's gaze fell on each of them in turn, her eyes glassy with tears. "But mostly she'd be so proud of the way you've pulled together. I'm proud as punch myself."

"Aw, thanks, Miss Della." Molly squeezed the woman's hand and blinked back her own tears.

The house phone rang, and Levi went to answer the call while the ladies finished setting the tables.

"So who's our summer guest?" Della asked. "Is he nice?"

"He's here on business, researching the area," Molly said. "And yes, he's very nice. It'll be good to have him around all summer."

Della gave her a curious look. "And is he single and handsome by any chance?"

"I meant, good for business," Molly said, but she could feel the heat rising to her face.

"Molly's got a crush on him." Grace smirked. "She's doting on him."

"I do not. I am not. For heaven's sake, he's a guest. I'll dote on all our guests. That's our job." Maybe she was protesting too much. She clamped her mouth shut.

"She thinks he looks like Ryan Gosling, which he totally does not."

"Is he the host from that popular music show?" Della asked.

"No, he's the actor from *The Notebook*."

"I just can't keep up with it all." She gave Molly a wink. "But it can't be so bad having a handsome man around all summer long."

"He's a *guest*," Molly reiterated as they found

their seats at the table. She'd called Adam as soon as they'd passed inspection and let him know all was clear.

"And yet you've roped him into your little romance project," Grace said, an impish gleam in her eyes.

Of course Levi chose that exact moment to enter the room, turning his dark gaze on Molly.

"That sounds intriguing," Della said. "Tell me everything."

Molly gave her sister the stink eye. "There's nothing to tell."

But of course Grace didn't see it that way and paid no attention to Molly's nonverbal cues. She rattled off the whole story, from finding the letter to reading its contents, and finally to Molly enlisting Adam's help.

Levi gave Molly a flinty look. "You asked our guest to help you?"

"He *offered* to help," Molly said with a thrust of her chin. "He *wants* to help."

"What did I tell you about—?"

"Oh, relax, honey." Della squeezed Levi's hand. "This sounds like a wonderful mystery. Now, what was the young lady's name again? Maybe I know her kinfolk."

"Elizabeth Van Buren," Molly said. "She went by Lizzie. I was going to ask if you'd heard of her or any Van Burens living around here back in the day."

"Hmm." Frown lines formed between Della's brows. "Not as I can recall. But I was just a babe in the sixties, and they could've been summer people for all we know."

"That's true," Molly said. "But she lived on Church Street. I can show you the letter later. It's up in my room."

"Oh, I'd like that. I'll bet they met at the old dance hall. It's where all the young folk of the day hung out."

Molly liked that thought. "It's a good possibility, I guess."

"For anyone who's interested," Levi said, "we have a party of three coming in at nine and staying for two nights. That's what the call was about."

"Well, that's great," Molly said. "Why didn't you say so?"

"Because I was too busy learning about all the lines you've been crossing with our very first guest."

A ding sounded from the bell in the lobby. "Pizza delivery!" a voice called.

Shooting her one last look, Levi got up and went to meet the guy.

Della gave one of her rich, throaty chuckles. "Now that's what I call being saved by the bell."

nine

Molly was behind the check-in desk by seven o'clock the next morning. They had house phones in their bedrooms, and Grace had been on call last night. No calls had come in, but it made for light sleeping. She was bleary-eyed when her alarm went off at six.

The previous evening she'd registered the guests—a husband, wife, and their adorable five-year-old daughter, Lily. They were in town visiting the wife's parents, who'd recommended the inn since their house was too cramped to accommodate the little family.

After that she'd helped Grace study for her algebra and English finals. Grace was smart, and she held herself to a high standard, which had only gotten worse with the passing of their parents. She'd nearly been in tears one night over a B on her midterms. Molly tried to help her keep things in perspective, but it didn't seem to work.

She'd hoped to see Adam when he returned, but he must've slipped in while she was helping Grace study. She'd heard the floor creaking in his room late last night, and his rental car was out front this morning,

She wondered if he'd had time to look into their project yesterday. She didn't want to bug him about it, but she was dying to know—no pun intended—if he'd found a death certificate for Lizzie or Benjamin.

The familiar clomping of Grace's steps sounded on the staircase, and Molly wondered anew that her slight frame could produce so much noise.

"Shh," she said when her sister neared the first floor. "We have guests now. You can't go tromping around the inn anymore."

"I can't help it. It's my last day of school!" Grace gave a little squeal as she hitched her book bag higher on her shoulder. "I'll officially be a senior. Summer vacation!"

Molly couldn't help but smile and refrained from reminding her that working at the inn would hardly be a vacation. "Good luck on your finals. I'm praying for you."

"Thanks. Have a good day."

"You too," Molly said, then watched through the window as her sister bounced down the porch steps and along the walkway. She really ached for her mom at moments like this. Her parents had already missed so much.

Molly heard movement overhead but couldn't tell if it was coming from Adam's room or the little family in the corner suite.

Other noises came from the kitchen where Miss Della was getting breakfast ready. The smells of vanilla and cinnamon—homemade granola—made her stomach growl.

The inn only served a continental breakfast, which had somehow made the licensing easier, according to Levi. They'd argued over this compromise since their parents had planned on offering a full-scale breakfast and a menu-based dinner, but Levi had been adamant. They'd start this way, he insisted, and shift toward a full-scale restaurant if the bottom line warranted it.

She heard sounds on the stairwell and recognized Adam's slow, deliberate steps. She moved her hair to the front of her shoulders, then rolled her eyes, remembering Grace's assertion that she had a crush. Nonsense. She just wanted to make a good impression.

He rounded the corner, laptop case in hand. Did his eyes brighten at the sight of her, or was that just a glare on his glasses?

Molly gave him a bright smile. "Good morning, Adam."

"Good morning. You have other guests already." He sounded pleased.

"They called last night. We'll have almost a full house this weekend."

"Good thing I got in on the ground floor then, so to speak." His warm smile was growing on her.

She wanted to ask about the research, but she checked her watch instead. "Would you like a table in the dining room? Miss Della's making her famous orange spice muffins and homemade granola this morning. You don't want to miss it."

"It smells delicious."

"Oh, it is. You won't be sorry." She led him into the dining room. "I didn't hear you come in last night. I hope you had a productive day."

"To be honest, I got a little sidetracked by your project."

She wilted a little and tossed him a look over her shoulder. "Sorry. Please don't feel you have to do me any favors. I'm sure I can figure out—"

"No, no, I didn't mean it in a bad way. I was looking for an excuse to avoid work, and I'm very curious about the whole thing."

"If at any time you feel you need to bail, please don't hesitate to do so." They entered the dining room and she gestured widely. "Take your pick."

He chose a table by the window overlooking the lake and pulled out the chair but remained standing. "I stopped by the clerk's office yesterday, but I wasn't able find a death record for Lizzie."

"Oh. Well, that's good."

"I checked with Benjamin's county also, and there's no death record for him there either. Of course, that only means they didn't pass away in the counties where they were living in 1964."

She sighed. "Right."

"So I did some looking online. I found obituaries for people who could be Lizzie and

Benjamin, but it's hard to say for certain since we don't have much information on them."

This was starting to look like a needle in a haystack situation. "Is it a dead end, then?"

"Not quite." He poked his glasses back into place. "I went to the library and did a little more research. I started looking through microfilm and found an ad for a general store—it was owned by Van Burens, so Lizzie was likely a resident."

"That must be the old mercantile. It burned down in the late sixties when the fire swept down the mountain."

"Maybe they left the area at that time. I also found mention of the family in an article. They attended St. John's—Lizzie's mother apparently did a lot of charity work for the church."

"Catholic. I wonder if there might be church records."

"I'll check into that next. A middle name or even a birth date would be very helpful."

"What about Benjamin?"

"I have a call in with the genealogical centers in Salt Lake and Fort Wayne. They're two of the largest genealogy libraries in the country. They might have records we couldn't find anywhere else. The librarians are supposed to call back today with anything they find."

"That's amazing. How do you know all this stuff?"

He ducked his head. "Research is my job. Look

at you . . . I could never run an inn. You're so good with people."

She chuckled. "Too good, according to my brother."

"Not at all. You're very hospitable."

Della appeared at the table with a carafe of coffee, and Molly introduced the two. Della poured him a cup; then, tossing Molly a wink over her shoulder, she disappeared into the kitchen.

Molly's face warmed. She hoped Adam hadn't noticed the wink. "I'll let you get on with your breakfast. Can I get you a newspaper or anything?"

"No, thank you. I'm all set."

"If you need directions or anything else, I'll be at the front desk most of the day."

ten

Adam had just arrived at St. John's rectory when his phone buzzed in his pocket. He turned off the engine and pulled out the phone, and saw *Mom* on the screen. He hesitated only a moment before accepting the call.

"Hi, Mom. How are you?"

"Hi, honey. Just fine and dandy. Thought I'd call and see how you're doing. I missed you over the holiday weekend."

Memorial Day at the Bradford house consisted of grilled burgers and a highly competitive game of flag football with an army of cousins. He could do without that particular humiliation.

"I missed you too. What's everyone up to?"

"Well, your uncles are already gearing up for football season, of course. Always strategizing, you know how it is. They were huddled up in a corner most of Monday, when they weren't playing football in the backyard. There's a transfer student coming in this year—a junior quarterback—they're all excited about."

His uncles and his father, now deceased, had coached his high school's football team in Austin, Texas. Last fall the uncles had finally led the Broncos to state, although they'd just missed earning the coveted state title.

"I'm sure they'll have a great year. How's Brody doing? I haven't talked to him in a while." His cousin was impossible to dislike, despite the fact that Adam's father had treated him more like a son than he had Adam. Partly, Adam knew, because Brody didn't have a dad—but also because Brody had inherited the Bradford athletic genes. He'd played quarterback under Adam's father.

"His job is going well. He just got his Class A driver's license, and he's got a job offer to work as an owner-operator."

"That's great."

"He'll be able to drive locally, so his mama likes that. He and Jessica are getting close to an engagement, I think. She's just a doll. You'll have to come for the Fourth so you can meet her."

"I'd love to, Mom, but I'm on a tight deadline right now."

"Oh, honey, you're always on a deadline. You have to make time for family. We miss you."

He had no doubt it was true. He missed them all, especially his mom, but distance was his friend when it came to getting along with most of his cousins. In a family from the *Friday Night Lights* state, Adam was as athletic as a penguin.

"I miss you too, Mom," he said, meaning it with all his heart. She had quietly supported his academic pursuits, his writing. "How are you doing?"

"I'm all right, honey. I mean, it's a little lonely around here sometimes, but I'm getting by just fine."

He worried about her since his dad passed away several years ago.

"I miss your dad, of course, but I guess we always will."

Adam was ashamed to admit, even to himself, that his life was actually easier without all that disappointment hanging over his head. Not that he hadn't grieved his father's death—but it was hard to miss someone who made you feel bad about yourself.

Adam had often wondered how someone like himself had been born into the Bradford family. They must wonder the same thing. But there was no disputing his genealogy. He looked very much like a younger, slighter version of his father.

His mom sighed. "Honey, this thing between you and your dad . . ."

"There wasn't a thing, Mom."

"Now you sound just like he did."

That rankled. "Well, at least I'm like him in some way. Hopefully he was proud of that."

"Honey, he was a flawed man. He placed far too much emphasis on athletics."

That was the thing. His dad hadn't just been disappointed in what Adam could or couldn't do on the field. He'd been disappointed in who his son was. Adam wasn't sure how to recover from that.

"Sometimes his love of sports blinded him from seeing all your finer qualities. You're one of the kindest people I know, Adam. You're compassionate and intelligent, and I've always been so proud of you."

"We both know Dad held little value for such things."

"I hate that his flaws damaged your self-worth. I know his relationship with Brody didn't help matters. I tried to warn him about that."

"Brody was the son Dad wished he'd had."

"Oh, honey . . . I wish you could be as proud of yourself as I am."

"I am proud, Mom. I just prefer to live a quiet life." That was his mantra, though it only told a small part of the story.

"Well, I suppose I can't blame you for that. Dora's daughter Ella is creating quite the stir in Hollywood, but she can hardly go anywhere without those photographers snapping shots of her. It's such an invasion of privacy."

Dora was one of her mother's friends from the auxiliary. He didn't bother telling her that authors—even bestselling ones—didn't draw the paparazzi.

"So what do you think of Bluebell?" his mom continued when he didn't respond. "Isn't it just the perfect setting for a love story?"

"You were right. It's beautiful. And perfect for this story."

His mom had come here in her twenties after trying to track down her birth mother. She found, unfortunately, that the woman had already passed away, but it was all her family research that had eventually led to her current occupation—helping people research their family trees.

"How's the outline going?" she asked.

"A little slow, to be honest, but I'm sure it'll be fine." At least that's what he kept telling himself.

"It'll be great. I can't wait to read the finished product."

Neither could he. Because that would mean it was done. But then he'd have to wring his hands, waiting for the professional reviews and readers' reactions. If they hated it he'd be devastated. And if they loved it he'd worry, because then he'd have to write another, and what if the well was dry again, or what if the story was awful?

That was just the writer's block talking. He loved writing. He did. It was just this stupid dry spell. The pressure congealed in his temples until the beginnings of a headache pulsed there. At least he had his heroine fleshed out.

"What's this one about? It's a love story, I assume."

"My outline isn't very far along, but it's going

to be about a famous singer whose career is in a free fall. She heads to a lake resort to recalibrate and meets a boat builder who has a link to her past."

At least that's what he thought it was going to be about.

"I can't wait to read it. Where are you working from up there? Did you rent a lake house?"

"Actually, I'm staying at an inn on the lake. It's just opened, but the owners are very hospitable, and the food's good."

"An inn—that's different for you. But you'll get your room cleaned and have towel service, so you can devote your time to writing. Very smart."

Adam glanced at St. John's rectory. Today's work had nothing to do with his book. Yesterday's hadn't either for that matter.

They chatted awhile longer about a committee she was chairing and the difficult personalities on the board. He commiserated with her. If these people couldn't get along with his easygoing mom, the problem was obviously theirs.

"Well, Mom, I should probably get off here and get some research done." And after that he'd go to the library and start his story. No excuses.

"Of course, honey. Send me some pictures when you get a chance."

"Will do. Tell the family I said hello."

"Love you, Adam."

"Love you too, Mom."

Adam hung up the phone, somehow feeling more lost and disconnected than he'd felt before the call.

eleven

Molly headed upstairs to see if Grace needed help with the rooms. The washing machine was already sloshing a load around, and the door to Adam's room was open, the cleaning cart parked in front of it.

"Grace," Molly called into the room. "You need any help in here?"

"I'm almost finished. You could fold the towels in the dryer, though, if you're just dying for something to do."

"All right." Molly was heading toward the laundry room when her phone buzzed with an incoming text. She checked the screen. Adam. Her heart gave a little flutter, which she quickly attributed to excitement about their little project.

New development in Project Lost Letter. I found Lizzie's birth date at the church. Heading to the library to see what else I can find.

It didn't seem like much of a find, but if he thought so, it must be significant.

She opened the dryer door and began folding the fluffy white towels. Could the new detail lead to a current place of residence?

She continued folding, and by the time she had the towels stacked in the linen closet, she'd made a decision. She pulled out her phone and tapped on Adam's number.

The phone rang twice before he answered in a hushed tone. "Hello?"

"Hi, Adam, it's Molly."

"Why are you whispering?" His voice held a note of amusement.

"Because you are."

When she laughed at herself he joined in.

"So you found Lizzie's birth date?" she asked.

"It was in the church's records. That's a very helpful detail."

She sensed hesitancy in his tone but pushed it aside. "Listen, Adam, will you be working on this for a while today?"

"Ah, yes, until lunch at least."

"Reason I ask is because it's my day off. I was wondering if you'd mind some company?"

There was a pause, and Molly winced. She'd just barreled across another line, hadn't she? She should start paying mind to Levi's warnings. "Listen, I shouldn't have—"

"I'd love that, actually," he blurted.

"Are you sure? I don't want to impose. It's so nice of you to look into this for me, and I know you have your own work to do. I can be a real pain in the butt, according to my brother."

"Not at all." She heard a smile in his voice. "I'd love the help."

"That's a bit of a stretch. But I'll bring my

111

laptop and maybe you can show me what to do. Or I can hunt down books or microfilm in the library—*that* I'm good at."

"Come down whenever you want. I'm at the little table behind the fiction section."

Molly smiled. "I know just the spot."

Adam couldn't focus at all once he got off the phone. Molly didn't really say when she'd be coming, so every time he heard the muted sound of footsteps on the carpet he looked up, expecting her.

He was excited at the thought of seeing her, of spending a little time together away from the inn. But he was going to have to tell her what he'd found after their phone call, and he dreaded that.

He drew in a breath, loving the musty smell of old books, the sound of hushed voices, and the quiet flutter of turning pages.

He went back to his search, using his laptop, but he was coming up empty. He'd hit a wall, and he wasn't sure where to go next.

At the sound of a nearby shuffle he looked up and spied Molly walking down the aisle toward him, her smile widening when she spotted him.

"Hi," she whispered, seating herself across from him at the study table. She dumped her purse and laptop bag in front of her.

"Hello yourself."

She looked so pretty with the daylight from the nearby window washing over her creamy skin.

Her shiny hair was down around her shoulders, falling from a side part, obscuring the corner of an eye. She wore a breezy white shirt with shoestring lacing at the top.

"How's it going?" she asked quietly as she settled her purse on the back of the chair and began removing her laptop. "Find anything new? I'm really good at library research, so if you need any help finding books or articles, I'm your— what? Why are you looking at me like that?"

He'd hoped to break it to her gently. He searched for the right words, but as was typical when he was speaking with a pretty woman, they were nowhere to be found. He should've texted it to her—the written word was his friend. But that seemed so cold.

"You found something, didn't you? Something bad. What is it? Did Benjamin die in the war? Tell me."

He had to put her out of her misery. "It's not Benjamin. It's Lizzie. But yes, she appears to have died."

The dread on her face was instantly extinguished, replaced by despondency, the depths of which seemed remarkable given that she'd never even met the woman. But he'd fully expected this reaction. He wondered how, when he'd only known Molly for a week.

"I'm sorry. I know you're disappointed. I am too."

"Are you sure it's her? Maybe it's someone else."

"I found the cemetery where she's buried. Once you have a birth date, it really narrows things down."

Her shoulders sank two inches. "We're too late. If only I'd found the letter earlier."

He shook his head. "She passed away a long time ago. Before you were even born."

"Oh." Her eyes became glassy. "I'm sorry, I don't know why this is hitting me so hard." She pressed a knuckle at the corner of her eye. "Who am I kidding? I've always been a bleeding heart."

"There's nothing wrong with that." It was one of the things he liked about her. "I couldn't find out much about her life, but she died when she was only thirty-five."

"So young!"

Across the way, another patron gave them a look over the top of her readers.

Molly lowered her voice. "What happened?"

"I don't know. I'm sorry it's not better news, Molly."

"She probably died thinking he didn't love her."

"We don't know that. He could've gotten in touch with her on his own before he left for war."

"That doesn't seem likely." Molly might be an optimist, but apparently not at the expense of reality.

"If not, she probably fell in love again and got

married. She had sixteen years between writing the letter and her death. She may have had many happy years after Benjamin left."

"That's true, I guess."

"I could probably find out a lot more about her life, but as soon as I realized she was gone, I switched to researching Benjamin. I was hoping to find some good news there before I had to tell you about Lizzie. Would you like me to find out more about her? Would it set your mind at ease?"

Molly shook her head adamantly. "No. I—I think I'd rather move on to Benjamin. I'd still like him to know what happened to Lizzie— that she'd changed her mind and tried to let him know. If he's still living, that is."

"That's what I thought."

She looked like a child who'd just dropped her ice cream cone on the pavement and didn't have enough coins for another.

"Listen, Molly, I know this isn't what you'd hoped to find, but all is not lost. Maybe we can still help Benjamin find some closure."

After a thoughtful moment Molly gave her head an abrupt shake, and just like that her countenance changed. It wasn't the beaming expression she wore as comfortably as yoga pants and a T-shirt. But there was a resolve to maintain a positive outlook. It showed the kind of inner stuff every heroine came equipped with.

"You're right," she said. "You're exactly right.

We'll focus our efforts on Benjamin. He deserves to know the truth."

"Thata girl," he said, feeling unreasonably proud of her. His face grew warm at his unwarranted familiarity. He started to put his hands over his keyboard.

But before he could move, she set her hand over his. "Thank you, Adam. Whatever we find isn't your fault; it's just what happened. You can't change the past. And whatever happened, I'm sure God has His reasons for it."

"Exactly right," he managed, though the warm softness of her hand on his muddled his brain and made the words more air than substance.

She gave his hand a squeeze before releasing it. "So have you been able to find anything else about Benjamin?"

"Unfortunately, I haven't. There are a lot of Benjamin Schwartzes out there. It would be helpful to find a middle name, birth date, or place of birth. We know he was here in Bluebell for at least one summer in '64, and we're reasonably sure he went to war that same year, but we don't know which branch. I've been looking at military records—we have an approximate age—but I'm not finding much."

"What can I do?"

"You could continue looking through old newspapers for his name. I left off on the third week of May 1964."

"Good idea. Back in the day they put all kinds of personal and social events in the paper. Even when and where people were going on vacation and when somebody was moving from one address to another."

"Well, maybe you'll stumble across something then."

And there was that beaming smile. "I'm on it."

Ordinarily, Molly could happily read old newspapers for hours. But Adam's news had left her unreasonably depressed. She felt stupid for shedding tears over a woman she'd never even met. What was wrong with her?

She got settled at the microfilm reader and forced herself to the task at hand, starting where Adam had left off. Back then Bluebell's paper ran twice a week, and she skimmed article after article looking for Benjamin's name.

As she read she delighted in all the delicious details of the daily lives of Bluebell residents, occasionally recognizing business names or surnames. The Randalls were going to Florida on vacation to visit Mrs. Randall's family. The Dorsetts were celebrating the birth of their first grandbaby—a girl. Pastor Frank was adding another weekly service to accommodate the summer people.

Molly got so swept up in the stories she had to keep reminding herself to focus on the task at hand. She found no mention of Benjamin through the end of May, but he likely hadn't come until Memorial Day weekend.

It wasn't until the first edition in June when her eyes stumbled upon some familiar names. Her eyes became greedy, taking in the article and the grainy photo. She jumped up from her chair and rushed to Adam's table, her heart pounding.

Somehow it hadn't felt quite real until now. Until she'd seen the names in the paper, in black and white. Benjamin had really been here in Bluebell. Had really fallen in love with Lizzie. The fire that had already kindled inside became a raging inferno. They had to see this through. Even though Lizzie was gone, they still had a responsibility to find and tell Benjamin.

Adam looked up at her approach, his expression turning hopeful as his eyes lingered on her face. "Find something?"

She couldn't hold back the smile. "Come take a look."

twelve

Lizzie had been looking for Benjamin since she'd arrived at Gibby's Dance Hall. The building, located across from the beach, was the place to be on summer weekend nights.

The zippy strains of "Runaround Sue" played from the speakers, couples spinning and twirling on a dance floor so crowded you could hardly tell who was dancing with whom. The smells of Chantilly and Tabu left only a hint of the earthy aroma of perspiration.

Lizzie's yellow party dress hugged her trim waist and flared generously over her hips and legs. It was perfect for dancing. She'd just worn it to her graduation party, and it was too soon to wear it again. But the person she'd worn it for had yet to see her in it.

Nonnie sidled up to her, sipping her fresh Coke. She looked exotic tonight, her black eyeliner turned up on the ends and her dark hair flipping up with meticulous precision.

"Have you seen him?" Nonnie yelled over the music.

"Not yet." Lizzie tried to appear nonchalant. But if he didn't show up tonight she was going to be so bummed. She'd thought about him all week and had gone back to the beach every day hoping for a glimpse of him. She'd taken such care with her appearance tonight—or rather Nonnie had.

"It's early yet. Did you see Earl? He's dancing with Cheryl Faulkner. I don't stand a chance."

"He's saving the best for last."

"Well, if he doesn't get around to it soon I'm going to find some other cat to hang out with, and then he'll be sorry."

"Well, look out for Charlie Watson. He's on the make tonight and he's blitzed."

Nonnie shuddered. "Of course he is."

Lizzie scanned the dance floor and found Earl's auburn hair, half a head above all the others. "You know he can hardly take his eyes off you—even when he's dancing with someone else."

Nonnie frowned. "Charlie?"

"No, silly. Earl."

"Really? Truly?"

"I wouldn't lie to you."

Nonnie pouted. "Well, why doesn't he just ask me to dance then?"

Just then Lizzie saw Benjamin near the entrance. Her breath caught. He wasn't but twenty feet away, and another boy she recognized from summers past accompanied him.

Benjamin was decked out in a dark suit and narrow black tie like most of the other boys. And yet something about him set him apart. It was those eyes, she determined. Those tilted-down eyes that might look sad if not paired with his crooked smile.

He started turning her way, and Lizzie whipped the other direction, not wanting to be caught staring.

Nonnie startled at her sudden movement, almost spilling her Coke. "Take it easy."

"He's here."

Nonnie looked over Lizzie's shoulder. "Who? Benjamin?"

"Don't look!"

Nonnie was smiling as her eyes returned to Lizzie. "Don't freak out, but he's spotted you. I think he's coming this way."

"Are you sure? Don't look!"

"I don't have to look. I have excellent peripheral vision, and he's definitely coming this way. And my oh my, doesn't he look boss tonight."

"What do I say? What do I do?" Her brain was suddenly mush, and her heart felt as though it might explode from her rib cage.

"Just play it cool."

A laugh came from her tight throat. She was anything but cool. She could tell how close he was getting by the tightening clamp of Nonnie's hand around her wrist.

"Excuse me," a baritone voice said over the music.

Lizzie tried for a casual expression as she turned and met those brown eyes. He was taller than she remembered. She only reached his lapel.

"Hi there." He was smiling at her, that crooked grin.

Lizzie couldn't help but return the smile. "Hi yourself."

"I was hoping to see you tonight."

She nearly swooned. No games. No dancing with other girls to make her jealous.

Nonnie prompted Lizzie with a nudge.

Her face went warm. "And here I am," she said a full five seconds too late.

The song ended to applause, and the familiar of notes of "Let's Twist Again" began.

Benjamin held out his hand. "Would you like to dance?"

"I'd love to." She put her hand in his and followed him to the dance floor. Halfway there, she looked over her shoulder to see Nonnie all but jumping up and down.

The floor was crowded, but they claimed a spot in the middle and began twisting to the popular song. It was too loud to talk, but she was delighted to see Benjamin was a good dancer. He swiveled his hips to the beat, working his arms like a pro.

Lizzie had been born with good rhythm, too, and matched his every move. Halfway into the song, he took her hands and led her in a few turns that had her dizzy and laughing. And happy. She couldn't ever remember feeling so euphoric.

She forgot about the crowd pressing in on them. Forgot about the DJ and about Nonnie waiting on the sideline. They moved together like they were separate halves of a whole. They communicated only with their eyes and gestures, and it was enough.

The song ended with flair. Lizzie clapped along with the others, her breath coming quickly as the DJ began spinning another forty-five.

The slower strains of "Moon River" began, and her heart fluttered as her gaze met Benjamin's.

His brows lifted, a question in his eyes as he held out his arms.

Without hesitation, Lizzie stepped into them. One of his hands settled on her waist and the other took her hand. She rested her palm on his stiff lapel and met his eyes.

"You're a good dancer," he said. The music was softer, allowing for conversation.

"So are you."

"I'm torn between wanting to dance with you all night and wanting to know everything there is to know about you."

Her face warmed. "We can accomplish both, I think. What would you like to know?"

His smile widened. "How old are you? What do

your parents do? Do you have a boyfriend?" He ducked his head at the last question.

For all his confidence, he was a little shy too. She liked that.

"I'm eighteen—almost nineteen. I just graduated. My parents own the general store in town." She paused until he met her gaze again, then held it for a poignant moment. "And no, I don't have a boyfriend at the moment."

"Must be something wrong with the boys around here."

She arched a brow. "Maybe I'm just fussy." She'd found her inner vixen, and she hadn't even known she had one.

His lips quirked, and the stroke of his thumb along the back of her hand nearly made her knees buckle. She'd danced with dozens of boys. She'd had crushes before. She'd even had a boyfriend or two. But no one had ever made her tremble with a simple touch.

She met his eyes and nearly drowned in the chocolate depths.

He gazed at her with affection. "Would it be too forward to tell you I've been thinking about you since Monday?"

"Is that so?" Her voice was breathy.

"Tell me more about you," he said. "Who's your friend?" He nodded toward the other side of the dance floor where Nonnie finally swayed in Earl's arms.

"My best friend since grade school, Nonnie. You're here with a summer boy, right? Patrick something."

"Patrick Lewis. His folks own a house out on Cottage Hill. They invited me to spend the summer with them." It was an older section of the lake where turn-of-the-century cottages stairstepped up the hillside.

"How old are you?" she asked. "And where are you from?"

"I'm nineteen—graduated last year—and I'm from a little town in Tennessee."

Her heart sank a little. So far away. But it was only the beginning of June; they had the whole summer ahead of them. Anyway, they'd only just met. She was getting way ahead of herself. But somehow she knew. She just knew this boy had the power to melt her heart.

"What do you do in Tennessee?"

"Right now I'm a custodian at an elementary school. They only keep one of us on when school's out, so I have the summer off. What are you planning to do now that you've graduated?"

She lifted a shoulder. "I have a scholarship to St. Anne's. It's a nursing school in Ohio."

His eyes twinkled. "I knew you were a smarty-pants."

"To be honest, I'm not sure I want to go." She had no idea why she'd admitted that. She hadn't told her parents or even Nonnie.

125

"Why not?"

"I like working at the general store with my folks. I like Bluebell. I can't imagine leaving and starting over someplace else."

"It's a big world. You might find someplace you like better."

She shrugged. "This is home. And what could be better than the Blue Ridge Mountains?"

"Well, I can't argue with that."

They'd grown closer together somehow. Their chests only inches apart. His freshly shaven jaw nearly touching her.

"Especially now," he said softly, stirring the tiny hairs at her temple.

thirteen

Present Day

ook, right there," Molly said before Adam could even get settled in front of the microfilm reader. "That's them, Benjamin and Lizzie. See, it says right here, below the photo."

Her finger trembled as she pointed to the dancing couple. The black-and-white picture included several people, but Benjamin and Lizzie were in the foreground. They looked as though they'd just completed a spin, her dress still flaring around her legs. Her head was tilted back, midlaugh, and Benjamin was grinning at her ear to ear.

Molly could almost hear the happy sixties music in her mind.

Adam read the caption aloud. "*Local girl Elizabeth Van Buren and summer visitor Benjamin Schwartz kick off the summer season at Gibby's Friday night.* Good work, Molly."

"Aren't they a handsome couple?" Lizzie was a natural beauty with delicate facial features, and Benjamin looked like a movie star of the day.

"They look comfortable together," Adam said. "Like they might've known each other a while."

"But it says he's a summer visitor, and lake season was just getting started."

"I wish it said where he was from. Is there anything about them in the article?" He was already scanning it.

"I'm afraid not." She was starting to come down from her momentary high. The article was only about the history of the dance hall.

He finished reading and, obviously familiar with the machine, used the buttons to center the page and print a copy.

Molly turned to the adjacent wall and pulled the oversize sheet off the copier, gazing at the grainy photo. She loved having a picture of them, of course. But she also realized it wasn't going to advance their search.

"What's wrong?" Adam asked.

"I feel silly. I guess I got a little overexcited. It's just a picture, after all. There's no new information. Nothing that'll help us find Benjamin."

"Not necessarily. A photo might help identify him if I stumble upon the right information. It could be important later."

"I guess so," she said over her shoulder. But she felt unaccountably useless, and the feeling had drained her energy and optimism.

"Hey," Adam said. "This is only the first edition in June. Keep looking and you might find just the clue we need." There was a brief pause, and then he said, *"Non ti dai abbastanza credito."*

You do not give yourself enough credit.

He spoke Italian—and quite fluently too. Her hands tightened on the copy. She turned, wanting to thank him for his kind words.

"It's Italian," he said before she could speak. A flush was rising to his cheeks. He poked his glasses into place as his eyes flittered back to the screen. "It means 'we're only just beginning.' "

She blinked at his translation, watching him work the machine with precision. She should tell him she was fluent in Italian, but his words had clearly embarrassed him. And she didn't want to make him uncomfortable by calling his bluff.

"Indeed we are," she said after a short pause. And she found that the prospect of future discoveries had once again lifted her spirits.

That, and Adam's sweet belief in her.

fourteen

Molly walked down the slope of the backyard beside Grace. It had been nonstop around the inn since Friday evening when their sixth guest had checked in. On top of cleaning and working the front desk, Molly had been doing everything from giving restaurant recommendations to busing tables to assisting guests with their in-room Keurig machines. They all had.

Currently she and her sister were tasked with cleaning out the boat, which had been used by a family of four that afternoon. Molly was hoping for a full night's sleep tonight. Six o'clock had come too early this morning.

"Have you heard from Sarah?" Molly asked as they walked across the recently mown grass toward the lake. Grace's best friend was in Florida for the next two weeks. The family deserved a vacation after making it through Mrs. Benson's cancer.

"We've been texting. She's so lucky. She's lying out on the beach all day, and I'm stuck working the inn the entire summer."

"Hey, that was part of the deal. You could be in LA right now, living in a strange city and getting ready to start your senior year there."

Grace sighed. "I know, I know. And I'm

grateful to you guys, really. But this weekend has been nuts. There's hardly even time to scarf down a sandwich."

"We're just getting into the swing of things. It'll get easier, you'll see." The old wooden pier shimmied as they stepped onto it.

"Ugh," Grace said as they neared the boat.

Molly stared down into the hull, frowning. Empty juice boxes, candy wrappers, and broken chips were scattered around the boat. Someone had spilled a drink on the bottom, and dead bugs had been caught in the sticky trap.

Molly handed Grace the trash bag she'd brought down. "I'll go get some cleaning supplies."

"We need to initiate some new boat rules," Grace said.

"They're in the rental agreement, but we already gave them back their deposit. Let's just get it cleaned up. From now on we'll check the boat before we give the refund."

Grace stepped into the boat as Molly turned and headed back toward the inn. Live and learn. She hopped off the pier, determined to keep a good attitude. Most of the guests were gracious and pleasant. There were bound to be a few bad apples.

"Hello, Molly."

"Oh!" Molly spotted Adam in one of the Adirondack chairs facing the lake. "I didn't see you there."

"You were chatting with your sister as you walked past, and I didn't want to interrupt."

Molly hoped he hadn't overheard them complaining about the guests, but the pier was far enough away to make that unlikely.

"I haven't seen you around the past couple days," she said. Not since the library research, which had turned out fruitless after finding the picture. She'd made it through June's issues and had called it quits when Levi called her for help.

"I've seen you running around the place, but you were always busy."

"It's been a little crazy. How's the research going? For your work, I mean. I'm not going to bug you about our little project every time I see you. I promise."

"My work's coming along all right," he said.

But something in his eyes gave Molly the feeling it wasn't.

"I'd rather be working on our project, if I'm honest. I didn't turn up anything new though. There are quite a few Ben and Benjamin Schwartzes living in the US, unfortunately. Also some deceased ones—one of whom could also be our guy."

"Let's hope not. If only he didn't have such a common name. Why can't he be Titus Dromgoogle or something?"

"Did you just make that up?"

"Maybe."

His lips twitched. "Well, I'm holding out hope we'll find another clue in the newspaper."

She had a thought. "You know, there might be some old-timers around here who remember them."

"Good thought. Especially Lizzie, since she was a resident. Maybe they'll have a birth date or middle name for us."

"It's Benjamin's information we need, so it's probably a long shot, but . . . Hey, what about the school yearbook? There are probably copies in the library. If we can find people who knew Lizzie and are still living here, maybe they'll remember Benjamin."

He tilted his head at her, his gaze laser-focused. "That's a great idea, Molly. I can check that on Monday when it opens."

Something about the way he looked at her made her cheeks go hot. "Well, it wouldn't hurt to check, I guess."

"If they have copies, I'll bring them home and have you look them over and see if you recognize anyone."

Bring them home. She liked his referring to the inn that way—because she wanted all the guests to feel at home. Or so she told herself.

He shifted a paperback book on his lap, and she automatically searched the cover.

"Oh, I read that one." She gestured to the Lee Child book. "All of the Jack Reacher novels are good."

"I stole it from your library. This is my first, but I like it so far."

"Why didn't you start with book one? I have them all in there."

He shrugged. "I liked the back cover copy on this one."

"No, no, no. How can you start on book six? Don't you want to know all the back story?"

His lips twitched. "The novels can apparently stand alone. I'm not lost at all."

"Well, yes, but—" She shook her head. "I can't read a series out of order. I mean, if I see a book I want to read, but it's the third of the series, I'll go back and read the first two before I start it."

He grinned. "You're an author's dream."

"Sometimes, if I have to wait like a year for the next book in a series to come out, I'll even reread the earlier books to refresh my memory."

He just smiled at her.

"What? That's perfectly normal."

"What are the most times you've ever read a book?"

"I don't know. Seven or eight, maybe?"

"And which book would that be?"

"Everything by Nathaniel Quinn." Grace butted into the conversation with all the grace of a lame giraffe. "She's read every book by Nathaniel Quinn at *least* ten times."

Molly's face went hot, and she nailed Grace with a warning look. "All right, Grace."

But her sister was just getting started. She shifted the bag of trash. "She's in looove with Nathaniel Quinn."

"That's enough." Molly's gaze skittered off Adam, too embarrassed to let it linger.

"Well, it's true," Grace said. "You talk about him all the time. Nathaniel Quinn this and Nathaniel Quinn that. Somebody put me out of my misery. If I have to listen to one more romantic paragraph I'm going to gag."

Molly gave her sister a flinty look, lifting her chin a notch. "I admire his writing. Now how about you go dump that garbage and get the cleaning supplies while you're at it?"

"Fine." Grace rolled her eyes as she started up the slope. She turned back to Adam and mouthed *Madly in love.*

Molly brushed her hair from her eyes. "She's such a child."

Adam was torn between being flattered and wanting to melt into the ground. That Molly admired his writing was extremely gratifying. She was well read and obviously bright.

He was also flattered by the fact that she seemed to have a little crush on him—or rather, on his alias.

But she was no doubt under the same illusion as most of his readers—that Nathaniel Quinn bore some resemblance to the tough, rugged heroes he wrote. Just the thought of Molly discovering his real identity, the thought of being such a disappointment to her, made him want to run far, far away.

He felt trapped in the chair. Worse, he felt exposed. His breaths were hot and stuffy in his lungs, the same way they'd felt each time his publisher tried to pull him out of hiding.

But he wasn't exposed, he reasoned with himself. Molly didn't know who he was, and she had no way of finding out unless he told her. And that sure wasn't happening. Especially now.

Molly was still talking. He had no idea what she'd said, but she was currently in some pretty heavy denial. Her cheeks were flushed, and he didn't think it was from the heat alone. Hard to say which of them might be more mortified by Grace's revelation.

"And he's a really good writer," Molly was saying. "I admire his skill, that's all. Are you familiar with his work?"

Adam rubbed the back of his neck. "Um, yes, I am, actually."

"He's good, right? I mean, it's hard to find such well-written romance, that's all. And he uses a pseudonym, so he's a mystery as well. And a bit of a recluse, I guess. Or maybe he's just shy."

Adam cleared his throat. "I've heard."

"So which is your favorite?"

His eyes flew to hers, dread lodged in his gut

at the thought of discussing his books, one by one, with her. Why hadn't he just said he'd never heard of the man?

But Molly was gesturing to the book in his hands. "Which author, I mean. I love Lee Child and his Jack Reacher series. I couldn't possibly tell you which one was my favorite though."

"I have a lot of favorite authors. David Baldacci, Richard Paul Evans, Daniel Silva, too many to name. *The Secret Servant* is one of my favorite contemporary novels, but maybe only because it was my first by Silva."

"That was a good one. There's something about that first, isn't there? Finding a new author you love? Especially when they have a long backlist." She tilted her head, a sudden flicker of appreciation in her eyes. "You know, I've really missed talking about books and authors. There's a book club in town, but . . . I don't know. The women who go aren't that passionate about reading. I haven't had anyone around who appreciates a good read as much as my dad did."

He felt a twinge of jealousy. What would it have been like to share something important with his father? To bond over books—over anything for that matter?

And yet Molly's words also warmed some place deep inside him. He loved sharing this interest with her. "I'm always available to talk books with you."

The back screen door slapped shut, and the sound of Grace's footsteps preceded her presence.

When she reached them she shoved a handful of cleaning supplies at Molly. "Brother dear needs me at the front desk. The boat's all yours." And with a jaunty little smile Grace was gone, having no idea of all the turmoil she'd just caused.

fifteen

Molly was working the front desk Monday evening when Adam returned to the inn. All but one couple had checked out yesterday, but they had another couple joining them tomorrow, celebrating their anniversary. Frankly, the quiet was a nice reprieve after the chaotic weekend. And they were gearing up for another full weekend.

"Hello, Molly." Adam smiled at her as he pushed the door closed. His messenger bag hung from his shoulder, and he cradled two large books in his arms.

"Hi." Molly beamed back, her gaze sweeping over the books. "Dare I hope you've come bearing yearbooks?"

"One from the year Lizzie graduated and one from her sophomore year. They didn't have the others."

"Yes!" Molly lifted her hand, palm out, and Adam met it with a high five. "Have you looked through them yet?"

"Only long enough to find her class pictures. I thought we could pore over them when you're off work." He ducked his head. "If you'd like, that is."

"I'd like that very much. I'm supposed to be

on for another hour, but Levi owes me one. Meet you in the library?"

"Sounds like a plan."

Molly called in her favor with Levi, and he took over at the front desk with only a minor scowl.

"Thank you, brother dear," she called as she fairly bounced toward the library.

Adam was sitting at the desk going through one of the yearbooks when she joined him. He'd pulled up a second chair.

Molly settled into it. "Find anything yet?"

He chuckled. "I'm only on page four."

What a lovely laugh. Deep and mellow, rumbling from his chest.

He opened the yearbook to the middle. "Here's her sophomore picture."

Molly leaned in, her arm brushing his. She caught a faint whiff of spicy cologne. Nice.

The picture portrayed a younger version of the Lizzie in the newspaper.

Adam opened her yearbook to a page he'd flagged with a yellow sticky note. "And here's her senior photo."

"She was so pretty." Molly stared at the image. "Kind of reminds me of that actress in *Enchanted*."

"I guess I missed that one."

"She's so young. Only about Grace's age here." Molly didn't even want to think about her little sister losing her heart to someone at her age, much less having it broken.

"So you go through that one," Adam said. "Look for any names you recognize. I'll see if I can find more photos of her."

Thinking of the index, Molly flipped to the back to see if she could find Lizzie's name and any pages she might be included on.

"I already tried that," Adam said. "I guess they didn't do indexes back then."

Molly started with the senior class, jotting down familiar names. By the time she was finished there were seven people she recognized as still living in Bluebell.

She started at the beginning of the yearbook and scanned each photo and caption. So far Adam had found photos of Lizzie in the glee club and National Honor Society, and Molly found her in both groups in her senior year also.

"Look at these glasses." Molly smiled at the cat-eye style one young lady wore.

Adam's eyes twinkled with laughter. "Far out."

"And this beehive."

"The boys wore slacks and button-ups every day."

"And the girls wore dresses and skirts. They all look so grown up and well behaved."

"I'm sure they got into their fair share of mischief. Lizzie didn't seem to play any sports. At least, not her sophomore year."

"I'm not finding anything her senior year either. But there didn't seem to be many options for girls. Just tennis and softball."

Molly turned the page to find pictures from the senior dance. At the bottom of the page a familiar face made her pause. She read the caption. *Friends Elizabeth Van Buren and Nonnie Ludwig take a break from dancing.* The two beautiful girls stood side by side, their arms around each other, their heads tilted close together.

"Look at this." Molly scooted the yearbook closer to Adam, pointing at the photo.

"There she is," Adam said. "Who's that with her?"

"Nonnie Ludwig, it says. There's a Nonnie Hartwell who lives in Bluebell; she goes to my church. That must be her. I mean, how many Nonnies could there be?"

He studied the picture. "They look close. As if they were good friends."

"They sure do."

He looked up from the book, his blue eyes piercing hers. "How well do you know Nonnie Hartwell?"

Molly's heart was thumping wildly in her chest. A big grin split her face. "Well enough to show up at her doorstep on a Monday evening."

"What are we waiting for?"

Nonnie Hartwell lived outside of town on the winding mountain pass leading toward Asheville. Her white clapboard house perched on a small rise. The yard was well maintained, though the house was sorely in need of a fresh coat of paint.

Adam got out of his rental and followed Molly up the porch steps. She'd been full of chatter on the short drive from town. Her face flushed with excitement, she was knocking on the door before he reached her side.

A moment later the door opened, and the older woman's face lit with a smile. "Molly! How nice to see you, dear."

"Hey, Miss Nonnie. How are you?"

"Oh, I'm just fine." The woman pulled open the door, revealing a full-figured body draped in a floral housecoat. Her thinning silver hair was short and curled, and her brown eyes twinkled with life. "Come in, come in."

As Molly embraced her warmly, Nonnie caught sight of Adam. "Well, who's your gentleman friend?"

"This is Adam. He's a guest at the inn. Adam, this is my friend, Miss Nonnie."

Adam shook her hand. "Pleased to meet you, ma'am."

"A guest, huh?" Miss Nonnie gave him the once-over, and he must've passed muster, because she invited him in. "I just made a fresh pitcher of tea. Come sit a spell."

A few minutes later they were settled in Nonnie's small living room. The evening light filtered through filmy curtains, softening the wrinkles on her face. She was somewhere in her seventies, and Adam hoped her memory was still intact.

Molly made small talk with Nonnie, asking after her grown children and grandchildren by name. She had such a warm way with people, putting them immediately at ease and making them feel important. He wondered if she knew what a gift that was.

After Nonnie inquired about the inn and Molly's siblings the woman got to the point. "So what brings you by, honey?"

"Well . . ." Molly looked at Adam for the first time since they'd sat down, then she turned back to Nonnie. "I was wondering if you could tell me anything about a girl you went to school with— Lizzie Van Buren."

Nonnie's sparse eyebrows shot upward. "Well, there's a name I haven't heard in a month of Sundays. We were best friends back in the day, you know. She was my partner in crime." Nonnie laughed, her eyes staring off into the distance as if remembering her friend fondly.

"Sounds like you have some wonderful memories of her."

"Oh, I do. I surely do. Now, where on earth did you hear about Lizzie? And how did you know we were friends? She's been gone for years— before you were even born, I'm sure."

"We saw a picture of you together in your senior yearbook."

144

Then Molly told her the whole story, starting at the beginning. About finding the love letter behind the wall, about discovering Lizzie had passed, and about their search to find Benjamin and give him closure.

The woman's face went from wistful to sad as Molly shared the story.

Adam's stomach filled with lead as he realized she might have bad news for them. If Benjamin was already deceased, the search was over. There would be no closure at all—for any of them.

"I'm sorry," Molly said. "I should've thought to bring the letter with me."

Nonnie waved the words away. "Oh, I know all about that letter, honey. Lizzie fretted over it for months after she sent it. So that's what happened to it. How tragic. How very, very tragic."

"She never heard from Benjamin again, after he left Bluebell?"

Nonnie shook her head. "Never did. Surprised me too. That boy was madly in love with her."

"Do you know what happened to him?" Adam asked, speaking up for the first time.

"I know he went off to war. When she didn't hear back from him, Lizzie went after him— much to her folks' dismay. But he was already gone."

"She must've been devastated," Molly said.

"Oh, she was. Hard enough having a fella at war, but to have been so thoroughly rejected and not know how he was faring or how he even felt about her. It was hard."

"And after the war?" Adam asked.

Nonnie gave a rueful smile. "Lizzie moved on best she could. She still hoped to hear from him, but she went on to college—nursing school."

"Did she fall in love again?" Molly asked. "Get married, have children?"

"Eventually she met a nice young man and settled down. But . . . I'm afraid she wasn't able to have children."

"That's too bad," Molly said.

"We kept in contact over the years, but she never did come back to Bluebell. Her folks owned the market in town, but it burned down in the late sixties. Instead of rebuilding they decided to move closer to Lizzie."

"It sounds as if she got over Benjamin, eventually." There was a hopeful note in Molly's voice. "Like she went on to have a good life."

"She did the best she could under the circumstances." Nonnie got a faraway look in her eyes. "Sometimes that's just all we can do."

"But what happened? If they were so in love, why did he leave like that?"

"I don't know the whole story—and it was all so long ago. By the end of that summer, they were so in love. Then there was some kind of big blowup. I don't remember exactly what happened or what all was said, but Lizzie was a wreck afterward. And Ben left town—the very next day, I recall. Lizzie was beside herself with regret. She was a very smart girl, but she was impulsive. I'm sure she said things she didn't mean."

"That was the gist of her letter," Molly said. "She was trying to make it right. But he never got the letter." Her eyes went glassy.

It was all Adam could do not to take her hand. He dug his nails into his palms. "That's why we're trying to find him. We want him to know she regretted her words and ultimately wanted to be with him. I know a lot of time has gone by, and it might not even matter to him. But we feel he has the right to know what happened."

"Well," Nonnie said, looking between the two of them. "That's surely a noble endeavor. But Lizzie turned over every stone trying to find him back then. I don't know how in the world you'd go about finding him all these years later, if he's even still alive."

"We have the internet today, though," Molly said. "We just need more information about him."

Nonnie's head tipped back. "And you were hoping I might have that information."

"His middle name or birth date would be particularly helpful," Adam said. "But anything you remember might be important."

"Oh, honey. My memory's still pretty sharp, but that was a long time ago. If I ever knew those things, they're long gone by now."

Molly's shoulders sank, but she gave Nonnie an encouraging smile. "Is there anything else you might remember? The letter was addressed to a town in Tennessee."

"That sounds about right." Nonnie's forehead wrinkled as she appeared to search her memory banks. "All the things I remember about him seem so inconsequential. He was here in town with a friend. I can't even recall the boy's name. Ben was a blue-collar worker, I believe. I can't remember exactly what he did. I'm sorry, honey. I'm no help at all."

Molly patted Nonnie's hand. "It's all right. Maybe something will come to you later."

Adam was touched by her desire to comfort the woman when she must be so disappointed herself.

"I'll give it some thought. Maybe go through some of my old boxes and see if I can find anything that jogs this old brain of mine."

"Thank you," Molly said. "That would be very helpful."

sixteen

By the time Molly and Adam arrived back at the inn, her mood had lifted. They'd spent an hour listening to Nonnie reminisce about the shenanigans she and Lizzie had gotten themselves into back in the day.

Though Molly was disappointed by the lack of information they'd gleaned on Benjamin, she felt as though she knew Lizzie much better. She didn't know why that was important to her, but it was. She and Adam rehashed the stories on the ride back.

Nonnie had taken to Adam, almost flirting with him as the evening wore on. Molly delighted in the way he'd ducked his head, a flush crawling up his neck. He was such a breath of fresh air. In high school and even after she'd been attracted to the heartbreaker types. But she'd learned her lesson there.

The stars were out in full force as they made their way up the walk, and the scent of jasmine hung heavily in the night air. The porch was lit with golden light, making the inn look homey.

"You know you have to show up at book club now, right?" Molly continued their conversation from the car. Once Nonnie had found out Adam was an avid reader, it had been a full court press.

"I thought you said it was all women."

"Well, it is, but only because we haven't been able to rope a man into coming yet."

He chuckled wryly. "Well, when you put it like that . . ."

"You have a whole week to read the book."

"That would be the novel titled *Hot Flashes and Cold Cream*?"

"It'll be educational for you. Besides," she added, tossing a coy look over her shoulder as she hit the porch, "Nonnie will be so disappointed if you don't come."

He gave her a look.

She was laughing at his discomfort as she pushed through the front door. "You know it's true. She was hanging on your every word."

Molly spotted Levi behind the front desk, hanging up the phone. He pinned them with those perceptive blue eyes. "Hello."

"Hey, Levi." She'd taken Adam through the back door earlier just to avoid the look her brother was giving her now.

"Hello." Adam shifted. Poked his glasses into place.

Levi crossed his arms, that bland smile she recognized so well barely curving his lips.

Adam cleared his throat. "I, uh, think I'll head on up."

"Take a cookie with you." Molly lifted the glass dome on the counter. "Oatmeal raisin—one of Miss Della's best. You won't regret it."

"My favorite." Adam took one, offering her a brief smile. "Thanks."

She replaced the dome as he turned toward the stairs. "Good night, Adam."

"Good night," he said to both of them before heading up.

Molly prompted Levi with a pointed look.

"Good night," Levi said belatedly.

Adam's footsteps receded, the stairs creaking in familiar places. Molly crossed her own arms, staring Levi down as the footsteps continued overhead all the way down the hall. A few seconds later Adam's door closed with a quiet click.

"You were rude to him," Molly said quietly. "And in case you forgot, he's a guest."

Levi snorted. "I'm not the one who's forgotten that."

"I'm a friendly person," she said with a thrust of her chin.

"You're getting awfully personal with him, Molly."

"Inns *are* personal. That's one of our many draws."

"This is beyond professional hospitality, and you know it. Hiding out in the library, running around with him at night . . ."

Oh, for— "We're working on a project together."

He rolled his eyes. "That's another thing. You

151

and that letter. It's taking up too much of your time. There's stuff to do around here. We have a full house this weekend and—"

"Don't you dare accuse me of neglecting my job. I've been working my butt off around here. I'm allowed to take two minutes to myself."

"We've already run out of complimentary shampoo—"

"A simple oversight. I've ordered more."

"And you never replaced the bulb in room three."

She huffed. "I'll do it now."

"Don't bother, I already did it."

Warmth prickled under her arms. Just because Levi was older and possessed a business degree didn't mean he was the boss.

"You're going to have to maintain some healthy boundaries with the guests, Molly. You can't get so involved in everyone's life."

She lowered her voice. "He's just helping me with the letter, Levi. That's all."

"Why does that letter matter so much to you anyway? Furthermore, why does it matter so much to him?"

"He's paying back a debt. He didn't like freeloading off us while we waited to get our permit—which was your idea—so he offered to help me. That's an honorable thing, Levi. Sheesh."

"I thought he came here to work. Don't you

find it a little strange that suddenly he has so much time to dig around on a personal project for you?"

"He's only doing this on the side. Of course his work comes first."

"And what is that exactly? Why is he here, other than to usurp all your time?"

"He does research."

"Research? What kind of vague answer is that?"

She narrowed her eyes. "I don't know, Levi. The kind he gave when I asked, and I was so busy keeping those boundaries in place that I didn't pry any further. Why are you so suspicious of him anyway? He's been nothing but kind."

He gave her a long, knowing look. The hall clock ticked in the silence.

Dread dropped like a pebble into the water, the ripples spreading outward, unstoppable.

Levi's left eye twitched. "I'm worried about you, Molly. You don't exactly have the best judgment where men are concerned."

Her chest constricted painfully. "Low blow, Levi."

She wanted to walk away, but she knew she'd regret it. She'd lie in bed stewing, feeling that clamp tighten around her heart until she was forced to go to her brother and make things right between them again. It seemed to be the way of things these days.

She drew a deep breath and blew it out, determined not to say anything that would drive a wedge between them.

"I'm just trying to look out for you, Molly."

The warmth in his tone made it a little easier to hold her tongue. "I know you are. But I don't need a babysitter, Levi. All right? I'm an adult. And I'm not going to shirk my duties around here."

He looked at her for a long moment, then finally gave a nod. "Fair enough."

Molly felt her chest loosen a bit. "All right. I'm going to bed now."

"Good night."

"Night," she said. Then, compelled by that inner nagging voice, she added, "Love you."

Levi gave her a strange look. "Love you too."

She'd been saying that more often since their parents' death, but it was an important thing to say. Because you never knew when it would be your last chance.

seventeen

A week and half later Adam was finally making some headway with his outline. He had a plucky heroine and an inciting incident. Perhaps the hero was still a little flat, but Adam would develop him as the story unfolded.

He shifted on the Adirondack chair, staring out at the still lake as he pondered the next plot point. A robin tweeted overhead, and a breeze ruffled the leaves. If he closed his eyes he could smell the damp earth from last night's rain and a charcoal grill someone had fired up nearby.

The lake lapped quietly at the shoreline. The boat was missing from its usual spot on the pier. Molly had taken an older couple for a ride a while ago. He realized he'd been anticipating her return and forced his eyes back to the screen.

Maybe he should work on a captivating first line. He really shouldn't be thinking about that so early in the story's development, but he did love a good opening line. If he could come up with something great maybe it would even inspire more material.

A text buzzed in, and he reached gratefully for the distraction. It was from his friend-turned-pesky-agent, Jordan.

Hey, how's it going? What are you up to?

Since the outline was finally coming along, he didn't prevaricate. Don't worry. I'm working as we speak. Outline is progressing.

He got a reply almost immediately. Finally, some good news. For a minute there I was starting to believe in writer's block.

Oh, trust me, it's a thing.

"Sounds like a convenient excuse to me."

Adam turned to see Jordan striding down the slope of the lawn, wearing jeans, a black T-shirt, and a smug grin.

Adam blinked, wondering for a second if his imagination had conjured up his friend. He set his laptop on the table and rose to his feet. "No way. What are you doing here?"

"Just checking up on my favorite author." Jordan grabbed Adam's hand and pulled him in for a shoulder bump.

But his friend was a good four inches taller, so his shoulder bumped Jordan's bicep instead.

"Lower your voice," Adam said, even though there was no one else outside. "When did you get here? How long are you staying?"

"Through the weekend. I'm here to crack the whip." Jordan made a whipping motion with his arm along with an impressive sound effect.

"No need. I'm well on my way to a solid story." Jordan moved in for a closer look at the laptop. Adam slapped it closed. "Not yet."

"You writers are a strange bunch."

"Tell me something I don't know. Where are you staying? Why didn't you tell me you were coming?"

"I'm staying here, and you would've told me not to."

Adam scowled, mainly because Jordan was right. Sometimes he questioned the wisdom of having a friend for an agent, but other than the fact that Jordan took certain liberties, he couldn't complain. His friend had gone to bat for him with Rosewood Press many times. That took guts. And loyalty.

The quiet hum of a boat engine drew Adam's attention to the water, where Molly was directing the boat toward the pier. Once it was in place she secured it and began helping the couple disembark. Their voices carried across the space, but he couldn't make out what they were saying.

"Did you hear a word I just said?" Jordan swung around to see what had distracted Adam.

"Of course." He'd been telling Adam about his delayed flight and the ensuing hassle with the rental car company.

"Is that boat available for inn guests?" Jordan asked. "Do they have fishing gear?"

"Yes . . ." Adam already knew what was coming.

"We should go fishing in the morning. I'll bet there are some nice bass in there just waiting for us."

"I'm here to work, remember?" Adam said pointedly.

"Who are we kidding? Your brain doesn't get into gear until at least nine o'clock, and we'll be done well before then. Come on, I can fry up our catch for supper on their grill."

Jordan was a beast at all that guy stuff. Gut the fish. Bag a deer. He might live in New York now, but he was a Montana boy, born and bred.

Adam wasn't even keen on fresh fish. But his friend had come all this way just to check on him. "Fine. But I'm not getting up before six."

Jordan tilted his head. "How about five?"

"Five forty-five."

"Five fifteen?"

"Five thirty," Adam said. "Final offer."

Jordan grinned. "Done."

Molly and her guests were coming up the walkway, still chatting.

Adam glanced at Jordan, who had obviously noticed Molly. It was impossible not to notice her infectious smile and melodious laugh. Or her long dark hair and shapely legs, which were currently exposed by a pair of crisp white shorts.

Adam wanted to rush her inside the inn, hide her from the interest in Jordan's eyes. But she'd already caught sight of his friend. Of course she had. Jordan might be as cerebral as Adam, but somehow he didn't wear it like a garish three-piece suit.

Her gaze slipped to Adam briefly before she parted ways with the couple. As she walked across the grass toward them both men rose to their feet.

"Hey, Molly," Adam said.

"Hey, Adam. Getting some work done?"

"Trying to." Adam was reluctant to introduce his good-looking friend, but basic courtesy required it. "This is my friend Jordan Ross. He's here for the weekend. Jordan, this is one of the innkeepers, Molly."

The two shook hands and exchanged greetings, holding eye contact for longer than Adam liked. Of course, a millisecond would've been longer than he liked.

"You're giving boat rides these days?" Adam nodded his head toward the couple that had just disappeared inside.

Molly finally pulled her hand back. "They didn't feel comfortable taking it out on their own. It was fun playing tour guide."

"That was awfully nice of you," Jordan said before Adam could get a word out. "Are innkeepers always so accommodating?"

"We try to be." Molly's smile had broadened on Jordan, but her eyes returned to Adam. "I didn't realize you had a friend coming."

"I, uh, I didn't either."

"I surprised him. I have a few days off and thought, why not? Called up and made a reservation."

"How did you guys meet?"

"We attended college together," Jordan said. "Roommates through most of it."

Molly's eyes teased. "And you still like each other?"

"More some days than others," Jordan returned.

Adam shifted. What if Jordan goofed up and mentioned his work? He knew the deal, of course, and had always been circumspect. But that didn't stop Adam's muscles from twitching. The thought of Molly knowing he was Nathaniel Quinn suddenly mattered much more than it ever had before.

"Well, I'll let you get back to your visit. It was nice to meet you. Let me know if there's anything I can do to make your stay more enjoyable."

"I'll do that. You have a beautiful property. I'm sure I'll be quite comfortable here."

With a final smile and wave Molly was gone. The men took their seats.

Jordan watched Molly until she disappeared inside, then met Adam's eyes with a laugh. "Now I see why you're hanging around this place instead of spreading out in your own lake house."

Adam squirmed in his seat. "What?"

Jordan gave him a knowing look, a smirk on his lips.

"Molly? Don't be absurd. They wait on me hand and foot around here. What more could I want?"

"Oh, I don't know. A pretty young woman looking up at you with a big dimpled grin?"

It was a sharp reminder that Molly was way out of his league. Somehow, spending all that time together, researching that love letter, he'd forgotten that.

His face warmed. "Get real. I'm here to work, remember?"

"Oh, *I* remember. I just hope you do."

"I have no personal interest in Molly." Except maybe as his muse. Yes, that's all she was. His muse. And maybe his friend. But that was absolutely it.

Jordan held up his hands, palms out. "All right, all right. I believe you."

Adam lowered himself in the chair, relief making his legs wobbly. He knew where he stood with the ladies. Back in college Jordan had been the girl magnet. He was a good-looking guy, and nice besides. Not like some of those arrogant fraternity types, only out to use a girl for a night or two.

Of course, Adam had had a few girlfriends over the years, but nothing serious. And lately, his secretive career had proved to be a real stumbling block. At what point did he confess who he really was? And what if, when they broke up, she outed him to *People* magazine or something?

"So what's her story?" Jordan drew him from his reverie. "How is it she's so young and running an inn?"

"She runs it with her brother and sister. Their folks passed away last year, and this was their family home." He could've expounded on that, but he was suddenly reluctant to draw a picture of just how courageous and selfless Molly was.

"How old are her siblings?"

"Her sister's still in high school, and her brother's older than Molly—and very protective." The last was meant as a warning, but it backfired.

Jordan arched a brow—challenge received. His special gift was charming people. Professors, editors, girlfriends' parents. A big brother would pose no problem for Jordan.

"So what else do you know about her? She have a boyfriend?"

Adam feigned interest in a passing pontoon boat. "I don't know much about her, really."

His friend was staring at the door Molly had disappeared into a moment ago, a contemplative look on his face. "I might just ask her out . . ."

Adam's internal body temperature shot up by a degree or ten. His gut felt hollowed and somehow weighted at the same time. He'd obviously done an adequate job of convincing Jordan that his feelings toward Molly were completely platonic.

"Why would you do that?" Somehow Adam

made his voice sound normal. "You live in New York."

Jordan hitched his shoulder. "Geographical challenges can be overcome."

"I'm not sure she'd date a guest," Adam said finally.

"Well, it's not like I'm here for the summer." Jordan gave a happy-go-lucky grin. "Besides, nothing ventured, nothing gained."

eighteen

Molly closed Adam's door behind her, set the trash bag on the cleaning cart, and pushed the cart to the suite at the back of the house. Last room of the day. She unlocked the door and propped it open. The Hendersons, a family of four, had left empty soda bottles, juice boxes, and various wrappers lying around. Area guides and maps lay here and there too, and pillows were hunched in random places as if the family had left mid pillow fight.

Molly stepped into the room and went to work, quickly disposing of the debris before giving the bathroom a good scrub. When it was lemon-scented and gleaming, she gathered the dirty towels and replaced them with a fresh, fluffy stack, taking care to hang them just so.

Next she proceeded to the beds, changing the linens and taking the time to fold crisp hospital corners. She replaced the pillows, since they'd been lying on the floor, fluffed up the new ones, and arranged them on the bed.

She dusted and vacuumed, then pulled back the drapes, letting the light flood in. She'd almost forgotten about the balcony—but of course the Hendersons hadn't. The inn's beach towels hung forgotten over the balcony railing, two coffee mugs sat on the little round table, and a well-read newspaper was scattered under the chairs.

She slid open the patio door and stepped outside. Warm, humid air brushed her skin, and she shooed away a fly that was hovering around the mugs.

As she reached for the mugs a familiar chuckle caught her attention. She peered over the railing to see Adam and his friend still sitting outside.

She'd been a bit disappointed that he had company for the weekend. They'd had little luck in their research over the past week and a half, and she'd hoped—selfishly—that Adam would have some free time over the weekend to devote to their search.

She took the mugs inside, depositing them on her cart and replacing them with clean ones. When she stepped back onto the balcony, she couldn't help but overhear Adam as she gathered the towels.

"Any word on the movie?" he asked. "Last I heard Claudia said the script was going through rewrites."

"I'll check with her Monday. These things always take time. They still have another several months on the option, but they'll likely have to re-up."

"And we thought publishing was slow," Adam said, a wry note in his voice.

Molly paused in the removal of the last towel,

ears pricking. Was Adam's friend in the movie or publishing business?

"Have you heard how sales are going on *This Time Forever*?" Jordan asked.

Molly's breath caught at the title of Nathaniel Quinn's most recent release.

"Not recently," Adam said.

"Well, it's still on all the lists six months after publication."

"That's all we need to know, I guess."

Molly waited, standing quietly. A squirrel shimmied through a nearby branch, making the leaves flutter. But all she could think about was the conversation going on below her.

These men were somehow tied to Nathaniel Quinn's books. She thought of the job description Adam had given her. Researcher. He'd never gone into detail, but maybe that was because he worked for the anonymous and elusive Nathaniel Quinn. Which meant—

Her breath caught in her lungs. She strangled the bunch of beach towels clenched to her stomach.

Was Jordan Ross really Nathaniel Quinn?

She replayed the conversation in her head and tried to puzzle it out. She'd recently read that one of Nathaniel's earlier books, *A Moment in Time*, was being developed into a movie. That must be what the men had been talking about. She couldn't construe it any other way. Why else would they care so much about the book's sales or the movie deal?

She supposed they could simply be part of his publishing team, but Adam was here to research something. And now Jordan was here too— possibly scouting out the setting of his next novel? Did fiction writers even have researchers? She thought she'd once read something about a bestselling novelist who used one.

She was so lost in thought that she missed something Jordan said. Now he was getting up and making his way toward the house, phone to his ear. A moment later he disappeared beneath the balcony. She heard the creak of the screen door as it opened and then a quiet slap as he entered the house.

Molly shifted to go. But as she did so the boards rubbed together beneath her feet, making a loud squawking sound that seemed to echo across the lake.

nineteen

Adam whipped back around to face the lake. He heard the slide of the patio door above him and imagined Molly disappearing inside the room.

How long had she been on the balcony? Had she overheard their conversation? They'd been talking quietly, but sound carried out here. He'd been cognizant of their surroundings and being overheard, but he'd never thought to look up.

He rewound his conversation with Jordan. They'd been discussing his sales and the movie. Had they mentioned anything that would tie the conversation to Nathaniel Quinn? Had they talked about specific titles? Yes. Jordan had mentioned *A Moment in Time*.

He winced. If she'd been out there long enough, she had to know the truth.

Biting back frustration, he sprang to his feet, grabbed his laptop, and made his way down the incline of the yard. He wasn't sure where he was going, but he wasn't going to stay here in plain view like a sitting duck. If she'd overheard them she'd seek him out. And he wasn't ready for that conversation. Not even close.

He ran a hand over his face. His heart was

thudding as though he'd just run five miles, and his lungs worked to keep pace.

Maybe she hadn't been outside long enough to hear anything. Maybe she'd even been wearing earbuds. She wore them sometimes when she cleaned.

When he reached the shoreline, he stepped onto the pier and walked the length of it. It creaked and wobbled under his weight. As much as he longed to go far, far away, he couldn't take out the boat—it had to be reserved and signed out. But there was a bench at the end of the dock that was all but hidden from the house by the trees. Good enough. He headed that way.

He had to plan for the worst. If Molly had overheard them she'd know he was Nathaniel Quinn. He'd have to own up to it. The thought was like a sucker punch.

He lowered his weight to the bench, his body drooping in dread. He leaned forward, elbows propped on his knees, fingers over his mouth.

It was always in the back of his mind—the fear of being found out. It had actually gotten worse over the years. Maybe he should've just put his real name on his books to begin with. But it was too late now. His secret identity had become a "thing," and the revelation would be significant.

And disappointing Molly was now a very real possibility. He remembered the way Grace had teased her about her crush. Molly would remember that same conversation, and she'd be mortified all over again. And after realizing who he was, those feelings would be null and void.

He closed his eyes, wishing he could make himself disappear as easily as he could obliterate the image of the lake. All those times he'd disappointed his dad rose to the surface like buoys, bringing a load of hurt and a feeling of unworthiness that went core deep.

The pier vibrated with footsteps. His eyes popped open. So much for hiding. He resisted the urge to turn around. He knew it was Molly. He could feel her presence.

If she was seeking him out, she'd probably overheard the conversation. He had to accept that. Had to apologize for not being more forthcoming, especially after Grace had ratted her out. If things were too awkward—for either of them—he could always find another place to stay.

For some reason that only made him feel worse. Dread swelled inside until he felt consumed by it.

"Hey," Molly said, caution in her tone.

He flickered a look at her, unable to hold her gaze. "Hi."

She edged around the end of the bench. "Can I join you?"

"Sure." He stared out at the water, not really seeing it. Her apple-y scent wrapped around him, and he found himself once again tongue-tied.

Molly drummed her fingers on her leg. "So . . . I have to admit that I overheard your conversation with your friend."

His eyes shot to hers. She ducked her head before he could get a read on her.

"I'm really sorry—I didn't intend to eavesdrop, but I was cleaning the room and the guests left things on the balcony, so I went out there to pick up and I couldn't help but overhear." A flush had crept across her cheeks. She bit her lip, her fingers still drumming.

It was hard to say which of them might be more embarrassed. "It's all right," he eked out, because he'd say anything to put her at ease. But there was nothing he could say to fix this.

She turned those wide amber eyes up to him. "I know the truth—I know that . . ."

She must be so disappointed to find out her writing hero—her crush—was him. Nerdy, boring Adam Bradford. He fought against a familiar flood of despair.

He flinched even as his heart sank down to the planks at his feet. "Molly—"

"I figured out that Jordan is Nathaniel Quinn," she finished.

Wait. What? He blinked.

"I mean, you were talking about a movie and then book sales, and you mentioned *A Moment in Time* by name, and that's my very favorite." Her hand pressed against her heart. "I mean, I love them all, but if I had to choose just one—I've read it a dozen times. Okay, maybe more like fifteen." She covered her face with both hands. "I can't believe he's here. I'm shaking. I'm shaking like a leaf. Look." She held out her hands.

They were indeed trembling.

She placed one hand at her throat. "Nathaniel Quinn, right here, staying at our inn . . . It's inconceivable. I can't believe it. I can't believe *the* Nathaniel Quinn is staying right here under the same roof as me. I know I already said that, but it bears repeating."

He had to correct her—didn't he? "Um . . . Molly . . ."

"So you came here to research the location of his next book, right?" Her eyes suddenly lit. "Oh, and don't worry. I won't tell a soul, I promise. I know his anonymity is a big deal and—what's up with that anyway? But no, never mind. None of my business. Mum's the word." She zipped her lips closed and threw an imaginary key into the lake.

He'd never even once considered the idea of Molly running her mouth. "Thank you," he managed.

"Of course. I'd never do anything to—well, and besides, he's a guest of the inn. We have to be discreet, you know."

"Um, he'll appreciate that. We both do." What was he doing? He was crossing a line. It was one thing to leave something important out of the conversation and quite another to go along with a lie.

"And, uh, maybe you can not mention to him what Grace said? About my little, you know, crush or whatever?" Her face turned a deeper shade of red. "I know it's silly but— Unless, you already told him? Please tell me you haven't told him."

"No. No, of course not." He deserved to go to hell when he died.

"Oh. Good. I feel so silly now that he's here. I mean, five million women are probably infatuated with him. Nathaniel Quinn isn't going to want to be stuck here with an innkeeper-slash-fan who's harboring a raging crush on him."

She might be surprised.

"I mean, I don't have any idea why he hides his identity, but he must be a little reclusive or not like attention or something." Her brows drew together thoughtfully. "Although now that I think about it, he didn't seem particularly shy. He seemed rather congenial, actually—and I'm totally not trying to pry information out of you. I promise. You must be sworn to secrecy. I get it."

Unable to conjure up actual words, he gave her a bland smile.

She suddenly sat up straight. "You know, let's just pretend I didn't hear a word. I know nothing, nothing at all. He's just a regular old guest. How's that? I don't want to make him uncomfortable. That wouldn't be very hospitable of me, and around here we have to be, above all else, hospitable." She paused, her brows raised.

He took that as his cue to respond. "Right. That's—a good idea."

"All right. It's settled then. I feel much better." She popped to her feet. "Whew! Glad to have that off my chest. Now I really have to get back to work. I've been ignoring Levi's texts, and he's fixing to hunt me down. Thanks, Adam. Have a great afternoon."

"You too, Molly."

He looked out to the lake. What in the world just happened? Whirlwind Molly had come along, making assumptions, and he'd just let her, that's what.

The dock gave a hard shimmy, and he turned in time to see Molly finishing up a little sashay at the other end of the pier. Obviously she was on cloud nine because Nathaniel Quinn was sleeping under her roof. She was absolutely right—and absolutely wrong all at the same time.

twenty

Nathaniel Quinn is staying right here at the Bluebell Inn.

Molly had been repeating this phrase to herself since yesterday afternoon, but it was only just beginning to sink in.

She'd been eager to see Jordan (Nathaniel Quinn!) again, but it seemed as though the universe was conspiring against her. Every time he and Adam left the building she was otherwise occupied. The same when they returned.

Saturday morning she ran some errands, and by the time she returned they were gone. She cleaned the four occupied rooms and moved on to her other chores only to find they'd returned in her absence.

In the late afternoon she relieved Levi at the front desk solely in hopes of catching a glimpse of her favorite literary genius. But so far she was striking out. He'd disappeared somewhere on the property. How was he so elusive—even when staying under the same roof?

She wandered into the library to "dust the shelves" but found it empty. She went out front to sweep the porch. And later she may have peeked out all the windows under the guise of watering plants. He and Adam must be upstairs, locked away in one of their rooms. Probably Jordan's—he'd booked the suite. Was he even now penning the words of his very next novel, right under her roof?

Her heart gave a stutter. She felt a little swoony.

Grace came in the front door. "Did someone already sweep the porch?"

"I did."

"Oh . . . thanks." Grace started to set her purse down behind the front desk.

"I'll take your shift," Molly blurted. "If you have something else you want to do, I mean."

Grace narrowed her eyes at Molly. "And why would you do that?"

"Can't a big sister just do something nice for her little sister?"

"What do you want?"

"Nothing! Sheesh, so suspicious." Molly wiped off the desk with a dustrag. She was bursting to tell her secret. Grace would know what a big deal this was for her. But she was sworn to secrecy. She bit her lip. Hard.

Grace was looking closely at Molly. "What are you doing?"

Molly tried for an innocent look.

"Your mouth is all . . . twisty."

"No, it's not."

"Ooo-kay. You're acting weird."

"Weirder than normal?"

"Good point." Grace hitched her purse back

on her shoulder. "Well, far be it from me to turn down free time. I'll be at Sarah's."

Almost an hour later Molly's good deed paid off. At the sound of footsteps above her she closed out the game on her phone, fluffed her hair, and picked up the dusting cloth.

Adam appeared at the foot of the steps first, followed by Jordan. Both men greeted her, but she could hardly take her eyes off Jordan. He wore a pair of jeans and a black T-shirt that hugged his muscular frame.

His eyes crinkled at the corners as his smile widened. "Hello, Molly."

"Hi," she breathed.

"We're heading out to supper," Adam said.

"Need any recommendations?" Her voice was less airy this time but it quivered a bit.

"No, thank you," Adam said, pulling open the front door. "We have it covered."

"I was craving pizza," Jordan said.

"I hope he's taking you to Buck's then."

"I hear it's the best."

"It's different from the New York style you're probably used to, but I think you'll like it. If you like cheese. And who doesn't like cheese, am I right?"

"That you are," Jordan said.

Adam was holding the door for Jordan, but his friend had stopped.

"I'll be right out," Jordan told him.

Adam paused a moment before his eyes flickered to Molly. "See you, Molly."

She gave a little wave. "Have fun."

Adam pulled the door shut, leaving Molly alone with Jordan. Completely alone, actually, because they were the only guests at the moment, and her siblings were off-property.

And Nathaniel Quinn was standing right smack in front of her, obviously wanting to talk to her.

He's just a guest. A regular old guest. Be professional, Molly.

Despite the heavy thumping of her heart she tried for a casual tone. "Is there something I can do for you? Is everything all right with your room?"

"Everything's great. I love this place—the inn, the town. I see why Adam's enjoying his stay so much." His eyes warmed on hers.

Butterflies swarmed inside at the look. Could he be talking about more than geography? "I'm so glad. If there's anything I can do to make your stay more enjoyable, just let me know."

"Well, now that you mention it . . ." He gave her a crinkly smile.

A flirtatious smile.

She swallowed hard. "Of course. What can I do for you?"

He put his hands in his front pockets, looking adorably uncertain. "I hope I'm not out of line here, Molly, but I wondered if you might be interested in catching a bite to eat with me sometime."

Her lips parted. She blinked. Nathaniel Quinn was asking her out. On a date. Nathaniel. Quinn. On a date. Had she already said that?

Say something, Molly. Anything. "Um . . . but you're checking out Monday morning."

Aaaand she'd just given away the fact that she'd peeked at his reservation. Her face heated, her skin prickling beneath her arms. Maybe he'd think innkeepers always kept track of their guests' comings and goings.

"Well, that's true. However, I plan to come back as the summer progresses, at least once or twice. But I was actually thinking tomorrow night, if you're not working. Do you like the Crow's Nest?"

"Everybody likes the Crow's Nest. There's not a better view of the lake, and it's kind of the place to go around here for proms and birthdays and anniversaries and whatnot—not that you need a special occasion to go there, of course. A regular old meal is reason enough—they have really good food. And Sunday nights are slow— here at the inn, I mean. Our slowest night of the week actually."

Shut. Up. Molly.

She bit her lip, then thought of Grace's twisty lips comment and stopped.

179

He tilted his head, his eyes twinkling. "Is that a yes?"

She nodded and tried to temper the excitement that buzzed through her veins. "Sure. Sounds great."

Adam glared at the inn's front door as if it had committed some atrocious crime. He knew Jordan. He knew what was going on in that lobby right now. And he knew how Molly would respond.

His conversation with her on the dock continued to rankle. Of course she'd assumed Jordan was the incomparable Nathaniel Quinn, Adam merely his assistant. It told him everything he needed to know. Reinforced everything he already believed to be true.

He rubbed a palm across his face. *Idiot.* What he'd considered yesterday to be his saving grace had actually been an enormous miscalculation. Adam had practically handed Molly over to Jordan on a big silver platter.

The front door opened and Jordan exited. He trotted down the steps and toward the car with that loose, easy gait of his. Adam would've known, even without his satisfied grin, that his little chat with Molly had been a raging success.

The car door opened, and Jordan slipped inside, his knees hitting the dashboard in spite of the fact that the seat was all the way back.

Adam checked both ways and pulled out of the slot. "You sure didn't waste any time."

"Well, I'm only here two days. Aren't you going to ask if she said yes?"

"I don't have to ask. You're practically levitating."

"She actually blushed," Jordan mused. "It was pretty cute too. You know, women in Manhattan don't blush. More often, they make *me* blush."

Adam gritted his teeth. "She's a nice girl." It came out like a warning.

"That's why she appeals to me." He gave Adam a sideways look. "And when have I ever been less than a gentleman?"

He hadn't. But apparently Molly brought out Adam's protective instincts. And now she thought Jordan was someone he wasn't. Probably felt as though she knew him or something.

This wasn't exactly fair to Jordan either, now that he thought about it. Molly would have high expectations where Nathaniel Quinn was concerned. She'd no doubt built him up in her mind as some kind of male paragon. That was a lot to live up to—even for Jordan. Adam should probably come clean.

"And don't worry," Jordan said. "I won't let on about who you are. I've got your back, buddy."

Adam winced. He hadn't even thought of that. "What are you going to say you do for a living?"

Jordan lifted a shoulder. "I'll tell her I'm a

181

literary agent. It's the truth, and there's no reason she'd think you're a client of mine. We already told her we've known each other since college."

"Sounds like you've got it all figured out." He knew he sounded a little bitter, but Jordan seemed to miss it. He'd never been particularly intuitive. Besides, he was obviously riding high on thoughts of Molly and their upcoming date.

twenty-one

The Crow's Nest was perched on a hill overlooking Snug Harbor. The winding road up to the restaurant took a bit of time to navigate, but Molly was glad for the chance to work out some of her jitters before they were seated face-to-face.

Conversation had flowed easily so far. She'd managed to keep her rambling under control and hadn't stuck her foot in her mouth yet. Of course, the night was still young.

As Jordan executed a hairpin curve Molly slid him a look. He sure looked handsome tonight in a nice pair of jeans and a black button-up. She'd chosen a turquoise sundress for the occasion—her favorite. It was fitted at the top and splayed out around the legs in a flattering manner. She'd curled her hair, leaving it loose around her shoulders, and had taken the time to apply makeup. The appreciative look on Jordan's face when she came down the stairs made it worth the extra effort.

She hadn't mentioned the date to Levi, as he would undoubtedly disapprove. Fortunately he wasn't around when they left. Besides, Jordan would only be a guest for one more night.

And he was *Nathaniel Quinn.* How was she supposed to turn that down?

They came around a curve and were treated to a beautiful harbor view.

"Wow," he said. "It's so beautiful up here. We don't get views like this in the city. The mountains remind me a little of home though."

"And where is home exactly?"

"Bozeman, Montana. I was raised on a ranch. My folks still run it."

She thought of the cowboy story he'd written a few years ago. No wonder he'd been able to write it with such authenticity.

"How did a cowboy end up in the big city?"

He chuckled. "Career opportunities. Much as I love home, Bozeman is kind of limited in that area."

She had to ask. It was a natural follow-up to his statement. "And what kind of career is it that you're pursuing?"

"I'm a literary agent. Of course these days an agent could live practically anywhere, with the internet and all. But it makes sense to be where the big publishers are. More opportunities for meetings and networking. And I didn't have anything tying me home other than my family."

"Of course." She was a little dismayed by how easily the lie rolled off his tongue. But what was he supposed to say? That he was a writer? The next question would inevitably be *What do you write?* Quickly followed by *Are you published?* and *Would I know anything you've written?*

She steered the conversation in a safer direction. "Are you close to your family?"

"Oh, yeah, we're a close bunch. I have five siblings—all brothers."

"You're kidding."

"My mom wishes I were. All that pregnancy and labor and not a single girl to dress up. But I say that in jest. She loved being a boy-mom. And believe me, she only had to look at us sideways to keep us in line."

"Where are your brothers now? Did they move away too?"

"They're all back home actually. Two of them work the ranch with Dad, and the other three followed other career paths. What about your family? I met your little sister. She checked me in."

"Right, that's Grace. Other than her there's just my brother, Levi. Our parents passed away last year—a car accident." Would she ever get used to saying it? She still hadn't quite gotten over the shock of it. Or the achy feeling of regret.

"I'm so sorry. That must be very difficult for all of you."

"It has been, but we're doing all right. The inn was their dream, and bringing it to life has been a labor of love for us."

"Do you enjoy it—running an inn?"

"Well, we haven't been at it very long, but yes, I do. My degree was going to be in hospitality actually, so it's a good fit."

"Was going to be?"

"I dropped out before my last semester to come back and open the inn."

He slid her a look. "That's quite a sacrifice."

She lifted a shoulder, feeling a little wistful about the internship she'd given up and her college friends, who seemed to be moving on without her.

"I'll finish eventually. Right now I'm needed more at home. We'll give the inn a good launch, two or three years of success, then we'll sell it."

They rounded the final curve, and he turned into the restaurant's sloped parking lot. He helped her out of the rental car and escorted her inside.

The sun had gone behind the mountains, ushering in the golden hour and swathing the lake in shade. She never wanted to take the views for granted. She was halfway up the walk before she even realized Jordan still had her hand.

Nathaniel Quinn is holding my hand. She gave her head a shake at the wonder of it.

The restaurant was just as she remembered from her eighteenth birthday—the last time she'd been there. Log elements gave the place a rustic feel, while soft lighting and white tablecloths lent a certain elegance. The two levels of the restaurant offered guests abundant views through the wall of windows facing the lake.

The hostess seated them at a table for two on the lower level. After giving props to the view, they looked over the menu and chatted about all the appealing options. Jordan finally settled on the rib eye, and Molly was eager to try the fresh trout.

"Do you cook at all?" she asked once they set the menus aside.

"Sadly, no. Though my mom did try to teach all of us. I eat out a lot, I'm afraid." He patted his flat stomach. "Which also means I have to work out a lot. What about you? Do you like to cook?"

"I can follow a recipe with the best of them, but it's not my one true love or anything. That's why we hired Miss Della. Now *she* can cook."

"Tell me about it. I've already eaten my body weight in muffins."

They were laughing when the server came to take their orders.

Once she slipped away, Jordan leaned forward, elbows braced on the table. "So . . . Adam showed me your well-stocked library. Let's talk books."

It was after eleven when headlights fanned across Adam's darkened room. He leaned over the nightstand and pushed aside the curtain just in time to see headlights go out. It was Jordan's rental, all right.

He felt a twinge of guilt for spying, but was it his fault his room faced the street?

The inn's porch lights carried far enough that he could see his friend exit the car and come around to help Molly out. He frowned as he watched the two exchange smiles. Halfway up the walk she nudged him, laughing at something he said, then they disappeared beneath the porch roof.

He let the curtain fall. So the date had gone well then.

Adam had turned off his light earlier even though he knew he wouldn't be able to sleep. The last thing he wanted was Jordan coming by his room, emotionally intoxicated, sweeter than ever on Molly. And Adam knew he would be. Who could resist Molly Bennett?

He set his glasses on the nightstand and lay back against his pillows, still listening for their entry downstairs. When he'd moved into the place he'd been pleased that his room was practically soundproof, but that amenity was not working in his favor at the moment.

He couldn't hear them down in the lobby at all. Were they still on the porch? What were they doing? How and where did one say good night to a date when staying beneath the same roof?

And why did he care so much?

She was *his* muse, he claimed in his own defense. Besides, he'd seen her first.

He scrubbed a hand over his face. Could he be more childish? He adjusted his pillows, staring up at the dark ceiling.

The last few hours had been agonizingly slow as he imagined every moment of the date.

He opened his laptop and tried to work on expanding his outline, but it was futile. He was too distracted by thoughts of Molly and Jordan. It only became more difficult as the night wore on. The restaurant closed at nine (yes, he checked), which was pretty much when the whole town rolled up the sidewalks.

That left only outdoor public spaces as possibilities. The park, the beach, or maybe some local version of inspiration point. He was sure Molly knew all the best spots and could give guided tours of them all.

He laced his hands over his abdomen. It was official. He had a massive crush on his muse. Which was most unfortunate since she seemed to have one on his best friend. At least Jordan was leaving in the morning.

Guilt pricked at him. Still, he couldn't help but be relieved at the thought.

Of course, with texting and social media the world was much smaller than it used to be. They could easily keep in touch if they wanted—and he couldn't help but think they would.

Adam still had his little project with Molly working in his favor. He could spend time with her. To what end, he didn't know. He just knew he craved her company. Would she pump him for information about Jordan? The thought of watching Molly mooning over his friend wasn't a pleasant one.

He heard a muted sound downstairs. They must be coming inside finally. Had Jordan kissed her good night? The thought made his stomach coil tightly. His fingers tightened around the quilt.

The steps creaked quietly, and a few moments later he heard Jordan's door close softly. He must not have walked Molly all the way to her door. Or she'd stayed downstairs to make sure the inn was locked up. Either way, she was safely home.

Only then did he allow his full weight to sink into his pillows. But he knew sleep would be a long time in coming.

twenty-two

The next morning Molly ran the dustrag over an armoire, her thoughts going over her date with Jordan as she cleaned. They'd lingered over their meal at the Crow's Nest, and by the time the restaurant was closing down they weren't ready to end their date. Since everything was closed for the night Molly suggested they continue their conversation at the park. It was well lit and had a nice gazebo overlooking the lake, but they settled at a picnic table instead.

Jordan regaled her with stories of growing up on the ranch, and Molly entertained him with some sibling stories of her own. She enjoyed their conversation. He was easy to talk to, and once her nerves wore off, she stopped worrying about what she said and how it might sound. Almost two hours passed before she knew it. She'd stopped thinking of him as Nathaniel Quinn and had begun thinking of him as just Jordan.

She'd only gotten nervous again as he walked her up the porch steps. She was surprised to find herself hoping he wouldn't kiss her. She liked to take things slow, but she feared he—being a city boy—might rush things.

But on the porch they wrapped up their conversation, and he'd simply hugged her good

191

night. Other than that he'd only touched her once throughout the evening—when he'd held her hand on the way into the restaurant. And he'd nearly let go before she'd even noticed.

He'd checked out early this morning to catch his flight, so they'd said their good-byes the night before. He'd gotten her number on the porch, promising to call once he was back in the city. He said he might return to Bluebell in a month or so.

The thought didn't excite her as much as she suspected it should have, and she wondered at that. She liked Jordan a lot. She'd like to get to know him better and hoped he did call her.

She gave her head a shake. It was possible she'd built up Nathaniel Quinn in her mind to proportions he couldn't possibly fulfill. He was only human, after all—brilliant literary genius though he might be.

Molly carried the bag of trash out to the hall where the cart awaited. She'd gathered the mini toiletries and a fresh stack of towels when the door to Adam's room opened.

He stepped into the hallway, his brows rising at the sight of her. "Good morning."

"Morning. You're up early. I hope I didn't wake you."

"Not at all. I actually got up to see Jordan off."

She wondered what Jordan had told him about their date. He'd seemed to enjoy their time together. "I had fun last night. He seems like a genuinely nice guy. Not at all arrogant. Very down-to-earth."

"He's a great guy." Adam pushed up his glasses as he ducked his head.

"I'd figured as much, since he's your best friend and all. And of course, I feel as though I know him somewhat through his writing. But you know, I'm always half afraid to meet an author I admire so much and find out he's really a jerk. It would forever spoil his books for me, and what a tragedy that would be."

"Well, no need to worry about that, obviously."

"How's your work going? Did you get any research done this morning? Is there anything I can do to help? Now that I know exactly what you're doing . . . feel free to pick my brain about anything." Just the thought of having some tiny part in one of Nathaniel Quinn's books was enough to give her goose bumps.

"I'll keep that in mind. I didn't get much done this morning, I'm afraid. My brain's not awake yet."

"Well, you should go have some coffee and muffins now that the kitchen's open. It's strawberry rhubarb today. A little sugar rush might be just the thing."

He placed a hand over his flat abdomen. "She's killing me with those muffins. I'm heading out for a jog first. I've gotten lazy since I've been here."

"I didn't know you were a jogger."

"My regimen has slipped since I've been here, but I'm usually in training for some half marathon or another—it keeps me motivated."

"I admire anyone who can run a marathon—or even half of one. Yoga is more my speed, and I haven't exactly been diligent about that lately."

"I'm sure you've had your hands full with the inn."

She pulled the stack of towels into her stomach. She wanted to ask him about their project, but she didn't want to push. He'd had company all weekend, after all, and was likely behind in his own work.

"Well," she said, "I'll let you get on with your day."

He tucked his hands into his pockets. "Would you have time later to work on our project at the library? I'd like to go through more microfilm."

"I'd love to. I should be finished by three."

He nodded. "I'll be downstairs most of the day in your library. Should we walk over when you're free?"

Molly gave him a winning smile. "Sounds like a plan. Have a super day, Adam."

Adam glanced at his watch for the fifth time in the past ten minutes. It was almost three o'clock. He'd spent an inordinate amount of his day anticipating his time with Molly.

His whole jogging time—when ideas usually flowed like water from a spigot. And his working time. All of it had been spent thinking of Molly and what they'd talk about on their walk to the library.

He'd planned to work at the downtown library today. He'd done more than enough research for his story, and he knew he'd be less distracted away from the inn. But when he'd discovered Molly would be available to work on their project he'd changed his plans just for the extra few minutes the walk would allow.

He was officially pathetic.

But his talk with Jordan this morning had left him desolate. His friend spent the few minutes raving about Molly and their date. Adam tried to be happy for him, but it was impossible.

If the relationship progressed, Molly was going to eventually find out Jordan wasn't her favorite author after all. And in finding that out, she would also learn that Adam was.

He shook the thought away. They'd only had one date. Chances were, the relationship would fizzle the way so many long-distance relationships did. After all, Molly was tied here because of the inn. And Jordan was committed to the city where he could stay on top of his career. Of course, Molly didn't know that. She fancied him an author who could live anywhere.

And then, of course, there was the deception.

But that was really a moot point. Molly might think she was in love with Nathaniel Quinn, but she wasn't. She was in love with the masculine heroes he wrote about. It was only natural to believe one was the same as the other.

A few years ago he'd attended a book signing of Lisa Scottoline, the popular thriller writer. Ever since then, when he read her books, he pictured her in the place of the female protagonists. He couldn't seem to help himself.

It was a similar phenomenon for Molly, only the other way around. She'd met Nathaniel Quinn's heroes and then pictured the author bearing their attributes. Who could live up to that kind of pressure? Certainly not him.

"Hey there."

Adam jumped at Molly's sudden appearance in the doorway.

"Sorry! I interrupted your work."

All day long, in fact. He shut his laptop, giving her a smile. "Not at all. I was just about to call it quits. Ready to head on over?"

"Quick, out the back, before Levi decides the fireplace needs cleaning out."

"Come along, Cinderella."

They slipped out the back and around the walkway toward the sidewalk.

"To be fair, he's a natural leader, and he only nags because he cares so much about the inn.

And I'll admit he takes more than his share of on-call nights, which I appreciate."

"What does that amount to? An on-call night?"

"At night any calls go to our room phones. In case there's an emergency and a family member can't get hold of a guest. Or one of our after-hour check-ins has a problem."

"Does that happen often?"

"Believe it or not, sometimes we even get a reservation at three a.m."

"How does that go?"

She laughed. "Not very well when I'm answering. Everything's on the computer, so we have to skulk downstairs in the middle of the night."

"All that skulking . . . must be exhausting."

"You laugh, but it's no fun trying to be congenial at three in the morning."

"Oh, I believe it. I'm rarely congenial before nine myself."

"It's just not natural."

The afternoon was hot and sultry, heat rising from the pavement. Somewhere out on the lake a speedboat throttled to life. The smell of apples wafted his way, sweet and alluring. He slid Molly a look from the corner of his eyes, his body buzzing with her nearness.

"Did you get much done today?" she asked.

"I made some progress." He searched for a way to change the subject, but he couldn't seem to distract himself from the sweet smell of her. Their arms swung at their sides, only inches apart.

It was too quiet between them. He struggled for something to say. "I was surprised to find that the population of Bluebell is fewer than fourteen hundred, though I imagine that number must go up by a few hundred during lake season."

"That it does."

"Did you know the average age of residents is sixty-five?"

"Sounds about right. All the kids seem to graduate and hightail it out of here. I was planning to do that myself. I guess I still will eventually." She gave him a sideways look. "You're like the Wikipedia of miscellaneous facts."

Smooth, buddy. He ducked his head. "Sorry. I collect useless information and tend to share it at the most random moments."

Her laughter made the awkwardness worthwhile. "Good thing I happen to collect trivial tidbits then. And don't forget my awkward habit of rambling on about nothing. At least your chatter has an educational benefit."

When they reached the sidewalk they turned toward town. The sidewalks were empty this time of day, the *Open* flags fluttering under sun-faded canopies.

"Have you thought of any other avenues for finding Benjamin?" she asked. "Other than microfilm, I mean."

"Not really. I did a little looking around online Saturday, hoping to find a record with his photo attached—now that we know what he looked like. But the search was unsuccessful."

"Maybe we'll find more information today. Or maybe we can find phone numbers for all the living Benjamin Schwartzes and just call them all."

"That's a lot of phone calls. And those numbers you find online are often obsolete landlines or old numbers. I feel certain we'll be able to narrow it down if we just keep looking."

"I'd really hoped Nonnie would remember something important."

"Has she hunted up old photos or anything else?"

"Not yet. She was a little under the weather last week. When I didn't see her at church I took her some chicken noodle soup. Poor thing seemed miserable."

He looked at her from beneath his lashes. "That was kind of you to take care of her like that."

"That's what neighbors do. She probably had more food last week than she could eat in a month."

"I miss that small-town kindness. You don't get that in the city."

"I don't expect you do. Where are you from originally? Every now and then I think I detect a little Southern drawl beneath that Yankee accent."

His lips twitched. "That's a Texan drawl you're hearing. What's left of it, anyway. I'm from a little town not far from Austin."

"What do your folks do there?"

"My mom stayed home with us, but she also worked a little—ancestry stuff. She was adopted herself, and after doing some legwork searching for her birth mother she ended up with a new hobby and eventually a career."

"Sounds like you got your penchant for research from her."

"Maybe so." He traded a smile with her. "My dad was a high school football coach—same school I attended."

"Was?"

"He passed away a few years ago—heart attack."

She winced. "I'm sorry. I know how hard it is to lose a parent. Especially when it's so sudden."

Somehow he didn't think the loss had been the same for him as it had been for her. "We weren't very close, I'm afraid."

She gave him a long speculative look. "Then I'm sorry about that too. Did your dad teach there—at your high school?"

Adam chuckled and hoped it didn't sound bitter. "This is Texas we're talking about. Football coaching is a full-time position."

"Ah, yes. I've heard as much. Did you play then, for your dad?"

Had he had a choice? "I did, but I wasn't much of an athlete. My cousins were, though. Brody, my closest cousin, was a quarterback, plus we had a wide receiver and a couple on the defensive line. I'm afraid I'm the runt of the family," he said lightly.

She gave him a long, thoughtful look. "I'll bet you're the scholar of the family. Nothing wrong with that."

He muttered something noncommittal.

"Brawn and athleticism fade," she said. "Brains endure a lifetime."

That might be true, but in his family one aptitude was valued over the other. And he was in possession of the wrong one.

Molly pulled her phone from her pocket and checked the screen, going quiet for a long moment.

Adam's gaze drifted her direction. She was reading a text, but he couldn't make out the sender's name. Not that it was any of his business.

She pocketed her phone. "That was Jordan. He made it safely back home."

And so it begins. Adam's stomach hollowed out a little. "Good to know."

A long moment of silence followed while he searched for something else to say. Some other topic. *No random facts.* A breeze stirred the air, and leaves scuttled across the sidewalk ahead of them.

"He said he was a literary agent," Molly said finally. "I guess that's about as close as he can get to the truth."

Adam scratched the back of his neck. That again. He could tell Jordan's "lie" bothered her. And he didn't feel right letting his friend take the fall for his own prevarication. "Don't let that unsettle you, Molly. He's a trustworthy guy."

She gave a thoughtful nod. "So this is how you do this? You go on location and do all the research, and he writes the books?"

He swallowed. Cleared his throat. "Once all the research is done, it frees him up to focus on the story. Otherwise it's a lot to manage all at once. Like spinning a bunch of plates in the air. He's a plotter, so he works it all out in advance. The first draft is actually done in a matter of weeks. Then there's the rewriting, of course."

"I read that somewhere, about the plotting. It surprised me. For some reason I thought an author had to let the plot develop organically in order for it to be right."

"The plot can develop organically just as easily during the plotting phase. As far as methods go, I don't think it's a matter of right or wrong. I suspect there are as many ways to write a story as there are authors to tell them."

"That's probably true." She kicked a rock down the sidewalk, and it rolled several feet away, landing in front of him.

When he reached it, he gave it a kick.

She smiled a little when it landed in front of her, and then volleyed it into his path. "I'd love to talk to him about his writing sometime. If he ever feels comfortable enough to tell me the truth, that is."

Adam kicked the rock, glad when it again landed where he'd aimed. Apparently all those years of his dad trying to make him into a decent punter were finally paying off.

"I thought he'd steer the conversation away from books last night," she continued, "but he didn't. We talked about our favorite authors and genres and all the classics—he likes them too, but I guess you know that already."

Something twisted inside. Straight-up jealousy, no doubt. He'd come to think of books as *their* thing. Although that was preposterous, he realized. As much as Molly adored books, she probably talked about them with every book lover she could find. Still . . .

"*Mi piacerebbe molto discutere di libri con te.*"

The words rolled smoothly off his tongue. How nice to be able to speak the unmitigated truth. Even if Molly didn't comprehend a word he said.

I would very much like to discuss books with you.

Molly's eyes cut to Adam. He said the sweetest things. And she loved that he was too shy to say them in English.

He pushed up his glasses, giving her a little smile. "Books are the windows into many worlds."

She blinked at him, preferring the actual translation to the one he'd made up. "That's a beautiful sentiment and entirely true."

She'd missed her turn at kicking the rock, she realized. And her heart was beating too fast for the pace they were keeping. Obviously she needed to get back to her yoga.

"Did you finish the Jack Reacher novel?" she asked.

"I did. I enjoyed it so much I went on to another one."

"Book seven? Or did you start over at number one this time?"

He gave her an impertinent smile. "Neither. I'm currently reading *The Hard Way*."

"But that's book ten."

His eyes twinkled. "So it is."

"I don't know if we can even be friends."

He chuckled, a low delightful sound. "That would be a pity when we have so many other things in common."

She nudged her chin up and gave a heavy sigh. "I suppose you're right. I guess I can overlook your ridiculous propensity to read series out of order."

"And I'll overlook your absurd compulsion to be so inflexible."

"I think I'm offended." Humor laced her words.

"Then I must apologize." He gave a mock bow, his eyes warm with laughter and something else . . . perhaps affection?

twenty-three

Molly rubbed the back of her neck. She and Adam had been leaning over the microfilm readers for almost two hours. They were slowly making their way through the summer of '64, but they had to be thorough. And it was too easy to get distracted by the stories of the day. Every now and then one of them would read aloud an interesting tidbit.

Molly leaned back in the chair, giving her eyes and body a break from the task. The small room was stuffy and dimly lit to aid in viewing.

"Any luck?" She leaned toward Adam. He was on the July fourth issue of the *Herald*.

"Nothing yet. It's rather tedious, isn't it?"

"We don't want to miss anything though." She leaned in farther, peering at a photo of a bride and groom smiling at one another. "They look so young. They were probably just my age."

"People got married younger back then."

"That's true. People are waiting longer these days. Especially in the city, I hear." She caught a whiff of his cologne or soap, something manly and fresh.

He continued to scroll through the reel. "It's true for the people in my circle. They want an established career before they settle down."

"Not a bad thing, I guess." She flickered a sideways glance at him, catching a glimpse of his profile, the light of the reader bathing his face in a silvery glow. "What about you? Any prospects in that department?"

He continued to scan the screen's content, his fingers tapping the buttons to adjust the view. "Not really. Nothing serious anyway."

She stared at his agile fingers for a moment. He had nice hands. His fingers were squarish, tapering down to nails that were clean and tidy, but not manicured. He wasn't a rugged guy, but even so, he definitely wasn't the salon type.

She wondered what Jordan's hands looked like. She hadn't noticed them last night except for the one thought she'd had early in their date— that those were the hands that wrote breathtaking stories.

"You?" he asked.

She looked at him, finding him closer than she'd expected. Her hand was on the back of his chair. She curled her fingers around the plastic back.

Was it warm in here? "I'm sorry, what?"

"I asked if there'd been anyone, um, special for you."

"Oh. I haven't really had time or opportunity to date since I returned from college. There was someone a couple years ago. We dated awhile but . . ." She lifted a shoulder.

"Didn't work out?" he asked.

That overused phrase didn't quite do it justice. "It ended badly. He just wasn't who I thought he was."

Adam cleared his throat. "I'm sorry to hear that."

"Yeah, me too." Her phone vibrated in her pocket with an incoming text.

She didn't check her phone but leaned into the reader and continued on to the community section. She didn't want to talk about Dominic. She may have gotten over him, but she lost a little piece of her dignity every time she recounted the story.

They'd met two summers ago when he visited her church. He was handsome and charming, and when he asked her out she said yes. He was easy to talk to and her family liked him. Skye was the only one with reservations, but Molly's friend was particular. Molly had no reason not to believe he was who he said: CEO of a home health care company in Charlotte and owner of one of the new mansions on the lake.

For the first time in her life, she felt herself falling in love. It was an enthralling experience, just as the romance novels promised. She was dizzy with the feelings he evoked. She shared her heart, her thoughts, her vulnerabilities, and he shared his too. Or so she thought.

They were five months into the relationship

when the real owner of the house, the real CEO, arrived and found them grilling out by the built-in pool. It had only taken a few minutes to realize Dominic was actually the property manager—and not even that by the time the homeowner was finished with him.

Molly and Dominic fought, and when she realized the depth of his lies, she walked away from him once and for all.

Afterward she was in shock. Levi had always called her idealistic, and she was beginning to think he was right. Still, Dominic had fallen so short of perfection, anyone would've been disgusted. She spent the next weeks sorting through the lies and wishing feelings could be blocked as easily as phone numbers. Skye had been a huge help in processing it all.

It took her a year to get over Dominic, but before her heart could completely heal, her parents died, throwing her into another tailspin. Who and what could she even count on? No wonder she was a bit of a mess.

"Hey," Adam said suddenly. "Look at this."

Molly leaned back over, her eyes following his index finger to the screen where there was a list in the sidebar.

She read aloud. *"Benjamin D. Schwartz, 2nd place, smallmouth bass, 2.6 lbs.* His middle initial!"

He shared a smile with her. "Bingo."

twenty-four

July 4, 1964

Lizzie leaned forward in anticipation as Benjamin reeled in his fishing line. The small boat dipped with the movement.

"It's a big one, I think." His voice was laced with excitement.

"Look how your pole is bowing."

He'd picked her up at the town harbor just as the sky began pinkening with dawn's muted pallet. She was sleepy, having been out late with him the night before. They'd spent a lot of time together in the past month. Sometimes with Nonnie and Earl and sometimes with his group. Other times all by themselves.

They'd eat out at the diner and go dancing at Gibby's on weekend nights. Sometimes they just sat on the swings at the park, talking, and other times they went out in the Lewises' boat. Benjamin would fish, and she'd bring a book that she scarcely ever opened.

She couldn't believe it had only been a month. She felt as though she'd known him her whole life. He was bright and kind, and he made her laugh. When he held her hand she felt as though her life was complete. And though he had yet to kiss her, she knew he wanted to. She was trying to be patient, but it wasn't her best virtue.

Currently the sun was hiding behind the mountains, and the morning fog still hovered over the water. They'd settled in a quiet cove on the east side of the lake. He'd discovered this fishing hole the previous week, and this morning it was paying off.

"There he is." Ripples sounded as Benjamin reeled the fish up out of the water, its fins smacking the surface.

Lizzie whooped as she grabbed the net and held it under the bass. "It's your biggest yet! Just look at him."

"It's a smallmouth." Benjamin lifted the fish from the net and removed the hook from his mouth. He held the bass aloft proudly. "Yep. He's a keeper all right."

"I'll say. You might even win the tournament with him."

His eyes flickered over her. "Win or no, I'm having a great time."

She smiled broadly. "Me too. Even if I did have to get up before the break of dawn." She couldn't help teasing him.

He put the fish in the cooler and began putting away his pole, still smiling.

She checked her watch. "Are you stopping? We still have another hour."

"I think I'll quit while I'm ahead." He leaned over the boat to rinse off his hands in the lake.

Lizzie grabbed on to the seat as the boat dipped.

Benjamin straightened, dried his hands on a towel, and settled beside her on the bench. Their thighs touched, and the length of his arm felt solid against her shoulder.

"It's so pretty out here," he said, his voice rumbling. "So peaceful."

It was quiet other than the gentle ripple of water against the hull. She'd put on a sweater to ward off the morning chill. But now she felt a surge of heat wash through her limbs at his closeness.

He glanced her way. "To be honest, I'm a little nervous about supper tonight."

Her mother and father had invited him over. They'd met him briefly on several occasions, but they wanted to get to know the boy who was usurping so much of their daughter's time.

"You needn't be nervous. You've already met them."

"I know but . . . this is different."

"My parents are very nice people." It was the absolute truth. But there was one subject she couldn't help but hope would not come up tonight. She considered mentioning it Benjamin, but she didn't want to make him even more nervous.

"I'm sure they are. But what if they don't like me?"

She nudged him with her elbow. "Of course they'll like you. What's not to like?"

He turned toward her and caught her in his serious gaze. He was so close. His breath brushed her cheek, making a shiver race down her arms. The smile fell away from her face.

"I've really enjoyed the last month, Lizzie."

"Me too." Was that her hushed whisper? She couldn't take her eyes from his. They simply mesmerized her.

His dark lashes swept down a moment before lifting again, stopping at her lips. "You've become very special to me." Once again he was making her swoon with that straightforwardness of his. She loved that she never had to wonder how he was feeling.

She leaned forward, pulled by a force she couldn't define, and brushed his lips with hers. The touch set off a ripple of awareness through her whole body. She swept her lips over his again, reveling in the way he responded.

He cupped her face softly, edging closer.

She slid a hand up the hard curve of his bicep. He was so strong. His job was physical, and she felt sure he was a diligent worker. But he had an old soul, a sentimental soul. The things he said sometimes made her wish for a pencil and paper. She committed the words to memory instead and let them play in her mind at night as she lay in bed.

Now she only wanted to think about what he was doing to her. She'd kissed other boys, but not like this. Never like this. Her head spun pleasantly, and her heart threatened to beat right out of her chest. A longing like she'd never felt before rushed upon her, leaving her helpless in its wake.

He drew back, a whisper away, his eyes hooded and focused on her. His breath was coming hard and fast too. At least she wasn't the only one so affected.

But she had been the one to kiss him, drat it. She'd gone and jumped the gun.

But she couldn't bring herself to truly regret it. Especially not now, with the way he was looking at her, those brown eyes filled with want.

"I could kiss you all day," he whispered finally. "All night. The rest of my life, Elizabeth Van Buren."

Her head swam with delight. She'd known he reciprocated her feelings, but this was the first time he'd spoken in terms of forever.

His head dipped down. He did this sometimes after revealing something personal, something that made him feel vulnerable. How did she already know this about someone she'd only met a month ago?

He stared down at fingers that twitched on his thigh.

She placed a finger under his chin and lifted

until his eyes met hers. A shadow of fear flickered in the depths.

She couldn't believe she'd found someone who set her soul afire. All those clichéd lines about love made sense now. Those feelings swelled inside her until she feared she'd burst with them.

Her lips curved of their own volition. But instead of telling him how she felt, she leaned forward and showed him.

Lizzie slid her spoon into the mashed potatoes. The clinking of silverware seemed loud in the silence. A light breeze fluttered through the kitchen window, cooling her heated skin.

"Supper's delicious, Mama." She turned to Benjamin, whose leg was bouncing under the table. "She makes the best meatloaf on the planet."

"I agree, Mrs. Van Buren. Best meatloaf I've ever had."

Mama gave her Sunday-best smile. "Well, thank you, Benjamin. It's my mother's recipe."

Another awkward silence hung over the table. Benjamin had been unusually quiet. Her father was never much of a conversationalist, tending toward brief statements of fact that sometimes bordered on brash.

"Benjamin won second place in the tournament this morning," Lizzie announced.

"Is that a fact," Daddy said.

"Do you fish often?" her mother asked.

"No, ma'am. Not much time for that back home."

"Lizzie said you're a janitor," Daddy said.

"Um, yes, sir. At least for the time being."

"What other aspirations do you have, dear?"

Benjamin shifted in his seat, his eyes bouncing off Lizzie. "I haven't quite figured that out, ma'am. I like what I do well enough, but I'd love to go to college eventually."

Benjamin was very smart, and Lizzie knew he'd do well in an academic environment. He just didn't have the money for it. He'd confessed that he'd thought about joining the armed forces to afford him the opportunity.

"What would you like to study?" her mother asked.

"I'm not sure. I like the sciences, but I also enjoy history and literature."

"Hard to make a living off that, isn't it?" Daddy said.

"He's thinking of being a teacher," Lizzie said, a bit of censure in her tone.

"A noble profession, to be sure," Mama said. "What does your father do, Benjamin?"

"He's a mechanic. He works at a local garage."

"How handy to have a mechanic in the family. And your mother?"

"She's been gone now for several years."

"I'm so sorry. You're awfully young to have lost a parent."

Lizzie squeezed his clammy hand under the table. He'd been close to his mother, and her death—the result of a fluke fall—had been a terrible shock. He'd been the one to find her on the kitchen floor when he returned home from school one day.

"Yes, thank you, ma'am."

"Where does your family attend church back home?" Daddy asked.

Lizzie stiffened, her grip tightening on Benjamin's hand. He glanced at her briefly before answering.

"Well, my father doesn't attend anywhere, I'm afraid. But I attend First Baptist Church there in Jasper."

"Schwartz is a Jewish name, isn't it?"

Lizzie's face heated. "Daddy."

"Yes, sir, it is. Actually, though, my folks never practiced Judaism. And I became a believer during high school."

"We're of the Catholic faith," Daddy said. "I'm sure Lizzie has shared this with you."

"Of course." Benjamin took a bite of meatloaf, his eyes on his plate.

Another awkward pause ensued, and Lizzie felt a trickle of sweat go down the back of her shirt.

Her mother changed the conversation, and the rest of the supper was uneventful, her dad mostly keeping quiet and her mother making a valiant effort to keep the conversation rolling. Lizzie couldn't wait until she and Benjamin could leave.

Benjamin spread out the quilt on the shoreline behind the Lewises' lake cottage. Bluebell's fireworks were one of Lizzie's favorite events of the year, and this year's were supposed to be spectacular. But since leaving her house she hadn't been able to think of anything but the tension at supper.

Benjamin had been quiet on the drive over. She'd tried to keep up the conversation, but she could tell he was distracted too. Her mother had been friendly enough, and Lizzie hoped Benjamin hadn't read her father so easily.

She was scared to death he'd pull away from her if he knew the truth. If he knew how loyal they were to the Catholic church, how her dad looked down on other religions. If he knew of her father's bigotry. She couldn't bear the thought of losing Ben when she'd only just found him. She didn't want to think of any of that right now.

She plopped down on the blanket as if she hadn't a care in the world. Benjamin sprawled beside her. It was growing dark, the sun having set behind the mountains. The stars were just becoming visible beyond the canopy of trees above them, and the muted sounds of firecrackers and laughter carried across the lake. The peppy melody of "Please Mr. Postman" filtered from someone's radio down the shore.

Lizzie gave Benjamin a sideways glance. "You're awfully quiet tonight, Benjamin Schwartz," she said lightly.

He turned on his side, propping his head on his elbow. It was impossible to read his expression in the waning light. "I don't think your parents like me, angel."

"What? Nonsense. Of course they like you." It wasn't entirely untrue. It wasn't him they disliked after all, but his heritage, and he could hardly help that.

"They don't like that I'm not Catholic."

"We believe in the same God, don't we?"

"They don't like that I'm Jewish either."

"Jesus was Jewish, and we like Him very much."

"Lizzie."

"What matters is who you are, down deep." She flopped over on her side and leaned in close. "And you, Benjamin Schwartz, are a very good man."

Fireworks sizzled in the distance. A cool breeze brushed her sensitive skin, chilling her.

"Yeah?"

The somber note in his voice turned her heart into mush. She hated seeing his confidence waver. Hated that her parents were the cause.

She'd do anything to reassure him. "Yeah," she whispered, leaning closer, and then she brushed his lips with hers, all else forgotten for the moment.

twenty-five

Present Day

Molly raised her backside into the air, going into downward dog position. The backs of her thighs stretched painfully. "Ouch."

"Didn't I tell you not to take so many weeks off?" Skye's long lean body was in perfect form. She held the position effortlessly, not a single sign of strain.

Molly felt the blood rushing to her head. "Nobody likes hearing 'told you so.' "

They were in Skye's dance/yoga studio on a slow Thursday morning. Molly had the day off, and her friend had no classes until ten.

Skye hadn't planned on this particular occupation. She was supposed to study psychology at Clemson. But her mom was an alcoholic, and Skye felt she had to stay behind and look after her. Molly knew all about giving up your dreams for the greater good.

Skye shifted into warrior position and Molly followed suit, going into the deep lunge with her hands stretched overhead.

Her front thigh trembled, and sweat beaded on her forehead. "You're killing me."

"That's what you get for ignoring me for weeks."

Molly felt a twinge of guilt. "If it's any consolation, I'm paying for it now."

"It does help, actually." Skye's lips twitched. "But for the record, I'm taking it easy on you."

"I've got to get back to some kind of routine."

"You've been hit-or-miss since the accident, even with book club. That's not like you. I've been worried about you."

"I've missed you. Does that help?"

"Immensely. And I know you've been through it. You're still grieving, and now you're also overwhelmed with the inn. And then there's that project you're obsessing over."

"I'm not obsessing."

"Or perhaps it's the cute guest you're obsessing over." Skye gave her a coy look as she transitioned to a new position.

"Adam? We're just working together on the project, that's all. He's very nice and easy to talk to. He's helping me. That's it."

Skye peeked at Molly from under her arm, her face slightly contorted as they were upside down at the moment. Her long dark ponytail reached all the way to the ground. "Um, I was actually talking about his friend. You know, the one you went on a date with?"

Molly's face heated, her core temperature going up about ten degrees. "Oh, him."

"Yes, him." Skye lowered her body to the

ground, going to upward-facing dog, her body arching gracefully back. "Interesting."

Molly tried for the same position and winced at the stretch. "What's interesting, that I have the flexibility of the average tree trunk?"

"No . . . that you assumed I was talking about Adam. I thought you said the date with Jordan went well."

"It did. We've been texting off and on since he returned to New York. He's nice."

"Nice?"

"Yes, nice. Is there something wrong with nice?"

"Not at all. I just wonder if you might be more interested in Adam, that's all."

Funny, Molly had been wondering the same thing. She just wasn't quite ready to admit it out loud.

Besides, Jordan was great. And he was, after all, the author whose work she loved so much. He wrote words that made her heart stutter. That made her feel understood. So what if she hadn't felt immediate in-person chemistry. They'd only had one date. She needed to give it a chance.

Molly was ready to talk about something else. "How's your love life going? Ever hear back from Coffee Guy?" A couple weeks ago Skye had bumped into someone at the coffee shop who'd caught her interest.

"Change of subject duly noted. But nope.

Never saw him again. I guess he was just passing through. Story of my life." They talked about Skye's prospects for a while, then the conversation moved on to work and family.

"So how's your little project going?" Skye asked when they'd exhausted the other topics. "Getting any closer to finding Benjamin?"

"We found his middle initial this week. Adam's going to ask his mom for suggestions. She helps people research their family history, ancestry and such. He thinks she might have some good tips. I just hope Benjamin's still alive."

Skye gave her a long, steady look. Before returning to her pose.

"What?" Molly asked.

Skye took her time transitioning to the next pose, a look of perfect peace on her pretty face. "Why do you think this is so important to you, Molly? Finding this man?"

"You know what a big romantic I am. I couldn't just throw that letter away and forget I'd ever read it, could I?"

"I know but . . . I just wonder if there's something deeper there. You seem kind of consumed by it." Skye eased lower into the position.

Molly followed, her muscles going rigid, both at the stretch and at her friend's prying. Skye could psychoanalyze with the best of them. Never mind that she was usually right.

"You've got to stop watching so much Dr. Phil," Molly said lightly.

Skye gave her a look.

"Sometimes an interest is just an interest."

"And sometimes it isn't," Skye said gently, stretching forward. "I know you were really upset about your last conversation with your parents. Do you think that might have something to do with it?"

"That was nothing. I'm over it." It wasn't as though she'd argued with her parents or anything. They'd simply called her at college, and she'd been on her way out. End of story.

You brushed them off.

That empty, achy feeling filled her middle as it always did when she thought about that last conversation. Her eyes burned. Okay, maybe she wasn't quite over it. Regret was a bitter and unwelcome friend.

She envied Levi, who'd been visiting home when the accident had happened. He'd been called to the scene and had exchanged last words with their father. Words of love.

Skye eased to a sitting position, knees outward, soles of her feet together. "I'm just wondering if all that might be driving this search, that's all. Maybe you're so intent on helping Benjamin get closure because you never got it with your parents."

Molly's eyes burned at Skye's compassionate

tone. At the words that clanged around inside her head like a gong. How did she do that?

Skye reached over and caught a falling tear. "I'm sorry, honey. I didn't mean to upset you."

Molly blinked. "No. You're right. You're absolutely right. And I hate it. I hate feeling like I ended things badly with them. And it's too late to fix it."

"I'm sorry you're having so much regret. But your parents knew how much you loved them, Molly. It was a sudden loss. If you'd known it was your last chance you would've talked to them all day. But you didn't know. You couldn't have known. And you did have class that afternoon."

"I know." It was nothing she hadn't told herself a million times already. "But if I'd just skipped that coffee run . . . I could've made time and I didn't. I'll always regret that."

"They wouldn't want you beating yourself up over this. You know they wouldn't."

Molly knuckled off a tear. "I know."

"You have so many good memories with them. Try and focus on those. Not everyone gets to grow up with an all-American family, you know," Skye said lightly.

"You're right. I'm grateful for it. I just need to let my heart catch up with my head."

"You'll get there. Just be patient with yourself."

"Do you think it's stupid, that I'm going to all

this trouble to find some stranger because of an old letter?"

"Not at all. It might even be very healing for you if . . ."

Molly knew exactly what her friend was thinking. "If we end up finding Benjamin, you mean. If he's still alive."

"Right."

But if he wasn't, Molly would feel that horrible loss all over again. That terrible unsettling feeling of leaving something forever open-ended. Unfinished. Incomplete.

Skye rose to her feet, going into the next pose. "I just don't want you to get hurt."

"You're a good friend, Skye. Even if you do love to torture me with painful stretches."

"All part of the job, girl. All part of the job."

Friday, late afternoon, Adam stared out the inn's library window, lost in thought. He'd made progress on his outline this week, partly because he'd only seen Molly as he'd come and gone. Partly because Jordan was constantly reminding him of that approaching deadline.

He needed the kick in the pants. It was too tempting to spend all his time looking for Benjamin. Finished for the day, he packed up his laptop and closed the case. He'd put in his hours. The weekend was here, and he was going to give his story a rest.

Something outside the window caught his eye. Molly, striding down the lawn in a pale-yellow flowy top, her dark hair fluttering behind her. The sunlight caught the strands and made them sparkle like copper.

A line of description came to him. He loved it when creativity struck. But he knew if he didn't write it down, it would be forever lost. His laptop already shut down, he grabbed his pen, reached for the inn's stationery pad, and began writing. One sentence turned into two, but he wasn't satisfied with what he'd written. He ripped off the sheet, wadded it up, and tossed it into the trash can. He grabbed the pad and began again. Yes, this was better. A keeper. He finished the thought and reread it, tweaking it as he went.

When he was satisfied he tucked the sheet into the side of his laptop case with all his other notes. Once he'd drawn up a solid outline he'd figure out how all these random thoughts and pieces of dialogue fit together. Then he would begin writing the story.

But right now he needed to make a call. He pulled out his phone and tapped the buttons. While he waited for an answer he watched Molly. She'd pulled out the hose and was watering the flowers lining the walkway.

"Hey, honey," his mom said on the other end of the line. "You picked a great time to call. I'm in the middle of cleaning out a closet and looking for an excuse to take a break."

"Happy to be of help. How are you, Mom?"

"Oh, I'm just right as rain. It's the same ol' same ol' around here. How's Bluebell? Are you getting everything you need for your story?"

And then some. Adam tore his eyes from Molly. "Sure, it's going great. Jordan came down last weekend for a visit."

"Oh? Business or pleasure?"

"A little of both. He got me out on the lake at o'dark hundred hours."

His mother laughed. "That Jordan. He's good for you, I think."

"He's not good for my sleep cycle."

"Well, we all need that one friend who pushes us out of our comfort zone."

Molly began winding up the hose and tripped over it. She glanced around to make sure no one saw her almost face-plant into the petunias. Adam ducked from the window, a smile tugging his lips.

Molly disappeared from view while he and his mom chatted. When they'd exhausted all the usual topics he broached the main reason for his call: the lost letter. He told her that Lizzie had already passed, and filled her in on the search for Benjamin, telling her what efforts he'd already made to find the man.

"Well," his mother said, "most of the people

I'm trying to find are already long gone. But I'm a member of a few sites that might be helpful in finding current information. Let me look around a little and see what I can find."

"That'd be great, Mom. Thanks."

He heard the back door of the inn open. A moment later Molly hurried past the library, making a beeline toward the front of the house.

"You could always hire a private investigator," his mother continued. "They can narrow it down to a list of possibilities, though a birth date or social security number would sure help. But that gets pricey."

Money wasn't an object. But he liked having this project with Molly. And as much as he wanted to locate Benjamin, finding him would mean the end of their search.

"We're not in a hurry or anything, so don't put your own projects on hold. Whenever you get around to it is fine."

"We?"

He could hear chatter at the front desk, and the lilt of Molly's voice as she welcomed guests.

"What?" he said.

"You said 'we' . . ."

"Oh, yes, the innkeeper, Molly. The one who found the letter. I'm assisting her with the project."

"Is she young and single?" There was a hopeful note in his mother's tone.

"It's not like that, Mom. She's just a friend."

"So, yes to the young and single."

"Mom."

His mother laughed. "All right, all right. I'll leave it alone. For now. The family is hoping you'll come down for Labor Day weekend. What do you think? Could you clear your calendar for that?"

"This story's due October first, Mom. I'll probably be working weekends at that point."

"Well, if you can't make it back home maybe I can come see you one weekend over the summer. See Bluebell again and meet your friend Molly."

He rubbed his temple. "Sure, Mom. That'd be great."

"I'm just teasing you, honey. But I do miss you, and I'd love to visit Bluebell again."

"Miss you too, Mom." He heard Molly approaching before he saw her. She was showing guests around, her voice strong and pleasant.

"And this is our library . . ." She pushed the door open and caught sight of him on the phone and stopped. The older couple nearly plowed into her back.

Sorry! she mouthed.

His mom was midsentence, so he just winked at Molly. He turned toward the window and palmed his forehead. Since when did he wink at women?

His mother was still talking, about what he hadn't a clue.

Molly had moved on with the guests, her voice growing quiet as she retreated down the hall.

"That sound all right to you?" his mom asked.

Try as he might, he couldn't rewind her words in his head. "Um, sorry. I missed that."

She laughed. "It's not like you to be so unfocused, Adam. You must be plotting your story. I should let you get back to work."

"I guess I am a little distracted."

He took off his glasses and pinched his nose. Molly Bennett had gotten under his skin, and he couldn't seem to get her out.

twenty-six

Molly went downstairs, then out back where she'd left the hose half wound. Her muscles were tight from her yoga session. She was going to hurt in the morning.

She stopped short when she spotted Levi finishing her task. "I was just coming to do that. Did you get that bed frame fixed?"

"Yeah, it's good to go."

Molly looked out over the calm lake where a lone sail drifted slowly over the water. She hoped to take out the boat later. She planned to float away until the inn was just a speck on the horizon, put down the anchor, and lose herself in a book. She might even get wild and crazy and leave her cell phone behind. Probably not.

She helped Levi drag the hose reel into place against the back of the house.

"Listen, I hate to ask," he said, "but can you cover the desk for a while? I have a few calls I need to make, and they really can't wait."

"Everything all right?" He hadn't mentioned any troubles in their first business meeting. Of course, she may have faded out a time or two. This might be why Grace had referred to the meeting as the Brain Drain.

"Yeah, no worries. Just some details I need to

take care of and an ad proof for *Carolina Country* I need to approve ASAP. There's a guest checking in early this afternoon, a couple. They should be arriving soon."

"No problem. I got it." She glanced wistfully at the lake as she headed into the house. The inn was a team effort, she reminded herself, and Levi had covered for her more than once.

Molly made herself busy up front. The flowers on the stand were wilting, so she dumped them and made a note to pick up a fresh arrangement. She dusted the living room and went to the library to get the shelves next.

In the library she thought of the look on Adam's face when she'd walked in on him with those guests. When he'd winked at her.

Her lips curved upward, and something pleasant stirred inside at the memory of it. Sure, he'd been on the phone. But winking was such an un-Adamlike thing to do. She couldn't help but feel special.

The phone was ringing, so she made her way back to the front desk. She answered the caller's questions and took a reservation for four at the end of the month. She put the reservation into the computer and finished the call.

She was in the living room fluffing the sofa pillows when she heard someone coming down the steps, and she straightened from her task.

"Hey, Adam." She gave him a welcoming smile.

"Hello, Molly. It's quiet around here today."

"That it is. We have more guests checking in soon. Did you get a lot of work done this week? I've hardly seen you."

"Sure did. But I'm officially taking a break for the weekend. I was actually thinking of taking the boat out this afternoon. Any chance it's available?"

"Oh, I was just thinking—" She bit her lip. She could hardly invite herself along. Then she remembered the twisty thing with her lips and let it go. "Never mind. Let me check the reservations. I'm sure it won't be a problem."

Adam gave her an inquisitive stare as he followed her to the front desk. "What was that look? Is there a problem with the boat?"

She shook her head as she opened the book. "No, no. It's fine."

"Does it have a dead battery?" There was a teasing note in his voice. "Is it running on empty? Does the hull have a gaping hole?"

She laughed. "Of course not. The boat's in perfect shape—and available the rest of the day, in fact."

Adam tilted his head as if remembering something. "Wait, isn't today your day off? I didn't mean to put you to work."

"No, it's all right. I'm actually filling in for Levi for a few minutes." She dangled the key, attached to a buoy designed to make the keys float if they were lost overboard. "Do you want to take it out now?"

Adam took the key from her, something hesitant in his action. In the way he avoided her eyes.

"You've . . . driven a boat before, right?"

"Of course. Is there something I need to sign?"

She waved him off. "I think we can dispense with the formalities."

"Would you . . . um . . ." He scratched the back of his neck. "Would you like to come along? After you're finished here, I mean. I'd love to, you know, hear all that lake history and everything."

It was so sweet the way he asked. His uncertainty. A pleasant change from guys who took their blatant appeal for granted. Suddenly her boat ride-and-read plan seemed like a snooze fest.

A smile bloomed on Molly's face. "I would love that."

Thirty minutes later the inn was growing distant as Adam maneuvered the boat along the shoreline. Molly took in a lungful of fresh air, enjoying the feel of the breeze stirring her hair.

This was clearly not his first time captaining a boat. Theirs was just a simple aluminum deal with two bench seats. He sat at the stern, guiding them with the tiller on the ten-horsepower outboard motor.

A cloud swept over the sun, a welcome reprieve from the heat of the afternoon. The boat slowed a bit, the motor growing quieter.

"What's that?" Adam pointed up the hillside where homes had given way to wider spaces. A big old building balanced on the hillside.

He'd been asking questions since they'd left the pier, and she was happy to play tour guide.

"That's the Bluebell Baptist Youth Camp. See the smaller buildings around the main building? Those are the cabins where the kids stay. The big building is sort of a community center. They've hosted breakfasts and other events for years, but mainly they cater to underprivileged children."

There were about a dozen kids splashing around in the roped-off section in front of the property, where inflatable floats and slides dotted the water.

"That's an expensive piece of property for a youth camp."

"Very. And they're struggling, I'm afraid. They've had serious issues with the building's foundation, and if they can't fix it they'll have to shut it down. This will probably be their last summer."

"That's too bad."

The recollection stirred up negative feelings. Two years ago when Dominic had found out about the camp's financial troubles he committed to saving it. He was vocal about it in town, getting everyone's hopes up. When he was exposed for the fraud he was, Molly felt as though she'd let down the entire community.

"Can't they do a fund-raiser or something?"

Molly gave him a wan smile. "The fix is very expensive—to the tune of millions of dollars."

"Yikes. That is a lot of money. And I guess selling the property wouldn't net them enough to start over somewhere else."

"Nope. It's a real shame too. They help so many disadvantaged kids. The property has an interesting history. The church bought it back in the late fifties. That main building used to be a dance hall, but the church wasn't happy with all the debauchery going on, so they bought the property from the brothers who owned it."

"Must've been a wild place."

Molly tossed a smile over her shoulder. "It was mainly just the dancing they objected to."

"I thought the old dance hall was in town, where that theater is now."

"Well, interesting story . . . Seems one of the brothers, Gibby, who sold the property to the church, wasn't quite finished with the idea of a dance hall."

Adam laughed. "I see where this is going."

"Yep. He decided to take his money and open a new dance hall. Right smack in the middle of town."

"I'll bet the church was fit to be tied."

Molly shrugged. "Nothing they could do about it, I guess. Gibby's was even more popular than the dance hall they'd sold. I guess it all worked out in the end. The youth camp has been a vital ministry. Too bad they'll have to shut it down."

They'd floated past the property and toward a large bay that was protected by the state. It was also picturesque because of the cliffs and a waterfall that dropped from staggering heights.

"It's beautiful back here," Adam said. "So secluded. Why are there no houses?"

"This is Pineview Bay. It's state property, so there are a lot of restrictions." She pointed to where the protected land began and ended. "Governor Jennings saw to that during his tenure. He saw the way it was building up and decided to preserve some of the land."

They meandered along the shoreline, appreciating the natural beauty. Molly told him about all the trails through the reserve and the swinging bridge that was back behind the cliff, spanning a huge gorge.

They were deep in the bay when a stiff breeze blew, giving her a chill. She looked up at the thick gray cloud obscuring the sunlight and drew in a deep breath.

"I think I smell"—a fat dollop of rain hit her nose—"rain."

"We should probably head back."

Before he could turn around the raindrops began falling steadily.

"Uh-oh." Adam looked around. "Should we take cover?"

"There's nowhere nearby." They were a long way from anything resembling a shelter. She looked back toward the inn, not even visible from this distance. "I guess we could make a run for it."

The rain came in buckets then, pummeling them with cold wet shards.

Molly shrieked, ducking her head against the downpour.

Adam picked up speed, making her grab for the bench seat. But rather than heading toward the inn he guided the boat toward the cove. The shelter of pine trees was the best they were going to do.

When they reached the inlet he pulled the boat along the shore, turned off the engine, and lifted the motor. They drifted toward shore until the boat scraped bottom.

The driving rain was so thick she couldn't see beyond the bay to the houses dotting the lake. The trees provided a little shelter, but the rain was so relentless, the wind kicking up, they were still getting wet. Molly's shirt and the tops of her thighs were already soaked.

Adam climbed over her bench seat, the boat rocking with his movements. He sat down on the bench and hoisted a jacket over them like a tarp.

"Better late than never," he said over the roar of rain.

Molly huddled underneath with him. "Where'd that come from?"

"There was a 32 percent chance of rain."

Of course Adam would be prepared for every eventuality. "I should've known this would happen. It always rains after I water the flowers."

"At least there's no lightning."

"Don't jinx it." She turned another smile on him, but she was unprepared for the sight of Adam. His hair was matted to his forehead, and his eyes were blocked by his rain-speckled, fogged-up glasses.

Laughter bubbled up inside her. "How can you see a single thing?"

Since both his hands were otherwise occupied, she reached up and lifted his glasses from his face. She started to wipe them off with her shirt, but it was soaked.

"I don't have anything to dry them on."

"That's all right. I can see better already."

She turned and found him inches away. Water dripped down his forehead and into his eyes. She was suddenly aware of the spicy scent of him. Of the warmth of his body. And those eyes. Unhidden by glasses, she was getting the full effect of that warm blue gaze. She couldn't look away. The heavy rain was like a curtain, cocooning them in their own world.

His gaze took her in, and she could only imagine what he was seeing. Her hair must be plastered to her head. Her face was wet, the little bit of makeup she had on probably making her look like a drowned raccoon.

She gave a wry laugh and ran a knuckle under her eye. "I'm a mess."

"*Tu es belle*," he whispered.

You are beautiful.

Her breath caught and her hand stopped midmotion. She really should tell him she spoke Italian. But she was reluctant to embarrass him. And, she had to admit, she loved being privy to his private thoughts.

Her eyes locked on him, her smile falling away at the longing on his face. His breath brushed her cheek, warm and soft, drawing her gaze to his lips.

And then she was leaning forward, her eyes closing. She brushed his mouth with hers. His lips were warm and soft and pliable. Her head spun at the brief touch, and a shiver of delight rippled through her.

Her eyes still closed, she put a sliver of space between them. Felt his breath on her lips. And then they were kissing again. His lips were deliciously warm and firm. Home. Her heart thudded in her chest, making her breaths shallow. She hadn't felt this way in so long. Not since . . .

Dominic.

Her chest tightened at the memory. Yes, his kisses had once made her feel amazing too. Until she discovered he wasn't at all who she thought he was. Until the truth had come crashing down, breaking her heart in the process. The ache in her chest swelled. Suddenly she couldn't breathe.

She pushed against Adam, unable to even look at him. She was afraid of the questions she'd find in his kind eyes. She'd started this, but she couldn't finish it. Couldn't even think about finishing it. She could barely even think around the panic building in her chest.

Fine time to realize she wasn't ready for this. And now she'd gone and made everything weird between them. So, so weird.

And, hello, you are kind of dating his best friend. Nathaniel Quinn. Remember him?

She put more distance between them and turned her attention to the lake, calling herself all kinds of fool. Water dripped from the rim of their tarp. She wanted to pull the jacket over her head and hide.

Adam's heart was thumping in his chest so loudly he feared Molly could hear it over the storm. He could still feel her, taste her, on his lips. Wished he could preserve those things for the rest of his life. That kiss. He'd been instantly lost in a fog of pleasure when her lips settled on his.

"I am so sorry." Molly looked like a puppy that had just been caught chewing her owner's favorite pair of shoes. "That was . . . This is . . . I shouldn't have done that."

He winced. Not that he fancied himself some kind of Romeo, but he was known for writing some darn good kisses.

"It's not you," she continued. "I made everything weird. I shouldn't have done that. You're a guest, and I'm making you uncomfortable. Oh my gosh, Levi was right, I have no boundaries. And then there's Jordan. What have I done?"

Ah, Jordan. Speaking of Romeo. Adam had completely forgotten his best friend. The one who'd had his back since forever.

"No, Molly. Please don't. It's all right."

She'd moved as far from him as possible given the narrow width of the bench. Her arms were wrapped around herself. Clearly she regretted the impulsive kiss.

It must've been the romantic setting—how many kisses in the rain had he written?—and possibly the irresistible allure of the Italian language. He couldn't discount that.

As much as he'd enjoyed the kiss, it would've been better if it had never happened, because now she was distancing herself from him. He could feel her withdrawal and feared that even their friendship was slipping away.

"It's fine, Molly. Really. I get it."

More than she could even know. Her spontaneous act hadn't really meant anything. He wasn't what she wanted. The kiss had probably disappointed her, and he was used to disappointing people.

As if a spigot had shut off, the rain stopped. Everything went quiet around them except the *drip, drip, drip* of raindrops falling from the branches above.

Adam carefully shifted the jacket behind them, letting the water run off into the hull, glad for something to do. His eyes flickered over her features.

Molly's fingers covered her mouth, and she was looking everywhere but at him. "I feel just awful. I don't know what came over me. I've never done that before. I mean, yes, I've kissed a man before, but I initiated this one, and that was very stupid of me."

He flinched. "Please don't give it another thought." He'd be doing enough of that for both of them. He tried for a smile, but it felt stiff and strained.

She wasn't looking at him anyway. She was messing with her wet hair, and the apple-y scent of her was wrapping around him.

"We'd better get back before the sky opens up

again." He climbed over the seat, eager to put some space between them.

She held out his glasses. "Don't forget these."

"Right."

He took the glasses and put them on, then tilted the motor down and turned the key. The hum of the engine was a relief after the weighty silence.

While the ride out to the bay had passed in a flash, the ride home seemed interminable. Molly sat in front of him, her back straight as a telephone pole, her shoulders rigid. How had everything gone so wrong, so quickly?

twenty-seven

When they reached the inn, Molly said an awkward good-bye to Adam and slinked into the back of the house. She was dripping all over the floor, a mess she'd have to clean up later. She was relieved to find the front desk vacant as she slipped upstairs and down the hall toward her room.

The cleaning cart was in front of the room across from hers and Grace's. The door to the room was wide open.

Entering her own room, Molly went for a towel in the bathroom and ruffled it through her wet hair. Next she grabbed some clean clothes and went back into the bathroom to change.

She wanted to hide in her room the rest of the day. The rest of the week. Maybe longer. This is why she should put boundaries in place. So she didn't make a total fool of herself.

She looked in the bathroom mirror. And yes, she did in fact look like a drowned raccoon.

Don't think about it. Just don't think about it.

Tomorrow she'd run into Adam on the stairs or out front, and she'd behave as though nothing had happened. As though she hadn't grabbed his face and forced a kiss on him. After going out with his best friend.

Argh! *Don't think about it.*

She left the bathroom and found Grace dusting their dresser. "Oh, hey."

Grace took in her wet, disheveled hair. "Did you just shower?"

"Got caught in the rain."

Grace gave her a once-over. "Your shirt's on inside out. And backward."

Molly looked down at the white tag at her neckline. She pulled off the shirt and turned it right side out.

"Thought I'd give the room a quick cleaning while I had the cart out."

"Thanks. It needs it." Molly put the shirt back on and smoothed out the black fabric.

"Is the Agony at two tomorrow?" Grace asked.

"The what?"

"The Brain Drain, the Agony, the Monthly. So many options. Why limit ourselves?"

Molly gave a wobbly smile. "That'll really get under Levi's skin."

"That's the plan."

Grace talked about volleyball practice as she moved the duster around the bureau's surface, but Molly couldn't focus on what she was saying. She was too busy wondering why that kiss had freaked her out so badly. Clearly she wasn't ready to date again.

And yet, it had been two years since Dominic. She should probably end things with Jordan rather than lead him on. But she hadn't had a hint of anxiety about him.

"What's going on with you and Jordan?" Grace asked, as if reading her mind. "Is he still texting you?"

"Yeah. And he called yesterday. We didn't talk long though. He was heading into a meeting."

As far as Grace knew, Jordan was just an agent from New York. Hard as it had been, Molly had kept her word to Adam; she hadn't told anyone about Jordan's alter ego. It was the secret of the century, and she gave herself props for keeping her mouth shut—she needed all the props she could get right now.

Because all she could think about was Adam and the feel of his lips on hers. She swore she could still taste his minty breath. For those few seconds she'd been lost in bliss. Because the kiss had felt so right. His lips had felt like home.

Oh, she had to stop this. She rubbed her fingers over her mouth. Not good enough. She'd brush her teeth. A nice fresh start.

She went to the bathroom and grabbed her toothbrush. She was going to wash away every trace of that kiss. Scrub him all away. Then she was going to forget it ever happened. They'd go back to being friends. Just friends.

Grace appeared on the threshold. "You all right? You seem a little . . . funny."

"I'm fine." If she could just rewind time and

take back that kiss everything would be hunky-dory. She spread the toothpaste onto her brush.

"Um . . . what are you doing?" Grace asked.

"Brushing my teeth." Molly stuck the brush into her mouth.

"That's not—"

"Blech!" Molly pulled the toothbrush from her mouth.

"Toothpaste," Grace finished.

Molly looked at the tube of travel-size toothpaste. "Clotrimazole . . . What is this?"

"Athlete's foot cream," Grace said evenly.

"Ugh!" Molly turned on the tap and rinsed out her mouth. Five times. It still didn't feel like enough. "That stuff tastes nasty."

"Well, in all fairness, it's not meant to go in the mouth."

"Did the tip come into contact with your foot? With your *fungus?*"

"You don't want to know."

Molly shuddered. She grabbed a washcloth and scraped her tongue with it. Disgusting. Well, at least her mouth didn't taste like Adam now. It tasted like antifungal cream.

Grace stared at Molly's reflection in the mirror, one eyebrow raised.

Molly capped the cream and made a point of moving it to the highest shelf of the vanity. "How 'bout we keep it up here from now on, hmm?"

She skirted Grace, heading back into the

bedroom. It was suppertime and she was hungry. But she didn't want to leave the room. She might run into Adam. It was too soon for that. She couldn't look him in the eye right now. She plopped down on the end of her bed, considering her options. Send Grace for food. Pizza delivery, right to her door. Twizzlers in her purse.

Grace was still studying her from the threshold of the bathroom, frown lines notched between her brows. She crossed her arms over her chest and slowly drummed her fingers against her upper arm.

"All right, all right," Molly blurted. "I kissed him."

Grace gave her head a shake as if trying to keep up. "Jordan? You mean before he went back home?"

Molly winced. "No, Adam. I kissed Adam. Today, out on the boat. In the rain."

Grace's head tipped slowly back. "Oh, right, Adam . . . Jordan's best friend." She gave Molly a pointed look.

Molly slapped a hand over her eyes and fell back on the bed. "Ugh! What is wrong with me? An innkeeper shouldn't go around kissing guests. Levi was right—but don't you dare tell him I said so. Much less guests who are also best friends with the guy with whom the innkeeper went out and with whom she's been communicating."

"Would it kill you to just leave the preposition

251

at the end of the sentence? I think you're missing the important part here."

"No, I think that about covers it."

"Um, no it does not. How was it? How was the kiss?"

Molly groaned. "That's the worst part of all. It was great. Amazing really."

"Um . . . I'm confused."

"He's a guest. He's Jordan's best friend. He lives in New York." And then there was that scary feeling she'd had just as she was losing herself in the kiss—the one that made her chest go all tight and twitchy.

"Jordan lives in New York too."

"Jordan can live anywhere; he's an—" Molly bit off the word just in time. "An agent. There's no future with Adam. He probably didn't even want the kiss at all. I made everything so awkward. Don't ever make the first move. It ruins everything."

"Wait, so did he kiss you back or what?"

"Well, yes, but what was he supposed to do? He probably felt sorry for me."

Grace lifted a brow.

"I probably embarrassed the poor guy. I made him uncomfortable, and now I have to tiptoe around here trying to avoid him for the next six weeks."

"What are you, twelve?"

"Hey. Who's the big sister here?"

"I'm starting to wonder. Listen, I'm sure the awkwardness will pass in time. The next time or two you see him might be uncomfortable, but eventually this will be just a little blip on the radar."

"You think?"

"Of course."

Molly sat up on the bed, her shoulders slumped. She'd gone out with Adam's friend, then turned around and kissed Adam, all within the same week.

"I'm a terrible person."

Grace rolled her eyes. "You're not a terrible person. Did it ever occur to you that maybe you're just more interested in Adam than you are in Jordan? There's no crime in that, you know. You said the kiss was great . . . Maybe you should see where it goes."

Molly shook her head. Grace didn't understand who Jordan was, and Molly couldn't even tell her. This Adam thing was just . . . temporary insanity or something. And scary. Had she mentioned scary?

"You only had one date with Jordan," Grace said.

"But we've been communicating, and I've promised him another date when he comes back."

Sure, Molly was attracted to Adam—no denying it. But she'd spent more time with him. One date with Jordan wasn't enough time to judge their chemistry. Texting and calls weren't conducive to judging chemistry either. When he returned and she got to know him better, things would be different. She'd forget all about this silly little crush on Adam.

Grace patted her shoulder. "It'll be all right. You'll see. Before you know it you and Adam will be back to your cute little investigative ways, and you'll have forgotten all about the kiss."

The project. Molly gave a deep sigh. She'd forgotten all about the project. So much for avoiding Adam the next six weeks.

twenty-eight

Molly managed to steer clear of Adam as long as she could. Or maybe he was steering clear of her. But she was working the front desk on Saturday morning when she heard him coming down the stairs. It was impossible to circumvent an encounter since she was checking out the Booths, a middle-aged couple who were celebrating their thirtieth anniversary.

Molly bestowed a smile on the couple, über aware of Adam coming around the corner and stopping hesitantly.

"Did you get over to Stone Gap Bridge yesterday?" Molly asked the couple.

"Sure did," Mr. Booth said. "Got some great pictures. It was amazing."

"It was terrifying!" Mrs. Booth laughed. "I'm afraid of heights, did I mention that?"

Mr. Booth curled his arm around his wife's waist. "You did great. She made it all the way across."

"And then I would've paid a million bucks to avoid going back."

Molly smiled. "I guess you figured out there is no other way back."

"My legs were shaking so badly. I just about collapsed when I made it back across. But I have to admit the views were stunning." She opened her phone to the photos and showed Molly.

The sunset views were beautiful. The rocky canyon reflected the pinks and purples of the sky. There were selfies of the couple on the middle of the bridge and photos of Mr. Booth taken by his wife from the safety of terra firma.

"These are great."

"I've already posted all our pictures on Facebook, and I tagged your inn's page."

"Thank you. I'll have to check them out."

"We had a wonderful time in Bluebell," Mrs. Booth said. "We're already planning to come back for our thirty-fifth."

"We'll splurge on the suite next time," Mr. Booth said.

"I'm so glad to hear it. We'd love to have you back." Molly handed them their receipt along with a white pastry bag. "I knew you'd be in a hurry to catch your flight, so I had Miss Della bag up some muffins."

"Oh, you're such a doll," Mrs. Booth said. "Thank you so much. You made us feel like family."

"My pleasure. You have a safe trip back to Philly. Take care now, and give that little granddaughter an extra hug for me."

The couple waved, then pulled their suitcases behind them and slipped out the front door.

And then there was nowhere to look but at

Adam, whose hands were tucked into the back pockets of his khakis. His presence seemed large in the space.

"Good morning!" she said, overly bright. She took her smile down a notch or two.

"Morning." His voice was morning gruff. He took a step closer, his eyes rising only as far as the counter. He obviously had something to say.

Please, God, not a reference to yesterday's unfortunate debacle.

He stopped half a body length away. "Um, I hate to be a bother, but the air conditioning unit in my room isn't functioning properly."

"Oh, no. That's not good." *Duh, Molly.* "And it's supposed to be a super hot one today. I'll let Levi know, and we'll get it taken care of as soon as possible. Will you be out today?"

"Yes, all day in fact. So whenever you can get to it is fine."

"Okay, we'll get it taken care of." *Already said that.* "I'm so sorry for the inconvenience." She couldn't seem to stop sounding so professional.

"It's fine." He poked his glasses into place, his eyes flickering to hers for the briefest of seconds. Maybe she wasn't the only one who was flustered. "It cooled off last night so I was comfortable enough."

Ah, yes. Cooled off. Because of the storm. All the images, all the feelings from yesterday's interlude swept over her. Man, that kiss. Heat flooded into her face. She fiddled with the tourist pamphlets on the counter, straightening them like a maniac.

"Right. Yes. Well. It's supposed to be hotter today." *Already said that too.* "So we'll get it fixed. Today. Levi, I mean. And if he can't take care of it, we'll find someone who can. Your room will be cool as a cucumber when you get back from, well, wherever it is you're going. It'll be great!"

He gave a nod, backing toward the door. "Thank you. I appreciate it."

"Great! Have a great day." Could she say *great* one more time?

"You too, Molly." He gave her a wistful smile, then slipped out the door.

At the final click of the door Molly collapsed on the counter and buried her head under her arms.

twenty-nine

A dam hunched forward over the library desk at the inn, scouring the website of the Bluebell Baptist Youth Camp Molly had pointed out on that fated boat ride more than two weeks ago. He hadn't been able to get the camp out of his mind, and he recognized the quiet nudging for what it was.

He was always looking for ways to give back, for worthy ministries to support. Writing had been a lucrative career, yet he was a simple man. He wasn't given to fancy sports cars, he didn't need a mansion, and traveling alone wasn't his idea of entertainment. The bottom line was, he had plenty saved up for a rainy day, and he was earning more money than he could possibly spend.

He liked what he saw on the camp's website. There was a donation page, but the progress thermometer was in the freezing cold zone. The site contained pages of glowing endorsements from children, parents, and adults who remembered going to the camp as youth. He read up on the church that owned the place and the people who ran it. He was still feeling that inner nudging.

There were many things he appreciated about

his anonymity other than just maintaining his privacy. He didn't have to wonder whether or not people liked him only for his money. Also, he could donate his resources to whatever ministry he chose without having to question his own motives or having others question them.

He jotted down the camp's phone number and closed out the page. He would schedule a meeting with the camp's manager, assess their needs, and determine if this investment was a good fit.

He should be working right now, but ever since that kiss he'd struggled to focus. He'd only seen Molly in passing the past couple of weeks. She was always bright and professional, but there was a new awkwardness between them. She was back to her run-on sentences. Ordinarily he found the trait adorable, but not when it was a reminder of his disappointing kiss.

He longed to put things back to normal, but he had no idea how to accomplish such a feat.

Slogging through his work had been consuming so much of his time that he'd made no progress on finding Benjamin. His mom was making some headway, she'd said earlier this week. She hadn't found an obituary yet, so that was encouraging. Maybe he could find some promising lead to put Molly and him back on familiar ground.

Behind him he heard someone clear a throat, and he turned to find the subject of his daydream standing on the threshold. Her hands were tucked into her shorts' pockets, and she looked beautiful in a red top that brought out the color in her cheeks.

"Hello, Molly."

"Hi . . . so, um, I ran into Nonnie at the market this morning." She had that familiar light in her eyes.

"Oh yeah?"

"She found some pictures and things in her attic. She said we could come over anytime and she'd go through them with us."

"That's terrific. I'd love to."

Molly seemed eager to accept Nonnie's invitation. And yes, it was because of the project, not because of him, but tell that to his thumping heart.

"So . . . I'm off work the rest of the evening, and I'm off on Thursday too. You don't have to go if you don't want to. I mean, I know you're trying to get your work done so . . ."

"I'd like to see this through, if that's all right by you." He applauded his direct response and felt a thrill of relief when she smiled.

"Great. I'd like that. I just didn't want to impose on your time. You've already helped so much."

"I'm not one to quit in the middle of a project. I spoke with my mom this week, and she said she's making progress with finding Benjamin. But

261

Nonnie might have information that expedites the search."

Molly perked up. She was practically bouncing on the balls of her feet. "I can't wait to see the pictures. I know we've already seen the two of them, but I just feel such a connection to them. I know that sounds crazy."

"Not at all." Adam tossed her a smile as he closed his laptop and stashed it in its case. "Let's get right on it then."

"I'm so glad you're feeling better, Miss Nonnie," Molly said as she sat on the living room floor at the woman's feet. The goods were piled in a shoe box on the floral ottoman, and it was all Molly could do not to start rummaging through it.

"It was one of those awful summer colds. I thought it would never go away." Nonnie wore another floral housecoat, but her silver hair was carefully styled, and a bit of makeup enhanced her features.

She patted the seat beside her, and Adam lowered himself onto the love seat on the other side of the ottoman, holding his glass of iced tea.

"Well, you're looking much better," Molly said. "I was worried about you."

"It was that chicken soup of yours—simply magic!"

Molly laughed. "I'd settle for edible. Mama didn't pass off her skills on me, I'm afraid."

"Oh, hogwash. You don't give yourself enough credit." Nonnie grabbed the glasses dangling from a chain around her neck and perched them on the end of her nose. "Now, let's see what we have here. This is where I keep my high school memorabilia. There's probably all manner of things in here, but I know I must have some photos from that summer Lizzie met Benjamin."

Nonnie pulled the box close, grabbed a stack of photos, and began looking through them. "I should've sorted these before you got here."

"Take your time," Adam said. "We're in no hurry."

Speak for yourself, Molly thought, her fingers drumming on her leg.

Nonnie sifted through the pictures and newspaper clippings, a pensive smile on her face. "Nothing here." She grabbed the next stack.

Molly wished she could dive in herself, but she didn't feel comfortable rooting through Miss Nonnie's personal things without express permission.

"Oh! Here we go. Just look at the lot of us." Nonnie handed Molly a photo of herself and Lizzie posing on the beach with two boys behind them, one of them Benjamin. They were all laughing.

"There's Lizzie and Benjamin," Molly said. "And that's you, Miss Nonnie? You're so beautiful." She passed the photo to Adam.

"Who's the guy behind you, Miss Nonnie?" Adam asked.

"That was Earl Foster. He was quite the scoundrel." The wistful smile on her face belied her words.

"Was he your beau?" Molly asked.

"Oh, not really. We just toyed with each other. He was a real flirt, though, I'll tell you that."

"Do you remember this particular day?" Adam asked.

"Like it was yesterday. We'd gone swimming and were having a marvelous time. Lizzie got one of our friends to snap the photo. After we swam we took a picnic out to Summit Ridge in Earl's new convertible—he was terribly spoiled."

"All of you went?" Molly asked. "Lizzie and Benjamin too?"

"Oh, yes. If Lizzie wasn't working at the market, those two were together. They fit together like two pieces of a puzzle. I remember Lizzie saying that from the moment she met him she felt like she'd always known him. I guess he must've felt the same, because they fell in love so quickly. Just seeing this photo, so many things are coming back to me."

"Do you remember any pertinent details about Benjamin that might help us find him?" Adam asked. "Did he have a birthday that summer?"

Nonnie started through another stack of photos, her hooded eyes narrowing in thought. "Not as I recall. Lizzie's birthday was in July though. Her folks threw her an nineteenth birthday party that summer at Patty's Place—a popular restaurant of the day."

Nonnie's fine brows puckered, something about the memory clearly bothering her. "There was some kind of tension going on that night. I don't remember exactly why. I just remember Lizzie was a nervous Nellie the whole time."

"Did it have to do with Benjamin?" Molly asked.

Nonnie slowly shook her head. "I can't rightly recall. It was so long ago. I sure wish I could remember something important."

Molly patted her knee. "You're doing just fine."

"Here's another." Nonnie smiled, gazing at the photo. "It's just me and Lizzie, but I think Benjamin must've taken it."

It was Lizzie and Nonnie at Stone Gap Bridge. They were posing in the middle of the bridge, and Lizzie was blowing a kiss to the camera.

Molly handed the photo to Adam. "It looks as though you had a wonderful summer."

"Oh, we did. So much laughter. So young and carefree." She sighed, a pensive look sweeping over her features. "We couldn't have known . . ."

Molly's gaze sharpened on Miss Nonnie. She seemed to be remembering something upsetting. "Couldn't have known . . . ?"

Nonnie blinked, her expression clearing. She gave Molly a placid smile. "Known what, dear?"

"You said 'we couldn't have known' and then you stopped."

"Did I? Oh, this mind of mine. I just can't seem to hold a thought anymore."

Nonnie proceeded to flip through the photos. Molly traded a look with Adam. What had Nonnie been about to say? Had it meant anything, or was it just the meaningless rambling of an elderly woman?

He lifted a shoulder, and they peeked over Nonnie's shoulders as she went through the next stack.

Nonnie continued through several photos, stopping to identify the people when she could remember. A white envelope surfaced next.

The script on it looked familiar. Was that Lizzie's handwriting? Molly leaned in.

Nonnie quickly turned the envelope over with the other photos.

Molly spotted another white envelope jutting out from the pile. Her fingers twitched.

Nonnie pulled out the envelope and put it facedown with the other.

It could've been anyone's handwriting really. But it had sure looked like Lizzie's. And if it was, why would Miss Nonnie keep the letters from them?

Molly's heart ticked away. She looked at Adam, who was gazing back at her, a question in his eyes. He'd noticed it too, then.

"Oh my, just look at this one. It's so romantic."

Nonnie held out a photo taken from behind Lizzie and Benjamin, who were kissing. They were sitting on a log facing Bluebell Lake. The sun had gone down behind the mountains, leaving swirls of pink and gold. Lizzie leaned into Benjamin, and he was cupping her face.

Molly warmed inside at the tenderness the photo had captured.

Nonnie sighed. "I remember taking this. It was quite late in the summer. They were so smitten with each other."

"If summer was drawing to a close," Adam said, "were they making plans to be together?"

"Oh, yes, they were talking about forever by the end of the summer."

"Well, something must've gone terribly wrong," Molly said.

Adam took a sip of tea. "I think we can infer from Lizzie's letter that her folks didn't approve of Benjamin—her father at least."

"Yes, that sounds about right," Nonnie said.

"Have you been able to remember where Benjamin worked?" he asked. "I haven't been able to find much on him in Jasper, but maybe if his place of employment still exists, they might have record of him."

"Oh, honey, I think that detail is long gone."

"What about the military?" Molly asked, remembering the mention of it in the letter. "Do you remember him talking much about that?"

"I think it was just for the GI Bill. He didn't have much in the way of material wealth."

"Did he mention a particular branch of the military?" Adam asked.

"Not that I recall."

"Did he mention what he might like to study at college?"

Nonnie shook her head. "I'm sorry. If he mentioned it, I surely don't remember. And in all honesty, we were far more likely to talk about a bunch of nothing than we were to talk of things of substance. It was all fun and games that summer . . ."

Until it wasn't.

Molly heard the unspoken ending of the sentence, and a glance at Adam confirmed that he had too.

thirty

Lizzie leaned into Benjamin's warmth, feeling the brush of his lips on hers. His fingers skated across her jaw, raising gooseflesh on her arms, and her head swam with longing.

She couldn't believe it was already August. They'd grown so close over the past two months. She'd never felt so close to anyone. Had never cared so much what another person thought. She wanted to be with him every waking moment. She wanted to be privy to his every thought.

She finally knew what all the songwriters were singing about. She was in love with Benjamin Schwartz. She believed he felt the same, though he had yet to say it.

His hand fell to her shoulder, a delicious weight. Over the past couple weeks he'd touched her in places she'd never let a boy touch before. When she sat in Mass on Sunday mornings she was consumed by guilt. She told herself she'd draw a line and ask him to respect it. He would, if she only asked. But his kisses were like fuel on a raging fire. She lost her head when he touched her.

She shifted on the log. She didn't have to worry about that right now. Nonnie and Earl were somewhere behind them, enjoying the sunset. The muted sounds of their chatter and laughter carried to her on a breeze.

Benjamin drew away from her, his eyelids weighted, his breath shallow. He undid her with that smoldering look of his.

"I can't believe we only have two more weeks of summer," he whispered.

"I know." He was headed back to Tennessee, then two weeks later she was off to nursing school in Ohio. It was so far from Jasper. She didn't want to go to college at all now. She only wanted to be with Benjamin.

He cupped her face, his eyes searching hers. "I don't want that to be the end of us, Lizzie."

Her relief seeped out in a sigh that seemed to come from her toes. "I don't either."

He wetted his lips, looking adorably unsure. "I know it's only been two months but . . . I love you, angel. I've never told another woman that, other than my mother."

She couldn't stop the smile that stretched her lips. "I love you too, Benjamin. So much."

He kissed her again, this time slow and gentle. Reverent. She was buoyed by his declaration. Her heart sang with joy. But thoughts of the quickly ending summer began crowding out her bliss. How could they possibly make this work?

Their lives would be in two different states.

And then there were her parents. She didn't even want to think about that obstacle.

She drew away, her mind spinning with worry.

He smoothed her brow, giving her a gentle smile. "What's bothering you?"

"You're going back to Jasper, Ben. And then I'm going off to college."

"I guess we need to talk about all that. I've been doing a lot of thinking . . . What if I moved to Ohio to be near you?"

Her heart felt full to bursting. She could hardly believe what he was offering. "You'd do that for me?"

"I'd do anything for you, angel. Don't you know that?" When he said it like that, when he looked at her like this, yes, she believed him.

"I don't even know if I want to go to college anymore."

"You got a scholarship. You can't just pass up an opportunity like that." She heard the censure in his voice. Sometimes, when she was with him, she felt a little spoiled.

"But what if you can't find another job in Ohio?"

"Have a little faith." He took her hand and held it gently. "And just so you know . . . My plans involve a future for us—a wedding and a family. I want all that with you, Lizzie. Does that sound like something you'd like?"

Her heart gave a heavy sigh. "It sounds wonderful. Oh, Benjamin."

He chuckled and ducked his head. "I've gotten way ahead of myself. You make me lose my head. I still need to ask your dad for his blessing."

A jolt of fear went through her. "That's not necessary, Ben. It's not the Dark Ages anymore."

"He's your father, Lizzie. I want his respect."

"It's too early for that; he hardly knows you. And it's my future, not his."

He gave her a placating smile. "Nonetheless, having his blessing is important to me. I want to start things off right."

The fear that jolted through her before multiplied into a million shocks. He didn't know how deeply rooted her dad's prejudices were. He would never accept Ben. Would never find him good enough for his baby girl. She had to get that through to Benjamin without scaring him off.

"You don't know him," she said. "Daddy won't be so easily won over." *He won't be won over at all.*

He patted her hand. "You worry too much. Just leave it to me."

"Let's talk about it later, okay?" Like after they'd moved to Ohio. And after they'd said their vows. They'd get married, and then her dad would have no choice but to accept Benjamin into their family. Right?

thirty-one

Molly put the finishing touches on the cake and carried it into the dining room where her siblings waited. It was a slow Thursday evening. They'd talked about going to the cemetery, but since they couldn't leave the inn unattended had decided to mark the occasion right here.

Someone had pulled the dining room door shut, giving them privacy. Grace shredded a napkin beside the stack of clean plates, her eyes a little bloodshot. Levi reclined in a chair, legs sprawled, looking about as excited for this as Molly felt.

She set the cake down on the table. Swirls were the only adornment on the vanilla buttercream frosting.

"Is it chocolate?" Grace asked.

"Mama's favorite recipe," Molly said.

"It looks good, Mol," Levi said. "Thanks for making it."

She hadn't bothered with candles since their mom wasn't here to blow them out. Molly blinked against the sting of tears. She needed to be strong for her siblings. Especially Grace. This was going to be a celebration, doggonit. Not a pity party. But it just seemed so unreal that their mother hadn't made it to her fiftieth birthday.

Molly began slicing the cake, Grace helping out with the plates. If their parents were here they'd be at the restaurant of their mother's choosing. Unlike the rest of the family, she picked someplace different each year, depending on her mood. One year when Molly was in elementary school they'd had sundaes at the Dairy Bar for supper and capped it off with the traditional chocolate cake when they got home.

Molly had loved that her mom would occasionally throw all the rules out the window. Once a year she'd allowed her kids to play hooky from school. They never knew which day she'd choose, but it always seemed to be when they'd needed it most. Mama would spend the whole day with them doing whatever they wanted.

The last piece of cake served, Molly sank into her seat, looking at her somber-faced siblings. She wasn't sure how this was supposed to go. She only knew the lump at the back of her throat was aching more with each passing moment.

Levi raised his milk glass. "To the best mother any kid could ask for."

"Hear, hear," Molly said.

"We miss you, Mama," Grace squeaked out, blinking hard.

They touched glasses and started in on the cake. Molly's appetite had evaporated, but she forced a smile to her face when Grace and Levi raved over the cake.

They reminisced about birthdays past and about Mama in general. The mood lightened as they recounted happy memories, but there was a heaviness inside Molly that belied the smile on her face. Why had God taken them? Why weren't they here, right now, celebrating with their kids?

Levi was recalling the infamous mouse-in-the-house incident when their mother's screech had brought their dad and them from their hidey-holes. They'd converged in the living room to find her standing atop the end table, her face as white as a swan, screaming, "There's a mouse in the house! There's a mouse in the house!"

Molly laughed at all the right places in the story—Levi was so good at telling it. She kept filling her face with cake, sorry she'd given herself such a large slice.

Grace recounted the time in seventh grade when she complained of a stomachache but Mom, knowing a big English test was on the day's docket, made her go to school anyway. Grace vomited all over her desk in first period science and was promptly sent home where their mother, awash in parental guilt, had waited on her hand and foot the rest of the day.

"You should've asked for a pony," Levi said.

"Darn it, you're right." Grace's smile wobbled at the corners. "Missed my chance."

"You couldn't even keep a fish alive," Molly said, trying to keep the mood light. "Remember Bubbles? How long did she last—two weeks?"

"I was only five. I forgot to feed her."

Levi pushed his empty plate back. "You didn't do much better with that bird of yours, Mol."

"He was already wounded." The robin had hit the front windowpane and lay stunned until Molly decided he needed her help. She put him in a shoe box on the porch, but he went to birdie heaven that afternoon. She'd written a poem about him, and she and her dad gave him a proper burial in the backyard.

A silence settled over the room, the three seemingly lost in their own thoughts. Forks scraped against the white plates. The air conditioner kicked on.

"I know it's been tough," Levi said a few minutes later. "But we're going to be all right. They'd be proud of us for pulling together."

It was true. They'd always enjoyed a close relationship, but this inn had brought them even closer.

Molly forced a smile. "You're right, they would."

A tear trickled down Grace's cheek, and Molly's heart squeezed tight. She pulled her sister into her side, swallowing against the lump in her own throat.

Levi, dry-eyed, wrapped an arm around Grace too.

Molly met his gaze, and they shared a look. This was the way it had been all these months. Levi being strong for both of them, and Molly trying to be strong for Grace. How was Levi coping with this weight? Because Molly wasn't sure she was holding up all that well.

"Thanks, you guys," Grace said as she dried her eyes. "I know I'm a pain sometimes, but I realize you gave up stuff to stay here, and I appreciate it."

"No regrets here," Molly said.

"Me neither," Levi said. "Even though you could do a better job sweeping off the porch sometimes."

"And remembering to take out the garbage," Molly added.

"Sheesh," Grace said. "Forget I mentioned it."

The lump in Molly's throat had grown to epic proportions. Her eyes burned. "Well. I've got some things to do upstairs."

Levi pushed to his feet. "And I've got the front desk."

"I need to update the website," Grace said. "But I'll get the dishes first."

"Thanks," Molly said. "Love you guys."

"You too," they said as they scattered.

Molly made a beeline for the French doors leading to the lobby, trying not to seem rushed. But the dark thing inside was swelling exponentially. She'd made it all day without breaking down, but now it seemed unavoidable—and imminent.

She took the steps quickly, swallowing down the emotion that threatened to surface. Not yet. Not yet.

At the top of the stairs she passed her room, where Grace would no doubt be working on the website soon. She went to the far end of the hall, to her parents' room, and slipped inside.

Tears escaped the moment the door snicked closed behind her. And there were some squeaky noises, maybe coming from her. Her chest was tight, the weight inside like a boulder. Tears flowing, she covered her mouth as she headed toward the antique burgundy chaise in the corner.

How many times had Molly snuggled up with Mama here? Her mother read to her sometimes, long after she could read for herself. Her father was the more avid reader, but it was her mother who always took the time to read her a book whenever the mood struck Molly.

She curled up on the chaise and let it all out, the sobs wracking her body. She'd already shed so many tears, it seemed unconceivable that she still had so much grief stuffed inside. It was a physical ache in her chest.

She pressed her palm against the ache.

God, I miss them so much. I know they're

happy in heaven right now, and I wouldn't call them back even if I could because that would be selfish. But I miss them so much. Her body shook with silent sobs, and the velvet material absorbed her tears.

Where are you, God?

Adam finished an email to his editor, reread it, then hit send. There were other miscellaneous business tasks that needed his attention. Rosewood Press needed a blurb for his current story—the one he hadn't actually started writing yet. They also wanted title suggestions. And he'd just received the galleys for the last book he'd written that would release next year.

But his rumbling stomach reminded him it was well after dinnertime. He'd walk into town and grab something quick, then come back and work a little more. It would take two full days to read the finished pages of *The Last Dance*, checking for errors. But that would be a breeze after struggling with his current work-in-progress.

He checked his hair in the mirror, smoothed it down, then slid his feet into his boat shoes. When he opened his door a delicious scent filled his nose. Something chocolate. Miss Della must be baking muffins for tomorrow. Maybe he'd slip into the kitchen and talk her out of one. Or two.

As he closed the door behind him, a sound caught his attention. His room was at the end of an unoccupied hall—unless they'd checked in a guest tonight. But he hadn't heard any luggage rolling down the hall.

He paused, listening. Nothing. Just the quiet hum of the air conditioning unit in his room. He took a step, and then he heard it again. A sniffle. Coming from the room across from his. He stopped.

There were more hushed sounds then. Someone was crying, a woman. It had to be either Molly or Grace.

He scratched the back of his neck. He should do something, but he didn't know what. He'd never been good with women, much less crying women. He tended to get tongue-tied or, worse, say the wrong thing.

A choked sob propelled him into action. Heart thudding, he lifted his hand and tapped lightly on the door.

The sound of weeping stopped. A moment passed. A sheen of sweat broke out on the back of his neck, but he rapped on the door again.

A voice cleared. "Yes?"

Molly.

"Um . . . it's Adam. Is—is everything all right?"

"Oh. Yeah. It's fine. I'm fine."

She was not fine. She'd been bawling her eyes out. He'd never seen her like that. Molly walked around the place like a beaming ray of sunshine.

Maybe he shouldn't intrude upon a private moment. But his worry for her outweighed his uncertainty. He turned the doorknob and stepped into the room.

She straightened on a lounge chair in the corner of the room. Her eyes were bloodshot, her cheeks damp.

Everything inside him softened with the need to comfort her. To soothe her wounded spirit. As soon as those thoughts surfaced something else rose inside him. Something unfamiliar—a shift from Molly's tears to the cause of her pain.

Adam suddenly understood the emotions of every protective hero he'd ever written. Whoever had made her cry was going to deal with him. His muscles tightened reflexively. He fought the urge to demand to know who'd done this to her.

Comfort first, payback later, he reasoned with himself.

Molly arranged her face into a haggard smile. "Do you need something, Adam?"

Always the hostess. Up close he could better see the roadmap of blood vessels in her eyes. The clumping of her lashes. The wobble of her chin.

His legs propelled him forward. "What's wrong, Molly? Talk to me."

She stood stiffly at his approach and waved him off, emitting a chuckle that gurgled. "Oh, I'm fine. Really. I'm just being—it's nothing. Have you had something to eat? There's cake downstairs, and Miss Della made oatmeal raisin cookies this afternoon; did you see them? She actually left out the raisins because she knows you prefer them without, so I guess they're just oatmeal cookies now. I think she's already wrapped them up for the night, but I can get them for you and heat them up in the—"

He pulled her into his arms. The sadness shadowing her eyes had been his final undoing. He couldn't stand to see his cheerful Molly so wrecked.

Her head rested in the cradle of his neck, her shallow breaths hot on his skin. But her shoulders were stiff and unyielding, her arms hanging down at her sides.

His eyes squeezed in a wince. He'd done the wrong thing. He'd just made things awkward between them. Again. His heart kicked into a new gear as he began wondering how to extricate himself from the awkward embrace.

But before he could move Molly sagged against him. Her arms came around his waist, and her body began jerking with sobs.

He tightened his arms around her, his palm coming to rest at the back of her head. He was holding her so tightly, their bodies shook as one.

She was killing him. "Aw, Molly."

He wanted to ask again what was wrong, but clearly she didn't have breath for talking. He wished he could take this pain from her, whatever it was. Just absorb it into his body one cell at a time.

Or better yet, find out who'd done this to her and bring him to justice.

He pushed for restraint. He could think about that later. Right now all that mattered was Molly.

She was trembling. He lowered them to the lounge chair, keeping her tucked into his chest. He stroked her hair; it was as soft as he'd imagined. He wondered idly if he was taking advantage of the situation.

A few moments later Molly said something, her words garbled, spoken into his chest.

"What was that?" he asked.

She took a shuddering breath and tried again. "Today's her—it's her birthday."

Her birthday? He'd missed the antecedent of the sentence. "Um, whose birthday?"

"My mom's." She sniffled, her stomach shuddering against him. "Today was her fiftieth birthday, and she isn't here to celebrate with us."

"Oh, Molly. I'm so sorry."

"I don't know why this is—it's been almost a year. I thought I was finished with this. I don't know why I can't—I was trying to hold it together for them, for Grace and Levi, and I was doing so well, but then I wasn't. I just couldn't hold it in anymore."

"You don't have to hold it in. You shouldn't hold it in."

She wept a little more. He murmured whatever came to mind. He hoped he wasn't saying the wrong things, making it worse. But she was probably too deep in her grief to comprehend what he was saying anyway.

The room was growing darker as the sun went down. There were no lights on. His eyes drifted over the suite, outfitted with cherry furniture and plush ivory bedding. Fussy draperies covered the large window, and a large en suite bathroom jutted out across the way.

Something occurred to him. "This was their room—your parents'."

She let a mewling sound. "Yes."

He set his chin on her head, letting loose a sigh.

"My mom used to read to me in this chair." Her voice trembled.

"What did she read to you?"

"All kinds of things. The Laura Ingalls Wilder books, Amelia Bedelia, Ramona, Madeline . . . so many books."

"Those are good ones." He drew in the scent of apples. "But I was partial to *Captain Underpants* myself."

She gave a gurgly laugh. "I found that series incredibly immature."

"I assure you, eight-year-old boys *are* incredibly immature."

She snuggled into his chest. "My mom taught me to read before I even started kindergarten. We had alphabet flash cards and all these beginner books. I could write my name in cursive at four.

Of course, there are only five letters in my name, and two of them are the same, so it wasn't that hard. She used to give me stickers. I lived for those stickers. The pony ones were my favorite."

He smiled against her hair, breathing in another lungful of apples.

"When I was four or five I wrote my name on my dresser in permanent marker. I was so proud I could write in cursive like my big brother. I got in trouble for that. But when my dad gave our furniture a fresh coat of paint a few years ago he didn't paint over it."

"They must've loved you very much, Molly." She was, quite possibly, the most lovable human being he'd ever met.

"They were the best." Her sentence crumpled like a pier collapsing into the lake. And just like that she was crying again.

He tightened his arms around her, rubbing the back of her head. He let her sobs fill the silence. As difficult as it was to hear her suffering, he knew tears could be healing. She needed to get it out.

God, comfort Your child in ways that I can't. Give her peace. Give me the words to say.

A few minutes later she took a shuddering breath. "I—I brushed them o—off. The last time I spoke to them I was at college, and I was on my way out the door. They called, and I didn't have class for another f—forty-five minutes, but

I wanted to stop at the coffee shop for a frappe on the way. A stupid frappe! I told them I couldn't talk and I'd call them later. But I didn't, and three days later they were gone and it was too late."

"Oh, Molly."

She wept hard, her body wracked with sobs.

His poor girl. His chest ached at her guilt and regret. He swept his thumb up and down along her temple, feeling the wetness of her tears.

He knew all about guilt. He was feeling it right now, in fact. Here Molly was, baring her soul to him, even while he hid his true identity from her. They'd become close, and she obviously trusted him. He was feeling pretty undeserving of that trust at the moment.

Her sobs began to subside. Her breaths deepened, coming in little hiccups that broke his heart.

This wasn't about him. He needed to focus on Molly. Find something helpful to say. He couldn't bear for her to go on thinking the worst of herself. She was such a positive force. Such an encouragement to everyone around her. Couldn't she see that?

He held her away from him and waited until she met his eyes. She needed to hear this.

Tears clung to her lashes. One of them made a crooked track down her flushed cheek. Those eyes—unbearably sad—tightened a vise around his heart.

"Your parents knew you loved them, Molly. You couldn't have known that would be your last chance to speak with them."

"I know but—"

He gave her chin a little pinch. "No. I didn't know your parents, but I know they loved you, and I know they wouldn't want you feeling all this guilt. I also know they must've been pretty darn proud of you, Molly Bennett. And take it from me, that's a wonderful gift to give a child."

She gave him a long steady look. "Your dad?"

"Yes, my dad." It was hard to admit it. Even to Molly. But he felt sure she'd somehow understand.

"You're a wonderful man, Adam. If your father couldn't see that, it was on him."

"Thanks." But he didn't want to make this about him. Not when Molly was so obviously devastated over their last phone call. "Your parents raised an amazing young woman. I'm sure they knew that, Molly. I'm sure they bragged about you to anyone who'd listen."

Her eyes filled again. "But I brushed them off."

"Do you think that, as wonderful as your parents might've been, that in the busyness of life with three kids, they never once put you off? They never made you wait while they finished their last bite of supper? Or held you off until they watched the last five minutes of their favorite TV show? Or put you to bed ten minutes early because you couldn't tell time yet and they were exhausted?"

She gave a strangled laugh. "Okay . . . You make a good point."

"That didn't mean they loved you any less, did it?"

Her breath stuttered on an inhale. "No."

"Well . . . there you go then."

She was silent for a long moment. Catching her breath. Thinking, he hoped, about what he'd said. Could it be he'd actually said the right thing at the right time? If so, he owed God a debt of gratitude.

She shifted in his arms, turning so her cheek was against his heart. He hoped she couldn't tell how hard it was beating.

"I think about it all the time. Like when I fuss with Levi or Grace or just say good-bye. I think *What if they die, and this is the last time I see them?* Then I try and resolve things so I can live with myself just in case the worst happens.

"And I think maybe that's why this letter thing is so important to me. I want Lizzie and Benjamin to have the closure I didn't get. Well, Benjamin at least. It's too late for Lizzie. Stupid, huh?"

"Not stupid at all."

"I didn't even realize what I was doing until my friend Skye pointed it out to me. She's always psychoanalyzing everything. It's annoying— especially when she's right."

"Sounds like a good friend."

"She is." She sniffled. "I want to keep looking for him though—Benjamin."

"Nothing wrong with trying to find a little closure—for Benjamin or for yourself."

He noticed a tissue box on the stand beside the chair. Duh. Why hadn't he thought of that five minutes ago? He pulled a tissue and handed it to her.

"Thanks." She wiped her eyes, but seemed in no hurry to leave his embrace.

And he never wanted her to leave. The thought packed a wallop, and his heart felt as though it were collapsing in on itself. It was true, and he knew what that signified. He was falling for this girl. This beautiful, intelligent, giving woman.

When Molly finished cleaning up, she wrapped her arms around his middle and gave him a tight squeeze.

"Thank you, Adam," she said on a breathy sigh.

Be still my heart.

"Anytime, *mia tesoro.*"

thirty-two

M*ia tesoro.* Molly stilled at the Italian endearment, a catch in her achy throat.

Adam's heart thumped against her ear, the only sound in the room. Until her phone buzzed in her pocket with an incoming text. She ignored it, still thinking of that Italian phrase.

Directly translated, the words meant *my treasure.* The same word was also used to mean honey or sweetheart or darling.

But if Adam had a good grasp of the language—and he obviously did—then he knew that *tesoro* was not a platonic word. It was strictly a romantic endearment.

Had his heart just accelerated, or was that her own heartbeat pulsing in her ears? Did Adam think of her romantically?

She had to see his face. Look into his eyes. She slowly drew back, giving only a momentary thought to what she must look like: blotchy skin, swollen eyelids, bloodshot eyes.

Her gaze swept up the column of his neck to his flushed cheeks. Her eyes met his and held. She had a clear view of his lidded gaze behind his glasses. Of his blue eyes, so soft and warm and focused steadily on her. Looking at her with fondness and affection, like maybe she was the prettiest woman he'd ever seen.

He made no effort to translate the Italian phrase, and she had no need to ask. If the endearment hadn't told her how he felt about her, the look in his eyes right now did.

Her phone buzzed repeatedly, an incoming call. His palm had shifted from the back of her head to her cheek, and his thumb brushed across the damp hair at her temple.

"Maybe you should answer that," he said softly.

She shook her head. Her hand clenched at the shirt at his waist. She could feel the warm puff of his breath on her lips, and she wanted his mouth on hers as badly as she wanted her next breath.

She leaned toward him, just a hair.

"Wait, Molly." He held her in place. "Wait. There's something I need to tell you. Something I haven't been—"

"Molly . . ." a voice called. Levi.

She held her breath as if her lapse of respiration might make time stand still, might hold her brother at bay.

"What?" she asked Adam. She wanted to get beyond whatever he had to say and right back to the kiss they'd been about to share.

"Molly!" Levi called again.

Adam's eyes closed briefly. His thumb stroked her temple again before his hand slowly fell away. He gave her a patient smile, poking his glasses up. "It can wait. Want me to go see what he wants?"

She let out the breath she'd been holding. The moment was gone. A weight she recognized as supreme disappointment dragged down her spirits.

She mopped up the rest of her tears with the soggy tissue. "No, that's all right. I got it."

"Molly!"

"Argh." Molly stood up and straightened her clothing, not quite meeting his eyes. "Thank you, Adam. Really. I feel much better."

That smile. "Anytime, Molly."

They walked toward the door, and he followed her out of the room.

Levi met them at the top of the stairs.

Conscious of her ravaged face, she was glad for the dim lighting. She narrowed her eyes and perched her hands on her hips. *"What?"*

Levi glanced at Adam, then the direction they'd come from. "Where were you?"

"I was—never mind that. What do you want?"

"We have an unexpected guest."

Okay. And he'd been hollering up the stairs like a hooligan?

Someone nudged past Levi. Someone tall and broad, someone armed with a suitcase and a winning smile.

"Surprise," Jordan said.

thirty-three

Adam tensed as he watched his best friend embrace Molly. Jordan's hand slipped around her waist, coming to rest at the small of her back.

He was momentarily glad Jordan's suitcase occupied his other hand.

"What a surprise," Molly said in her usual sunshiny voice. No trace of the sadness that had overwhelmed her only moments ago. "What are you doing here? You didn't say anything about coming."

Yes, a little warning would've been nice. Adam resumed breathing as Jordan and Molly eased apart, and he managed a stiff smile as his friend extended a hand to him.

"Hey, buddy." Jordan pulled him in for a shoulder bump.

"How you doing?"

"Not too bad." Jordan's gaze returned to Molly. "I was a last-minute substitute at a writers conference in Charlotte. I gave myself an extra day when I booked my flight back. I needed to talk to this guy and figured I may as well do it in person."

Adam was sure that a certain innkeeper had no bearing on Jordan's decision to travel eighty miles out of his way.

"Well, darn it," Molly said. "I wish you could've come last night. Today was my day off."

If she was faking her disappointment, she deserved an Oscar.

"I know, but I was hoping I might take you to breakfast in the morning? I don't have to be on the road until one."

"Sure. I don't have to work until noon, so that works just fine."

"Great." He looked at Adam. "You doing anything tonight, buddy? Want to grab a pizza or something? I'm starving."

"Sure."

"I'll let you guys catch up," Molly said, backing away. "I'm heading to bed. It's been a long day."

An understatement. Adam wanted to say something to recognize the truth of that assertion. Do something to show her he understood. But he had no idea what that might be. So he simply exchanged good nights and followed Jordan to the room next to his.

"I think I surprised her," Jordan said a moment later as he dropped his suitcase on the colorful quilt.

"It would appear so."

"I thought about forewarning her, but I figured it would be more fun this way. She seemed happy to see me."

Indeed she did. Adam nodded, but Jordan was rooting through his suitcase.

Adam took a seat on the corner chair, his stomach filling with acid. Had he imagined that whole moment between the two of them in her parents' room? He'd felt so close to her. There'd been an intimacy between them—the kind that came from sharing innermost thoughts and vulnerabilities. He hadn't just imagined the progression in their relationship. Surely he wasn't that inept at reading women.

"You all right?" Jordan glanced at him as he pulled out some clean clothes and closed his suitcase.

"Sure." Adam scratched the back of his neck. "Uh, how was the conference? Find any promising new talent?"

"Listened to pitches until my ears were numb. But I did request a couple manuscripts—a general contemporary, nice voice; and a thriller, high concept, but the writing's a little raw. We'll see. Some of the Rosewood team were there—Kimberly, Amanda, Paul. I touched base with them."

"Great." It was always good to stay in contact with the publishing team. Adam knew there was more to the conversation, but he was reluctant to ask.

Jordan sank onto the end of the bed, giving Adam a long, steady look as he exhaled.

"What? The outline's coming along. It's great." Not entirely true. But he had developed the idea into a solid story. There was a sympathetic protagonist with a compelling problem and a stoic hero. The plot had a hook, high stakes, and a by-the-book story arc. All the right ingredients.

He simply had no passion for the tale—and therein lay the problem. But he was running out of time. He needed to start writing the actual story.

He looked away from Jordan's piercing look. "I'll email you the outline, and you can forward it to Elaine. That should allay their fears."

"We didn't even talk about your WIP. They're more focused on that *Newsline Tonight* interview. The show agreed to promote it heavily."

Adam's pulse quickened. A sweat broke out on the back of his neck. "I already said no to the interview."

"I know how you feel about all this, buddy, and I know they've always bent to your will, but they're digging in more than usual. Readers want a relationship with their favorite authors these days, and publishers rely on authors to promote their own work. And with social media so prominent, that's never been more true."

He'd heard it all before. Still, like a nefarious weed, anxiety pushed to the surface. "I value my privacy, Jordan. You know this."

"At what cost? At ticking off the house that's made you a bestseller?"

Adam narrowed his eyes at Jordan. His friend knew about his insecurities stemming back to his father. Jordan had told him from the beginning he'd have his back. That didn't seem to be the case anymore. Five minutes alone with the team and he'd already switched sides.

"They're making plenty of money off me. If they don't want to adhere to my directive, I'm sure I can find a publisher who will."

"I don't think it would be as bad you imagine. Most people have no idea what authors look like. It's not as though your face is constantly on the screen like most celebrities. Only your biggest fans will know what you look like. You'll still be able to go out in public. Wear a ball cap. Have a spare pair of glasses that look nothing like those. It doesn't have to be that big a deal."

"I thought you had my back."

Jordan planted his elbows on his knees. "I'm always on your side, Adam. You're my friend first. Always. I would never try and talk you into something I didn't believe was in your best interest. I just think it's time you worked through this unfounded fear that you'll disappoint your readers."

"This isn't what I want."

"Just think about it. Pray about it. I'm not asking for an answer tonight. I'm just asking you to be open to the idea. All right? Can you do that?"

He could barely even breathe past the tightness in his chest. "Fine. I'll think about it."

Jordan stood and clapped his shoulder. "Good man. All I'm asking. We can discuss it more over dinner. I'm going to change real quick and I'll be ready to go."

Jordan disappeared into the bathroom, and Adam's mind spun. He couldn't really do it, could he? Just the thought of it nearly brought on an anxiety attack. But maybe he had been making too much of it. Was it possible it wouldn't be the big deal he'd feared? That he wouldn't be the disappointment he was afraid he'd be?

Rosewood Press apparently didn't think so, or they'd never push so hard for it. Was it possible this stigma was all in his head? He glanced in the mirror, seeing only the nerdy guy his father saw. The disappointing son.

He shook the thought away, his mind going another direction. In the morning Jordan would be taking Molly out again. The thought left him feeling sucker-punched.

He'd decided one thing. Regardless of her feelings for Jordan—or for him—he needed to tell her the truth about who he was. He felt like a lowlife for keeping it from her, especially with the way she'd opened up to him tonight. Maybe she'd be disappointed that he was Nathaniel Quinn. But he was starting to feel as though she might be even more disappointed that he'd deceived her.

A few minutes later Jordan emerged from the bathroom, dressed casually, on a cloud of Creed Aventus, his signature scent. He stopped at the hall mirror and finger-combed his thick dark hair.

Adam had to tell Molly who he was, and soon. Before she found out some other way.

"Don't tell her who I am," Adam blurted.

"What?"

"Molly. Don't tell her who I am."

Jordan spared him a glance. "Have I ever let it slip to anyone, ever?"

"I know but—I'm going to tell her myself. Soon. And I don't want her finding out in the meantime, that's all."

Jordan's hand fell to his side as he looked at Adam. "You're going to tell her the truth."

Just the thought of it had Adam's heart racing and his palms damp. "Yes."

Jordan studied him for a long moment. "Hmm."

Adam stood, making sure he had his wallet and phone. "You ready? We can take my car."

"Uh, sure. Whatever."

Molly was nowhere to be seen as they exited the house, and even the front desk was vacant. He'd tell her tomorrow as soon as Jordan left. Maybe it wouldn't be as awful as he thought.

thirty-four

Molly leaned back in the red vinyl booth as the server refilled her coffee mug. The Country Skillet was full this morning, the servers bustling around with trays and carafes of coffee. The sounds of chatter and clanking silverware and the savory scent of bacon and sweet maple syrup combined for sensory overload.

Molly and Jordan picked up right where they'd left off after his last visit. He shared amusing stories from the writers conference and caught her up on his family's activities. Molly updated him on her life, skipping over the part about her mom's birthday yesterday.

He was easy to talk to, easy on the eyes, and it would be oh, so easy to slide right into a relationship with him. But if she were completely honest with herself, there was no chemistry between them. And no amount of reminding herself he was Nathaniel Quinn changed that fact.

She was beginning to realize she'd liked the idea of Nathaniel Quinn much more than she liked the reality. It had been immature of her to assume she would swoon over the author simply because she swooned over his words.

And she was all right with that discovery. She

would go on loving his stories—but she would never love the man. Not like that.

Jordan pushed back his plate. "You're quiet over there. Too much to eat?"

Molly put her hand on her stomach. "Way too much. How could you let me order that? Friends don't let friends order Big Mama's Breakfast."

"I helped you out with the bacon, didn't I?"

Molly frowned at her empty plate. "I ate three pancakes, two eggs, four sausage patties, and a biscuit."

Jordan's eyes twinkled. "Don't forget the gravy."

Molly laughed. "You're no help. I'll need five hours of yoga to work this off."

Jordan checked the time. "Well, I ate just as much. And I'd love to suggest we walk it off, but your shift is starting soon."

"And you don't want to miss your flight." He'd already checked out of his room and put his luggage in the car.

After Jordan settled up with the server the two made their way to his rental. Molly's nerves clattered. She needed to tell Jordan how she was feeling before he left. Maybe he felt the same way. As though they could be terrific friends but nothing more.

As he was pulling from the street slot his phone buzzed with a call. He checked the screen and winced.

"I'm so sorry, but my mom's been trying to reach me all morning. Do you mind if I take it?"

She felt a guilty moment of reprieve. "Of course not. Go right ahead."

"I'm going to put her on speaker. My phone's not synced to the car."

"No problem."

He answered. "Hi, Mom. Sorry I missed your call. You're still having computer issues?"

"This stupid thing." The sound of keys being punched came over the line. Her voice was mild and warm despite her obvious frustration. "I'm writing a paper for that class and it's frozen."

"What do you mean by frozen?"

"I put the curser where it goes, and no matter what keys I punch nothing happens."

"Did you try to close down the program?"

"No, I was afraid I'd lose my work."

Molly stared out the window at the lake, shimmering under the late morning sun. It was a short drive back to the inn, and she had a feeling the call was going to take a while.

While Jordan directed his mother Molly worked out in her head what she'd say. There would be no way to avoid awkwardness, especially if he didn't feel the same way.

Before she knew it Jordan was pulling into the slot in front of the inn. He was now trying to help his mom restart the computer.

He put the car in park and left the engine

running. "I'll be there in a minute," he whispered to her. "Sorry."

"It's all right." She opened the car door.

"Who's that?" his mother asked. "Are you with someone? I thought I heard a woman's voice."

"Yes, Mother." He rolled his eyes at Molly. "Is your computer off yet?"

Molly closed the car door behind her and checked her watch as she made her way up the walk. She had twenty minutes before she had to cover the front desk, and he'd have to leave shortly after that. When Jordan was finished with the call she'd invite him to sit on the front porch where they could talk in private.

She winced, dreading the conversation. It wasn't as though they were serious. They'd just been talking. Still, she'd only ever "broken up" with Dominic, and righteous indignation had made that task supremely easy.

Jordan was a nice guy. But he also seemed to have a healthy self-esteem. How could he not, bestselling author like him? She didn't expect him to be crushed or anything.

It was hot enough that she bypassed the porch swing in favor of air conditioning. When she entered the building Levi was at the front desk on a phone call. He nodded in greeting.

She probably shouldn't go up to her room just yet. A spin around the dining room showed it to be cleaned up and empty. The kitchen was vacant,

Miss Della already gone for the day. She bagged a few leftover muffins—blueberry strudel—for Jordan to take with him and set the bag on the flower stand. A peace offering. Levi was still on the phone.

Hearing the sound of typing coming from down the hall, she wandered back to the library. A smile lifted her lips as she thought about Adam. About the way he'd held her last night and the way he'd made her feel. As though she were coming home.

She'd lost her sense of home since her parents had passed, she realized. She had the inn, of course. But that was only temporary. Adam had felt like her forever home—and that was a scary concept. No wonder the kiss had made her anxious. But she could work through that, couldn't she? Clearly her heart was ready to move forward.

She wondered if Adam felt the same about her. He had his work, but he traveled a lot and it didn't sound as if his family had felt much like home, at least where his dad was concerned. Could she be home for him too?

Mia tesoro. Her smile widened at the memory of the endearment and the smoky tone of his voice when he'd said it.

She walked around the corner and spotted him at the desk. He'd paused in writing and was staring out at the lake, chin propped on his hand.

His hair was a little ruffled as though he might've just run his fingers through it.

"Hi there," she said.

He whipped around. Something dark lingered in his expression though his lips lifted in a wan smile. "Oh, hello. You're back. Where's Jordan?" He faced his laptop again, pushing the lid shut.

"He's still in the car. He's on a call. You all right?"

"Sure. Of course. I'm just trying to get some work done."

Was she bothering him? He seemed a little guarded, but could she blame him? He was probably confused. They'd shared a moment last night, and now she'd just returned from a date with his best friend. She wanted to tell him she wasn't interested in Jordan, but it didn't seem right to tell him first.

She sat on the little bench next to the desk and looked at him.

He was stuffing everything into folders and back into his laptop case. She longed for the Adam from last night instead of this distracted, distant version sitting next to her.

"Adam . . . I . . . Thank you again for last night. I was so upset, and talking to you really helped."

He spared her a glance. "No problem. Happy to be of help."

"You were more than that. You were—" She

swallowed against the emotion rising in her throat. "You were perfect."

He finally met her eyes. Really looked at her. There was something lurking in those blue depths. Something sad and vulnerable. "I'm glad, Molly. You're too hard on yourself. I hope you can give yourself a little grace. I think your parents would want that for you."

"Yeah . . . I'm going to work on that."

He scratched the back of his neck. "Did you have a good breakfast?"

She smiled, thinking about her conversations with Jordan. "Um, yeah. I ate way too much though. I'm skipping lunch and maybe dinner too." Her chuckle sounded forced.

She could see his eyes now. They were piercing in their intensity. Serious.

"*Perché non vedi la verità?*" His voice was low and throaty.

Why can't you see the truth?

He leaned forward, his elbows on his knees. "*Lo sono l'autore, non lui.*"

I am the author, not him.

Her breath tumbled out. Her lungs forgot how to refill. *I am the author.* Her eyes held his as she tried to work that out in her head to be something other than what it seemed to mean. But there was no other way he could've meant it.

Adam was the author. Adam was Nathaniel Quinn.

"What?" Her single word packed a lot of emotion.

Adam blinked once. Sat back in the chair. The intensity in his expression shifted to confusion. "What?"

Her mind spun. The memory of that day she'd been on the balcony and overheard Jordan and Adam talking. The memory of her subsequent conversation with Adam. She'd only assumed Jordan was Nathaniel Quinn. And Adam had let her believe. For how many weeks—five? Six?

"You know Italian," he said flatly.

She gave him a flinty look, her breath resuming, quick and shallow. "You've been lying to me."

She couldn't believe this. He was no better than Dominic. Something dark and heavy rose up from deep inside her. Heat suffused her face, making her ears go hot.

He held up his hands, palms out. "I was going to tell you."

The scornful laugh sounded foreign. "Sure you were."

"I was, Molly. I swear. Today, right after Jordan left. I was about to tell you last night."

"Why, Adam? Why did you lie to me? We sat right down there on the pier and talked about what I'd overheard." She flung her hand toward the lake. "Why didn't you tell me the truth right then? Why can't anyone just tell the freaking truth?"

She sprang from the bench and out the door, her heart feeling as if it might explode from her chest. She barely registered Levi at the front desk as she zipped past and out the front door. She was about to bound down the porch steps when Adam gripped her elbow from behind.

"Wait, Molly. Please."

She jerked her arm away as her eyes fell on Jordan, still sitting in the car.

"I'm sorry," Adam said. "I'm really sorry."

She whipped around, her eyes locking on his. She saw something desperate and pleading in their depths. His neck was splotchy pink, and his shoulders heaved with shallow breaths.

Just like that all the anger seemed to drain out of her, leaving her hollow inside. Empty and achy. Hurting.

She wanted the anger back.

"I don't understand." Her voice was wobbly, and she seemed to be crying, darn it. "I feel like such a fool."

"You're not a fool. This is my fault, not yours."

She gave her head a shake, trying to understand. "Is this some kind of game? Are you and Jordan just . . . toying me with me or something?"

"*No.* No, Molly, that isn't it at all. I would never do that to you. Please believe me."

"How can I believe anything you say now? You've been lying to me for weeks, both of you."

He dug his hand into the hair at the nape of his

neck. A shadow flickered in his jaw. "No, it's all my fault. I didn't want anyone to know the truth."

"Even me? As close as we've become? Don't you trust me? I trusted you. I trusted you last night when I spilled my guts about something very private."

He winced. "I know you did and I—"

Footsteps fell on the steps behind her. "Everything all right?" Jordan's voice was tentative.

"Can you give us a minute, please?" Adam said.

Something rose, hot and quick, inside her. Molly whirled around.

Jordan's eyes widened. His lips parted.

"No," Molly said. "No, I think he should stay for this since he was obviously in on the little joke."

Jordan's cautious gaze toggled between them. "What's going on?"

"She knows who I am."

"Oh . . . right."

Molly thought back to everything Jordan had said on their dates. Was any of it real? The conference stories . . . his occupation . . .

"For crying out loud," she mumbled. "You really are an agent."

"Um . . . yeah."

And here she'd thought he was just spinning things to cover his real job. She'd been more or

309

less all right with that since they didn't yet know each other well.

"Jordan didn't know you thought he was Nathaniel Quinn," Adam said.

"She what?" Jordan asked.

"She overheard us talking out back last time you were here. She assumed you were the author."

Molly gave Adam a flinty look. "And you let me believe it."

"Oh," Jordan said. "I see."

Molly's mind spun quickly, trying to separate truth from fiction. Just as she'd done when she'd caught Dominic in his web of lies.

How had she let this happen to her, not once but twice? What was wrong with her? She cupped her forehead. "I'm such an idiot."

"No, Molly." Adam reached out.

She sidled away. "You know what? I'm just—I have to work now. You two . . . I don't know, go do whatever you need to do."

"Molly—"

She nailed Adam with a look. "Stay away from me." She held the look until he wilted a little. Then she walked around him and through the door.

thirty-five

Adam paced the length of the porch. He couldn't believe this was happening. Why hadn't he just told her the truth when she'd confronted him about the conversation she'd overheard?

"So she thought I was you," Jordan said. "She thought I was Nathaniel Quinn."

Adam stopped at the swing and laced his hands behind his neck. "I'm sorry. I know that wasn't fair to you."

"No, it wasn't." Jordan had come up on the porch. "That's probably the only reason she went out with me. Talk about a blow to the ego."

"I'm sure that's not true."

"Don't worry; my self-esteem can handle it. So you told her the truth, and she obviously didn't take it well."

"I didn't tell her. She—she found out before I got around to it."

He'd literally been minutes from revealing his identity. Although technically he *had* ended up telling her the truth. In Italian.

He shook his head. All those things he'd said to her . . . His face went hot. He was such an imbecile, thinking he was so clever, telling her what was in his heart. She'd known what he'd been saying all along. Had his words meant anything to her? Or had she only been patronizing him all this time?

"That's unfortunate," Jordan said. "Are you all right?"

"Not really." He'd made her cry. Just last night he'd been ready to throat-punch the guy who'd made her cry, and today he'd put the tears in those eyes. He deserved a beating.

"Want me to talk to her?"

He faced Jordan, hands on hips. "And say what? This isn't a contract clause you can negotiate or a bad title we can replace. I lied to her. She has every right to be angry with me."

"Technically . . . You just let her believe what she wanted to believe."

He flinched. "Technicalities only matter in contracts. This isn't business, this is a relationship." One that had been on the precipice of something more than friendship—at least he'd thought it had been. Maybe it was time to be honest with his friend about that too. Why not? Everything else was on the table now.

"Jordan . . ." He drew a deep breath and forced his eyes to meet his friend's. "I have feelings for Molly." There. He'd said it.

Jordan smirked. "You don't say."

"I know I should've—Wait, you knew?"

"Not till last night, if I'm honest. Then today,

Molly seemed pretty distracted. I got the feeling she was going to friend-zone me, but then my mom called, and Molly went inside and . . . What happened in there anyway?"

"I don't want to talk about it."

"Do you think she'll keep quiet? I should probably talk to her about signing a nondisclosure agreement."

Funny, Adam hadn't even considered that. "I thought you wanted my identity revealed."

"Not like this."

"That's the least of my worries right now."

Jordan's brows rose. "Really. Because it kind of seemed like the most important thing in the world to you yesterday."

"Yeah . . ." Adam said, still reeling from everything that had just happened. "That was yesterday."

Molly blotted her face with a tissue. After leaving Adam and Jordan on the porch she'd gone up to her room. Levi had been on the phone, making it easy to slip past.

She powdered her face to help cover her blotchy skin and used eye drops to get rid of the redness. But it wouldn't work if she kept tearing up like this. Darn it.

The vacuum cleaner came on down the hall. She was glad Grace was busy cleaning Jordan's room. Glad Jordan had already checked out.

Maybe he'd be gone by the time she went downstairs to take her shift. *Please, God.*

But Adam would still be here. She'd have to face him every day. How would she do it? She was so stupid! She'd trusted him. How had she not seen the truth? How had he so blithely let her believe Jordan was Nathaniel Quinn? What was his deal anyway?

She was swearing off men until she figured out why she let herself be so easily duped. Was she just a magnet for con artists?

She balked at the slur. No matter how angry she was with Adam right now, he wasn't a con artist. Dominic, yes, con artist. But there was something else going on with Adam.

However, it wasn't her problem. *He* wasn't her problem. Her eyes stung again, but she blinked away the tears.

A quick glance at the clock showed it was a couple minutes after noon, so she headed downstairs to take her shift. She'd keep busy and refuse to think about Adam.

When she came downstairs Levi was looking inside the bag she'd left on the flower stand. "What's this?"

She glanced out the window, relieved that Jordan's car was gone. Adam's too. "I guess Jordan forgot them."

She slipped behind the desk. "How are we looking for the weekend?"

"Great. We're full up."

"Great."

He studied her a long moment, his keys jingling in his hand. "Everything all right?"

"Just peachy."

He looked toward the porch, then back to her. "You seemed upset earlier. You guys have a fight? Do I need to beat somebody up?"

"Just me," she mumbled. After all, she was the idiot who kept believing people's lies.

"What?"

"Never mind. Everything's fine. I'm good. I've got things covered here if you need to go somewhere."

She busied herself by checking the reservations, waiting for Levi to head out. He'd warned her about getting too close to guests, and he was probably fixing to remind her. He'd been right, after all. She hated to admit it to herself, and she sure wasn't going to admit it to him.

She focused on the screen and made note of the special requests for tonight—extra pillows and a crib. She sent a text to Grace, asking her to fulfill those requests while she was upstairs.

"You're sure you're all right?" Levi was still teetering on the threshold. Maybe he wasn't going to throw her mistake in her face.

The warmth she felt for him just then produced a convincing smile. "I'm fine, Levi. Really." Or she would be. Eventually.

thirty-six

Molly checked out the last of the weekend guests and sent them off with a bag of muffins and two coffees to go. Normally, after a busy weekend, Monday mornings were a bit of a relief, but she had mixed feelings about an empty house today.

One, she'd have more time on her hands, giving her too much opportunity to think about Adam. Two, all of her convenient buffers were gone, and chances of awkward encounters with him had just risen exponentially. They currently had no guests scheduled until Wednesday.

Outside, the lawn mower's engine growled to life, and a moment later Molly saw a flash of red through the picture window as Levi rode by.

Adam had been away much of the weekend. He left before she was working and came home after she was off—obviously avoiding her. She'd only seen him twice since their blowup Friday, and both times there'd been guests nearby. She'd kept everything professional. Levi would've been so proud.

She'd had a few days to calm down, though, and now a terrible unsettling feeling had begun rising up inside. The one that said she needed to make peace with Adam. Because people didn't last forever, and if anything happened to him she'd never forgive herself for leaving things so badly.

It annoyed her that she assumed the responsibility for clearing the air. She hadn't done this. She hadn't been the one to lie. The one to break trust. And yet, there it was, this nagging need to rectify things.

Yesterday when she'd awakened to find his car gone again, she'd had the horrible feeling he wouldn't return. What if he had a car accident? What if he had an undiagnosed aneurism? What if an oversize tome fell off a library shelf and conked him on the head?

It was irrational, she knew. But was it really? Hadn't her parents' accident been just as random and yet so very real?

Her chest tightened, and she pressed her palm against it. She had to clear the air with him. She knew it was the only way to relieve this awful anxiety. And she wanted answers, doggonit. Why hadn't he trusted her? She'd thought they were friends.

Friends, Molly? Really?

Her thoughts went back to Thursday night when he'd held her in her parents' room. She'd never felt so comforted in her life. Had never felt more cherished. The way he'd looked at her, those eyes warm and full of affection. She wanted to go back in time and be in his arms again where she'd felt so complete.

But even then he'd been lying to her. There was no excuse for what he'd done. She didn't understand it, and she sure didn't trust him anymore. But she'd gone off on him Friday, and she couldn't just leave things that way. She was going to have to hunt him down today. She couldn't stand this much longer.

Jordan had texted her when he'd gotten home Friday. They'd cleared the air between them, but he hadn't given her any answers either. *Please talk to Adam* was all he'd said.

Maybe she'd been dating Jordan, but she'd been falling for Adam. She hadn't realized how far she'd fallen until Friday when her heart had hit the ground with a resounding thud.

She heard the rolling thump of a suitcase overhead and frowned at the ceiling. The last of their guests had already checked out. She looked at the screen just to be certain she wasn't losing her mind. No, everyone was gone. The distant hum of the vacuum cleaner kicked on upstairs as Grace cleaned the recently vacated rooms.

Footsteps sounded on the stairs, and a moment later Adam rounded the corner. He hadn't shaved this morning, giving him a haggard look. Or maybe it was the dark circles, visible even through his glasses.

His lips curved in a sad smile. "Good morning, Molly."

Her eyes fell to his suitcase, and her heart

seized. He was leaving. Of course he was leaving. It was that or live under the same roof with the freak who fancied herself in love with an author—with him. He was probably afraid she'd turn into a psycho stalker and start rooting through his trash can for souvenirs.

Swallowing back a knot of humiliation, she forced a professional smile to her lips. "Good morning, Adam. Are you . . . checking out?"

"I am. I—thought it might be best, considering . . ." His words fell off. His weight shifted. He poked his glasses into place.

Molly's heart was beating a million miles per hour, thoughts of those potentially fatal incidents stealing him away forever.

"Oh?" She cleared her throat and began the process of checking him out. "Are you heading back to New York then?"

"No—I still—I'm sticking around town for a few more weeks. I found a house on the lake that's available. But go ahead and charge me through the end of the month."

"No, that's okay. It's fine."

"I reserved the room, Molly. I don't mind paying for it."

"Cancellations are part of the business. No worries." She gave him a placid smile as she clicked a few buttons. The printer whirred to life. When it stopped she grabbed the receipt and handed it to him.

"There you go."

She started to ask which house he'd rented but didn't want him to think she'd become that stalker. And all she could think was that he was about to walk out the door, and she might never see him again. Bluebell was small, but it wasn't that small. And she had a feeling he'd be avoiding her. Plus there was that accident thing.

Her chest tightened, and she fought the urge to press her palm there. She couldn't let things end like this.

"Do you have a minute?"

"I owe you an explanation."

They spoke at the same time. Then stopped, each waiting for the other to continue.

Molly swallowed against the swelling in her throat. "Go ahead."

A beat later he stepped closer, his eyes more intent than she'd ever seen them. "I just wanted to apologize again. I am so sorry for hurting you, Molly. I feel just awful that I've let you down. I assure you, that was never my intention."

She gave a little nod. "I know that."

"I wanted to try and explain. I've never told anyone this, not really. Not even Jordan, fully. It's hard for me to talk about."

"Okay . . ."

"I don't want you to think I'm making excuses, but I want to explain why I write under a pseudonym—why I keep my identity a secret. I didn't really understand it myself at first. I said I just valued my privacy, and I do. But over the years I've come to understand it's much deeper than that.

"I told you a little about my family. I wasn't like the rest of them. They're athletically gifted and I'm not. That probably sounds petty, but I always felt . . . like a misfit. Like a big disappointment. Especially to my father."

But Adam was so smart. So kind. So gifted. She shook her head.

His cheeks were flushed, and he shifted on his feet. "Remember, I come from Texas, Molly. Football was my dad's life. My value was largely based on what I could do on the field—and in that arena I amounted to a big zero. One of my cousins was particularly close to him. My dad treated Brody as more of a son than he did me. I guess he didn't know what to do with me. He was such a man's man, and I was so cerebral. It left me feeling pretty insecure about myself."

Her heart twisted of its own accord. "But you're a wonderful person, Adam. And you've been so successful."

"I know it might seem that way, but . . . those insecurities go deep. It's humiliating to even confess all this to you. But you deserve to know why I did what I did."

"I still don't understand. I wouldn't have judged

you the way your dad did. We were friends—or I thought we were."

"We are." His eyes flickered down to the desk. "We were. But when you overheard Jordan and me talking shop . . . all those insecurities rose to the surface. I know how you feel—felt—about Nathaniel Quinn. I knew you had high regards for him and such high expectations—"

"Yes, I did. So why wouldn't you want to claim that, Adam? Especially with me? You know how much I value books and great writing. Didn't you trust me to keep your identity to myself? I would never out you like that."

"I know. I know you wouldn't! That's not—" He scratched the back of his neck.

"Jordan mentioned something about a nondisclosure agreement. I told him I'd sign it and I will."

He frowned. "I asked him not to do that. I'm sorry."

"It's fine."

"No, it's not. You don't need to sign it. I trust you."

Well, at least there was that. But if he trusted her so much, why had he been so reluctant to tell her the truth?

"Listen, Molly, I'm fully aware that readers form . . . attachments to authors."

Oh, boy. Her face heated at the memory of what Grace had said about her little crush on the author—on him. She closed her eyes briefly, wishing she could crawl behind the counter.

"I'm not the man women are picturing when they envision Nathaniel Quinn, Molly." He gave her a direct look. "I'm not the man *you* were picturing."

He was so much more than the man she'd imagined. She blinked at him. It was unbelievable that his insecurities had led him so far astray. "That's not true, Adam."

"You're just trying to be kind, and I appreciate it. But I know what kind of man you imagined me to be."

She had no idea he was so stubborn. "Seriously? You can read my mind now?"

"Admit it, Molly. You assumed I'd be like my heroes. Tall, rugged, handsome, masculine. Few men can live up to that—certainly not me."

"I wasn't infatuated with your heroes, Adam, I was infatuated with your *words*. With the way you strung them together in a way that made me feel understood. How shallow do you think I am?"

A stricken look came over his face. "I don't think that at all."

"Yes, you do. Did it ever occur to you that I might care more about what's on the inside? Not to mention, there's absolutely nothing wrong with the outside either."

She skimmed him, head to toe, taking in his

aristocratic features, his strong shoulders, his lean frame. Maybe he wasn't the stuff of fantasy, but he wasn't exactly hard on the eyes. And his brain . . . The creativity housed in that head of his was a thing of beauty. How could he not know that?

Adam's face heated under Molly's slow perusal. He felt like a scrawny gelding on the auction block next to a noble stallion.

"I don't understand how you can think so little of yourself." She was shaking her head. "You're so smart. So creative. You're a *New York Times* bestselling author, for crying out loud."

"Look, I know I have a valuable gift. But I'm not what readers expect. I don't want to be a disappointment. I've already been that and it's the worst. Writing is just what I do. It's not who I am." He gestured to himself. "This is who I am, Molly."

Her eyes snapped. "I *liked* who you are."

She gutted him with her use of past tense. He swallowed back the disappointment swelling in his throat. That's why he was leaving. She was finished with him, and having him around would only make things harder on her. He'd seen the strain it was taking for her to simply be hospitable.

"I trusted you, Adam, and you've been lying to me all this time. And it doesn't help that this isn't the first time a man's made a fool of me."

He steeled himself against the quaver in her voice and fought the rising tide of jealousy. He had no right to be jealous though. Especially since he'd let her down just like the man she spoke of.

He was used to being a disappointment on the football field. He was not used to being a disappointment in the arena of moral failure. This felt immeasurably worse.

"I'm so sorry, Molly. I never meant to open an old wound, but I can see that I have."

She looked at him for a long moment. "My ex-boyfriend—Dominic, the one I told you about. He lied to me about who he was . . . and now I just can't abide—"

"You don't owe me anything. Least of all an explanation."

He'd never even dreamed she could be his. Not really. Despite what she said, when she'd overheard the conversation between him and Jordan, she'd jumped to the conclusion that Jordan was Nathaniel Quinn. Not him. That had told him everything he needed to know. Anything he might've seen in her eyes the night he held her had only been wishful thinking.

No, she didn't want a relationship with Adam now, even knowing who he was. Add his deception to that, and any chance he'd ever had with her—virtually nil—was completely gone.

"It's okay, Molly. I understand."

She drew in a breath, looking down at where she gripped the countertop, her knuckles blanched. When she looked back up at him, her eyes were so sad it was like a punch to his throat.

"I owe you an apology too," she said.

"No, you don't."

"I knew what you were saying when you were speaking in Italian—obviously. And I should've told you."

"Why didn't you?" The question was out before he could stop it. Then he held his breath in dread of what she might say. Until her eyes went bright with tears; then he wished he'd kept his big mouth shut.

"I liked it," she whispered. "I liked knowing what you really thought. But it wasn't fair to you. I deceived you, and I regret that."

Regret . . .

He rocked back on his feet. She was trying to make peace with him. Trying to avoid more regret. And after the way he'd hurt her, the least he could do was give her the closure she needed. He'd do anything to take the sadness from her eyes. Anything.

He stepped up to the counter and carefully placed his hand over hers. He waited until he had her full attention. Until her amber eyes were trained on his.

He squeezed her hand gently. "You didn't do

anything wrong, Molly. This is all on me. Every bit of it. All right?"

Her eyes flooded with tears.

He tried for a smile, took her in one last time, committing those features to memory. Then he gave her hand a final squeeze and turned to leave.

thirty-seven

A week had passed since Adam left the inn, and he hadn't run into Molly at all. In fact, he'd hung around the lake house so much he was going stir-crazy. He took in the sleek cottage. It was a new contemporary, two stories full of glass panes and lake views. It had clean lines, neutral décor, and a lot of stainless steel. It was beautiful and sleek, much like his flat in the city. But it made him long for old glass doorknobs, squeaky wood floors, and the sweet scent of baking muffins.

He tried to stay busy. When he wasn't working on his outline, he looked for Benjamin Schwartz. Giving Molly the closure she needed had become his number one goal.

He'd taken the long list of living Benjamin Schwartzes that his mother had given him and pared it down to twelve possibilities, and phone calls had already ruled out more than half. The next number had a Tennessee area code.

Adam pulled out his phone and tapped the numbers. It was dinnertime, a good time to catch people at home.

The phone rang and rang. He was ready to hang up when a woman answered. "Village Life, Marion speaking, may I help you?"

"Hi, my name is Adam Bradford, and I'm looking for a Benjamin Schwartz."

"One moment, please."

The line went silent. Did that mean a Benjamin was there or was she just redirecting his call to an operator? The phone began ringing in his ear. She was only redirecting. Disappointment swamped him. The other numbers had been dead ends. No Benjamin Schwartz at all or the wrong one.

"Hello?" An older gentleman's voice sounded on the other end of the line.

"Hi, I was wondering if you could tell me if there's a Benjamin Schwartz living in your community."

"This is he." His voice was gruff and a little loud.

Adam blinked and raised his voice in case the man was hard of hearing. "Oh, hello. This might sound a little strange, but I'm looking for a Benjamin Schwartz who spent time in Bluebell, North Carolina, during the summer of '64."

There was a long beat of silence, and Adam feared the man had hung up. "Hello? Are you still there, Mr. Schwartz?"

"What is this regarding exactly?" He sounded cautious.

Who could blame him? But he hadn't instantly denied being the man in question, as the others had.

Adam got to his feet and began pacing the open

living room. "It's a long story, sir. A friend of mine found a lost letter at an inn here—used to be the old post office. We've been trying to reach the intended recipient of that letter for a couple months now."

"What kind of letter?"

"A personal letter. They found it behind a wall during renovations. It was where the mail slot used to be. Obviously the letter never made it out of the post office."

"What—who was this letter from?"

"A Lizzie Van Buren." Adam paused, letting that sink in a moment. "Are you the man we're looking for, Mr. Schwartz?"

"Lizzie Van Buren . . ."

Adam thought he detected a wistful note in the man's voice, but maybe he was only trying to jog his memory. For all he knew Mr. Schwartz had dementia and couldn't even remember where he'd spent last Christmas, much less the summer of '64.

"Mr. Schwartz, are you still there?"

"Yes. Yes, I am. You've caught me off guard. I haven't heard that name in years." Mr. Schwartz's voice was thick with emotion.

Adam's breath escaped. "It's you then. You were here at Bluebell Lake."

"Best summer of my life. And the worst. Funny how those two things can both be true."

"I can't tell you how glad I am to have finally

located you. My friend will be so excited. We've been trying to find you all summer."

"Have you opened the letter?"

"Yes, sir. I'm sorry, but we did. It was so old, and we had no idea it would be so personal."

"It's all right. What does—" Mr. Schwartz began, then stopped. "I'm not sure I even want to know what it says. This is all quite a shock. All this time I'd thought—"

Adam suddenly wondered if the man was aware Lizzie passed away years ago. And he suddenly feared having to be the one to tell him. He didn't want to deliver upsetting news over the phone. He should've thought this through.

"She's gone now, you know," Mr. Schwartz said. "Lizzie."

Adam breathed a sigh of relief. "Yes, we found that out early in our search. I'm sorry for your loss."

"A friend of mine reached out after he'd heard. I was sorry to hear it. She was a lively girl, and a delightful young woman. Gone much too soon."

"Yes, sir. I'm sure my friend would love the chance to speak with you if you're willing."

"She's from Bluebell, you say?"

Adam stopped pacing and stared sightlessly out at the lake. His heart was trying to explode from his chest. "Yes, sir. She owns the inn where the letter was found."

"Not so far from here then. Maybe she could

come visit me. I'm afraid my health doesn't allow me to travel very far anymore."

"I'll certainly pass along the invitation to her. I hope my call hasn't upset you, Mr. Schwartz. I'm sure it has dredged up all kinds of memories."

"Mostly wonderful ones. I guess this ticker of mine can still handle a shock or two after all."

Adam gave Benjamin his phone number and wound up the conversation, telling him Molly would get in touch with him soon.

Then he went to find Molly.

Molly swiped the back porch with the stream of water from the garden hose, clearing off the dirt and debris. The storm last night had left leaves and twigs all over the backyard.

She'd been keeping busy since Adam had checked out. When she wasn't working she found herself in the kitchen helping Miss Della or outside doing odds and ends.

Adam hadn't said anything about hearing from his mother or continuing their search for Benjamin. And his last words to her had seemed pretty final. She assumed he was finished helping with their little project.

Maybe she should be too. But the letter lying upstairs in her nightstand drawer just wouldn't leave her alone. She'd done a bit of computer research in her free time, but there were so many hits for "Benjamin Schwartz" that she always ended up dizzy with options and unable to decide where to go next.

Maybe she'd scrape together enough money to hire a professional investigator as Adam's mom had suggested.

"Molly?"

She jumped a mile, letting loose of the trigger. Water splattered over her bare legs. She palmed her chest, her heart recovering.

Adam approached from the back door, holding up his hands. "Sorry. Didn't mean to scare you. Grace said you were out here."

What could he want? Maybe he needed a place to stay for a night or two. She could do this. Be professional. Be hospitable.

"No problem." She gave him a polite smile. "What can I do for you, Adam?"

He took a few steps closer, his eyes clear blue in the evening shade. She'd missed those eyes. Those faded denim eyes. And as he grew nearer she caught a whiff of his familiar scent. He poked his glasses into place. She'd missed that nervous habit too. That shy, unassuming way of his.

Do not get sucked back in. Do. Not.

"With the way we left things," Adam said, "we didn't really talk about pressing forward with your project. But I've continued this week." His eyes sparkled with excitement as he held up a sticky note. "And I found him, Molly. I found Benjamin."

333

She blinked. Reached out for the note. A phone number was scrawled on the paper. "You found him? Are you sure?"

"I just spoke with him. I hope you don't mind that I talked to him, but I had quite a few numbers, and I just kept calling them until . . . I found him."

The paper in Molly's fingers trembled. "What did he say? What did you say? Where does he live? Oh no, does he know about Lizzie? That she's already gone?"

His smile was a little sad. "Yes, he already knew. I was worried about that too. He's living in Knoxville at a retirement home. He was curious about the letter. I think he was also a little afraid to know what it said. Just talking about her seemed to awaken a lot of memories."

"I can only imagine." Molly stared at the number as if it might make more information appear. "I can hardly believe it. I have so many questions for him."

"He's expecting your call. He'd like for you to go see him if possible."

"You bet it's possible. I could go Thursday— though I can barely stand the thought of waiting three more days. What about you?"

"What about me?"

"Do you want to go?"

His mouth opened, then closed. He swallowed.

"I—didn't think you'd want me to. And that's fine, Molly. I get it."

"You should come—if you want to. If you have the time. I know you're on a deadline though."

He scratched his neck. "Are you sure you wouldn't mind having me along?"

Despite the way he'd deceived her, Adam had put even more time into this than she had. She didn't feel right excluding him at this point.

"We should see this through together," she said.

He gave her a smile that warmed her from the inside out. "Thank you. I'd like that very much."

thirty-eight

August 17, 1964

Lizzie couldn't believe she had to close the store tonight. Benjamin was leaving in just two days, and she wanted to spend every last moment with him. Their future plans were set. He'd go back to Jasper, give his boss notice, and start packing his things. He'd already begun inquiring about jobs near her campus in Ohio.

Lizzie's parents would take her to St. Anne's the last weekend of August, and she'd settle into college life. Benjamin would join her as soon as he got a job. She hoped she didn't have to wait long. She'd become hopelessly addicted to his company.

They'd grown much closer since they'd confessed their feelings two weeks ago. She could hardly stand to be away from him, and when they were alone together, she could hardly keep her hands off him. The feeling seemed to be mutual.

One clear night when they'd been stargazing on the quiet banks of Bluebell Lake, Lizzie had given herself completely to him. They hadn't meant for things to go that far, but once they had it was like trying to leash a tiger. Despite the guilt that plagued them both and despite their best intentions, they'd slipped twice more.

Ben's imminent departure—and her father's obvious disapproval—only made Lizzie more frantic to snatch every last second with him.

That's why it had been so frustrating tonight when a summer person had come in at two minutes until nine and browsed every shelf before finally leaving with only a can of Aqua Net.

She was meeting Benjamin at the movies at nine thirty, and she wanted to go home and shower first. She locked up the store and headed down the sidewalk at a brisk pace.

The sun had set almost an hour ago, and the last remnants of light glowed midnight blue on the horizon. The night was sultry, only a slight breeze blowing in off the lake. Nature sounds abounded: the high-pitched chirping of crickets, the oscillating buzz of cicadas, the quiet rustling of leaves overhead. She drew in a lungful of air, taking in the smells of freshly cut grass and damp earth. She loved Bluebell so much it would be hard to leave. But anticipation of her wonderful future with Ben took the sting out of it.

The stars were already out, sparkling brightly on a dark canvas. If, after the movie, she and Ben headed to their private spot on the other side of the lake, the sky would provide a well-lit canopy. She shivered in anticipation of his touch and tried to quell the inner voice that told her that would be another mistake. He'd be in Ohio soon enough. And then they'd get married, and she could be with him all the time without this feeling of impending doom hanging over her head.

She rounded the corner and saw that the lights were still on at her house. She tamped down disappointment. Her parents were often in bed by now, as the store opened bright and early. Though they knew she was still dating Benjamin, they had no idea how serious things had become. She knew they were simply biding their time until his departure, thinking that would be the last of him. A "summer romance," her mother called it.

And that was for the best. Just a few more weeks, and she and Ben would be together again, this time forever. She hoped to talk him into eloping when he got to Ohio. Daddy was never going to approve of her marrying Ben, much less agree to walk her down the aisle.

She didn't need a big white wedding anyway. She only needed Benjamin.

As she neared the house, she saw someone leaving by the front door. The shadow moved swiftly down the front porch steps.

Her heart caught in her throat at the familiar gait. What was Benjamin doing at her house? Had he been confused about their meeting place?

He'd already reached his friend's Buick, a hulking silhouette in the waning light.

She quickened her steps and called down the sidewalk. "Ben!"

He turned, the streetlight casting a glow over his features. His shoulders were slumped, his face drawn, and the look in his eyes nearly made her blood freeze. Something terrible had happened.

She cut across the lawn even as dread swept over, engulfing her like a tidal wave. "What—what's going on? What's wrong?"

He stuffed his hands in his front pockets and looked at the ground, eerily silent.

"Why are you here?" Her voice quavered. "We were supposed to meet at the theater."

"I know."

She shook her head in frustration. Why wasn't he talking to her? She took in his sloped eyes, always a little sad looking. But tonight, his whole countenance looked completely hopeless.

She glanced back at the house, dark now beyond the living room sheers. A horrible feeling of dread seeped into every cell of her body. Her father. Her stupid father was going to ruin everything.

"Talk to me," she demanded. "What happened? What did he say to you?"

He gave her a smile that didn't come close to reaching his eyes. "Maybe we can talk about this tomorrow, angel. I need—I need some time to think things through."

Dread morphed into terror. She grabbed his

arm. "No. There's nothing to think about. What happened in there, Ben? Tell me what he said to you. You're scaring me."

He gave her a long hopeless look. "I just don't see how this is going to work out, Lizzie."

Her heart skipped a beat. "That's ridiculous. We have a plan in place. Of course it's going to work out. Everything's all set."

His eyes sharpened on hers. "I asked for his blessing. Your father doesn't approve of me." The words seemed weighted with a thousand anchors.

Oh, she wanted to strangle her father! And Ben! "I told you not to talk to him! Why did you do that?"

"I couldn't ask you to marry me without his blessing, Lizzie."

"Who cares about his blessing? It's my life, Ben, not his. We're moving to Ohio, and we're going to get married. He'll come around in time. He'll have to. What choice will he have?"

Ben palmed the back of his neck. "I'm a janitor, Lizzie. I barely make enough to support myself. You deserve much better than that."

Her ire rose, prickling her skin with heat. "Is that what he told you?" She had a few things to say to her father, and they wouldn't wait.

She darted toward the house.

Ben grabbed her arm. "Don't, Lizzie. It won't do any good. I don't want to come between you and your parents. That was never my intention."

Heat prickled behind her eyes. "He shouldn't have said that to you! He shouldn't have made you feel less than. You're a wonderful man. I couldn't find a better man if I searched the whole world over!"

"Aw, honey . . ." He thumbed away the tears on her cheek. "He didn't say anything that wasn't true. Look at the life you live. I couldn't begin to provide all this for you."

"I don't need all this! I only need you, don't you understand that?"

He shook his head slowly. "That's not the way the world works. A couple needs more than love, Lizzie. You haven't struggled like I have. It's not fun. It's not easy. It's bound to cause all kinds of problems. I don't want that for us."

"It won't be like that. I love you."

"I love you too, angel. But I think we need a new plan."

The words gave her a bit of hope. She'd been so afraid he was breaking up for good. She waited for him to continue, not liking the resolve that was coming over his face.

"I want to make something better of myself. I want to go to college and get a real career and be able to support you the way you deserve."

"That costs a lot of money, Ben. And we don't need that anyway. When I graduate, I'll be able to get a good-paying job, and we'll be just fine. You'll see."

He was already shaking his head. "I'm not living off my wife's money, Lizzie. It's my job to provide, not yours."

"I've been working since I was fourteen. I want to work, Ben. I enjoy it."

"Be that as it may, I aim to have a real job, a career, and to get one I need a college degree." His tone was resolved to the point of obstinacy.

Maybe she was going to have to compromise a little. "All right. All right then. After I get my degree I'll get a good job, and then you can go to college—"

"I'm enlisting in the military, Lizzie."

Her stomach bottomed out. Her lips parted, but no words were forming on her tongue. The military? That was a four-year commitment. They wouldn't be married for *years*. He could even die over there. What if he never came home to her?

She shook her head adamantly.

He took hold of her arms. "Just listen, Lizzie. If I enlist they'll pay for my schooling. When I get out you'll be graduated, and we can get married then. I'll be able to make something of myself. Make your dad see that I'm worthy of you."

"Ugh! You're already worthy, Ben! Why can't you see that?"

"You have to look at things from his point of view, Lizzie. His only daughter is going to nursing school on a full academic scholarship,

342

and she wants to marry some no-good elementary school janitor. Assistant janitor, even. You could do so much better."

She jerked out of his hold. "You're a good man, Ben! And you don't understand a single thing. You'll never get Daddy's approval, because you can't change what he despises most about you!"

He blinked, going still.

She hadn't wanted to say it, but all the cards were on the table now. And the stakes were high. So very high. "Daddy's prejudiced, Ben. I'm ashamed to admit it, but he is, and you'll never get his approval for that reason alone, even if you became the president of the United States!"

She hated the hurt, the hopelessness, that washed over his face. Hated that she'd put it there. But she had to make him understand that there was nothing he could do to earn her father's approval. That they didn't even need it.

"So you see, there's no reason for you to enlist. It won't change anything. And if you want to get your college degree, you can do it later when I have a good job. We don't have to change our plans at all. We're a team, you and me. We'll make this work. We'll do whatever we have to do."

He was quiet for a good long time. The crickets in the nearby copse of trees chirped, filling the silence.

She closed the gap between them and touched

his arm. He was helpless under her touch—he'd told her so. She stroked the smooth flesh of his arm, the springy hairs tickling the pads of her fingers.

His face softened, his eyes intent on hers.

She breathed in the smell of him, willing him with her eyes to see things her way.

A look of tenacity came over his features. He cradled her face. "I know you want to get married now, angel. I do too. I'm only asking you to wait for me. It'll only be four years, and you'll be busy getting your education, so time will fly—"

She leaped back, making his hands fall. "No! Aren't you listening to me? I won't wait, Ben. Four years is forever, and anything could happen in that time. You could die over there, don't you know that? Men go to war and never come back."

"I'll come back to you, Lizzie."

"You don't know that! No! I won't wait. I can't do it, I just can't."

The crickets had ceased their chirping. Only the ragged sound of her breathing broke the silence.

"I can't marry you right now, Lizzie. Not like this. I have to earn his respect. I have to do right by you. It's about honor. It's more important to me than anything. If we're meant to be—"

"*If* we're meant to be?" She took a staggering step backward.

"—four years won't change that. You know what I mean."

She gritted her teeth, daring the tears to fall. "I'm not waiting. Especially not for someone who isn't even sure I'm worth waiting for."

"You know that's not what I meant, Lizzie. I love you and I always—"

"Just go, Ben! Just go ahead and leave now if that's what you want to do. Go off to war and never come back, and see if I even care!"

"Lizzie . . . you don't mean that. You're just angry right—"

"I do mean it! If you enlist I don't ever want to see you again!" She turned around and fled into her house, too angry even to look at him.

It only took twelve hours for Lizzie to regret everything she'd said. But the next morning when she drove to the Lewises' cottage Ben was already gone.

thirty-nine

Present Day

Molly bent forward from her seated position on the mat and reached toward her toes. Her hamstrings cried for mercy.

Beside her, Skye was folded in half, her flat stomach against her thighs, her forehead resting on her knees.

"That is not normal," Molly said.

"You'll get your flexibility back. Just keep at it."

"I wasn't that flexible when I was four."

"Everybody's different. It's not a competition."

Molly wasn't competitive at all. She was happy to let others win. But she'd been on edge since setting up the meeting with Benjamin, and waiting until Thursday was about to kill her nerves. She'd gone over the potential conversation in her head so many times she was about to drive herself crazy.

"So did you hear about the youth camp?" Skye asked.

"No, what about it?"

"Someone bailed it out. There's an article in today's paper."

"That's great. Who was it?"

"I don't know. It was an anonymous donation. But that's awesome news, right? That place was a real escape for me. They showed me who God is—and who I am in His sight. I'll always be grateful for that."

"I'm so glad. Whoever saved it, I hope they know how thankful the whole community is."

"I'm sure they do." Skye eased back on the mat, lying down flat, then pushing her belly upward in a perfect bridge.

Molly followed suit, her bridge obviously in need of major reconstruction.

"So I heard Adam checked out," Skye said.

"Was that in the paper too?"

"Grapevine."

Molly had told Skye they'd had words, but she hadn't gone into detail—she couldn't without giving away Adam's true identity. And even if he'd broken her trust, she wasn't about to reciprocate.

"He rented out a lake house."

"Must've been some argument."

"It's for the best."

That's what she kept telling herself every time she heard a creak overhead and thought, just for an instant, that Adam was still upstairs. Every time she glanced out the front window and saw his usual parking space empty.

"Still . . . it's too bad. I liked him. He really seemed like a genuine guy."

Right. Molly rolled her eyes, glad Skye was staring at the ceiling. At least she wasn't the only one he'd duped.

Okay, a little harsh. Molly kept rehashing what he'd told her about his dad and all those expectations he couldn't live up to. She could empathize with him, even though she'd been blessed in the parental department.

She was still working on forgiving him though.

Just as Molly's back was about to give out, Skye lowered to the mat and sat up, easing into a seated twist.

"Okay . . ." her friend said dryly. "I guess we're not going to talk about that. Let's talk about Benjamin. You're going to see him Thursday, right? And don't forget your breathing."

Molly drew in a deep breath and blew it out. "Yep. He's in Knoxville, living in a retirement village."

"Want some company? I have three classes on Thursdays, but I can get Leanne to take them. She's been begging for more hours."

"Um . . . Adam's coming along with me actually."

"You don't say."

"Don't make too much of it. I just figured he deserved to be there since he's been as invested in this mystery as I've been."

"Interesting."

"Not really."

"If you say so."

Molly shot her a look.

"What?" Skye asked, all innocence.

"Aren't we supposed to be focusing on our mental well-being?"

"We are." Skye switched sides, stretching toward the mirrored wall. "So how much longer will he be in town?"

"Another week or so, I guess." She rolled her eyes at her friend's reflection. "Just go ahead and spit it out, Skye. You know you want to."

"I'm trying not to be pushy."

"Not possible. Let's just get it over with."

"I don't know what you and Adam argued about . . . but are you sure it's important enough to call it quits over?"

"Call it quits? It never even got off the ground." Never mind the rebellious thumping of her heart or the squishy lump forming in her throat.

"I saw the way you looked at him when I was over a few weeks ago, Molly. And you know what? When you weren't paying attention, he was looking at you the same way."

Molly swallowed hard, but the lump didn't budge. Her eyes were starting to sting too, doggonit.

"He broke my trust, Skye. That's all I need to know."

"All right. I won't push you on this, especially since I don't have all the facts. But he didn't seem like Dominic to me. I didn't get those smarmy vibes from him."

"It's true that Adam's offense was different from Dominic's," Molly said. "Less . . . flagrant. He's not a bad person. But after what happened with Dominic . . . I just don't have it in me to go through that again. I need someone I can trust."

A long pause ensued as they eased onto their backs and pulled their knees into their chests.

"Remember five years ago when my mom got fired?" Skye asked. "And then she couldn't get another job because, you know, nobody wants to hire a drunk?"

"Right."

"Remember how freaked out I was about my future? I was afraid I was going to end up working in that greasy diner till I was forty-five and coming home to a houseful of cats."

"You do have a houseful of cats."

"Only three. But then Miss Mirabelle gave me a job here, and it changed my life. God worked everything out. I'm part owner, and I love what I do. But the point is, I was dealing with some major fear for a while, so I know what that looks like. I know what that feels like. And girl— you've got a fear thing going on."

Molly blinked at her, her back going stiff even though she was lying down. "How do you figure?"

Skye pulled in her other knee. "You're afraid

of leaving things badly with people you love in case they die before you see them again. You hug me three times every time we part ways, do you realize that? We haven't even had a decent argument since your folks passed away."

"We've never argued, not really."

"Fuss, squabble, bicker, whatever. You're so careful to keep things congenial, even with me, and you know I love a good fight."

"Is that a crime? And what does all this have to do with Adam anyway?" Did she really just bring the subject back around to him?

"You're afraid of getting hurt again, Molly. I mean, I know Dominic did a job on you, I get that. What he did was inexcusable. But you've been so busy trying to protect yourself you won't let anybody in."

"I just haven't met the right person, that's all."

"Are you sure? You met Adam, and you genuinely liked him. I get the feeling you might be using this little snafu with him to keep him at arm's length."

"So I have a little trust issue. Is it any wonder after Dominic?"

"It's more than that, Molly. And I'm only saying this because I love you. But doesn't it seem a little telling that your only infatuation since Dominic has been with an author?"

Molly's eyes shot to Skye. Had she somehow figured out that Adam was Nathaniel Quinn?

"I mean," Skye continued, "it wasn't safe enough to become infatuated with just any old author. You had to go and find an anonymous, reclusive one just to be absolutely certain he was safe."

Molly breathed a quiet sigh. "Well, at least I didn't go for an inmate on death row. And he's not reclusive, just . . . a little shy."

Skye sat up. "That's your defense?"

Molly sat up, bristling. "I shouldn't have to defend myself. Maybe for once in your life you should just butt out, Skye." Her raised voice echoed through the studio.

"I wouldn't say this if I didn't care about you, Molly. Nathaniel Quinn was safe. He wasn't going to hurt you because you were never going to meet him."

And yet that's exactly what happened.

But Molly couldn't even digest that because she'd just raised her voice at her best friend, who was only trying to help. What was wrong with her?

She looked at Skye, her eyes watering. "I'm sorry. I didn't mean to yell, and I shouldn't have said that."

Skye gave her a pointed look, and Molly realized she was doing just what her friend had said she'd been doing—avoiding arguments, making sure she left things well. The fear roiling in her belly right now was proof enough that Skye was right. About everything.

"It's fine." Skye put her hand over Molly's. "If you don't think Adam's worth fighting for, that's one thing. I just don't want fear to keep you from someone who could be really good for you."

There was that word again. Fear. It seemed to be coming up a lot lately. She never used to have this problem. She'd always considered herself to be well adjusted. Fairly brave, even.

God, what is wrong with me? What's happened to me?

"You know," Skye said, "when I went through all that with my mom and my future, you know what I figured out? Fear is often just a lack of faith. I wasn't trusting God with my future."

Molly stared at her fingers. Started pushing back the cuticles. "I don't know why I'm being so defensive. You're right. I have been anxious since my folks passed, about a lot of things. It hasn't been fun. But I don't have a clue how to get beyond it."

"It's going to take some time, Molly. Losing your parents like that, so suddenly—it was devastating. It was bound to leave its mark, one way or another."

"I guess so."

"I have some scriptures that really helped get me through that time. I can text them to you if you want."

"Sure. Yeah, it wouldn't hurt, I guess." She needed something to help her figure this out. She didn't want to live a fearful life. She didn't like feeling uptight and anxious all the time.

Molly's phone vibrated on the end of her mat, and she checked it just in case it was an emergency. That was another accommodation she'd made since her parents died, she suddenly realized. She made sure her phone was charged and within reach at all times.

She frowned at the screen. What could Nonnie want? Molly had left a message with her yesterday about finding Benjamin and their plans to go see him Thursday.

"It's Miss Nonnie."

"Go ahead," Skye said. "I think we're about finished here anyway."

Molly answered the phone.

"Hi, Molly." Nonnie sounded upset. "I got your message."

"Are you all right, Miss Nonnie? You're not sick again, are you?"

"No, honey, I—I'm just a wreck over all this, that's all. I've been praying about what to do since I got your message."

"A wreck? About me going to see Benjamin?"

A long silence ensued. She traded a glance with Skye and shrugged. She would've thought they'd lost their connection except she heard something rattling in the background.

"Honey, I think you need to come over." There were tears in her voice. "There's something I need to tell you. Something about Lizzie. Can you come over yet today?"

"I can come over right now if that's all right."

"Yes, yes, that would be wonderful. I think I just need to get this off my chest."

Molly shook her head. What could it be? "I'll be there in fifteen or twenty minutes, all right? Sit tight, and don't worry. Everything's going to be fine."

"What's going on?" Skye stood with Molly and followed her to the door.

Molly shouldered her purse. "I don't know. She said she needs to tell me something about Lizzie, and she seemed pretty upset. Sorry to rush off like this, but I'm a little worried about her."

"No, it's fine. You should make sure she's okay."

Molly paused awkwardly in the doorway when she'd normally hug her friend—three times apparently.

Skye gave Molly a rueful smile and pulled her into an embrace. "One time is perfectly normal. Now go check on our friend."

forty

Molly was getting out of her car when a vehicle slowed on the road and pulled into Miss Nonnie's drive behind her.

Adam. She must've called him too. Molly had been so worried about the woman she hadn't even thought of calling him, but she was glad he was here. Whatever Miss Nonnie had to say seemed important.

Molly gave a little wave, her heart pounding at the sight of him behind the wheel. She'd only just seen him yesterday, but her eyes drank in the sight of him anyway. He looked so debonair in his sunglasses and crisp white shirt. How could he not know how handsome he was? Her heart gave a little tug at the memory of their conversation on the patio.

She glanced down at her yoga attire, wishing she wasn't slick with perspiration, her hair pulled up into a messy bun. Oh well. Her appearance was irrelevant. Their relationship wasn't headed in that direction anymore.

"Is she all right?" Adam asked as he exited his car, a frown tugging his brows.

They walked together toward the door. "I don't know. I just got here."

"She seemed upset on the phone."

"I know. I rushed right over."

His gaze flickered over her. "Yoga with Skye?"

"Yeah. Miss Nonnie wants to tell us something about Lizzie."

"That's what she told me too."

"I can't imagine what it would—"

Nonnie pulled open the door before they reached the top of the porch. Her eyes were bloodshot, and her hand trembled on the doorknob.

"I'm so glad you're here," she said.

"Are you all right?" Molly asked. "You sounded upset on the phone."

"Oh, I'm fine. Just an emotional old woman. Thank you for coming on such short notice, kiddos. I didn't mean to make you fret." But Nonnie had obviously been fretting herself.

The woman led them into her small living room and dashed off to get them some tea, despite Molly's offer to help. When Nonnie returned she settled on the armchair catty-corner to Molly and Adam.

Molly noticed the box on the end table—the one that held Nonnie's memorabilia. The letters, the ones Molly had spied last time, sat beside the box. Molly glanced at Adam and saw he'd noticed them too.

"I've been praying about this since you first came to me," Nonnie said. "I just didn't have clear direction on what I should do. I promised

Lizzie I wouldn't say anything, and even though she's been gone so many years now, I wanted to keep my word. She was a dear, dear friend. But in trying to be loyal to her I was dishonest with you, and I feel just terrible."

"What's all this about, Miss Nonnie?"

The woman reached over and took the letter from the table. Her hand trembled as she passed the envelope to Molly. "You should just read it for yourselves, I think."

The letter was from Lizzie and addressed to Nonnie, but the return address was a Louisiana one. The postmark was dated October 12, 1964.

Molly traded a look with Adam as he moved to the middle of the sofa so he could read along with her.

She withdrew two sheets of stationery, unfolded them, and began reading.

Dearest Nonnie,

I know you must've noticed that I'm mailing this from Louisiana and not from Ohio. I am not at college anymore. I'm staying with my great-aunt near Shreveport.

I don't know how else to say this, so I'll just come right out with it. I'm pregnant, Nonnie. When my parents found out they came to get me. I had to drop out of school. I should've told you before now, but I was too ashamed.

At first I was almost glad about the news because I dreamed a baby might convince Ben to come back to me. But he never responded to my letter, and when I tracked him down through his place of employment I found out that he'd already enlisted.

He's clearly done with me. My heart is truly broken. I didn't know it was possible to weep so many tears.

When my parents came for me I thought at first they might allow me to live with Aunt Georgia and raise the baby in Shreveport. But I couldn't have been more wrong. Aunt Georgia barely tolerates my presence—and my morning sickness. My parents are insisting I give my baby up for adoption. They say I won't get a dime from them if I decide to keep it.

Oh, Nonnie, my heart is so heavy as I write this. I don't have any way of supporting a child. Ben wants nothing to do with me any longer, and even if a baby might somehow change this, he's a world away in Vietnam somewhere.

My parents plan to find an adoptive couple. They want me to give my baby away and come home for the summer and pretend I just spent my first year away at college! As if I could just go on like normal! But they're embarrassed and just want to sweep this pregnancy under the rug. They seem more concerned about losing their standing with the Catholic Church than they are about me and my baby.

I am so afraid for the future, Nonnie. Afraid of giving up a baby I already love. Afraid for my baby's future. I feel hopeless, and I just had to tell someone. I know I can trust you to not tell a soul.

Please pray for God's will in this. I feel too ashamed to ask for His help when it was my sin that got me into this to begin with. But I know He'll hear your prayers. So pray for me as you never have before, friend! And pray for my precious, innocent baby. I already love this child so much I can't bear the thought of losing him or her.

If you write back, please don't refer to any of this. I believe Aunt Georgia opens my mail—that's just the way she is. I'll call you next week if I can get her out of the house for a few minutes.

Yours truly,
Lizzie

Molly's eyes were wet by the time she finished reading the letter. She met Adam's gaze, her heart in her throat. "Poor Lizzie. Pregnant and all alone."

"I know I told you Lizzie couldn't have children. But that was only true later."

"It's all right," Molly said, still trying to digest the letter. "I can't believe her parents would be so cruel."

"I know it's hard to fathom in this day and age," Nonnie said. "But there was such a stigma back then. I wanted to invite her to come back here with her baby. To come live with my family. But there were eight of us living in a small house, and money was tight. Anyway, it was obvious Lizzie's folks didn't want her anywhere near Bluebell."

"What happened after this?" Adam asked. "Did she have the baby? Did she give it up for adoption?"

"There's another letter that explains what happened. Mostly we talked on the phone, but it was expensive, so she didn't call often." Nonnie handed over another letter.

It was all Molly could do not to rip it out of its envelope and devour its contents. She forced herself to slow down.

Adam leaned in closer as she pulled out the single sheet of paper and unfolded it. She was momentarily distracted by the warm strength

361

of his thigh against hers. She drew in a deep, steadying breath, and the spicy scent of his cologne drew her.

Focus, Molly.

The letter was dated March 18, 1965. She began reading to herself.

Dearest Nonnie,

Everything is all set. Mama and Daddy have found a couple in Texas who want to adopt my baby. I am not allowed to meet them, but Mama and Daddy interviewed them. The woman is a homemaker who is unable to have children of her own. Her husband is in banking. They attend a Catholic church and have been longing for a child for years. They sound like wonderful people who will give my baby a good home and loving family.

I know I should be grateful, but I can't get past the idea of losing my baby. Deep inside I am so angry with Mama and Daddy for forcing me to do this. I know I shouldn't be, as I got myself into this mess. It's a bitter pill to swallow, Nonnie.

I only have two more months until the baby is born, and I'm dreading it with every fiber of my being. Until then I will treasure every moment that my baby's heart beats beneath mine.

As much as I want to see you again, I don't know how I will return to Bluebell in May. How can I simply pretend none of this happened? I will never be the same again.

And yet, God forgive me, if I could go back and do things differently, I'm not sure that I would. I don't have it in me to regret this child. I only pray that God has mercy on my baby despite the sinful circumstances that brought him or her into this world. It would mean so much to me if you would pray toward that end.

I have to be strong. I have to find a strength I don't feel capable of in order to get through these next weeks. I will need every one of your prayers.

I love you, Nonnie, and I miss you so much.

Yours truly,
Lizzie

"Oh, Miss Nonnie." Molly knuckled away a tear, her chest tight and achy. "How did it all work out? Is there another letter?"

Nonnie dabbed at her own eyes. "I'm afraid that's the last one. But yes, the adoption went through as planned. I spoke to Lizzie on the phone shortly after the baby arrived. It was a little girl, and she didn't even get to hold her. Something went wrong, and she had to have a hysterectomy. Lizzie was weeping so hard I could hardly understand her. About broke my heart."

"I can't even imagine giving up a child. And then finding out she'd never have another. It must've been so awful."

"It surely was."

"What happened when she came back to Bluebell?" Adam asked.

"She never did come back for the summer—or ever again, for that matter. She got a job in Louisiana. A few years later her parents' store burnt to the ground. They moved down there to be with her, though their relationship was strained after what they'd put her through.

"Eventually Lizzie met a nice man and settled down. I don't think she ever felt as strongly about him as she had Benjamin. But then maybe it's unfair to compare such a young love with a more mature one."

"Was she happy?" Molly asked. "Did she ever get over giving up her baby?"

"I believe she was happy. She made what seemed like a nice life for herself. But I don't know that you ever truly 'get over' something like that."

Adam shifted toward Miss Nonnie. "So . . . what you're telling us is that Benjamin Schwartz has a daughter he doesn't even know about."

Molly sank back into the sofa, pressing her palm against her thumping heart. This had mushroomed into so much more than she'd ever dreamed.

"I've been praying about this since you first contacted me," Nonnie said. "As reluctant as I was to give away Lizzie's secret . . . In light of all that's happening, you finding Benjamin and all . . . I felt God leading me to tell you the whole truth. I hope you can forgive me for not being forthcoming before."

"Of course. You've been a very loyal friend to Lizzie. But . . . how can we tell Benjamin he has a child he never knew about?"

Adam's eyes met hers. "Especially when we don't even know her whereabouts."

forty-one

Adam leaned away from his laptop, massaging the back of his neck. He'd been sitting at the kitchen table, researching ways for adopted children to find their birth parents. There were adoption registries for people who were searching for their birth family. Social media was also commonly used.

Those methods took time, though, and they were going to see Benjamin tomorrow.

He and Molly had been a little stunned when they left Nonnie's house the day before. They talked awhile by their cars, processing the new information. As far as telling Benjamin about his child, Nonnie had left that to their discretion.

Mr. Schwartz was old and in a nursing home. His health might not be very stable. And besides, what good would come from finding out he and Lizzie had a child out there whom he'd never know? They decided they'd wait and assess the situation before deciding what to do.

When Adam's phone buzzed an incoming call, he was glad for the distraction. Deep down he hoped it was Molly. She'd said she'd see if her sister could work a little online magic today. Maybe Grace's search had been more fruitful than his.

However, when he checked the screen, he saw it was his mom. Popping the little bubble of disappointment, he tapped the button to answer and greeted her.

"You must be feeling inspired," she said by way of greeting. "We haven't talked in almost two weeks."

"Sorry, Mom. Things have been a little crazy lately." He'd texted her at least. Since she'd helped them find Benjamin he wanted her to know they had located the man and were going to visit him soon.

"With your story, you mean? It's going well?"

"Not that so much. Just . . . other things."

"Could it have anything to do with your pretty innkeeper, Molly?" his mom asked in a teasing tone. "I looked up the inn's website and saw her picture. She's just darling."

That didn't even begin to describe her. "I actually moved out of the inn over a week ago. I rented a lake house."

"Oh no. Did something happen? Not that a lake house doesn't sound lovely."

"It's . . . complicated, Mom. And I'd rather not get into it right now if you don't mind. I'd much rather talk about you. How's your work going? Any new projects?"

"It's going great. And yes, I do have a new family tree project. In fact, it turns out the woman's uncle worked with your grandpa at the bank. Can you believe it? It's such a small world."

"You know what they say about six degrees of separation."

"That's true. And yet those connections always surprise me. I mean what are the chances that my client, a woman living in Idaho, has an uncle who worked with my father in Austin, Texas?"

Two things connected at once. Banking. Texas. Adam flashed back to Lizzie's letter, processing all the information at lightning speed. His heart rate accelerated, and it seemed suddenly warm in the room. He stood and began pacing across the white tiled floor, assimilating the facts.

"Honey, did you hear me?" His mom laughed. "You're plotting again, aren't you? You creatives can be so hyperfocused. You surely didn't get that from me. I'm as distractible as can be."

"Mom . . ." The rush of adrenaline sent tingles through his limbs. "What was your mom's name? Your birth mother, I mean?" He wasn't even certain she'd mentioned it in the past. On the rare occasions she'd referred to the woman she'd always just said "my birth mother."

"Well, that was out of the blue. Only reason I even knew it was because your grandparents felt it was important for me to have her name in case I ever wanted to search for her. They gave it to me when I turned eighteen, and as you know, I did look for her. Unfortunately, I was too late."

"Right, but . . . what was her name?"

"It was Elizabeth Van Buren. Why do you ask, honey?"

Adam's breath released in a great *whoosh*. A chill swept over him, and his legs trembled beneath him. He lowered himself into the nearest chair. This was . . . How could this even . . . He couldn't believe . . .

Lizzie had given birth to a girl, and her parents had arranged an adoption with a banker and his wife from somewhere in Texas. His mother was adopted, and her birth date was May 3, 1965.

It seemed like an impossible coincidence that he'd come to Bluebell to research for his book and had stayed in the very building where Lizzie's letter had been mailed.

And yet, he'd chosen Bluebell on his mother's recommendation. And she'd come here because it had been her birth mother's hometown.

Benjamin was his mom's birth father. Benjamin was Adam's grandfather. A fresh wave of chills washed over him. He blinked at the unfamiliar burn behind his eyes. His mind was officially blown.

"Honey, are you all right? Why did you ask about my birth mother?"

He sucked in a few breaths. "Mom . . . I have to tell you something."

"Well, gracious, honey, what is it? You sound so serious."

"You know that project I've been working on with Molly . . ."

"Of course. You're going to see the man soon. What's all this about? You're scaring me."

"Mom . . . I'm fairly certain the man we've been searching for—Benjamin—is your birth father."

A heavy pause hung on the line. "What? Oh, honey, that can't be. I couldn't find any information about him at all, not even his name."

"The woman who wrote the lost love letter was named Elizabeth Van Buren, Mom. She went by Lizzie. We have letters from her to her best friend. Elizabeth Van Buren was involved with Benjamin the summer of '64—and she got pregnant."

He went on to explain the rest of the story while his mother listened, probably in stunned silence. "We only just read the letters yesterday. We didn't know about the pregnancy and subsequent adoption. I didn't connect the dots until you mentioned Grandpa and his job at the bank. Mom . . . we've found your birth father."

"Oh my word." Her voice quivered with emotion. "Are you sure, honey? I mean, it all seems so . . ."

"I know. But your birth mother was from Bluebell. How many Elizabeth Van Burens could there have been in this little town?"

"You're right. I know you are. I'm just . . . I

have to catch my breath here. Did Benjamin know about the baby . . . about me?"

"No, he didn't. Doesn't. He doesn't know about you, Mom. As far as Miss Nonnie knows, he and Lizzie never reconnected after she discovered she was pregnant."

"Oh my. I'm just . . . I can hardly think straight. I'm shaking."

"Are you all right? Are you glad to know? Maybe I shouldn't have said anything." But his mom had searched so hard for her birth mother. She'd surely want to know about her birth father. Her *living* birth father.

"No, honey, I'm glad you told me. I'm excited. And a little scared, I'll admit." She gave a choked laugh. "What if he doesn't want to meet me? Is he married? His wife might not welcome this news. I probably have siblings—but they might not welcome the news either."

"I guess we'll have to play all that by ear. I don't know what his health is like. He mentioned something about his heart, but I couldn't tell if that meant he had heart problems. I imagine this will all come as quite a shock."

"That's right. You mentioned he was in a nursing home. He might be in poor health. Maybe you should feel out the situation first. I don't want any harm to come to him, and I don't want to cause his family any grief." But he could tell by her tone the idea saddened her.

They talked it over and decided that would ultimately be the best thing.

Now he just had to tell Molly what they'd discovered.

forty-two

Molly smiled at the retired couple who had just checked in. "Here are your keys. I'll show you around a bit, then take you to your room."

As she stepped from behind the counter the desk phone rang. Letting calls go to voice mail was a good way to lose business.

Fortunately Levi waltzed over at just the right time. "I can show them around if you want to get the phone." He gave the couple a winning smile. "I'm Levi, one of the owners. I'm so glad you could join us."

"Fred and Joann Baker. Nice to meet you."

"What brings you to the area?" Levi asked as he led them toward the library.

The Bakers in good hands, Molly took the phone call and was glad she'd caught it. The woman was calling on behalf of a company that wanted to book a staff retreat. Molly answered her questions and felt like dancing a jig when she booked every room for four days in November.

When she finished the call it was almost her shift's end. She was eager to get upstairs and see if Grace had made any progress locating Lizzie and Ben's daughter. She'd checked in midafternoon and there'd been nothing to report.

Molly knew it was a long shot. But Benjamin deserved to know the truth, and it would be hard to deliver the news when they had no clue where his child was.

She tidied up the counter, remembering her talk with Adam outside Miss Nonnie's house. Even though the circumstances had been serious, it was good to chat with him. She'd missed the sound of his voice, the scent of his cologne, and his shy mannerisms. Even now, she was more looking forward to tomorrow's two-hour drive than to meeting Benjamin at long last.

She gave her head a shake. *Not good, Molly. You have to forget about Adam.*

But she couldn't help but think of what Skye had said yesterday. She had been avoiding relationships since Dominic. And then she'd started letting Adam in—who was she kidding? She'd completely fallen for Adam.

Her chest constricted at the thought. True, he shouldn't have let her believe Jordan was Nathaniel Quinn. But what he'd done wasn't the same as what Dominic had done. Now that a little time had passed she could see that clearly. Especially in light of his sincere apology and explanation.

But she wasn't sure she was ready to trust anyone with her heart again. Skye had been right about all of it, darn her. Somewhere along the way Molly had let fear take root in her life. It had sunk down deep, gaining a death grip.

Molly pulled out her phone and found the scriptures Skye had sent her. She'd been reading through them, letting them soak in, praying over them, every chance she got. It was the only way fear would ever loosen its grip. None of the verses was new to her, but they'd taken on special meaning. She held tightly to them.

She read her favorite again, absorbing the promise. *We know that all things work together for the good of those who love God: those who are called according to His purpose.*

In her mind, she knew it was true. But she wanted to believe it with her whole heart. She wanted to be so certain of the promise that she didn't question when bad things happened or when people did hurtful things. She wanted to be so certain that she could lay her heart on the line, knowing that God would use any hurt for her own good.

She wasn't there yet. But she wanted to be.

Her phone buzzed in her pocket, and her heart rate accelerated when she saw the name on the screen.

She cleared her throat and tapped the button. "Hey, Adam."

"Molly. I'm glad I caught you. Are you working right now?"

"Um . . ." She checked the time. Her heart rate

was twice what it had been before his call. "I'm actually getting off right now. What's up?"

"Is there any way we can meet somewhere? Or can I come over? I have something I need to tell you—it's about Benjamin and Lizzie's child."

"Did you find something? Grace isn't having much luck, I'm afraid."

"You should probably call her off. I think we have all the information we need."

She blinked. "Oh! That was fast."

"Tell me about it."

She should probably just have him tell her over the phone, but she couldn't resist the chance to see him. Maybe he felt the same since he was asking to meet. The thought set butterflies loose in her stomach.

"I can't wait to hear. Want to meet at the park? Say, in twenty minutes?"

"Sounds good. I'll see you then."

Just then she heard Levi's footsteps on the stairs as he returned from showing the Bakers to their room.

Molly skirted the desk and passed him on her way upstairs. "Your turn. And I must say your timing has been stellar today."

"I try. Has the Murdock party checked in yet?"

"No, they'll be here after check-in hours. They already know the drill."

"Where are you headed in such a rush?"

"Meeting Adam at the park."

"Adam? I thought you guys had a falling-out."

"It's complicated," she said over her shoulder.

He muttered something as she reached the top of the staircase.

She opened her mouth to tell him she loved him. Then she closed it again. She was pretty sure he already knew.

Twenty minutes later Molly pulled into the park. She'd loosened her hair from her ponytail and put on her favorite white shorts with a red top that Adam had complimented her on once before. As she scanned the park for him, she tried not to think too hard about why she'd taken such pains.

She found him sitting on top of a picnic table in the gazebo. He was facing the lake, elbows planted on his knees.

Molly followed the paved pathway along the grassy peninsula. It was a beautiful park, well maintained and full of colorful blooms. The scent of jasmine carried over on a breeze, its sweet scent reminding her of her mother. Two swans floated by, their movements so fluid on the water they seemed to be gliding.

The white gazebo, straight ahead, was large enough to seat about a hundred guests, making it a popular wedding venue during the warmer months. Currently it was empty except for a few picnic tables—and Adam, of course.

He wore khakis and a blue polo that she knew

matched the shade of his eyes perfectly. The warm breeze tousled his hair as he stared out over the lake. He seemed deep in thought, and she wondered again what he'd discovered.

It occurred to her that it might be bad news. What if Lizzie and Ben's daughter had passed away? Maybe that's why he wanted to tell her in person—he knew she'd be upset. Her heart sank at the thought. What would they tell Benjamin then?

Adam spotted her and gave a wave as she neared.

"Hey," she called, trying to assess his mood but coming up short.

His smile seemed a little off, and his eyes looked strained at the corners. His fingers beat out a tempo on his thighs. She'd never seem him fidgety.

Her heart twisted in dread. *Please, God. Don't let it be bad news. Help us give this poor man some closure—the good kind.*

When she reached the table she perched on top, leaving plenty of space between them. The surface of the table was rough and warm against her palms.

"Thanks for coming," he said. "I realized after we got off the phone that I should've suggested dinner. You're probably hungry after working your shift. But I couldn't eat right now if I tried."

Her smile faltered. "What's going on, Adam? Is it bad news? Is their daughter dead?"

He met her gaze. "No. It's not bad news. Sorry to worry you. It's actually good news . . . It's just been a bit of a shock. I don't even know where to start."

Relief washed over her. "Okay, well, how about the beginning?"

He gave a wry laugh. "That goes back a ways. But all right. I suppose that's as good a spot as any."

She waited a moment while he collected his thoughts.

"So my mom—I mentioned that she was adopted . . ."

"Yes, you said that's how she developed an interest in ancestry."

"Right. Well, when she turned eighteen her parents—the ones who raised her—gave her the name of her birth mother. They wanted her to have the chance to find her if she chose. So before I was born Mom started looking—and unfortunately she discovered that her birth mom had passed away some years earlier."

"Oh, how sad. She must've been so upset." Molly wondered if this project had stirred up negative emotions for his mother. She'd helped them with the search after all.

"I'm sure she was. But she had terrific parents who loved her like crazy, so I think she was able to process it in a healthy manner and move forward with her life."

"What about her birth father? Did she ever search for him?"

"She never found out anything about him." Adam's eyes connected with hers and hung on with power that was magnetizing. She couldn't look away even if she tried. There was something there in that intense look . . . but she had no idea what.

"Molly . . ." he said finally. "My mom's birth mother's name was Elizabeth Van Buren."

Molly blinked even as a chill swept over her, lifting gooseflesh on her arms. She stared into Adam's blue eyes.

"What?" Her voice was no more than a breathy whisper.

"I know it sounds crazy." His voice was low and fervent. "But I spoke with my mom on the phone today, and she said some things that jogged my memory. Her dad was a banker—I'd forgotten about that—and they're from Texas, of course. I'd never heard her birth mother's name, but when she told me . . . She was from Bluebell, Molly. Benjamin Schwartz is my mom's father."

Molly was shaking her head, trying to assimilate the facts. It didn't add up. It was too big a coincidence. Adam being here in Bluebell, at her inn. He was from New York, his mom from Texas, both hundreds of miles from here.

"But how . . . how could it be that you happen to be here, and I find the letter and . . ."

"Yes, I know. The timing is inconceivable. But I came to Bluebell on my mom's recommendation. She visited in her twenties after she found out who her birth mother was. I guess she wanted to connect with her in some way since she'd already passed. She fell in love with the place. She's been telling me for years I should set a story here."

He ducked his head. Of course he'd never mentioned this to Molly because she hadn't known he was an author. He'd been trying to keep his "research" vague.

"So when I got stuck for an idea," he continued, "I decided to come here and see if it was all she said. I was hoping for a little inspiration."

Now that the missing pieces were filled in, it was all making sense in some bizarre, miraculous way. The scripture she'd been repeating whispered in her heart. *All things work together for the good of those who love God . . .*

"Can you believe it?" Adam asked, chuckling in wonder. "Benjamin Schwartz is my grandfather, Molly."

She put her hand over his, looking into his eyes. "Oh, Adam . . . That's so wonderful. Have you told your mom yet?"

"I have." He laughed. "I think she was shell-shocked. She's been texting me every two minutes since we got off the phone."

"I can only imagine."

His smile fell away, his look becoming intent again. "Molly . . . I've never had God's work in my life be so . . . blatant. I mean, I've seen Him work in my life so many times. But this particular situation is so convoluted and layered, it would be impossible not to see it as His handiwork."

"Yes, I see what you mean." She realized her hand was still on his and drew it away.

But he caught it in his, wrapping his other hand around it too.

Her face heated at the touch. At the look in his eyes.

"You were a huge part of this, Molly. You found the letter and needed answers. You invited me along on the journey. And no matter what happens . . . I'll always be thankful for that."

No matter what happens . . . Her eyes stung with tears.

"I know I have no right to ask. But later, when we've had a chance to digest all that's happened, I hope . . . I hope you might be able to forgive me. And I hope you might even find it within yourself to give me a chance—to give *us* a chance. I know I blew it. But I really care about you, Molly. I hope you know that."

Her heart melted at his words. At the sincerity so obvious in his expression. She'd already forgiven him, and Adam was worthy of a second chance.

But Dominic had seemed sincere too. And she'd been so wrong about him. And even if Adam was the man she believed him to be, he still had the power to break her heart. At just the thought of it, her heart felt as though it might explode from her chest, and the muscles in her chest tightened painfully. The burgeoning fear rising up in her was all the proof she needed.

A tear slipped down her cheek. She tried to remember the scriptures she'd been repeating to herself, but she couldn't think past the powerful swell of emotion.

"I do forgive you, Adam, but—" She couldn't even put into words the fear that held her back.

Adam squeezed her hand, then let it go, a pained smile on his lips. "It's all right, Molly. I get it. Thank you for forgiving me. That's more than I deserve. It's been a real pleasure getting to know you."

Molly breathed a laugh. "You sound like you're saying good-bye."

"Not just yet. But I'm heading back to New York day after tomorrow. I've already arranged my flight."

Panic spread through her body like a poison. "But . . . but what about your book? Don't you have a lot of work left to do on it?"

"I'll figure out the rest back home." His sad smile about broke her heart. "It's time I go home."

The ache in Molly's chest spread outward. At the thought of his leaving, that familiar fear swamped over her. But this wasn't the last time she was seeing Adam. They'd be together all day tomorrow.

No, this was different. This time the fear wasn't about parting badly. It was about lost opportunity.

Who are you kidding, Molly? It's about lost love.

A knot swelled in her throat even as her breaths grew shallow. *Oh, God, do I really love him? And what am I supposed do with that? You know I'm not ready for this. I can't even—*

He slid off the picnic table, coming to his feet. "Well . . . I should probably call my mom. She's full of questions about tomorrow."

Molly swallowed hard, trying to shove all the emotions down deep. "I'm sure she is. We can handle that however she wants. I'm sure she'd love to meet him."

"Yeah, we can talk about that tomorrow on the drive up. I'll pick you up at eight?"

Two hours alone in the car with him. She suddenly didn't know if her heart could take it. She dredged up a smile. "Yeah. Sounds good."

He backed away, the pained smile lingering on his lips. "See you tomorrow, Molly," he said. And then he was gone.

forty-three

The next morning Adam had a lot on his mind. Molly's rejection battled with worry over his upcoming meeting with Benjamin for top spot. But since he'd mostly stewed over the former all night, the latter took precedence this morning.

When he picked up Molly she was her usual sunshiny self.

She handed him several copies of the newspaper photo of Benjamin and Lizzie dancing at Gibby's. "Thought you and your mom might want copies. Did you get much sleep?"

"Enough. Good idea, thanks. Benjamin might like a copy too. Got the letters?"

"Right here." She held up three envelopes: the original lost letter and the two letters Nonnie had given them.

As they headed out of town Molly launched into a conversation about their rapidly approaching meeting with Ben. Once Adam had explained his mom's feelings on the matter, they agreed to play it by ear. Adam would make the final call. If Benjamin was in poor health or if Adam felt it might cause him hardship they wouldn't give him Nonnie's letters or tell him about Lizzie's pregnancy—at least not today.

After that was settled Molly began quizzing

him on his writing process. He squirmed at first, as this was the thing that had come between them. But he soon forgot that in light of her insatiable curiosity. He wasn't used to talking about writing with anyone outside his publishing team. Molly wanted to know everything there was to know, and he found the time flying by.

As they drew closer to Knoxville his thoughts turned to Benjamin, and his palms grew damp against the steering wheel. What would he be like? Would Adam be able to see any of his mother in the man? Any of himself?

Would he have the chance to tell Benjamin who he was? He'd been praying for wisdom since yesterday. He wanted to do the right thing, but it would be difficult and disappointing to walk away without telling Benjamin the truth.

"You all right?" Molly asked. "You're looking a little pale over there."

He ran his sweaty palms down his legs one at a time. "I don't know why I'm so nervous."

"Because you're about to see the grandfather you've never met?" She gave him a wry smile. "It's going to be all right. God didn't bring us this far to let us down now."

He darted a look at her. She amazed him sometimes. *Sometimes?* Who was he kidding? Most of the time.

"You're right," he said as he merged into the Knoxville traffic. "You're absolutely right."

• • •

Twenty minutes later they walked down the halls of Village Life Retirement Community. The facility looked more like a nice apartment complex than a nursing home. Beige carpet padded their footfalls, and potted plants and welcome mats greeted guests at each doorway. There were wall sconces beside each door, giving the homey illusion of porch lights.

"Nice place," Molly whispered.

Adam could only nod. His throat was dry, and he wished he'd brought in his water bottle. He spotted room 107 just ahead to the right and made an effort to regulate his breathing.

The white five-panel door was closed like all the others. They came to a stop on a generic green welcome mat.

Molly looked his way. "Anytime you're ready."

Adam tapped on the door. He wished he had a clue what Benjamin looked like now. He kept picturing the photo from 1964, but that was decades ago. There was so much riding on this meeting. So many things to tell Benjamin regarding Lizzie and the letter. So much Adam wanted to know. He was also nervous on his mom's behalf. He wanted to have good news for her.

A moment later the door swept open. A man about Adam's height leaned against a walker, peering at him through a pair of black-framed glasses. Though his face was lined with age, his dark hair now white, Adam could still see traces of the younger Benjamin in the sloped eyes and thick brows.

Adam cleared his throat. "Mr. Schwartz? I'm Adam Bradford." He shook the man's hand. "We spoke on the phone."

"Pleased to meet you, young man. You're right on time."

"This is Molly Bennett."

"The innkeeper." Benjamin shook her hand. "The one who found Lizzie's letter." Nothing wrong with his memory.

"Yes, sir," Molly said with a heart-stopping smile. "It's nice to finally meet you. We've been looking for you for weeks."

He returned her smile. "I've been right here all along. Please come in."

They followed him into a room that resembled a small hotel room with a few personal effects. Sunshine flooded through a picture window, making the room feel bright and cheerful, and the faint scent of pine cleaner hung in the air.

Benjamin's shoulders were slightly stooped, his movements a little slow as he trudged behind his walker. "I usually entertain in one of the community areas, but I thought this conversation could benefit from a little privacy, yes? I'm sorry; I should've offered you something to drink. Would you like some coffee or tea? I have one of those new-fangled pod machines."

"No, thank you," Adam said, and Molly also declined.

They seated themselves around a small circular dinette table.

"I have to admit," Benjamin said, "hearing from you the other day was quite a jolt. I've thought of Lizzie often over the years, but knowing she tried to contact me way back then leaves me with mixed feelings."

"I'm sure it does, Mr. Schwartz," Molly said. "We did bring the letter if you'd like to read it."

"Oh, wild horses couldn't stop me. I've driven myself crazy wondering what she might've said. And please, call me Ben."

Molly explained in detail how she'd found the letter and a little about their search. Adam slipped in a detail or two when he could stop studying the man long enough to contribute to the conversation.

When Ben laced his hands on the table Adam noticed a simple gold wedding band circling his finger. He met Molly's gaze and saw she'd noticed also. Adam quickly scanned the room for pictures of his family, but they were too far away.

"Here's the letter." Molly pulled it from her purse and slid it across the table. "Maybe we should give you some privacy. We could wait out in the lobby?"

Ben patted her hand. "No, that's quite all right,

dear. It's been a lot of years. I'm more eager than anything, so if you don't mind . . ."

"Go right ahead," Adam said.

The man pulled out the sheet and began reading.

Wanting to give him a modicum of privacy, Adam turned to Molly. She gave him an encouraging smile before her gaze began drifting around the room.

He did the same. There was a twin-size bed, neatly made, and a bureau, covered in photos and greeting cards. Beside the bureau was a waist-high bookcase, its shelves bowing slightly under the weight. Adam could read a few authors from where he sat: C. S. Lewis, Stephen King, Kurt Vonnegut. Quite the variety. He couldn't help but smile as he wondered at genetics. He also couldn't help but scan the shelves for his own books, but he didn't see any.

There was a hand-stitched wall hanging that read *Be still and know that I am God*. He shared another smile with Molly, his eyes lingering on hers for a moment, soaking in her composure. Her presence calmed him, he realized, and he was glad she was with him today.

"I will wait for you to come back to me," Ben read softly. *"I will wait four years or however long it takes, and we will become husband and wife as my heart has longed to do all along."*

Hands trembling, Ben folded up the letter, then

slid it back into its envelope. When he removed his glasses, his dark eyes were clouded with tears. He cleared his throat. "My goodness. I didn't expect it to hit me this hard."

Molly slipped him a tissue she must've fished from her purse. "It's an emotional letter. It's obvious how much she loved you."

"She sounds just as desperate as I felt at the time. I can't believe she wrote this. For years I . . . I thought she meant what she'd said. Not at first. At first I just thought her temper had gotten the best of her. But later . . . when I never heard from her . . . when I wrote her and never heard back . . ."

"You wrote her?" Adam asked.

"Several letters. I apologized for upsetting her so, and I begged her to wait for me."

"Her parents," Adam said.

"They must've intercepted the letters," Molly added.

Ben put his glasses back on. "I'm afraid you must be right."

A beat of silence ensued as though they all needed a moment to digest the revelation. It was staggering how such an action could change the course of a person's life. Multiple people's lives: Ben, Lizzie, Adam, and his mom, just to start.

Had Lizzie's lost letter and her parents' interference advanced God's will or gotten in the way of it? Maybe they'd never know. But here they were today, meeting Adam's grandfather. And Adam knew this meeting had been divinely orchestrated. It gave him the courage to continue.

"What brought on the argument, Mr.—Ben? If you don't mind my asking."

"That night I'd gone to her house to ask for her father's blessing. She warned me not to, but I didn't understand why until much later."

"Understand what?" Molly asked.

"Her daddy let me know in no uncertain terms that I wasn't good enough for his little girl. I was a janitor at the time, you see. Lizzie was of a different class. Her parents owned a store, and they were well to do.

"I felt lower than a worm by the time I left his house that night. Asking for Lizzie's hand had taken every bit of courage I could muster, and his rejection was a huge blow.

"Then I ran into Lizzie outside and we argued. She tried to tell me her father was prejudiced—I'm Jewish, you see. But I hardly registered what she was saying. He'd played on all my insecurities—and it worked. But I wasn't going to give up. I was determined to prove my worth. I was going to enlist so I could go to college and get a degree—and I did. I was blind to the fact that, in his eyes, I would always be nothing. I only realized later that I'd been in no frame of mind to be making important decisions. But Lizzie pressed me, and I just reacted."

"That's so sad," Molly said. "That one night, one mistake, could alter your future that way."

"It took me four years in the army, four years at university, and several years beyond that to realize Lizzie had been right all along. My worth had nothing to do with a job or a paycheck. My worth, everyone's worth, is based on God-given value.

"I tried to find her when I got out of the army, but her parents had moved away, and her friend wasn't there anymore. Nobody knew where Lizzie had gone. It was as if she'd just disappeared into thin air.

"It took a lot of years to get over her. Lizzie was . . ." Ben shook his head, a wistful smile playing over his lips. "She was something. I was head over heels for her."

Adam's gaze flickered down to Ben's hand. To the simple band, encircling his finger. "But you met somebody else, I see."

Ben twisted the band. "Yes, I did. My Rosa Lee. We met at the school where I ended up teaching. She was a kindergarten teacher, and it was her first year also. She befriended me, but I was still heartsick over Lizzie and a little reticent to have my heart broken again. Rosa Lee was patient with me. I finally got a clue and asked her out." He chuckled fondly. "We got married the next summer and taught in the same school through most of our careers. She was so good with children. It always grieved me so that—"

At his sudden silence Adam darted a look at Molly. She subtly lifted a shoulder.

"I'm afraid we weren't able to have children. I was grieved over it, but not like Rosa Lee. She poured herself into every child who passed through her class."

His mom had no siblings then. And now their news was even more significant. Because Ben did have a child after all.

But he also had a wife. Would she welcome a child another woman had been able to provide him? Adam wasn't a woman, much less a childless one, but it seemed as though that might be a bitter pill for any woman to swallow.

"I'm sorry," Molly said. "But I'm glad you were able to move on from Lizzie and find happiness with another woman."

"Yes, we were very happy. She was my best friend."

Were? Was? Adam's heart rate kicked up. He traded looks with Molly. Guilt stabbed at the hope he felt.

"She's been gone for four years now—complications with diabetes. She monitored it very carefully, but it's a tricky disease. I was always healthy as a horse, but it turns out my bones are quite brittle, and I fell and broke my hip a while back. Never fully came back from that, and here I am. It's a nice place though. Having no family, I like having a community so close."

"Do you get many visitors?" Molly asked.

"I have a wonderful church family where Rosa Lee and I served for years. They have a service here on Sundays just for me—well, it started out that way. Now, a dozen or so of my new friends attend too. And if they fall asleep my pastor doesn't seem to mind." His chuckle was deep and rich.

His health—his heart—was apparently fine. He had no wife. The last of the potential obstacles were gone; the pathway was clear. There was no reason not to tell Benjamin Schwartz that he did, indeed, have a child. That at this very moment he was sitting face-to-face with his grandson.

forty-four

Adam could feel Molly's gaze on him. She was waiting for him to make the next move.

Ben leaned back nonchalantly, just beginning to relax with them.

Adam hated to introduce shocking news, but there was no getting around it now. He shifted in his seat, taking a deep breath. "Ben . . . We brought two more letters with us. They're letters Lizzie sent to her friend Nonnie. You remember her?"

Ben smiled, as if remembering Nonnie fondly. "Oh, yes. We were pretty tight that summer. That Nonnie was a real character."

From his peripheral vision, Adam saw Molly reach into her purse.

"Lizzie wrote Nonnie these letters over the next year after you enlisted. I think it's important that you read them."

Ben's smile fell from his lips. He straightened in his chair, as if bracing himself for whatever came next. "All right."

Molly slid a letter over. "This is the first one. It was written in October of '64."

"Lizzie would've been in Ohio then, for her first semester at college." Ben frowned at the envelope, then his gaze slid between them. "Louisiana?"

Adam nodded at the letter.

Ben slid the paper from the envelope, unfolded it, and began reading to himself.

Molly gave him an encouraging smile and a tiny nod. He tried to remember what information the letter contained. That Lizzie had dropped out of college and had gone to live with her aunt. And the big news: that she was—

"Pregnant?" Ben whispered, looking from Adam to Molly. "She was pregnant?"

Before they could answer he was reading again. His breaths had turned ragged. His gnarled hand grasped his shirtfront.

The signs of distress worried Adam. He felt Molly's hand slide over his. She gave him a reassuring smile.

"Oh, dear God," Ben said, still reading. "They wanted her to give up our baby."

Adam closed his eyes. *Please, God.* It was all he could think to say. He could only imagine the shock Ben was feeling. The fear and regret that would surely follow.

When Ben finished reading he lowered the letter and removed his glasses. His eyes were wet with tears again. "How could they do that to her? She thought I didn't care about her? I would've moved heaven and earth—"

Molly covered his hand with hers. "Of course you would have."

"Did she have the baby? What happened to Lizzie? What happened to our child?"

"I know this is a lot to take in," Adam said. "I'm sorry to deliver such shocking news."

"Do you need a moment to catch your breath?" Molly asked.

A tear slipped down Ben's cheek. "I need to know what happened."

Adam gave Molly a nod, and she slid over the other letter. "This one was written in March."

Ben's fingers trembled so much he struggled with the envelope. When he finally had the letter in his hands he slipped on his glasses again and began reading.

This one explained about the adoptive couple and expounded on Lizzie's grief at having to give up her child. It was heartbreaking, and Adam wished he could spare the man from knowing of Lizzie's misery.

Most of all he hoped the forthcoming news would make it all worthwhile.

Ben lowered the letter, his gaze connecting with Adam's, then Molly's. "Did it happen then? Did they make her give up our baby?"

"Yes," Adam said. "I'm afraid they did. To the couple she mentioned in the letter. Nonnie filled in the rest of the details for us. She was in contact with Lizzie for a while, but as you can see she was sworn to secrecy."

Ben stared at Adam, but he was obviously lost in thought. Lost in another time and place, where grief and misery were close companions.

Adam leaned forward, placing a hand on the man's arm. "Ben . . . You have a daughter."

A tear trickled down the man's cheek. He removed his glasses again. "I have a baby girl. Only she's not a baby anymore, is she? My goodness, she'd be—in her fifties by now."

"Yes," Adam said.

"I've missed so much. I can hardly believe this."

"I'm so sorry for all that's happened," Molly said. "For all you've missed. But I promise all the sadness will be worth it."

Ben's eyes darted between Adam and Molly. "Do you know where she is—my daughter? I have to find her. Is there any way to find her?"

Molly gave Adam a pointed look.

His heart stuttered at what lay ahead. He hoped Ben would be delighted by the news. But what if it backfired? What if his grandfather found him just as lacking as his father had?

Desperation flickered in the man's eyes. "I have a daughter out there somewhere."

"Yes, sir. You do." Adam's insecurities faded in light of the man's distress. He swallowed hard against the lump swelling in his throat. "And we've already found her."

He'd planned, if it came to this, that he would back up and tell the man the whole story, starting years ago with his mother's adoption. But the desperation in Ben's eyes begged Adam to skip to the chase.

"Your daughter"—Adam's voice trembled—"is my mother."

Ben blinked at Adam. Confusion furrowed his brow.

The air conditioner kicked on, humming quietly.

"My mother was born Catherine Sue Mays on May 3, 1965. She was adopted by my grandparents. He was a banker and she was a stay-at-home—" He gave his head a shake. He was getting too bogged down in details.

"I don't understand," Ben said. "This doesn't make sense. You just happened to be in Bluebell, and this gal here found the letter while you were there, and it just so happens that your mother is my daughter?"

It really did sound absurd, and Adam knew he should elucidate. Too bad emotions were crawling all over his mind, spinning a sticky web that trapped all his words of explanation.

Molly squeezed Adam's hand. "I know it must sound impossible, Ben. But here's how it happened."

And then she told the story of his mother's search for her birth mother years ago, which had led her to Bluebell. "Lizzie had already passed by then, but Catherine fell in love with the town. And so when Adam was searching for a place to set—" She stopped suddenly, her gaze darting to Adam, seeking guidance.

"I'm an author." Adam couldn't tell the man anything but the full truth. And, in truth, it felt good to say it out loud. Really good. "I needed a place to set my next novel, and I went to Bluebell to find inspiration—on my mother's recommendation."

"He came to my inn, and I found the letter and asked for his help. The rest is history."

"When we discovered Nonnie had been friends with Lizzie, we enlisted her help too."

"But she didn't tell us about the pregnancy," Molly added. "Not until just this week."

"And then yesterday when I was talking to my mom, she happened to mention my grandfather being a banker, and I suddenly put two and two together. I asked her what her birth mother's name was, and she told me—it was Elizabeth Van Buren."

Ben shook his head, looking starstruck. "That sounds . . ."

"Impossible?" Molly asked on a wry laugh.

Ben stared intently at Adam. "Providential."

Adam cleared his throat, his insecurities rising like floodwaters. "Of course, we can do a DNA test if you like. It's a simple matter of a mouth swab."

"But we're 100 percent certain Catherine is your daughter," Molly said. "There was only one Elizabeth Van Buren in Bluebell, and she was Catherine's birth mother. Which, of course, makes Adam—"

"I know this is a lot to take in." Adam's heart was beating like a bass drum in his chest. "But my mother lives in Austin, Texas, and she's very eager to meet you if you're willing."

"There's nothing I'd love more." Ben stared intently at Adam for a long moment. "You're my grandson."

Adam swallowed hard. "Yes, sir."

"Your only one, apparently," Molly added. "Adam's an only child."

His grandfather's eyes drifted over Adam's features. The man seemed to see everything with those eyes of his. Right down to his soul.

The back of Adam's neck heated at his scrutiny. He shifted in his seat, thinking of all the reasons Ben might find him lacking. His unremarkable height and build. His nerdy demeanor. His social incompetency.

"You have her eyes," Ben choked out. "The same color, like a stormy sky, I used to tell her. And you have my hairline." He chuckled, palming his forehead. "Well. The hairline I used to have."

Adam breathed a laugh.

Ben's smile fell away, a look of wonder sweeping over his features. "My *grandson*." He reached out and pulled Adam into an embrace. "Imagine that. Just imagine that."

Adam's arms wrapped around the man's frail shoulders.

"Do you see this, Rosa Lee?" Ben's voice warbled. "Just look at my fine young grandson. Thank you, God. This is beyond belief. My heart is so full. How can I love someone so much—someone I only just met?"

Adam closed his eyes against the sting, swallowed against the knot in his throat. He felt so many things in the arms of his grandfather. Acceptance. Belonging. All of it instantaneous. His heart thumped wildly at the foreign concept.

His grandfather trembled in his arms, and when he drew away he was wiping his face. "And you're an author, you said?"

"He's very famous," Molly inserted. "And an exceptional writer."

Adam shot her a look even as his face warmed at the pride on her face.

"Of course he is," Ben said. "That's wonderful. I used to write a bit, you know. Well, it was just poetry, probably a bunch of schmaltzy drivel, but you must've gotten some of that aptitude from me, yes?"

His hopeful tone made Adam's lips quirk. "It's quite likely, sir."

"Grandpa," Ben corrected, his face beaming. "You must call me Grandpa. Now tell me everything about you. And don't leave out a single thing."

forty-five

Molly watched the rolling landscape pass as they headed east on 40, a smile permanently etched on her face. They'd stayed at the nursing home for over three hours, some of which she'd excused herself for—Adam and his grandfather needed time alone. The sound of their laughter when she returned was music to her soul. As was the serenity on Adam's face as they left the home.

She knew just enough of his insecurities to realize what his grandfather's acceptance must mean to him. She'd been holding her breath as Adam made the announcement, praying the man would receive the news gladly. She'd wept tears of joy when they embraced.

Molly gave a happy sigh. *Well, God, that sure was an amazing thing You did.*

Looking back, she was in awe of how everything had transpired this summer. She was even finding closure for her own wounds. They were healing more by the second. She could feel God working in and around her to complete His good work.

Thank You.

"We took pictures," Adam said into his headset. He'd been talking with his mom since they'd left Knoxville. "I'll send all of them to you . . . Yes,

yes. He's very eager to meet you too . . . I don't know. The sooner the better, I think . . . Yes, I know . . . Well, we'll have to work all that out."

Adam chuckled. "You're going to love him, Mom. He'll be able to tell you all about your birth mother too. He really loved her. He was so distraught when he first heard about Lizzie having to give you up that he cried . . . I know. It was difficult to watch."

Molly didn't want to think about that part of the day. She wanted to remember the look of wonder that had come over Ben's face when he realized he was sitting across from his grandson. Precious. Eyes watering, she placed her palm against her chest. Her heart felt so full.

The blurry landscape passed as they grew closer and closer to Bluebell. To home. Her home, not Adam's, she reminded herself. The thought that had been trying to push to the foreground for days surfaced now.

He was leaving in the morning. Flying back to New York. There would be no reason for him to return to Bluebell. The town would just be a pleasant memory he'd revisit as he wrote his story. She didn't know if she'd even be able to bear reading it when it released. But how could she keep from it when it would be her only connection to Adam? Her only chance to "see" him again?

She pressed her palm harder against a heart

that had gone from full to heavy in the span of a minute. He'd be dropping her off at the inn soon. Maybe a clean break was for the best. She had some groundwork to do herself. She needed to learn to trust again. She couldn't bring fear of getting hurt into a relationship—certainly not a relationship that had already been scarred by a small betrayal.

Plus he was leaving. That again. The clock was ticking down. The tires were quickly eating up the miles between Knoxville and Bluebell.

Adam's chuckle drew her from her thoughts. He'd begun repeating parts of the story, his mother obviously feeding off every detail. Who could blame her? Molly could hear Adam's love for her in his patient tone. She had a feeling that the closeness they enjoyed would soon grow to encompass the elderly man they'd just left.

Molly would comfort herself with that thought when memories of this summer threatened to drag her under. And she was certain they would.

Adam didn't hang up until they were nearly to Bluebell. "Sorry about that. She was so excited."

"Of course she was."

"She said to tell you thank you for all you've done to make this happen."

Molly shrugged. "I just stumbled upon a letter."

"You did a lot more than that."

"When will she come to see him?"

"She's going to have to figure that out. She has a few things on her calendar to work around, but she's hoping to make the trip within the month. She's going to call him tonight though. Can you imagine? Meeting your father for the first time at her age?"

"Not to mention Ben meeting his child for the first time at his age. Good thing he has a strong heart."

"No kidding. The poor guy received a lot of shocking news today. He held up pretty well."

"He was a trouper." She gave Adam a warm smile. "He discovered he has a wonderful daughter and grandson to love. That must be the best kind of day."

He cut her a look. "It went really well, didn't it?"

"Couldn't have gone better. I'm so happy for you, Adam. Seeing you with Ben was really sweet. The way he looked at you was something to see."

"I'm still a little astounded, I think."

"Who could blame you? It'll settle in, though. You'll be just fine." He would be. She suspected all of this had changed him in some really good ways.

They rounded a curve, and Bluebell Lake came into view, sparkling in the late afternoon sun. She was home. Adam would drop her off and say good-bye, and that would be that.

The ache blossomed in her chest, spreading outward. She cleared her throat. "So . . . I guess you're leaving in the morning."

"Bright and early. Ten a.m. flight out of Charlotte. I haven't even packed yet. I was too focused on today."

"I imagine it'll be good to get home again."

There was a long pause. "I have plenty to keep me busy. Lots of writing ahead of me, and a release coming up next week."

"That's right. *Under the Starry Sky*. I'm looking forward to it."

"I hope you enjoy it."

It was as if they were strangers. She closed her eyes against the sting. She had nobody to blame but herself. She was the one who'd shut him down. But now—after such an emotional day— wasn't the time to resurrect any of that.

"I'm sure I will," she said.

Adam put the car in park, his heart tripping in his chest. He couldn't even look at Molly. Instead he stared out the windshield, his eyes zooming in on the sprawling inn.

That's where it had all begun. Where he'd found Molly. Where he'd mistaken her for his muse, only to find she was actually the keeper of his heart.

He tightened his sweaty grip on the steering wheel.

Molly's seat belt detached with a click. "Well, I guess this is it."

"I can walk you to the door."

"No, that's all right. You have a lot of packing to do."

A vise tightened around his heart. It was as if she wanted to be rid of him.

"It's been an amazing day," she said.

"An amazing summer." And all because of Molly's persistence. He turned to her, taking her in one last time. That silky soft hair, those amber eyes, so serious just now.

"Thank you for inviting me on this journey with you," he said. "If you hadn't, I never would've found my grandfather."

"It was meant to be." She twisted the straps of her purse in the silence.

He kept waiting for her to rattle on in that endearing way of hers. Nervous energy. But she seemed short on words just now, and the car remained quiet. The air seemed to be charged, a low hum thrumming in the background.

Did she still have hard feelings about what he'd done? She said she'd forgiven him, but he didn't want to leave anything unfinished. "I really am sorry, Molly, about before. About hurting you. I'll always regret what I did." She had no idea how much.

Molly just waved him away, giving him a warm smile. "We've already covered that. It's been a pleasure, Adam." The tremble in her voice about broke his heart. "You're a kind, wonderful man, and I'm glad you came to Bluebell. I'm glad you stayed at our inn. And I'm glad I got to know you."

The lump in his throat swelled. Her words were kind and gracious. But there was something in her eyes, a little flicker of fear that reminded him of the night of her mother's birthday.

Her glassy eyes tugged at his heart. He loosened his grip on the steering wheel and took her hand. It felt so delicate in his. He lifted it, pressing his lips to the back of it. Her skin was silky smooth and scented with jasmine.

He forced words past his achy throat. "The pleasure was all mine, Molly Bennett."

"Take care, Adam." Her smile wobbled as she released his hand. And then she was gone. Slipping from his life as suddenly as she'd slipped in to it.

forty-six

The sidewalks bustled outside the glass windows at the restaurant where Adam and Jordan were meeting for dinner. Inside the restaurant the sounds of clinking silverware punctuated the low buzz of conversation. The delicious aroma of grilled steak made Adam's stomach growl.

He took a slow sip of ice water.

Jordan was droning on about movie rights and contractual obligations, and Adam resumed watching the passersby, rushing from work to home or wherever they were going after their busy days at the office.

He liked the city. It was an environment he'd always thrived in. He often wrote at a coffee shop, preferably at the bar where the blur of life continued just beyond his laptop screen.

This past week he hadn't been writing much though. He'd mostly been ruminating. And he'd been on the phone with his grandfather and with his mom. She'd gone to meet him earlier this week, extending her stay in Knoxville to three nights. It seemed the two had bonded quickly. It was good to hear his mom so enthusiastic.

Jordan had shifted the topic to Adam's next novel and was about to start pushing him about his deadline. He could smell it coming.

It was probably time to tell his agent what had been building inside him over the past week. He did feel inspired to write—more than he had in a long time.

Just not by the plot he'd been working on all summer. Another story was now living and breathing inside him, aching to be told. It featured a strong, cheerful innkeeper, a lost letter, and a happily-ever-after.

Well. He'd have to use his imagination on that last part.

Sure, the hero wasn't Nathaniel Quinn's usual type. He was flawed and rather ordinary. But he was special in his own way. The heroine would recognize that and so, he hoped, would the reader.

"And when it airs," Jordan continued in business monotone, "it'll premiere first on Mars, then Jupiter and Uranus and so on and so forth."

"If we're going in order it would be Saturn next, not Uranus. But if you're going by size it would be Mercury, Mars, Venus, then Earth, followed by—"

"All right, all right. You can daydream *and* listen. But you have to admit you've been a little spacey lately, pardon the pun. And I have a feeling you're still on planet Earth." Jordan gave him a pointed look. "Just not necessarily in New York."

"You're right. You're right. I've mostly been in Bluebell—the setting of my work-in-progress."

Jordan gave a nod of approval. "Well at least you've been writing. I'll count my blessings."

"Yeah . . . about that."

Jordan's hand paused, his glass midway between table and mouth. A look of dread moved over his features. "Adam . . . please don't tell me—"

"You can scrap the outline I sent you. I'm starting fresh."

"Your deadline is in—"

"Eight weeks. I know. Don't worry; I'll make the deadline." Having vocalized the idea that had been swelling inside for days, relief washed over him. He was suddenly more certain than ever that this was right.

"I already sent your outline to Rosewood Press, and Elaine loves it."

"That's unfortunate. But she'll like this one better. And so will my readers."

Jordan leaned in on his elbows. "There's nothing wrong with the story you were working on. It's good. It has all the elements readers expect in a Nathaniel Quinn story."

"You're right. There's nothing wrong with it." Adam paused pointedly. "But it's not the story I need to write."

Jordan slunk back in his chair, studying his friend. They'd been together a long time. No one knew Adam better.

Slowly, resignation crept over Jordan's features.

He drew in a breath and blew it out. "Fine. Send me the outline. I'll look it over."

"I don't need an outline for this story. Trust me, Jordan. I've got this. And while you're at it . . ."

He took a moment to reassess his decision, making certain. His grandfather's words had played repeatedly in his mind. It had taken Ben years to realize that his worth or lack thereof wasn't based on his job or paycheck or even his ethnicity. And Adam's certainly wasn't based on someone else's expectations, not even his father's. In fact, his father's disappointment hadn't been caused by a deficiency in Adam at all, but a deficiency in his father.

Adam was sufficient just the way he was, because he'd been lovingly and intentionally created by God Himself. Molly and his grandfather had helped him see that.

"And while I'm at it . . ." Jordan prodded, obviously growing impatient.

Adam leaned on his elbows. "You can tell Rosewood Press I'll do the interview with *Newsline Tonight*."

Jordan's eyebrows popped. He gave his head a quick shake before he homed in on Adam, studying him through the eyes of a friend. "Who are you?"

He was Adam Bradford—and also bestselling author Nathaniel Quinn. The truth felt real. Good. Freeing.

He was ready for this. Adam's lips turned up. "I think I'm ready to embrace my true identity, my friend."

Jordan broke out into a smile. "Well, hallelujah. It's about time."

forty-seven

Molly slouched against her pillows, holding the book in her hands—Nathaniel Quinn's newest release. She'd been at the bookstore bright and early this morning as Mr. Delbert was flipping the *Open* sign.

She ran her fingers over the cover, over the raised letters of Nathaniel's name. It was a beautiful image: a night setting, the starry sky seeming to stretch on and on. In the foreground a couple cuddled in the bed of an old red truck. As beautiful as the cover was, she was certain the story inside was even better.

She had yet to open it though. And it wasn't as if she hadn't had time today. It was a slow Tuesday. After cleaning two rooms and helping Miss Della with kitchen cleanup, she'd gone to Skye's studio for yoga. Molly filled her friend in on all the details of the Knoxville trip, while neatly dodging the questions about Adam. Skye hadn't been fooled.

Molly wasn't ready to go there yet, not even with her best friend. She was . . . mourning, she supposed. It was the only word that adequately described the hollow, achy feeling in her chest. She missed Adam the same way she missed her mom and dad. The only difference was . . .

She looked at the cover, her heart squeezing tight. Adam was still living. But somehow that only made it worse. Right now he was walking around Manhattan somewhere, living his life as if he'd never met Molly at all.

And it hurt. She'd had a lot of trauma the past two years. But Skye had helped her through Dominic and the loss of her parents. She'd help Molly through this too.

"Molly!" Grace hollered up the staircase, loud as you please. "Molly, come here!"

Molly started to reprimand her, but what was the point? They had no guests tonight anyway.

Still, she got up from the bed and padded over to the railing. "Have you ever heard of an indoor voice? Or texting? I could've been—"

"You have to come here! Right now." Grace dashed toward the living room.

Molly rolled her eyes even as she followed orders. Recipe crisis? Nail emergency? Local tragedy? No, she wouldn't think that way. Grace seemed excited, not upset. Maybe she'd booked a winter wedding party. That would be worth whooping over.

But when Molly entered the living room, Grace and Levi were standing behind the couch, staring at the TV, blocking her view.

Levi turned to her. "Did you know about this?"

"Know about what?"

And then she saw it. Him. On the TV. He

looked so handsome in a V-neck sweater with a collared shirt. Her heart stuttered at the sight. He looked a little nervous. Well, who wouldn't be? He was on national TV.

"What is this?" she croaked.

"Adam is that author you love," Levi said.

"Turn it up, turn it up!" Grace said.

Levi complied.

Adam's words reached Molly's ears, that familiar low voice making her heart turn over in her chest.

"I was just channel surfing and there he—"

"Shhhh!" Molly and Grace said.

On the screen Adam paused, nudging up his glasses. The familiarity of that gesture sent a ripple of longing through her.

"That's a good question, Martina," Adam was saying. "I guess the most authentic answer is that I'm known for writing larger-than-life heroes— and yet I've always felt so ordinary myself."

Martina Lopez appeared on the screen, wearing that infamous compassion like a cozy sweater. "Is that why you wanted to keep your identity a secret?"

"I guess when it comes down to it I was a little afraid of disappointing my readers."

The camera focused on Martina. "It's hard to believe that an author who has, literally, millions of fans might be dealing with any level of insecurity."

"And yet I was. I write characters who deal with all sorts of issues because it's real. It's true. We all have flaws we have to sort out and obstacles we need to overcome. That's just part of life."

"And yet here you are, on the release date of your highly anticipated next novel, on national TV, telling the world who you are. What happened to change your perspective?"

Adam paused, breaking eye contact with the host. A sheen of perspiration had broken out across his forehead.

Molly was rooting so hard for him she wanted to jump in front of the camera and answer for him.

"A lot happened to me this summer," Adam said finally. "Personal things I'd rather not get into. Suffice it to say I met a lot of amazing people, and I learned so much about myself. But mostly I've come to realize that we're all just ordinary people."

"So this sort of coming-out . . . It's going to be life-changing, you know. You have millions of readers, and now they know who you are, what you look like. Do you think you're ready for that?"

"I hope I am. I know it feels authentic. It feels freeing to be honest about who I am. And while my desire for anonymity may have allowed me to live in comfortable obscurity for a while—it also cost me the one thing I most value."

Martina tilted her head. "And what is that?"

Adam gave a wistful smile, those intelligent eyes glittering under the studio lights. "Love," he said simply.

Martina's dark eyebrows rose. "It sounds as if that might apply to someone in particular."

He gave a furtive smile. "It definitely does. But I'm not telling *all* my secrets tonight."

"And there we have it," Martina said. "The mysterious and elusive author Nathaniel Quinn— still a bit of a mystery. And maybe that's exactly as it should be."

The camera panned out as the show's theme music began, then Martina wrapped up the segment.

Molly's hand was clutching the material of her pajama top. Her breaths were shallow. She was unable to tear her eyes from the screen even after the network broke for a commercial.

Adam had just revealed his identity. On national TV no less. Molly wondered at the courage that act had taken. He'd just changed the rest of his life. More important was the motivation behind the act: Adam had obviously come to a place of peace about who he was.

Because of Benjamin Schwartz. Because of that letter. Perhaps a little bit because of Molly herself. But mostly because God had sent him on a journey of discovery this summer.

All things work together for the good of those who love God . . .

Gooseflesh raced down Molly's arms.

She thought of Lizzie and Ben, needlessly separated from each other. She thought of her parents, taken from her so suddenly.

But Adam was still here.

"Did you know?" Levi's question snapped her from her reverie. "Did he tell you?"

Molly gave a wistful smile. "Yes, he told me." *In Italian.*

Grace grabbed her arm. "He was talking about you, wasn't he? He's in love with you."

"I—I don't know."

But she did know, didn't she? She remembered the look on his face last week just before he'd pressed that kiss to her hand. She remembered his exquisite kindness and the last overture he'd made that night in the park. It must've taken such courage for him to try again.

And she'd told him no.

Why in the world had she told him no? Sure, she was still afraid. Nobody liked having her heart broken. But why was she letting fear keep her from the thing she wanted most? Isn't that just what Adam had been doing all these years— hiding from the public? She'd been hiding from love.

He'd been brave. She could be brave too.

Molly turned toward the stairs. "I have to go now."

"What are you doing?" Levi asked.

"I need to see him."

"Ever heard of the phone?" Grace asked.

"I can't do this over the phone."

"You can't drive all night either." She heard the worry in Levi's voice. "That's not safe. Wait till morning."

Molly stopped at the first step. "There's no way I'll be able to sleep tonight anyway."

"Give me five minutes," Grace said. "I'll book you a flight."

"I don't have that much in savings."

"You're in love with the man, and anyone could see he makes you happy. We'll pitch in, true love and all that." Grace gave her brother a pointed look. "Won't we, Levi?"

Levi sighed, looking hard at Molly. After a moment his eyes began softening.

Molly could almost see his purse strings loosening, one stiff thread at a time.

"For once I agree with Spendy here," Levi said reluctantly. "Go ahead and book the flight, little sis."

forty-eight

Adam's morning had been as chaotic as he expected. He'd been on the phone, starting early with drive-time radio interviews, scarfing down breakfast between shows. Having seen the coming wave of publicity, Rosewood had arranged a landline to be installed in his flat yesterday.

After last night's reveal, Jordan had gotten calls and emails from all the major national networks. It seemed everyone wanted an interview. His publisher was over the moon at all the publicity opportunities and was already rushing to a second printing.

A last-minute release tour was in the works too. Adam would leave next week on a thirty-day tour. He'd requested a stop in Knoxville and Austin because he had personal business there. He'd been tempted to suggest Charlotte or Asheville too, but why torture himself?

In light of his upcoming schedule Rosewood had even offered to extend the deadline on his work-in-progress.

But the story was burning like an inferno inside him. He'd gotten up at three, restless, and had penned the first words of his new novel. The first four chapters had poured out of him before his first radio interview, and he couldn't wait to get back to it.

This amazing feeling of inspiration and freedom was dampened only by his grieving over Molly. He missed her. He'd never missed anyone so much in all his life.

Adam chased the thought away as he paced his kitchen. He was currently on hold while WOWO out of Fort Wayne, Indiana, broke for commercial.

"And we're back with Adam Bradford—AKA bestselling author Nathaniel Quinn," the DJ said. "Adam, you just had a book release . . . *Under the Starry Sky*. Looks intriguing. Tell us a little about the story and what inspired it."

Adam went into automatic, describing the plot as succinctly as possible and going into the back story. It was set near his hometown in Texas and inspired in part by a childhood friend who'd served in the Marines and lost a limb in Afghanistan.

He was answering another question about the book when his doorbell rang. Adam frowned at the door. He'd placed a hold on his landline and shut off his cell so he wouldn't be interrupted during the live shows. But he hadn't thought to put a Do Not Disturb sign on the door.

Hopefully it was UPS or FedEx, and they'd simply drop the package and go.

But no, the doorbell rang again. Adam cringed at the background noise. He rushed across his apartment, regretful for the first time of the spacious living area. He twisted the lock, trying to follow the host's line of questioning, and whooshed open the door, already lifting his shushing finger.

His breath froze in his lungs. His finger paused midair. His brain ceased functioning, and his chest tightened until he thought he might be having a heart attack at the ripe old age of thirty. But no, that was just anxiety talking. Adam blinked, in case he was hallucinating.

Molly gave a sheepish smile and waggled her fingers.

Nope. Still there.

Molly.

In the city.

Standing right here on his doorstep. For all of ten seconds now.

He opened the door wider and gestured her inside. The apple-y scent of her wrapped around him like a favorite memory.

"Mr. Bradford, are you still there?" the DJ was asking.

The interview. Dead air. "Um, yes, sorry. Go ahead."

"I was just asking about your writing process. Do you plot out your books or do you tend to write by the seat of your pants?"

"Right, right." Adam waved Molly toward the sofa, soaking up her presence.

She really was here in his apartment. She must've seen the interview. Which meant she'd heard him talk about love. Heat flooded his face. Why had he mentioned that? On the other hand . . . She was here, wasn't she? That seemed promising.

Dead air. He gave his head a shake, facing the wall of windows so he could concentrate.

"Ah, I'm definitely a plotter." Adam managed to rattle on about his process for a solid minute before he let himself look at Molly again. She gave him a nervous smile. She was twisting her purse straps. Biting her lip.

"And that's about it, as far as my writing process goes." He had to wrap this up. "I really appreciate your taking the time to interview me this morning, but I, ah, I have to go now." He winced at the clumsy ending, but it couldn't be helped. How could he possibly think straight with Molly sitting here, watching him?

And why exactly was she here again?

"Uh, of course," the DJ said. "Thank you for joining us, Mr. Bradford."

The DJ began wrapping up the show, including all the information about his book, website, and upcoming tour, which would make his publicity team happy.

Molly's heart was hammering against her ribs as Adam paced the gigantic room. His apartment was luxurious, all beige and black, leather and steel, with clean simple lines.

There were a few pictures and personal effects strewn about. A photo of Adam on a gondola ride with, presumably, his mother. Venice. Adam with an older couple in a mountain setting. A quilted throw that looked out of place on his sophisticated sofa. A stack of magazines and such. Oh, those were from Bluebell. She spotted their local things-to-do directory and the brochure for the Bluebell Baptist Youth Camp. There was a phone number scrawled in Adam's neat handwriting.

She blinked at it.

And then Adam was hanging up the phone. He set it on the nearest table. "Molly . . ." he said finally. "You're here."

The scrape of his voice abraded her heart. "It was you," she said.

"What?"

She gestured toward the pamphlet. "The youth camp. You were the anonymous donor. The one who saved the camp."

He ducked his head, pushed up his glasses.

She should have known. He was nothing like her ex-boyfriend. While Dominic had practically shouted to the world that he had the means and desire to save the camp, Adam had just quietly gone about it. So Adam.

"I can't believe you're here." Adam perched on

an overstuffed armchair across from her. Too far away. Looking right at her.

His appraisal sent her heart into overdrive. He looked amazing in a white button-up, rolled up at the sleeves. His six o'clock shadow and tousled hair gave him that derelict, Ryan Gosling, end-of-*The-Notebook* vibe.

But unlike Noah Calhoun, Adam's disheveled appearance no doubt had more to do with a sudden life change than a heartbreak over a woman. Over her.

But was he glad to see her? Even just a little? She thought she'd be able to tell at first glance. But he'd been on the phone—a radio interview, no less—and his expression had given away nothing. Well, surprise. There had definitely been that.

"I'm sorry I interrupted your interview. I should've called." Because maybe he was going to reject her, and wouldn't that have been so much easier to handle over the phone?

He was looking at her with an inscrutable expression. What she wouldn't have given for just a little clue to his thoughts.

"What are you doing here, Molly?"

Her laugh was too loud in the quiet space. "Good question."

She was starting to wonder that herself. Because Adam was suddenly the most intriguing man in pop culture. Millions of readers were clamoring for more of him. Female readers. Unfortunately, she hadn't really thought of that until now. His talk of love on last night's interview might've even been a publicity stunt. Also a new thought—and not a happy one.

"I assume you, ah, saw the interview?"

"Yes, the last bit, at least." Molly shook her head. "I still can't believe you were on national TV."

"I'm still coming to grips with that one myself."

"It's great, though, Adam. Obviously it's paying off big . . . radio interviews, a book tour . . ."

"It's been a little crazy around here this morning."

"Right. Again, I'm sorry to disrupt your morning, and I hope I can say this without sounding condescending but . . . I'm really proud of you, Adam. A little in awe too, frankly. That took tremendous courage—and that's coming from someone who's been working on that particular trait. You make it look easy. I'm babbling. Sorry. I guess I'm nervous."

"Trust me, I can relate."

Nervous for last night's interview or nervous right now, with her? And all this talk of courage reminded her she'd flown all this way for a reason. She had something to say that couldn't be said on the phone. And just because she was suddenly feeling uncertain and insecure didn't mean she could just call it off. She was working on courage, and come hell or high water, she was going through with this.

"Adam, I heard what you said about, uh, love." She stared at her fingers because she couldn't bring herself to meet his gaze. "I don't know how much of it was . . . Well, I guess it doesn't matter anyway because I'm going to say what I came to say even if—is it hot in here?"

The air in her lungs felt hot and stuffy. The back of her neck was warm, as was her face and everything but her hands, which were strangely cold.

"My flat faces the east, and sunny mornings can raise the temperature by as much as seven degrees." He got up and pointed a remote, and the blinds slid neatly over the windows with a quiet hum.

"Oh, that's handy."

"I can turn up the air if you like."

The closing shades instantly changed the room's temperature and mood. "No, that's good. Thank you."

She got up, too nervous to remain seated anymore, and walked toward him, reminding herself with every step to be brave. She stopped when she was an arm's length away and forced herself to meet his gaze.

"So I flew a long way to be here, and you must be wondering why. The thing is, I heard what you said, about love, I mean, and I don't know if you meant it or not, but I knew with sudden clarity that I'd made a mistake before—that night in the park. I was afraid—just like you were of revealing your identity, only I was afraid of getting my heart broken again, given what Dominic did, and I know that's not really fair to you, but I'm just putting that out there. The thing is, I've really missed you since you left, and when I saw you on TV last night, I knew. I just knew."

"Knew what?" His voice was low and smoky. And was that an almost smile hovering around those familiar lips?

"Um, right, that." Now or never. Fight or flight. Fear or faith. She gazed into his soulful eyes. The pools of blue were as inviting as a swimming hole on a hot summer day.

"I knew that I loved you," she breathed. "Still love you, I mean, present tense. I *love* you. Wow, it shouldn't be that hard to say it, should it, but I think I've felt that way for quite a while now, only I was too afraid to take a leap of—"

And then his mouth was on hers, strong and firm and confident. And what was a girl to do but lose all train of thought? She threw herself into the kiss with equal abandon, relishing the familiar feel, touch, and taste of him.

He palmed her face, his fingers pushing back into her hair, sending shivers down her arms. She put her arms around his waist, her hands coming to rest against the hard planes of his back.

But it was his lips . . . The man knew how to kiss. She was pretty sure he'd ruined her for every other man.

But as perfect as this was . . . he hadn't said the words. And she needed the words.

"Wait." She pressed back, allowing just enough space for their breaths to mingle. "Wait, do you . . . do you feel the same way? I mean, it's all right if you don't, but I'm not going to lie, I definitely have a preference—"

He put his fingers gently over her lips, a twinkle in his eyes. "I thought the kiss made it fairly obvious. But yes, Molly Bennett. I *loved* you, and I *love* you, past and present—and also future."

Her chest gave a snug squeeze and her eyes stung just a little. "Aw. That was really nice. Maybe you should be a writer or something."

Somewhere on another planet a phone was ringing.

"Shoot." Adam drew away, checking his watch. "I have another interview, and it's live. I forgot to call in. Some crazy woman showed up on my doorstep, distracting me with talk of love."

Lips twitching, Molly pushed him toward the phone. "Well, you'd better take it. Your public awaits."

Her heartbeat began to steady as she watched Adam take the call. She heard him expound upon the story he'd written as well as the story of his life. All the while he watched her right back. And she couldn't help but think that as much as she adored all of his stories, she would always love theirs the very best of all.

Epilogue

The hot summer months gave way to a cool, crisp fall. The leaves were turning shades of gold and red that made Molly stop and stare in wonder at the mountains surrounding her beautiful little lake town.

Business had fallen off a bit but not to the point that Levi was panicking. They'd anticipated this and set back some of their profits to make it through the slower season.

Grace had started her senior year, and volleyball season was underway. The slower pace allowed Molly and Levi to take turns attending her games. For senior night they'd closed the inn, and flanking Grace, they'd walked her proudly across the court. Though they wished their parents could've been there for the honor, they were a team, a family, and nothing was more important than being there for each other. There hadn't been a dry eye in the house. And Molly may have blubbered like a baby.

As for Molly and Adam, they talked on the phone every day, Skyped often, and he even—be still her heart—sent her the occasional love letter in the mail. Those went a long way toward balancing the difficulties of a long-distance relationship. But the time spent talking from afar had also given them a chance to grow closer.

In early October she drove to Tennessee for a Bradford family reunion. There she met Adam's mother, who immediately grabbed Molly and wrapped her up in a big Texas hug. They took Adam's grandpa to Gatlinburg for the weekend and rented a "cabin," which was actually an extravagant lodge. Adam obviously enjoyed spoiling his family.

Molly missed him as October flowed into November. His tour was over but he was still traveling for interviews and speaking engagements and writing when he had the chance.

The inn had hosted a wedding party over the weekend, which kept the Bennetts busy and helped their revenue stream. But seeing the happy young couple, so in love, made Molly long for her man.

Levi and Grace had tolerated her heartsick sighs with eye rolls.

Molly ran a dustrag carefully over the flower stand—yes, the very flower stand Adam had assisted her in assembling. A wistful grin tugged her lips at the memory of his entrance into the inn, into her life. She should've known she was a goner right then.

The stool behind the counter scraped the floor as Levi stood, stretching. "Can you watch the desk a few minutes? I have to go upstairs."

"Can't Grace do it? I was about to get my clothes out of the dryer."

"This won't take long."

"Well, hurry, I don't want my clothes to wrinkle. You know how I hate to iron." She raised her voice because he was already halfway up the stairs.

"I think we got a package," Levi called down. "Can you check the porch?"

"Sure, why not?" she mumbled to herself.

She dropped the dustrag and opened the door. Sure enough, a padded manila envelope sat midway between the door and steps. She stepped out and picked it up. The package was heavy and thick.

She turned it over, frowning at it. Odd. It didn't have a return address. Or even a mailing address for that matter. Confused, she looked up, looked around.

And that's when she saw him, sitting calm as you please on the porch swing.

Her lips parted. "Adam!"

He stood up just in time to catch her. His laughter rumbled right through her chest. "Glad to see me, are you?"

She hugged him hard. "Of course I am. What are you doing here? Why didn't you tell me you were coming?" She caught his face and laid a big one on him. Oh, it was so good to see that face. "You could've called, you know. A girl likes time to put on makeup and maybe dress for the occasion."

His blue eyes pierced hers, and her heart gave a heavy flop. "You couldn't possibly look more beautiful to me than you do right now."

Well. What was she supposed to say to that?

The heavy package was between them, poking her in the ribs. She eased away and suddenly things clicked into place. "Wait, did you . . . Is this from you?"

There was a mischievous look in his eyes. "Yes, ma'am."

She squealed. "What is it?"

"Open it up."

"I love surprises."

He gave her a tolerant look. "You don't say."

She reached inside and pulled out a thick stack of papers, bound with a sturdy rubber band. The first page read simply *Untitled by Nathaniel Quinn*.

She sucked in a breath. "Your manuscript! It's done already? You didn't tell me you finished it. With all the traveling you've been doing?"

Of course, he'd told her he was writing their story and that he'd want her input when he was finished. But he'd started it less than two months ago.

"It just flowed right onto the page, and Rosewood wants to rush it to print to capitalize on the recent publicity. But first I want your input."

She hugged the manuscript tight to her chest, beaming at him. "I love it! I absolutely love it."

He gave her a wry look. "I'd feel more confident in that assessment if you'd maybe read it first."

"Of course, I'll read it. I can't wait to read it. But I already know it's your best book yet."

He pulled her closer and nuzzled her nose. "Well, it's already my favorite, but I might be a little biased, seeing as how I'm in love with the protagonist."

"Hmm . . . What a coincidence, because I'm in love with the author. I can't believe you came all this way to bring me this. You could've mailed it or even emailed it. Isn't that the way you authors are sending things these days?"

"I wanted to deliver it in person. But there is one other thing . . ." Something shifted in his eyes, in his face. He poked his glasses up, looking a little shy. A lot adorable.

"One other thing . . . ?"

"It seems my studio lease will be up soon—at the end of December."

Her heart raced. "Oh, yeah? And are you planning to renew it?"

"Actually, I was thinking a move might do me good. Perhaps someplace farther south. Studies show that southern residents are happier than people residing in most other states. In fact, New York ranks dead last in those studies."

Molly squelched a smile. "Well, nobody can blame you for wanting to be happy."

"Weather is also a concern. Manhattan has 3.5 warm months per year and averages 51.7 degrees, while North Carolina has 7.4 warm months and averages 59.8 degrees annually."

"You make a good argument."

"And I can't overlook the cost of living. A two-bedroom apartment in North Carolina costs roughly one-third what the same apartment would cost in Manhattan."

"I see you've done your research."

He slipped his arms around her waist. "Bluebell, in particular, holds special appeal to me."

She quirked a brow. "Is it the mountains? The lake? The small-town atmosphere?"

"Naturally those are all draws." He eased her closer, seriousness entering his eyes as they pierced hers. "But mainly it's the big-hearted girl I want to be with every minute of the day, more or less. I'd very much like to live in the same town as my girl. What do you think?"

Molly's heart heaved a happy sigh. "I think there's nothing I'd like better. Only . . ."

He tilted his head. "Only?"

"Will you still write me love letters? Because I'd really miss them if you didn't."

His lips stretched into a big smile. "I think that can be arranged."

"I'll understand if you run out of things to say."

"I'll never run out of things to say about you. Read the manuscript and you'll understand why."

She couldn't wait. Already she was itching to get started. "How long can you stay?"

"Three days . . . What's wrong? You don't look happy."

"How am I supposed to decide between spending time with you and diving into this epic love story?"

His lips curled up in a grin. "How about if I hold you on the porch swing while you read it?"

Molly beamed as she pulled the rubber band from the manuscript. "That's what I love about being with an intelligent man—all those clever ideas."

He pulled her onto the swing, settling close beside her. His hand skimmed her arm. "Don't you worry. I have lots of clever ideas."

She grabbed his hand, eyeing him. "Oh no, you don't. No distracting me. I have a very important story to read."

The swing swayed gently beneath them. His breath stirred the hair at her temples, making her shiver.

"Go ahead and read," he said. "We have all the time in the world."

Acknowledgments

You don't write thirty-five books without realizing the monumental team effort it takes to get a novel from the page to the shelf! I'm so incredibly blessed to partner with the fabulous team at HarperCollins Christian Publishing fiction team, led by publisher Amanda Bostic: Jocelyn Bailey, Matt Bray, Kim Carlton, Allison Carter, Paul Fisher, Jodi Hughes, Kristen Ingebretson, Becky Monds, and Savannah Summers. Not to mention all the wonderful sales reps and amazing people in the rights department—special shout-out to Catherine Zappa and Robert Downs!

Thanks especially to my editor Kim Carlton for her incredible insight and inspiration. You help me take the story deeper, and I'm so grateful! Thanks to editor L. B. Norton, who saves me from countless errors and always makes me look so much better than I really am.

Author Colleen Coble is my first reader and sister of my heart. Thank you, friend! This writing journey has been ever so much more fun because of you!

I'm grateful to my agent, Karen Solem, who's able to somehow make sense of the legal garble of contracts and, even more amazing, help me understand it.

The town of Bluebell was inspired by the little town of Lake Lure, NC. Don and Kim Cason, innkeepers of the beautiful historic Esmeralda Inn (which once functioned as a post office!), were so kind as to host my husband and me for a few days and answer all my pesky questions. If you're looking to visit Chimney Rock and Lake Lure, I highly recommend it! Visit theesmeralda.com for more information.

Kevin, has it really been thirty years? You've supported my dreams in every way possible, and I'm so grateful! To my kiddos, Chad, Trevor, Justin and Hannah, and my beautiful new granddaughter, Aubrielle. Every stage has been a grand adventure, and I look forward to all the wonderful memories we have yet to make!

Lastly, thank you, friends, for letting me share this story with you. I wouldn't be doing this without you! Your notes, posts, and reviews keep me going on the days when writing doesn't flow so easily. I appreciate your support more than you know.

I enjoy connecting with friends on my Facebook page, facebook.com/authordenisehunter. Please pop over and say hello. Visit my website at the link www.DeniseHunterBooks.com or just drop me a note at Deniseahunter@comcast.net. I'd love to hear from you!

Discussion Questions

1. Which character did you relate to most? Why?
2. Have you ever found something old and precious? If you had found Lizzie's letter would you have searched for the lovelorn couple? Why or why not?
3. Molly felt guilt and regret about how she'd handled her last conversation with her parents. What advice or scripture would you give a friend who found herself in a similar situation?
4. Adam's father left him with insecurities about who he was. Has anyone ever made you feel insecure about your identity? What was the result? How did you overcome it?
5. If you owned an inn, which living author would you want to come for an extended stay?
6. Both Benjamin and Adam struggled with their self-worth. What are some things we often use to prop up our self-worth?
7. What parallels can you draw from the present story of Molly/Adam and the past story of Lizzie/Benjamin?
8. Discuss Romans 8:28 as it pertains to the events in the story. "We know that all things

work together for the good of those who love God: those who are called according to His purpose." Discuss a time you have found this to be true in your own life.

9. Skye told Molly that fear is often a lack of faith. Do you believe that to be true?

10. Molly and Adam found "home" in each other. Discuss reasons why they each might've needed a person to call home.

About the Author

Denise Hunter is the internationally published bestselling author of more than thirty books, including *A December Bride* and *The Convenient Groom*, which have been adapted into original Hallmark Channel movies. She has won the Holt Medallion Award, the Reader's Choice Award, the Carol Award, and the Foreword Book of the Year Award and is a RITA finalist. When Denise isn't orchestrating love lives on the written page, she enjoys traveling with her family, drinking green tea, and playing drums. Denise makes her home in Indiana, where she and her husband are currently enjoying an empty nest.

DeniseHunterBooks.com
Facebook: Author Denise Hunter
Twitter: @DeniseAHunter

| Books are produced in the United States using U.S.-based materials | Books are printed using a revolutionary new process called THINKtech™ that lowers energy usage by 70% and increases overall quality | Books are durable and flexible because of Smyth-sewing | Paper is sourced using environmentally responsible foresting methods and the paper is acid-free |

Center Point Large Print
600 Brooks Road / PO Box 1
Thorndike, ME 04986-0001 USA

(207) 568-3717

US & Canada:
1 800 929-9108
www.centerpointlargeprint.com